Praise for
All That We Carried

"*All That We Carried* is a deeply personal, thoughtful exploration of dealing with pain and grief. Erin Bartels makes it shine."

Life Is Story

"Bartels proves herself a master wordsmith and storyteller."

Library Journal

"Bartels delivers another immersive tale set in her home state of Michigan, drawing on some of her own adventures, in *All That We Carried*—a story about the complexities of grief, faith, and sisterhood."

Family Fiction

the Lady with the Dark Hair

the
Lady
with the
Dark Hair

A NOVEL

ERIN BARTELS

Revell

a division of Baker Publishing Group
Grand Rapids, Michigan

© 2024 by Erin Bartels

Published by Revell
a division of Baker Publishing Group
Grand Rapids, Michigan
RevellBooks.com

Printed in the United States of America

Library of Congress Cataloging-in-Publication Data
Names: Bartels, Erin, 1980– author.
Title: The lady with the dark hair : a novel / Erin Bartels.
Description: Grand Rapids, Michigan : Revell, a division of Baker Publishing
    Group, 2024.
Identifiers: LCCN 2023035445 | ISBN 9780800741662 (paperback) | ISBN
    9780800745578 (casebound) | ISBN 9781493444717 (ebook)
Subjects: LCGFT: Novels.
Classification: LCC PS3602.A83854 L33 2024 | DDC 813/.6—dc23/eng/20230815
LC record available at https://lccn.loc.gov/2023035445

This book is a work of fiction. Names, characters, places, and incidents are the product of the author's imagination or are used fictitiously. Any resemblance to actual events, locales, or persons, living or dead, is coincidental.

Baker Publishing Group publications use paper produced from sustainable forestry practices and postconsumer waste whenever possible.

24 25 26 27 28 29 30   7 6 5 4 3 2 1

"What more can we expect from women if throughout the world this sex has not produced one single great mind, nor one complete and original work of art, nor, in anything, one work of lasting value."

—ARTHUR SCHOPENHAUER

❖

"Women, who know only themselves, who, in their adorable, childish way, find it impossible to ever see beyond themselves . . . have no concept of the logical order."

—HUGUES LE ROUX

❖

"True to their instincts, women embrace by preference the easy genres, those that require elegance rather than energy and invention."

—EUGÈNE MÜNTZ

❖

"Women in general love no art, know nothing about any form of art, and have no genius."

—JEAN-JACQUES ROUSSEAU

❖

"Women have produced no masterpieces in any genre."

—HENRY HAVARD

❖

"Woman is inferior to man."

—AUGUST STRINDBERG

for the women

PART
ONE

Chapter
ONE

◆

SOUTHERN FRANCE, 1879

Viviana—no, it was Vivienne now—dipped her brush, squared her shoulders, and began to scrub. Beneath the stiff bristles, the crusted remains of some long-forgotten ragoût broke away from the edges of the cocotte, and the copper pot began to sing. It was the eighth pot she'd scoured so far, and it would not be the last. Lisette had seen to that.

Though it was Lisette's laziness and Madame Dorset's indifference that had the cookware in the Renaud home looking so shabby to begin with, it was Vivienne's muscle that would bring it back to life. The task was a punishment, that was clear. What was hazier to Vivienne was precisely what she was being punished for. She could understand quite a bit of what was said to her in French if it was said slowly and with helpful gestures to supplement—it was not completely unlike her native tongue, after all—but Madame Dorset only occasionally released her tightly clasped hands to point, and Lisette spoke so fast Vivienne was lucky to pull two or three clear words from any given sentence. She suspected Lisette did this on purpose.

Whatever she'd done wrong, Vivienne was sure she'd do it again. Or if not that, something else. Her new employer seemed as difficult to please as her last one. If she could call the last one an employer—she certainly had not been paid for her service. Still, she was determined to keep this position at all costs. She could not go back to living on the streets of Toulouse, and she could not go back home. Ever.

When her fingers could detect no trace of the ghosts of meals past, Vivienne dried the inside of the cocotte with a soft cloth, then picked up half a lemon, dipped the cut end in a dish of salt, and began polishing the exterior of the pot with it, ignoring the sting as traces of the mixture found their way into the cuts on her fingers. Somehow the salt combined with the acid of the lemon in such a way that the gray-green patina on the copper was stripped away, leaving only the warm glow of the pure metal beneath. If only it were so easy to remove the tarnish on a life, to scrape the memories of the past decade—no, more than that—from one's mind, leaving only the good parts behind. It was a silly notion. If such a thing were possible, Vivienne would find little of herself left at the end of the process.

When the cocotte was polished to a high shine, Vivienne set it aside, pulled the cap from her head, and finally scratched an itch she'd been trying to ignore for the past twenty minutes.

"Madame Dorset said you had to cover your head," Lisette snapped from the doorway.

Vivienne understood the word *head* and knew exactly what Lisette must be saying. She smoothed back her shamefully short hair, replaced the cap, and secured it with pins. Until it grew longer than her shoulders, she was never to appear without a head covering outside of the bedchamber she shared with Lisette.

"Vivienne," Lisette said slowly, "Monsieur Renaud needs a copper pot upstairs for a still life. Take one to him."

Vivienne glanced across the kitchen counter, which was practically covered in copper. "Which pot?"

14

"How am I to know which one?" Lisette shrugged.

Vivienne tried not to panic. One mistake, whatever it had been, had earned her hours of scrubbing and polishing. What might happen should she arrive in Monsieur Renaud's studio—a place she had already been warned not to enter under any circumstance—with the wrong pot?

"You bring?" Vivienne said in heavily accented French. "He asked you."

"No, he asked Madame Dorset to send someone up with one, and Madame Dorset asked me to find someone who wasn't busy."

Lisette spoke so quickly this time that beyond the name of her direct supervisor, Vivienne could pick out only the word *no*. She lifted her hands slightly to indicate the piles of pots she had yet to scrub, dry, polish, and put away.

"Do you want me to tell Madame Dorset you refuse?" Lisette said.

Vivienne looked around the room for the pot that seemed like it had the most potential to please. Out of the corner of her eye she could see Lisette smirking at her.

"He's waiting," she intoned, drawing out the words.

Vivienne picked up a poêlon in one hand and a saucier in the other and headed slowly up the steps, careful not to trample her skirt. At the top of the stairs, she hesitated.

When Madame Dorset reluctantly took her on, she'd entered through the back servants' entrance and immediately went into the kitchen. She knew how to get from the kitchen to the root cellar to the lavatory to her bedchamber, but she had never actually been in the Renauds' living quarters.

Where was the studio? She considered going back downstairs to ask Lisette, but she doubted the haughty girl would stoop to help her. Instead, she tiptoed down a hall, hoping to avoid running into Madame Dorset, Madame Renaud, or Graciosa and Percinet, the Renauds' spirited spaniels, which terrified Vivienne despite their relative good cheer and smiling faces. Her only experience with dogs was with the packs of strays that roamed the streets of the poorer parts of Barcelona.

She made her way undetected past the dining room, the library, a sitting room of some kind. While she was no follower of design movements and the grandest places she had ever set foot in were churches, Vivienne had a sense that the carpets, draperies, and furnishings in these rooms were of another era, and though much of it had the look of being expensive, the colors seemed faded and the frames around paintings and the rich, carved wood of tables and chairs were covered in a thick layer of dust. Whatever Lisette did with her time when she was not bossing Vivienne around, it was not cleaning.

Vivienne heard the sound of a man's voice speaking French but with a faintly Spanish accent. Her lungs seized up within her chest. Had they found her after all? Had Madame Dorset suspected something was amiss and contacted the authorities? She forced her feet forward and followed the sound to a door that was not quite closed. She peeked through the opening to find a white-haired man in a paint-smeared smock before a large canvas. No soldiers, no officials. Taking a steadying breath, she pressed the door open with the back of her hand. "Monsieur Renaud?"

"Yes, what is it?" he asked without turning around.

She took a step into the chaotic room. "I have pots."

"What?"

"Pots. Lisette said you need a copper pot?"

Finally, Renaud looked her way. "I beg your pardon? Pots?" Vivienne held up the pots in her hands. "Good?"

Renaud was now fully facing her, both fists on his hips, a long, thin brush poking out from one of them. "I don't recall asking for any pots."

"Pots."

"No pots."

"No pots?" She lowered her hands. "I'm sorry. There was a mistake." Such as listening to Lisette at all.

He waved a hand in the air. "Never mind that. Come in here a moment, uh . . . "

"Vivia—no. My name is Vivienne."

He was waving her in. "Vivienne, come in here and have a look at this, will you? Just put those pots anywhere."

Vivienne carefully picked her way across a number of sketches that were scattered across the floor like lily pads on the surface of a pond, all the time looking around for a clear surface to accommodate the pots. None was forthcoming. As she approached Monsieur Renaud and the expansive canvas in front of him, she could see that he was not painting a still life at all. Instead, the large rectangle stretched out in front of the artist was filled in with the details of a complex interior scene—tapestry-covered walls, ornate tables, leaded glass lamps, a pile of books, a Persian rug, all surrounding a settee upon which an irregular, oblong shape was left blank, the warm underpainting of a yellowy-brown hue popping through.

Vivienne admired the intricate picture. How incredible that it had started out as nothing at all, that the thoughtful application of color on canvas created a world where there was none. She reached the master of the house, pots still in hand. "Beautiful."

"Don't you think he should be reading a book?" Renaud said.

Vivienne glanced at him. "I'm sorry?"

He motioned impatiently at the canvas. "A book, girl! Don't you think he should be reading a book? Or a letter? He wouldn't be lying there doing nothing, would he?"

Her eyes searched the canvas. "Yes," she answered, though she still wasn't sure who he was talking about.

Renaud raised his voice and shouted through the canvas, "You see, Vella? I'm not the only one who thinks so."

Vivienne leaned to her left and peered around the canvas. There, not ten feet away, was the whole scene—tapestries, rug, tables, settee, lamps, books—but in place of the unpainted blob on the settee was a man dressed in breeches and a loose-fitting white shirt, open at the neck. A military jacket of unfamiliar origin was draped over the end of the settee, and a pair of boots was crumpled by it on the floor. The man was dark-haired and dark-eyed, with skin the color of fine leather. In fact, he did not look unlike Vivienne herself looked when she spent time in the sun. If he wasn't Spanish, he was something quite close to it. And yet, inexplicably, upon his head was a turban.

"I don't care what either of you say, Monsieur Renaud," the man said in French. "A man who had just come home from war would not lie down and pick up a book." He locked eyes with Vivienne. "He might lie down with a beautiful woman . . ."

Vivienne quickly turned away and put the canvas between them again. She understood the last two words he said.

"But not a book," he finished.

Monsieur Renaud looked down at Vivienne then, truly looked at her. "Why do you have those pots?"

Vivienne started into her explanation again, but Renaud cut her short. "Never mind." He put the paintbrush between his teeth and took the pots from her. "Go on," he said through the brush handle, nodding toward the canvas, or rather, what was beyond the canvas. He tossed the pots aside with a clatter and took the brush out of his mouth. "Just go over there a moment and we'll see who's correct: the master artist who has been painting for more than thirty years"—he raised his voice—"or the brash young colorman who's gotten too big for his breeches and is far more difficult to work with than his father was."

"His father was never asked to sit around doing absolutely nothing in your studio for hours without payment," the man countered.

Renaud leaned in close to Vivienne's ear and whispered, "That's because his father was tremendously fat and would take up too much paint—which, of course, he sold at a tidy profit for himself—were I to attempt to represent him on canvas."

Vivienne tried to work through the many sentences she had just heard. "I'm sorry," she finally said. "I do not understand."

Renaud examined her. "You're not French."

"No."

He pursed his lips. "It doesn't matter. He isn't either. The two of you will fit together quite nicely."

Vivienne couldn't imagine what he meant, or what she was supposed to do now.

"Well?" he said, motioning to the settee. "Go on."

At a loss and now longing for the uncomplicated—if extensive—pile of copper pots awaiting her scrub brush downstairs, Vivienne did as she was told and walked around to the other side of the canvas. She avoided eye contact with the man reclining on the settee, though she could feel his gaze upon her as she crossed the room and entered the scene. She turned toward Renaud and said to the backside of the canvas, "Where?"

"Here," the man on the settee said, in Spanish this time, patting the space in front of him.

The spot he indicated was a strip of threadbare nectarine-orange jacquard upholstery the width of a loaf of bread. If she sat there, she'd have to press up against this stranger to avoid sliding off the edge onto the floor. Perhaps sensing her reluctance, the man scooted toward the back of the settee. The space for her to sit grew, but not by much.

"What's the matter?" the man said, in Spanish again. "Do you understand what I'm saying?"

"Yes," she said in Spanish, "but—"

"My dear, will you please get yourself situated?" Renaud said brusquely, motioning toward the window. "Too much longer and I'll lose the light."

Vivienne perched on the edge of the settee.

"Fine," Renaud said. "Now lean toward him and place a hand on his head."

Hand. Head. She understood that. She touched her own

head, but the man on the settee took her hand and put it on his head.

"Like this," he said.

"No, not like that," Renaud said. "Soothingly. He has come back from war and you are grateful he is home, yet you worry about his state of mind. Vella, stop smiling. You're a broken man. Come, girl, you can do better than that. Look deep into his eyes. You thought you'd lost him but here he is, safe again."

The man—Vella—quickly translated Renaud's directions into Spanish.

"There, that's a little better. The positions at least are correct. Don't move. I will fix your faces tomorrow."

Vivienne looked back toward Renaud, whose head could be seen around the edge of the canvas, and said in French, "Tomorrow?"

"Don't move!" he snapped, and she whipped her head back into place.

"Yes, my dear," the man on the settee whispered to her in Spanish. "He has to finish as much as possible by tomorrow because I must move on to Paris. I told him I'd only stay to model for him if he bought extra product."

"You're a merchant?" Vivienne whispered back.

"I'm a colorman," he said, regarding her. "I sell pigments to artists and artisans. The men in my family have been traders and merchants for generations. But I'm expanding the business. I'm an art dealer now as well. And a bit of an artist. I may be a great one someday." He adjusted his position slightly, eliciting a frustrated sigh from Renaud. "And you, Vivienne? What do you do?"

"I've just started working in the household recently." For some reason she did not want to tell him she was a scullery maid.

"And your family?"

"I have none."

The corners of his mouth turned down.

"Vella," said Renaud, "you are happy, relieved, relaxing for the first time in months. Stop frowning."

Vella rolled his eyes. "You're not French," he said to her. "No."

"And you're not Spanish. Your accent betrays you."

Under her cap, Vivienne's scalp began to itch. "I am Catalan," she admitted.

"Ah, Catalan! Then we may find we have much in common. We are both from crossroads. My family is from Gibraltar," he said. "We're Spanish and Genoese and Maltese and, rumor has it, just a little bit of English and Scottish. Quite a mix of cultures." His eyes drifted up toward the turban he was wearing. "Though not Indian."

Vivienne relaxed a little. "What war are you supposed to be home from anyway?"

"Who knows? Renaud is not a stickler for historical accuracy, as you can plainly see from how my imaginary house is decorated. And look how you're dressed. Are you my servant or my wife? If I'm an Indian, you should be in a sari and wearing an alluring veil. Or dancing and clacking those little finger cymbals together to celebrate my longed-for homecoming . . . to Toulouse."

Vivienne giggled.

"No, no, my girl," Renaud said. "No levity here. He will never be the same. Your life will never be the same. There will always be a part of him that has been left upon the battlefield, and you feel that you will never truly know him now. Your love is fractured by pain."

Vella stifled a laugh and translated, but Vivienne could not quite find the humor in what Renaud said. Not after all she had witnessed—all she had done—at Alpens, at Bocairente, at Seu d'Urgell. She knew war—probably better than either of these men. She knew every texture, every sound, every color, every smell. She knew what it was to feel drunk on victory, nauseated by defeat. She knew what death looked like, what it sounded like, when the soul was separated from the body. She knew what it was to lose friends, to lose family, to escape with her life only to find, to her horror, that she then must go on living.

"Vivienne?" came Vella's voice. "What's wrong?"

She focused in on him. "Nothing."

He narrowed his eyes.

"Nothing," she said again, then smiled as if to prove it.

"No smiles," Renaud said sharply.

"No smiles, no frowns," Vella said to him in French. "You are impossible."

For the next hour, the two models spoke in Spanish in hushed tones. Well, Vella spoke. He regaled Vivienne with stories of his constant travels across Europe and the Middle East and North Africa, buying and selling pigments, smuggling tobacco, fraternizing with people from all walks of life. His vivid descriptions of places she had never seen, would never see—Paris, Brussels, Vienna, Venice, Algiers—painted pictures in her mind that distracted her from the pain that began to radiate from her shoulders and neck after staying in one position for so long. He spoke of treacherous roads and colorful company, rough waters and gentle sea breezes, mysterious and exotic peoples speaking a cacophony of languages.

It wasn't fair. Men could live such rich and exciting lives if they wanted to, while she knew of few women who even traveled outside of their own towns. She only had because of unhappy circumstance—because of a mistake. A terrible mistake. And her adventures, while perhaps exciting, were never pleasant. Not for the first time, she wished she'd been born a boy.

Renaud cursed from behind the canvas. "We've lost the light."

"That is a shame," Vella said in Spanish, holding Vivienne's gaze. "I have rather grown accustomed to the most excellent view." Vivienne sat up straight and stretched the spasming muscles in her back and shoulders. "It is not a shame to me. You got to lie on your back that entire time while I had to hunch over you like a vulture. I'll have a permanent hump, I'm sure." She stood and rubbed her neck and felt her bones crackle.

Vella swung his feet to the floor, removed the turban, and raked his fingers through his sweat-slicked hair. He smiled up at her. "Shall we take a walk to stretch our legs?"

"Vivienne! There you are!" came Madame Dorset's irritated voice from across the room.

Vivienne straightened her shoulders and clasped her hands in front of her. "I'm sorry, Madame Dorset, but Lisette—

"Never mind that, Madame Dorset," Renaud said in a voice one might use to calm an angry dog. "Vivienne is here at my request. And I will need her tomorrow as well. Send her in no later than eight o'clock."

"But monsieur, the breakfast dishes—"

"Will surely keep," Renaud finished. "Better yet, have Lisette take care of them. I need Vivienne here. Vella is right. She is much more interesting to look at than a book."

Madame Dorset seemed to bite back another comment, then said demurely, "Certainly, monsieur. But can you spare her now? I've need of her elsewhere."

Renaud nodded and waved his hand toward the door. "You may have her for now. But tomorrow."

"Eight o'clock," Madame Dorset supplied.

"Indeed," Renaud said.

Vivienne glanced down at Vella, who offered up a shrug and a smile. "Hasta mañana," he said.

Vivienne walked swiftly to the door, doubled back to retrieve the copper pots from their landing places on the floor, and then followed Madame Dorset into the hall. When the door had closed behind them, Madame Dorset's expression changed from obsequious to outraged.

"You'll never pull such a stunt again, my girl, if you hope to remain in the employ of this house."

"Lisette—"

"Never mind Lisette. See to your own affairs." She started for the kitchen, and Vivienne fell in behind her. "Honestly, that man knows nothing about what it takes to run his own household."

Back in the scullery, Vivienne ignored Lisette's sneers and attacked the remaining hoard of copper pots with a renewed spirit, her mind retracing the far-flung trade routes the man on the settee had opened to her imagination—and lingering just a bit on the memory of sitting so close to him.

Chapter *TWO*

◆

E sther Markstrom had never left a flea market empty-handed. She didn't always—ever?—go home with just what she'd been looking for (and frankly was beginning to think that perhaps her ideal score existed only in her mind), but she always managed to find something she could talk herself into buying.

Usually it was because she was the only one at a particular stall and she couldn't make herself leave unless another prospective buyer entered. She felt a deeply Midwestern sense of guilt about the whole thing and so bought something out of pity for the vendor, whom she always assumed must be on the verge of utter financial ruin.

Still, she was beginning to think that today might be the exception. Today might be the day she drove home with nothing in the trunk or even on the passenger seat. She'd nearly given up hope, in fact, when she spied the rather tattered cover of an herbal on top of a stack of discolored 1970s high school science textbooks.

She wasn't the least bit interested in flowers as a concept, but she was interested in supplementing her income by cutting out, framing, and selling prints on her Etsy site. After all, she was close to financial ruin herself.

She picked up the oversized book and began haphazardly leafing through the pages. She quickly ascertained that there were, regrettably, no color prints. Such decorations were really not her cup of tea, and there was no free wall space to speak of in her house anyway. But if Pinterest was to be trusted, they were still desired pieces to grace the walls of the kind of people who seemed to enjoy knocking *out* walls in older homes in order to make them more "open concept."

Savages.

She was about to ask the vendor how much the book cost when her off.

"How much is that footstool?" she said in a gratingly sweet voice, pointing a perfectly manicured finger toward the opposite end of the large open-sided tent.

The footstool in question was covered in worn gold brocade fabric, the dingy ghosts of heel marks digging concave depressions in the middle. Esther immediately knew what this woman would do with it. In her Pinterest wanderings, she'd seen a resurgence of footstools, always re-covered in jewel-toned or animal-print (or jewel-toned animal-print) plush velvet fabric that didn't quite match the rest of the room. Statement pieces, they were called. In its current condition, the statement this particular footstool was making was something along the lines of "Burn me. Please."

Esther would bet all the cash she was carrying that this young woman was not going to reupholster it herself but would instead pay far more for someone else to do it than she would spend if she'd just bought a new footstool from IKEA. But then, "IKEA" was such a boring and bourgeois answer to the envious, wide-eyed question "Where did you get *that*?" How much better to be able to relay the story of the hunt, the shrewd negotiations, the choosing of the hideous fabric.

"Hello?" the woman said when the silence had stretched on too long. "I asked you—"

"$175," the vendor said, not looking up from the pulp science fiction book he was reading. He had obviously been following trends too.

"For that?"

Here we go.

As the dance began, Esther stared at the back of the woman's head. Her long hair was styled in waves that must have taken her a half hour and a fair amount of product to perfect (and they *were* perfect). A slight turn of her head and Esther could see that she had taken great care with her makeup. From one of the woman's bare shoulders hung a beautiful slouchy brown leather purse. Her legs were tan and shapely, ending in pedicured toenails peeking out of the pair of stylish wedge-heel sandals she was wearing. To an outdoor flea market. In a field. That was nearly always soggy after heavy rains. Which they'd had in the area just two days prior.

In contrast, Esther was bare-faced and ponytailed, no hair-spray even to tame the flyaways. She was wearing dirty sneakers, secondhand jeans, and a twenty-year-old Hope College T-shirt that she routinely wore when painting or mowing the lawn. Her spending money was tucked into the old fanny pack her mom used to wear to flea markets back when they went together. Back when she would still leave the house.

Esther let her eyes travel back up the woman's perfect figure until they found what they were looking for: a flaw.

Ah. There it was, when she raised her arm just slightly: the white residue of her deodorant, caking the edge of the dress's arm holes. Esther relaxed a little, took one step to the right, and waved the book in the air.

"$24.95," the vendor said.

"That's better," the woman said.

"Not you," he said.

The woman turned and fixed Esther with an irritated glare.

"Excuse me, we're in the middle of a negotiation here."

"You're wasting your time," said Esther. "And mine. He's not going lower than $150, I can tell you that." She turned her attention to the vendor. "I'll give you $15."

"Sold."

She stepped around the woman and held out the ten and the five she already had in her hand. The vendor took it with a smile and a "Have a nice day." Then the smile disappeared like a blown-out flame as he faced the increasingly agitated woman in front of him. Esther tucked the book under her arm and walked out from the shadow of the tent into the May sunshine.

She ambled past a booth of textiles, one that was mostly glassware, one that showcased an array of vacant-eyed dolls in various stages of rot and disrepair. One man's trash . . . was most often still trash. But for some people it was tantamount to sacrilege to throw anything away if there was even the slightest chance someone was out there who wanted it. And truly, there always was someone, somewhere, someday.

It was funny. If just one person was interested in an item, the price went down, but if many people were interested, the price went up. The item itself never changed except to get older, rustier, more threadbare. Its value was completely dependent on interest. And how arbitrary that was. Where had footstools been five years ago? Where would they be in another five? Just another passé home decor notion.

Longevity was one of the benefits of being off trend, though Esther could not remember ever having made any purposeful personal choices in the matter. It wasn't that the Markstrom family couldn't afford to be fashionable. Quite the opposite, in fact—until fairly recently. It was simply that when you knew who you were, you didn't feel the need to strive to be somebody else. Someone more stylish, more likable, and ultimately more common.

The Markstroms were uncommon, and they liked it that way. It was in their blood. Not many people in the world could say that they were descendants of one of the finest—though scandalously underappreciated—painters of the late nineteenth century. Not many people could say that they worked for a respected—though perhaps in recent times rather shabby—museum named for an eccentric relative who obsessively painted the same woman again and again, but whose own visage was a complete mystery because he never completed a self-portrait. And no one but Esther and her mother, the last living leaves on Francisco Vella's family tree, could claim ownership over his finest work—*La Dama del Cabello Oscuro. The Lady with the Dark Hair.*

Ultimately, she supposed, it was a good thing that Vella was not so celebrated as his contemporaries (who, frankly, were not so celebrated in their own lifetimes as one might be inclined to think by their near-universal adoration today). Otherwise, it would have been impossible to have amassed even the small number of his paintings currently showcased at the Vella-Markstrom Museum and Gallery in downtown East Lansing, Michigan.

No, it was always better to be just slightly on the outs with popular culture.

After another forty minutes of casual searching, Esther sensed it was time to go. Her mother had been home alone for a few hours now, and the drive would be at least ninety minutes, not counting delays for construction crews and accidents. It wasn't smart to leave Lorena on her own for too long. Bad things happened.

Esther was making her way to the car with her one purchase when she had the distinct feeling that she was being followed. She looked back over her shoulder, fully expecting to see green-dress girl gearing up to give her a piece of her mind—maybe a footstool to the face. But it wasn't the blond with the deodorant stains. It was a man she sort of recognized but couldn't quite place.

"Esther?" he said, smiling broadly. "I thought that was you." With as few people as she interacted with on anything more than a superficial level, she really should know who this man was.

"Well, hi there!" she said, hoping her chipper tone would throw a cloak of invisibility over her brain's mad dash to pull his name from some dusty file drawer in its right anterior temporal lobe.

"It's been a while," he said, extending his hand for her to shake.

So they were handshake acquaintances, not hug acquaintances. Though that detail admittedly didn't help her much. She could count on one hand (and less than half of that) how many people she felt comfortable hugging. Her own mother didn't make the cut.

"Yes," she agreed, "a long time." She frantically cataloged observations. Muddled British accent indicating a long time spent in the States. Olive skin hinting at ancestry somewhere other than the pasty British Isles. The thinning and graying hair of a man pushing sixty—perhaps more. Dark eyes behind dark-rimmed glasses.

"It's so wild to run into you here," he said. "You didn't move to the Detroit area, did you?"

"No, still in East Lansing."

"Still at the museum, then?"

He knew where she worked.

"Yep."

"Still going strong, eh? That's marvelous."

"And you?"

"Still teaching, same place. I do believe I'm apt to die there, though if someone had suggested such a thing when you were a student, I would have laughed them out of the room. Still haven't gotten used to the winters."

Of course. Her brain quickly filled in more and darker hair, switched the glasses for an earlier wire-framed model, and added back at least seventy pounds, and there he was. Dr. Ian Perez, native of Gibraltar and professor of art history at Hope College in Holland, Michigan.

"Well, I guess I'm glad you've stuck it out, Dr. Perez." Esther made sure to pronounce it the way he had in class—*PEAR-ez*, short and clipped, with the emphasis on the first syllable—rather than the Americanized *pah-REZZ* that so many of her fellow students had insisted on using despite his gentle attempts to correct them. "Otherwise, I doubt we would have run into each other again."

He waved his hand in the air. "Ian, please."

"What brings you all the way out here? After something special?"

"As a matter of fact, yes, but I didn't find it." He motioned to the herbal in her hand. "You?"

"Oh, this?" she said, lifting it a little. "Not really. I spend some time at a flea market or antique fair a few weekends each summer. Looking for art."

"For the museum? Or yourself?"

"Maybe a bit of both."

He nodded. "Ever find anything good?"

"Never," Esther said. "But I keep trying. Habit. My mom and I used to do it together when I was little. Those were some good times."

"Oh, I'm sorry. Has your mother passed on?"

"Oh, no. She's not dead. She's just . . . not here." Esther shifted her weight. "What were you looking for?"

Perez put his hands in his pockets and rocked back on his heels. "Would you believe I'm searching for the same thing you are? Always hoping to find something interesting—either a new-to-me artist or perhaps something on the obscure side where the vendor doesn't know what he's got." He held up his hand and quickly added, "Or she."

Esther grinned. Ah, yes. Dr. Perez was the professor with whom she'd had that semester-long argument about the non-universality of the masculine pronoun back in 1999. Funny how those do-or-die moments of youth fade away and become less earth-shattering as one careens into one's mid-forties. She routinely used the masculine pronoun in its old universal sense even though the world had caught up and then some. She didn't even think about it.

"Though I must say," he continued, "if you're out hunting, there's little hope for me finding anything of worth before you do. You had one of the keenest eyes of any of my students, and you were certainly one of the more competitive."

Esther turned away toward the car for just a moment to hide the color she could feel rush into her cheeks. How nice to be remembered by someone you hadn't seen in over twenty years. And to be remembered so specifically.

"Well, I won't keep you," Perez said. "We both have a drive ahead of us."

Esther suddenly remembered her mother. "Yes. Well, it was nice seeing you, Dr. Perez."

"Same here, Esther," he said.

She opened the car door, then hesitated. It wasn't often that she ran into someone worth keeping in touch with. Someone who shared her interests and could talk intelligently about them. All she really had was Lorena, and conversations with her rarely went in a satisfying direction.

"You should come by the museum sometime if you're ever in town," she said. "I'd love to hear what you think of some of Vella's work. And we have a temporary exhibit of plein air paintings by local artists going up for the season soon. There are some nicely executed pieces in the collection. Are you teaching over the summer?"

"No, I'm not." He sighed. "I'm supposed to be writing."

"Supposed to be?"

"Yes. It's hard to make myself sit down and do it, though. I love the research aspect of publishing, but the writing . . ."

"Gosh, that's the part I think I'd love," she said. "The research, not so much."

"You always did write a nice paper."

She scoffed. "I seem to remember getting a lot of pretty mediocre grades in your classes."

He chuckled. "That's because your research was sloppy. Your writing was lovely."

"I was lazy," Esther admitted.

He regarded her. "I'm not sure that's it. I think perhaps you were just a bit too romantic about art."

She dropped the book on the driver's seat and shut the door. "Too romantic about art? Someone who thinks you can be too romantic about art should not be teaching art history. Art *is* romance. It's seeing something and having such deep affection for it in that singular moment that you're compelled to capture it so you can revisit it again and again and again. So you can share it with other people. So you can make them see the worth in what you see."

She stopped. Her former professor was looking at her with a bemused smile, and she realized that, had he had that look on his face when he first said hello, she would have recognized him immediately. It was how he had always looked when she got off on some impassioned tangent during his classes. She'd had a lot to say back then.

"Well put," he said. "As always. I'm glad to see you haven't lost your passion over the years."

Hadn't she, though? Hadn't the last twenty-some years slowly but surely drained her of that animating force to make room for more practical things, like knowing how to hold her tongue, how to navigate the twisty halls of the mental health care system, how to stretch every dollar to its limit?

"And I would like to visit the museum," he continued. "On a day you'll be there."

"I'm always there."

"Except when you're out antiquing on the weekends."

"We're only open on weekdays. Well, Tuesday through Thursday, eleven to four, and Friday nights from five to eight."

He nodded. "Okay then. Maybe I'll see you soon. During one of those very specific times."

Esther opened her door again. "Looking forward to it." She sat down in the car, right on top of the book she'd bought. She put on her seat belt and turned the key in the ignition, then checked the rearview mirror. Dr. Perez was turning away, a broad smile stretching across his face. She fished the book out from under her legs and tossed it on the passenger seat, feeling that somehow she'd made a bit of a fool of herself during the last few minutes but not quite understanding just how or why.

Then she glanced at the clock on the dash and all thoughts of herself dissipated. She had to get on the road, and quickly. Lorena was waiting, and she didn't wait well.

Chapter

THREE

◆

SOUTHERN FRANCE, 1879

"Vivienne, let your hair down," Monsieur Renaud commanded. "You look like a servant in that cap."

They were all back in yesterday's positions. Vella reclining and translating, Vivienne appearing to fuss over him, Renaud behind the canvas occasionally barking orders.

"I am a servant," Vivienne responded. "Removing my cap will not give you the look you are hoping for in your painting."

Vella relayed the message in French.

"Mm, and why is that?" Renaud said.

"I had to cut my hair very short and it has taken longer than I expected to grow back."

"Sickness?" Vella ventured.

"No."

He frowned. "Convent?"

"No."

He brightened.

Renaud was coming around the canvas toward them. "Vella, it's none of your business why a servant in my household had to cut her hair. As for you, Vivienne, whatever your hair's defects, I at least need to get this infernal white thing off your head."

With a tug and swipe, the cap was gone. Renaud pulled a few pins, tousled Vivienne's dark hair, which only reached her chin, and attempted to tuck some behind her right ear. It fell forward immediately, and Renaud clumsily pinned it back.

"There. That will have to do." He made his way back behind the canvas.

"Was it lice?" Vella whispered.

Vivienne laughed in spite of herself. "Sorry," she said to Renaud. "No," she whispered to Vella. "Though that is what I told Lisette."

"Do you have to share a room with her?" he said.

"Unfortunately, yes. She would not even speak to me last night, she was so angry I was gone for so long. It was quite pleasant, actually. And anyway, it is her fault I ended up in this room to begin with."

"Then I will have to thank her when I see her," he said. Vivienne felt herself blush and glanced away. They were quiet for a moment, and she thought, with some measure of relief, that he might forget the question of her hair altogether. But then he said, "So why did you cut your hair?"

Vivienne considered. What harm could there be in telling him? He wasn't a Spaniard, after all. He did not stand to gain anything by turning her in. Most likely, he wouldn't believe her, would think she was playing games with him. And he had told her so many exciting stories the previous day, several of which showed him to be a man whose respect of the law and rules of society was anything but absolute. Perhaps she should share a bit of her own story.

"I posed as a boy in order to serve alongside my twin brother during the last war between the Liberals and the Carlists."

She wasn't sure how she expected Vella to react, but the sly smile that took over his face was not it. He did not seem shocked or offended by her revelation. He didn't even seem all that surprised. He almost seemed . . . impressed.

"Is that so?"

She raised her eyebrows slightly. "Do you doubt it?"

"I don't know you well enough to doubt it," he said. "So I suppose I shall believe it and allow that morsel to serve as the appetizer for a meal I would very much like to consume. Now then, mysterious Vivienne, tell me more. Satisfy my hunger for knowledge of you. Being Catalan, I assume you sided with the Carlists."

"Of course," she said indignantly.

Renaud cleared his throat.

She lowered her voice. "When Alfonso XII was installed during the coup, my brother, Ignasi, wanted to fight for a free Catalonia with the forces that Don Carlos was gathering. It was all he could talk about for over a year. I could not dissuade him, and I did not want to be left all alone."

"Where were your parents?"

"Our father died in the war with Morocco before we were born. My mother died not long after we were born. Her sister took us, but she died as well—yellow fever—and her husband wanted to remarry so he sent us to an orphanage. We ran away from the orphanage when we were thirteen. Well, Ignasi did, and I didn't want to be left behind. I suppose I was always following him."

He frowned. "And how old were you when you followed him to war?"

"Fourteen."

"Seems a foolish thing to do. A beautiful young girl among all those men."

She blushed again. "It was fine. We planned it out. He cut my hair—almost down to the scalp. I bound my chest. I said, 'Yes, sir,' and 'No, sir,' to the officers, but otherwise I rarely spoke. Ignasi talked more than any boy I'd ever known or heard of anyway, so it worked out just fine."

Vella appeared to think. "But that was nearly four years ago. How is it your hair has not grown back yet?"

"I kept cutting it, for a while anyway, after I left Catalonia." At his puzzled expression, she added, "It is far safer when one is living on the street to be a boy than a girl."

"No, no, no!" came Renaud's voice. "This is not right. It is not right at all." He came around from behind the canvas, raised his arms, and dropped them dramatically. "You still look like a servant."

"She is a servant," Vella said. "What do you want from her? You're the one who put her in the picture."

"My dear, you must change your clothes," Renaud said.

Vivienne sat back. "I have nothing else to wear, monsieur."

"Of course you don't. But Madame Renaud does. Just go upstairs to her room and choose something from the armoire. Something bright, please. *Not blue.* What Vella charges me for ultramarine is criminal."

"What I charge you for ultramarine barely nets me a profit," Vella remarked, then he translated Renaud's instructions, adding, "Something yellow, to complement your coloring."

"Did you just say yellow?" Renaud said. "No, no. Red would be better for the scene. And I could test the efficacy of this synthetic alizarin you keep going on about, Vella."

Vella touched Vivienne's hand and mouthed the word *ama-rillo.* Then he whispered, "Don't touch the walls."

She gave him a quizzical look, but he glanced toward Renaud, who was heading back to his canvas, and shook his head almost imperceptibly.

Confused, Vivienne stood and looked toward the studio door with trepidation. Would Madame Dorset catch her roaming the halls? Surely Madame Renaud, whom she'd never before laid eyes on, would object to her scullery maid rooting around in her armoire and wearing her fine clothes. And what could happen if she touched the walls?

"Go on," Renaud urged. "Up the stairs, down the hall, the last door on the right. Hurry now."

Vivienne trotted quickly out of the room and shut the door behind her, listening for a moment to the muffled male voices—Were they discussing colors? Were they discussing her?—before setting her course for the stairs that led from the two-story foyer up to the private parts of the house she had yet to see. Her eyes darted about for Madame Dorset, but as it was nearing time for the noon meal, the fierce woman was likely in the kitchen bemoaning the absence of the girl she'd taken on to do all the dirtiest and most taxing tasks. Lisette was almost certainly furious.

Vivienne climbed the grand curving staircase and passed beneath an enormous portrait of a woman. Her sumptuous gold-brown hair was braided and coiled and curled and piled on her head, adorned with a simple ribbon and an understated trio of small white flowers. She stood in a garden, surrounded by thick green foliage and blooming yellow vines. At her feet lay a spaniel. On her face, the hint of a demure smile. And from regal head to dainty toe, she was swathed in blue satin. Whoever it was, this was a woman worthy of ultramarine.

If Vivienne had to guess, the subject was likely Monsieur Renaud's wife. As she continued up the stairs, she wondered when he had painted it. Was it made in order to woo her? Was it a wedding gift? Perhaps its creation was more recent and his wife far younger than he? Or was it possible he had a daughter no one had spoken about?

Lost in thought as she was, Vivienne quite suddenly found herself at the end of the hall, staring at the last door on the right. She took a deep breath, thanked God that Madame Dorset had not seen her, and tapped lightly on the dark wood. When there was no answer, she pushed the door open and said in a quiet voice, "Madame Renaud?"

Nothing.

Vivienne opened the door just wide enough to slip through and found herself in a dim room enveloped in green walls. The large windows were obscured by unending folds of white linen that filtered the light from outside so effectively that all that could get through was a dull glow. A carpet of green and white swallowed the sound of her footsteps as she crept past the large bed, upon which a veritable mountain of white pillows and blankets was haphazardly tossed. It was clear that the colors chosen for this bedchamber were meant to evoke the freshness of a spring garden. But in the weak light the entire room took on a sickly pallor.

Though she was clearly alone, Vivienne opened the armoire as quietly as possible. She wanted to simply take whatever she first laid her hands on and flee from the room, but Vella had insisted that yellow would be best.

Why should she follow his directive rather than the artist's? Renaud was the expert, after all, and he was also master of the house and the person who paid her wages. When Vivienne was taking aim over a broken-down wall in Seu d'Urgell, she followed the orders of her superior officer. She made ready when commanded. Aimed when commanded. Fired when commanded. Even when she feared that the movement she'd seen was from their own troops, caught between the lines of scrimmage. Even then, she had done as commanded.

And look where it had gotten her.

Seeking light, Vivienne went to the nearest window and pulled back the drapery, careful not to touch the wall as she tucked the fabric behind the brass curtain knob. She was about to go back to the now far more visible contents of the armoire when a small white hand speckled with brown shot out from beneath the bedcover and gripped her own. She let out a yell, then clapped her free hand over her mouth. There, nearly lost in the voluminous bedding, was a pale face cast in anemic green light. Patches of darker skin around the eyes and temples gave the face a hollow look, as though it were already in the process of shrinking back into the skull.

Vivienne's heart pounded against the walls of her chest as she stumbled over an explanation. "I am sorry. Very sorry. I—Monsieur Renaud said—I need a dress—for a painting—he paints—"

"Shhh," the woman in the bed soothed. "You are not in trouble." She tugged weakly at Vivienne's hand. "Sit down and catch your breath."

Vivienne did not understand all the words, but the tone was clearly meant to be calming. She allowed herself to be pulled down onto the bed by this specter, though every impulse within her wanted to flee.

"There," the woman said. "Now settle down and tell me who you are."

Vivienne took two slow breaths. This was just a person. Just a woman. A sick woman. Who was, until Vivienne had entered the room, all alone.

"My name is Viviana." She shook her head. "Vivienne. My name is Vivienne."

"Viviana. It is nice to meet you," the woman said slowly. "I am Madame Renaud. But you may call me Monique in here. In this room, I am Monique." She smiled without revealing her teeth, and it was only then that Viviana could recognize a shadow of the woman in the rich blue dress in the portrait.

"I work in the house, madame. But Monsieur Renaud—"

"You are his new model," she supplied. "And you have been sent to retrieve a dress."

"A dress. Yes. I did knock. But you did not hear. I am so sorry." She stood. "I will go."

"Yes, I suppose you must not keep Valentin waiting." Madame Renaud—Viviana could not think of her as Monique—gave her a critical look. "There is a yellow dress in there that would be perfect for you."

Two votes for yellow. "Thank you, madame." She walked over to the armoire and found the buttery yellow dress in question.

The skirts were in the newer, slimmer style, meant to be worn with a bustle rather than over hoops. The bodice was low-cut, stiffly boned, and trimmed with delicate ruffled ribbons and hand-painted porcelain buttons. It was absolutely enchanting, and Viviana had little notion of how to put it all on. "Thank you, madame," she said again. She gathered up the skirts and started for the door.

"You'd better change in here," Madame Renaud called from the bed. "There's a screen just there, in the corner, for modesty's sake. Though I must say if Valentin has chosen you to model for him, that will be a moot point soon enough."

Viviana looked up from the mass of cloth in her hands and tried to string the woman's words together in her mind. "I beg your pardon?"

Madame Renaud laughed lightly and spoke slowly. "You saw the paintings in the hall?"

She hadn't. She had been so focused on that magnificent portrait over the stairs, she'd passed the smaller works by without so much as a glance.

"Dear, you'll need my crinolette. It's just there, in the trunk."

Viviana followed the trajectory of Madame Renaud's finger. She hurried across the room to retrieve the foundation garment to add to the mounds of fabric already spilling out of her arms. How silly women's fashions were. The pantaloons she had worn when she lived as a boy were far more practical and more comfortable than any of this appeared to be.

"I imagine you'll be up on that wall soon enough," Madame Renaud pronounced. "You'll be the seventh muse, no doubt. And then there will be just two more to go."

Viviana stepped behind the screen to hide her confusion more than her body as she removed her functional black work dress and apron and attempted to piece together the puzzle of the yellow frock, starting with the crinolette.

The woman could not be saying what Viviana thought she

was hearing. If Monsieur Renaud thought she would pose nude for him, he was sorely mistaken. She had done a number of immoral things in her life, but never unless driven to it out of desperation. Yes, she had stolen food. Yes, she had dressed as a boy and lied to people about who she was. Yes, she had killed people in battle. But she had been ashamed of all of it. She had confessed her sins in the church in Saint-Gaudens as she followed the Garonne River down out of the Pyrenees Mountains after escaping Seu d'Urgell. And she had eventually taken the priest's advice to find honest employment in a good household and to live out her days cleansing her soul through hard physical work that would keep her hands from sin. She would not now do something to tip the scales back toward judgment.

Viviana slipped the skirts into place and then pulled the bodice on over her chemise. It was a little tight, but she managed to secure everything in its proper place. She practiced breathing shallowly but slowly in the constrictive garment—so like the strips of cloth that had once bound her growing breasts—then came around the screen and stood by the bed for inspection, spinning slowly when Madame Renaud twirled a thin finger in the air. The skirts rustled like a warm spring breeze through new leaves.

"My girl, what on earth happened to your neck?"

Neck. Viviana's hand shot up to cover the long and ugly scar. She had not considered that it would be visible now that she was no longer wearing her high-necked work dress.

"It is fine. It is old."

Madame Renaud eyed her but did not press the matter. "Come closer. The skirts are not hanging quite right."

Viviana did as she was told, standing close to the edge of the bed so that Madame Renaud could reach the poufs of fabric sprouting out from behind.

"I wore this dress the last time I went to Paris with Valentin. We saw those odd little experiments—well, some of them were quite large—at the exposition of the Société Anonyme des Artistes. I guess they are calling them Impressionists now," Madame Renaud winced and sucked in a breath.

"What is wrong?" Viviana asked, turning slightly. She had not understood what Madame Renaud said, but a pained gasp was universal.

"Nothing, nothing. Just my hands feel tingly, that's all. Too long in bed."

Viviana could feel her fingers probing at the fabric again, telling the folds where to fall.

"That was in the springtime in 1874," Madame Renaud continued. "I wanted to attend the next one—those paintings were so interesting, though most people didn't care for them. Valentin certainly didn't. But my health began to fail."

She was speaking slowly, but Viviana could not tell if it was because Madame Renaud knew from her new servant's accent that she did not speak French well or if it was because speaking was laborious for the sick woman.

"He went to Paris in 1876 without me," she continued. "He did go to the next exhibition, despite his criticisms of the first, and he did return with some measured praise for Caillebotte, but the others did not make a great impression." She snickered at the pun, which turned into another sharp intake of breath.

"Madame Renaud—"

"You know they have had three of those exhibitions now. Another is planned for this year. I should very much like to go, but my health won't allow it. There, you're all fastened." She tapped Viviana on the shoulder and motioned for her to turn.

"Thank you, madame."

Madame Renaud was smiling at her, that close-lipped smile.

"You look lovely." Then the smile faded.

Viviana stood there, waiting for her mistress to say something more. Waiting to be dismissed. Time ticked by on the clock on the bedside table.

Finally, Madame Renaud said flatly, "Close the curtains before you go."

Viviana snapped into action. She released the folds of linen from behind the curtain knob and allowed them to fall back into place, shutting out the outside, cocooning Madame Renaud once more in a suffocating green shell.

"Thank you, madame," Viviana said at the door.

The woman in the bed did not answer her. Viviana backed out the door and pulled it closed, leaving just a crack—in case Monique Renaud should want to get out.

Chapter

FOUR

✦

MICHIGAN, PRESENT DAY

Esther reentered 1745 Chesterwood Parkway exactly five hours and twenty-three minutes after she'd left it that morning to find her mother topless and staring at herself in the gilt-framed mirror to the left of her easel. On the canvas in front of her was a rough sketch of the basic shapes of her face, neck, and bare shoulders in raw umber over a burnt-sienna underpainting. Esther knew the colors without looking at the tubes on the tray. Lorena was a woman of habit.

This was also why it didn't surprise Esther to find her mother topless near an open window. Each year, as spring shifted to summer, Lorena painted herself, recording the aging process in an experiment that reached back to her days as an art student at Cranbrook. The open window was to let the light in, and Esther supposed that their neighbors at the sorority house across the back fence were used to it by now. The girls were quite kind, actually. Always keeping an eye out for Lorena and texting Esther if they witnessed anything of concern.

"I brought you something to eat," she said, setting a glass of water and a plate of Honeycrisp apple slices and Manchego cheese on the little table next to her mother.

Lorena didn't look away from her reflection, nor did she acknowledge Esther's presence with even the smallest of sounds or gestures. She was completely still but for her breathing and the slight movement of her hair at the warm breeze through the window. Esther pulled a wooden chair up next to her and sat down, silently invading her mother's reflection.

A moment later, Lorena frowned and sighed. "What is it?"

"A snack," Esther said. "And your afternoon pill."

Lorena turned to face her daughter. "This couldn't wait?"

"No, I'm afraid it can't wait." She picked up the pill and the glass of water and held them out to her mother, who eyed them suspiciously but accepted them anyway. "It's that time again," Esther said, gesturing toward the canvas.

"Yes," Lorena said, popping the pill into her mouth.

Esther watched her throat as she washed it down with the water, then looked expectantly at her mother's face, a habit she'd acquired after Lorena was hospitalized following an episode and then admitted to the doctor that she had been crushing up her medication and mixing it into her paint, claiming artistic expression. Esther knew exactly which portrait—the third one going up the stairs—had been adulterated in this way, and she wasn't about to let it happen again. Lorena opened her mouth and lifted her tongue to prove she'd swallowed the pill, then handed the glass back to her daughter.

"You need to eat something," Esther said.

"I guess I may as well," Lorena said. "Now that you've interrupted me, it will take me an hour to get back into the right frame of mind." She picked up an apple slice and took a bite.

"Do you want your robe?" Esther suggested.

"I'm fine."

They sat there together, eating apples and cheese, mother

topless, daughter still in her old T-shirt, mostly silent but for the chewing and Esther's occasional attempts to force some intimacy through benign questions about her mother's new painting. Would it be in a particular style? What tone would it strike? Would there be a background scene?

One question she did not ask because of the agitation it would likely elicit was where Lorena thought she'd put the painting when it was done. Except for Esther's room, the walls of their home were already suffocated by her mother's self-portraits. Close-ups, full length, clothed, nudes, warm tones, cool tones—everywhere you looked, Lorena looked back.

Off-putting as it might seem to others, Esther didn't really mind—they never entertained anyway. And having so many paintings of the same woman seemed appropriate given their pedigree; after all, Francisco Vella had painted the same woman again and again over his entire career. It did mean there was precious little real estate for Esther's own work, which was okay too. Her mother was a far better artist than she was. When Esther painted her own self-portrait, it never came out quite right. Taken alone, each individual feature was accurate—the eye, the nose, the mouth, the ear—but taken as a whole, the painting didn't actually look like her. It looked like a sister might have looked if she'd had one. Or perhaps how she might look in an alternate dimension. But the essence of Esther herself remained elusive.

Growing up with an artist for a mother, Esther had sketched and painted from a young age and was rather talented, if her schoolteachers were to be believed. But as much praise as they heaped upon her, only one person's opinion really mattered. And she was not so liberal with words of affirmation.

"There's no personality in that," her mother said once over her shoulder as she drew pictures at the kitchen table. "You must put yourself into your art. Show the world what only you see." Despite her mother's criticism, Esther would arrange her fin-

48

ished pictures on the fridge herself, already carefully staging her little exhibits at age six or seven. But just once she wished her mother would take a picture from her and, smiling with pride, put it on the fridge, up on the freezer door where Esther couldn't yet reach. Way up at the top.

As an adult, Esther had a better understanding of her mother's condition. She knew she couldn't take these things personally, knew that Lorena would never show genuine excitement about her daughter's achievements. Because she couldn't. She wasn't wired that way. And while medication could mitigate some of the scarier symptoms—the voices, the hallucinations, the paranoia—it was more difficult to treat the apathy, the asocial behavior, the inability to form strong relationships.

No, Lorena was Lorena and always would be. And Esther was a happier person when she remembered that.

When the apples and cheese were all gone, Lorena turned back to her reflection and Esther brought the plate and the glass down to the kitchen sink. She washed and dried them and put them away, then retired to her room with the herbal she'd bought. But instead of getting out her metal ruler and an X-ACTO knife, she took up her palette and her brushes and stood before her own easel.

She hadn't painted a self-portrait in many years and didn't intend to do so now. For the past week she'd been working on a landscape—well, a lakescape. Something she'd seen on a weekend trip up to Tawas earlier that year. She hadn't gone there for an art fair or a flea market. Nothing like that would be going on in March. Too cold. It was just a short escape during one of those rare hospitalizations for her mother. With Lorena under constant monitoring by the doctors and nurses at St. Lawrence, Esther was afforded thirty-six precious consecutive hours to herself. Being a true Michigander, she used that time to get to one of the big lakes.

She drove up to a bed-and-breakfast in East Tawas, where

she ordered in dinner and read a novel from beginning to end, stopping only to sleep, eat a delicious breakfast alone—she was the only guest, it being very much the off-season for tourists—and catch the first sunrise of spring at Tawas Point State Park.

Twenty degrees below freezing with a biting wind and big pancakes of ice still floating on the surface of Lake Huron like tectonic plates—and a sunrise that was what God must have had in mind when he set the earth in place at just the right distance from its star. Pink and orange and white, with seagulls calling as they glided across the frigid expanse of indigo blue. It was simply magical.

Entranced as she was at that effervescent moment, Esther had taken no pictures. She was glad she hadn't. Painting from photos created in her the overwhelming urge to copy what she saw, which inevitably led to disappointment with herself when colors didn't precisely match, when contours were a little off. Painting from memory was far more forgiving. When you painted from memory, there was simply no way for anyone to compare the real thing with the interpretation. No way to find a flaw.

The canvas before her was nearly finished. She had only to add the highlights. For the next hour, she mixed soft pastel tones and tapped them into place with detail brushes, careful not to lose her darks. The darker the darks, the lighter the lights. She stepped back from the canvas from time to time to examine the effect of each stroke on the whole composition, until finally she deemed it complete, cleaned her brushes, and removed the wet paint from the palette with a palette knife. Then she pulled out a razor to scrape away the dried paint from earlier sessions.

Other artists might feel that it was the addition of their signature that meant a painting was finished, but for Esther it had always been this—the systematic erasure of the evidence that a painting had been painted at all. Though years of art education had revealed that of course even great artists went through a process—building up a painting glaze by glaze, stroke by stroke, correcting here, changing there, until the final result was perfect (or nearly so)—when it came to her own attempts to get the picture from her head to the canvas, she'd rather no one be privy to all the false starts and mistakes she made along the way. She was not a great artist and none of her works would ever end up in a museum collection. Certainly no one would ever bother to x-ray them to discover the secrets of her technique like they did with the Caravaggios and da Vincis of the world. But cleaning up the evidence of the crime was always a satisfying endeavor.

When everything was neat and tidy again, Esther went down to the kitchen to make dinner for herself and her mother. After dinner she'd give Lorena her nighttime meds, slip beneath the sheets, and read a few pages of one of the many books stacked by the bed before falling asleep. Tomorrow she would begin the weeklong process of getting the herbal prints ready for selling online—slicing them from the book; cutting, gluing, and clamping the frames, which would then have to be painted or stained; cutting the glass for the front and the board for the back; then putting all the pieces together and tediously listing them one by one in her Etsy shop. With all the materials and time involved, she really didn't make much money off of them, but some money was always better than none.

Admissions to the museum had been falling longer than Esther had been alive. The Markstrom family had kept up with expenses for a while, attracting some wealthy patrons here and there and selling off some of the relics of the family's more auspicious past—an apartment in New York, a garage full of classic cars, a small collection of minor works by major artists. Precious little of that money made it into reinvestment in the museum, though. Most of it was swallowed up by old debts and business ventures gone south.

But it was her mother's first diagnosis, incorrect and antiquated though it was, that seemed to have been the last nail in the prosperity coffin. Hysteria was something women in gothic novels had, not something that should plague women born in the latter half of the twentieth century. Yet that was the word scrawled on the mimeographed paper that was handed to Lorena's father. Eventually they'd get it right, though. And no matter what you called it, where she was once a talented-though-eccentric artistic prodigy who could be forgiven her odd behavior and brusque, unfeeling manner because she created such exquisite work, at some point before Esther was even born, Lorena had become a woman to be medicated and pitied and avoided in social situations. And social situations were the life-blood of the arts community. Without networking, net worth suffered.

At the rate they were going, Esther would have to do something drastic before the year was out. If she didn't, she'd have to live with the shame that the Vella-Markstrom Museum and Gallery had failed under her watch. She'd also have to figure out if there was any other paying job in the universe that a former art history major was qualified to do.

Which seemed unlikely.

✦

SOUTHERN FRANCE, 1879

Vivienne turned away from the door and toward the hall she had not noticed on her way to Madame Renaud's bedchamber. It was indeed lined with paintings. Three on either wall, each depicting a lithe young woman, either nude or nearly so. Holding a garden hoe and carrying a vine laden with grapes. Playing a flute. Dancing in a wooded glen. Smiling and holding a comic mask. Weeping and holding a tragic mask. Holding a trumpet and a book. Attached to the bottom of each frame was a small brass label with words engraved onto them. Their names, she supposed, though she could not read. No two women had the same features—and one of them looked remarkably like Lisette.

Suddenly sensing just how long she must have been gone, she hurried back down the curved staircase and down the hall to the studio, pausing just outside the door when she heard raised voices. The men were clearly arguing, but they spoke so quickly in French that she could only pull out a few words.

Vivienne breezed through the door as though she had just arrived. "Sorry I am slow," she said, heading straight for the settee. "This dress is difficult. Madame Renaud helped me."

Anger was still etched into Renaud's features, but Vella was grinning at her.

"The yellow is very fetching on you, Vivienne," he said.

"Madame Renaud was awake?" Renaud said, frowning.

Vella translated.

"I didn't mean to wake her," Vivienne said. "I didn't know she was there."

"Did she look . . . well?" Renaud pressed.

She most certainly did not, but Vivienne didn't think it would do to say so. "She is well."

Renaud sent Vella a pointed look. Vivienne attempted to sit on the settee and nearly landed on the floor, but Vella's reflexes were quick and a well-placed hand at her elbow kept her upright.

"How do ladies sit in these contraptions?" she said in Spanish.

"They don't," Vella said. He switched to French and said dreamily, "They dance in them. They walk about in fine rooms and draw the eyes of everyone else—men out of allure and women out of envy."

Renaud scoffed. "Listen to him. As if he has ever been a guest at such an occasion. Vivienne, put your hand where it belongs."

Hand. While Vivienne had understood little of what the men had just said, she did know that word. She had not noticed she was covering the scar on her neck with her hand. Reluctantly, she got back into position. From where Renaud stood, the scar was still hidden, but Vella clearly noticed it. He said nothing, however, and the three of them—the artist, the colorman, and the scullery maid—settled into a comfortable silence for a moment.

"How was she, really?" Vella whispered in Spanish more quietly than ever. At Vivienne's questioning look he sent his eyes in the direction of the stairs. "She looked very sick, didn't she?"

Vivienne nodded slightly. "What is wrong with her?"

He glanced toward the canvas behind which Renaud was laboring. "Arsenic poisoning."

Vivienne's eyes grew wide. "He—?"

"No, not like that. The walls. The dye in the wallpapering. They've known for years that it's poisonous. But people still manufacture it and many still sell it. Not me. Renaud bought it from someone else, at a discount, because he is so miserably cheap. And the longer she stays in there, the sicker she will get."

Vella stopped talking as Renaud's head appeared around the side of the canvas. "Stop filling her head with whatever nonsense you're peddling, Vella. Vivienne, you know better than to be seduced by the likes of him. He'll leave you in some dirty little foreign port when some other girl catches his eye, and then where will you be?"

Vivienne blinked, uncomprehending.

"Never mind that," Vella said, sending a glare across the room. "I am not filling her head with nonsense." He smiled at her. "Not yet, anyway."

AN HOUR LATER, the light was gone and the luncheon bell was ringing. Vivienne could barely move, sore as she already was from posing the day before. Her right hand was asleep, and a sharp pain shot from her tailbone up her spine and into the back of her neck.

"I'll return the dress," she said. "Then I will work."

"No, no. There is no need to take the dress back up yet. I need you for one more day," Monsieur Renaud said. "Vella, you may go. I'm finished with you, and I know you must be on your way to Paris. I'm sure Madame Dorset can send you with a basket."

Vella took off the turban, stood, and began taking off the blousy shirt he'd been wearing.

"Really, Vella. You couldn't wait to do that until she was out of the room?"

Vella regarded Vivienne. "Unless I miss my guess, Vivienne has seen plenty of men in all manner of undress." He winked at her and began putting on his own tailored shirt, which had been lying over the arm of a chair at the edge of the room.

"Vella!" Renaud said.

Vella explained to her what he'd said.

"It's fine," Vivienne said in French. "He is not wrong." She switched to the more comfortable Spanish. "But not for the reason you might be supposing."

Vella translated.

Renaud looked a bit shocked. "What possible reason could there be?"

"Renaud, you wouldn't believe it if she told you," Vella said, buttoning his waistcoat. "Our Vivienne is full of surprises."

"She is not *our* Vivienne, young man. She is my Vivienne, and I think she would be better off giving you a wide berth from now on." Renaud beckoned her with a hand. "Now go and change out of that dress but keep it in your own quarters. Be back here tomorrow morning at eight o'clock sharp. Dress on, hair down."

After Vella's translation, Vivienne gave him a small curtsy. "Yes, monsieur." She briefly locked eyes with Vella, trying to convey without speech that she had enjoyed her time talking with him. His face said clearly that he too had enjoyed her company—and that he was not done with it yet.

LATER THAT NIGHT, after Lisette stopped sighing and began to snore, Vivienne lay on her back in the dark, thinking through the past two days. She'd met and then been left by a charismatic and handsome stranger who seemed to have an unending supply of engaging stories about far-flung places she would never see. She'd met and then abandoned a frail, sick, and clearly lonely woman whose own bedchamber was poisoning her. She still had yet more copper pots to scour and polish. Pots that had not so very long ago seemed preferable to even speaking to the master of the house in which she worked. And now tomorrow she would be back in the studio in that beautiful dress so that he could paint her. Could paint her.

Only a few years ago, she had been stumbling over rocks, half-starved as she sneaked out of a country she did not want to leave and into a country that did not want her. For many months, she had alternated between begging on the street and doing odd jobs for business owners who gave her food in return for her work. Just weeks ago, she'd been nearly desperate enough to—no, not quite that desperate, she insisted to herself. May God allow her to die before it ever came to that. And here she was now, respectably employed and in a warm bed, her belly full, her life unrecognizable once more.

A tap at the window caught her attention. Through the glass she saw Vella, the whites of his eyes and his teeth shining in the moonlight. She quickly threw on a dressing gown and her thin slippers and snuck out the kitchen door. He was already there, waiting for her.

"I thought you'd left," Vivienne said.

"I did." He scratched the back of his neck. "I got to the other side of the city and suddenly I just couldn't go any further."

"Did something happen to your cart?"

"No, to my heart."

Vivienne almost laughed at his melodramatic tone and his play on the words *carro* and *corazón*, but then stopped. She had misinterpreted men's words before. And though she could speak Spanish far more fluently than French, it was not her first language. "Are you ill?"

He chuckled and reached out for her hand. "Perhaps. But if I am, it is your fault."

She did not put her hand in his. "My fault?"

He let his hand fall to his side. "Of course. I was minding my own business, perfectly content with life, until you walked into that studio yesterday."

Vivienne crossed her arms over her chest and glanced back at the doorway through which she'd come. "I did not come into that room to meet you. I shouldn't have even been there."

Vella followed her gaze, then his eyes darted to the dark windows. He tipped his head to beckon her, and she took a few steps down the limestone path with him.

"But don't you see?" he said. "Neither should I. I am not an artist's model. I should have been long gone before you arrived with those copper pots. And yet, there we both were, in a room we shouldn't have been in."

"So?"

"So? I assumed you were a person of faith."

"Of course I am," Vivienne said, though truth be told, she was anything but sure about that anymore. Her brother had been so certain of God's blessing on the Carlist cause, and yet it had failed. "But what does that have to do with it? Are you saying you think that God brought us into that room together?"

He shrugged. "Is that so outlandish? To think that God, who can control the rise and fall of nations and rulers, might also be able to draw together the paths of two ordinary people?"

She turned back toward the house. "I imagine God has bigger things on his mind."

He caught her elbow. "Perhaps. But it still seems like quite a coincidence."

"Maybe. But so what?"

"So what?" He smacked his forehead with the heel of his palm. "So what? So come with me. You don't really want to stay here with Lisette and that slave driver Madame Dorset. Come with me to Paris, to Brussels, to Vienna, to Rome! There's nothing here but more pots to polish. Wouldn't you rather see the world?"

For just a moment, Vivienne let herself consider it. She placed herself into the stories that Vella had told her the day before. She imagined the delicious food, the colorful people, the magnificent buildings, the trains and the ships. Had God orchestrated this? Had he caused the Garonne River to flow through Toulouse so that she would follow it to her destiny as a world traveler?

No. Of course not. It was the most egotistical and vain notion she'd ever allowed herself to entertain, and she was ashamed to have thought it at all. If it were true, that would mean that the events leading up to her being in the mountains at that time and place would also have been part of his plan. Which would mean . . .

She could not allow herself even to consider it.

"I am lucky to have found this position in this household," she said. "It's more than I could have hoped for, much more than I deserved. And what kind of a person would I be if I left in the night with a man I just met? What kind of a woman do you imagine me to be? You would have done well to keep moving rather than coming back here to insult me like this."

"I didn't mean to—"

"Señor Vella, you have overstayed your welcome here. I suggest you go. I have to get to sleep. Monsieur Renaud requires me in the morning, and I doubt he will be happy if his model has dark circles under her eyes."

As she talked, Vella's expression slowly morphed from surprise to penitence to indignation to hardened resolve. She had seen that look before. She had wounded his pride, which was a dangerous thing to do to a man. Still, she stood firm and waited for what he might say next.

After a moment of silence, he gave a resolute nod. "I'm sorry. I overstepped. I hadn't thought how it might seem from your point of view. And you're right, of course. We did just meet. It was rude of me to approach you with such a proposition. Please forgive me."

Vivienne could not hide her surprise at the change in his tone, his entire demeanor. She could not remember a man ever having apologized to her before.

"It's just," he continued, then shook his head. "Listen, I will be back around to Toulouse within six months. Nine at the most. And I would very much like to get to know you better. Would that be okay?"

She uncrossed her arms. "Yes."

Vella brightened. "Then I may write to you in the meantime?"

"I cannot read."

"Oh." He was quiet a moment. "Then I will send you sketches of the places I am and the people I see. How about that?"

She smiled. "Yes. I'd like that very much."

Chapter

SIX

Michigan, Present Day

Esther's chance meeting with her old professor had briefly slipped her mind when she was home attending to her mother and working on getting the prints ready for market, but when she was at the museum the following Tuesday, it came roaring back. That day she made her regular rounds through the exhibits with new eyes.

The Vella-Markstrom Museum and Gallery was housed in a former fraternity house on a side street across from the far eastern end of the campus of Michigan State University. Esther's grandfather, Richard, had purchased the building in 1978, thinking at first that it might work as an artists' colony. But the age of such hippie nonsense was ending—and besides, there was no money in it—so he made it into a museum. There was no money in that either, so the first floor became a gallery where living artists consigned their paintings. There was also a small gift shop, an office, a bathroom, and an information desk. On the second floor was the permanent exhibit of Francisco Vella's work. The third floor was storage.

As a child, Esther had spent more hours roaming these rooms than she did in her own home. She took a CATA bus from school to the stop on Grand River Ave. and Bogue St., then zigzagged through the crowds of college students at top speed, tingling with the excitement of spending time alone with the creative vision of her ancestor. She dispensed with homework while wolfing down animal crackers and juice under the supervision of Eddie the custodian. Then she divided her time between roaming the exhibit, pretending she was an eccentric wealthy collector deciding what to buy for her mansion, and poking through the dusty storage areas, imagining she discovered a long-lost painting that would change the course of history.

On one occasion, she invited a friend to play at the museum with her after school; she never had friends over to the house for fear of her mother's erratic behavior. Kristy or Christie—she could never remember how it was supposed to be spelled—was fun for about twenty minutes, but she quickly tired of Esther's playacting and began looking for pranks to pull on Eddie. But Esther loved "Steady Eddie," as she thought of him, and she hadn't been interested in tricking him or making him feel bad for cleaning floors and toilets.

Now as Esther walked every inch of the place she knew by heart, she wondered, How would Ian Perez experience the museum she so dearly loved? Would he notice the burned-out bulb or the scratched-in graffiti on the bathroom door or the divot in the hardwood floor where a delivery man had dropped a bronze bust seven years ago? Would he be impressed by the Vella collection? Would he be disappointed in the new exhibit of local artists? Would he buy something from the gift shop? Would it be out of pity? He hadn't been brought up in the Midwest, but he had been here for the better part of three decades—plenty of time to internalize the region's particular neuroses.

That week she'd made a list of chores that needed doing and handed it to Eddie, who still did his best to maintain the building despite the nonexistent budget and the inevitable march of time. By the time she sat down the next Friday night on the small couch in her crowded office to leaf through an old issue of *Art Market* magazine, most of the list had been checked off, with the notable exception of "Find whatever is making that smell on the third floor and deal with it." Some problems just didn't have ready solutions.

The desk phone rang, and Esther rose to answer it, tripping over a stack of art books on the way. While she kept her home studio immaculate (and secretly wondered if that was why she was not a better artist), her office was always a disaster.

"Yes, Kylie?"

"There's a man here to see you."

"Does this man have a name?"

A pause. "Ian?"

"Are you asking me?"

"It's Ian. Parrish." A muffled voice. "Paris?"

"I'll be out in a moment."

Esther wished she could offer a better pay rate for working the information desk. The crop of college students who applied were not usually the most professional, yet for the people walking through the door each day (well, some days), they were the face of the institution.

She retucked her shirt and ran a hand over her hair, which she'd pulled into a haphazard ponytail when she was stopped at the light at MAC Avenue. She frowned then shook her head. This was an old college professor, not a blind date.

She walked out to the information desk. "Well? Where is he?"

Kylie looked up from her phone. "Huh? Oh, um . . ."

Esther shook her head and waved her hand. "Never mind. I'll find him."

After a moment she spied Dr. Perez in the gallery, hands in his pockets, bending slightly at the waist, examining a small landscape executed with a palette knife. Trees in various shades of green. Cloud-scraped blue sky. Sunlit creek tumbling over brown rocks.

"What do you think?" Esther said as she approached.

Dr. Perez looked up and took a step back. "Nicely captures a summer afternoon. I can almost feel the heat and the wind. Too bad it's not bigger."

"Oh?"

"Well, summer feels big, doesn't it? Expansive. Unending."

"Perhaps the artist is saying something by putting summer into so small a box," she suggested.

Perez looked back at the painting. "And what do you suppose he or she is saying?"

Esther shrugged. "Perhaps she doesn't get to experience summer as she'd like. Maybe this little sliver is all she has time for."

He examined the card on the wall next to the painting. "Do you know the artist? There appears to be no signature, and the label just has a number."

"Of course I know the artist. It's my gallery, after all."

He stood straight and smiled. "It's good to see you again." She held out her hand to him and he shook it. "Glad you made it in."

"Do you ever have the artists here for events?" he said.

"We nearly always do when there's an exhibition where the artist is living and can make the trip. This particular exhibit isn't actually supposed to be open until *next Friday*." She tried to catch Kylie's eye, but the girl was deep in her phone again.

"Oh, it's not her fault," he said. "I saw the ropes and the sign plain as day. I just sneaked around them. I assume you'll have a big shindig next week then?"

"Yes, I'm sorry you came this week. As you can see, we still have pieces to hang." She pointed to a corner full of boxes and hardware. "And by we, I mean me."

"You do the displays yourself?"

"Eddie helps with the really large ones. He's the maintenance guy. We're down to a skeleton staff in the summer. Most of the students are gone at this point—except the Kylies of the world. She's retaking a class and working this summer. It's pretty quiet. I'm hoping this exhibit might liven things up a little when it opens. But it'll probably just be you and me tonight."

He smiled. "Well, that suits me fine. I'm always up for a gathering, but I think perhaps for my first time at the Vella-Markstrom, a personal tour might be more rewarding."

"Let's start the tour then." She waited a moment for him to follow her out of the gallery. He was looking at the little landscape again. "Shall we?"

"Oh, yes. Sorry."

They walked to the front desk, where Esther retrieved a brochure and handed it to Perez, pointing out the map on the back. Not that there was much need for one.

As they walked up the large, twisting front staircase to the second floor, Esther quickly relayed the house's history as a fraternity, its purchase by her grandfather, and its conversion to its present state. "The collection that was moved here from Detroit was a bit smaller than it is now. Richard continued to acquire other paintings as he was made aware of their existence and had the funds. Then when he died, my father was helping my mom run things for a short time. Then he left the family. He'd married into it, you know. Didn't love it quite like my mom and I do." *Didn't love my mom and me quite enough.*

"And if I remember correctly from having you in class all those years ago, you said you're descendants of Vella?"

She nodded. "Through my grandmother Marian. Francisco was her great-great-grandfather. But I never knew her. Or my grandfather, for that matter. They were all dead by the time I came along."

They paused at the top of the stairs, where the Francisco Vella Memorial Gallery began with a silhouette and a long paragraph of text etched on plexiglass.

"We begin the exhibition with this image of a generic silhouette because there are no surviving pictures of the artist," Esther began. "Even though Vella lived during a time when people could be photographed, no photos have ever been found, and he never, as far as can be ascertained, painted a self-portrait. He's not identified as the subject of any other artist's portraits either, so we don't know what he looked like. There's not even a gravestone that we could take a picture of. The story is that he emigrated to America aboard the *Prometheus*. It departed from the port at Gibraltar, actually. Strange coincidence, isn't it? You're the only person I know from Gibraltar."

"Not so strange, really," he said. "There are many of us expats about. You'd be surprised how many Gibraltarians I keep in touch with, and very few of them actually live on the Rock. But regarding the ship and the trip to America—you sound dubious."

Esther pressed her lips together. "Well, it's problematic. The ship did exist, and there is a Francisco Vella on the manifest, but I haven't been able to find any record of him in the US after the ship leaves Gibraltar. And he had a family in France. It seems strange that he would leave them behind. Not impossible, though."

"Hmm. Intriguing. You certainly have my interest." He motioned to a painting on the wall to the right. "Lead the way."

For the next hour, Esther led Dr. Perez through Francisco Vella's paintings. There were several landscapes and a few still lifes, but much of his work was figural in nature. Rather than religious motifs, history paintings, or the personification of mythical figures, the scenes generally depicted small, intimate moments that captured men and women engaged in their regular, day-to-day lives in various locales—village squares, desert cisterns, red-light districts, cathedral steps. The paintings ascribed dignity to ordinary people doing ordinary work, erring to neither the side of sentimentality nor the grotesque. And many of them included the same beautiful woman somewhere in the scene, sometimes the focal point, sometimes filling in the background.

They were works never featured in textbooks or coffee table books—Esther had seen none in her entire time as an art history major. Vella was considered a minor artist, and an unimportant one at that. He never showed his work at any of the significant Salons or exhibitions of his time. He had no famous patrons. He was not schooled at the academy, nor did he apprentice under a well-known master like Monet or Degas. But those were all things she admired in her ancestor. That he was a rustic, self-taught man. That he painted out of love for the subject matter rather than out of obligation because of a commission. That he didn't let his relative obscurity keep him from creating.

It was how she painted as well. Oh, she'd had some training, of course, but nothing formal. She'd learned mostly by watching her mother. She did exhibit here and there, but not anywhere important, and never with her name attached to the work. She liked to maintain some distance from its reception. And she hated talking about it with people. At exhibitions like the one that would open the following weekend, she marveled at artists who could chat with viewers and prospective buyers about their vision, their purpose, the message they were sending out into the world. They all seemed so sure of what they had to say.

Painting had never been like that for her. It had always been rather private, sometimes frustrating, and always first and foremost for *her*—no one else. Not even her mother.

As they came to the end of the gallery, Esther cleared her throat. It had been some time since she'd talked so much for so long, and her voice was getting rough. "So, what do you think?"

Perez rubbed his chin. "He was a fine painter, and you're a fine tour guide."

Esther wanted a bit more than that. "But what do you *think*? Do you think he's just a minor painter?"

The question hung in the air a moment, long enough that he

didn't actually need any words to answer her. But he made an attempt anyway.

"I think," he began slowly, "that perhaps that's a question to discuss over a drink." He looked at his watch. "After all, it's past closing time here."

Esther looked at the watch on her own wrist. It was 8:07 p.m. Kylie had almost certainly already left—without so much as a "See you next week."

"So it is," she said. She hesitated a moment. "You don't need to get on the road?"

"No, I decided to make a weekend out of it. I'm staying at the Graduate."

"Nice." She hit a few light switches, then started down the staircase. "And what are you doing tomorrow?"

"I'm not exactly sure," he said, a few steps behind. "I thought perhaps a couple bookstores. Maybe I'll stop into the Broad."

"The Broad? You like modern art?"

"It's not my favorite. But you never know. There might be something interesting there."

They reached the first floor. The front desk was empty.

"So what do you say?" Perez prompted. "Shall we discuss your venerated ancestor over cocktails?"

Esther smiled sadly. "You know, I'd love to, but . . ."

He held up his hand. "No obligation. I don't want to make you uncomfortable."

Esther felt a moment of pity for him and his entire gender; they had to be so careful nowadays not to say the wrong thing, not to come too close, not to imply any pressure, lest they get knocked over by the merciless justice of the swung pendulum.

"It's not that. I just—" She sighed. "I have to go home and check on my mom."

He brightened a moment. Then, "Is she okay?"

"She's— Hang on a sec." Esther popped into her office and grabbed her phone, checking for message notifications before slipping it into her purse. She straightened a few things on her desk—a pointless endeavor amid the chaos—then left and locked the office door behind her. When she was back out front, Perez was gone. She found him in the gallery again, looking at the little summer landscape. "You're really drawn to that one, eh?"

He came to meet her at the doorway to the gallery. "There's something about it. I don't know. Will the paintings in this room be for sale next week?"

She switched off the light. "Most of them." She led the way to the door, then stopped in front of it. "Anyway, what I was saying about my mom. I just have to check up on her, give her her meds, and make sure everything's locked up tight."

"Okay, great. Well . . . I walked here from the hotel. I'll just walk back that way, and when you're done you can meet me at the bar on the top floor."

He followed her out into the bright summer evening. She locked the door and yanked on it for good measure, then pulled out her phone. "Maybe I should get your number. Just in case I can't make it for some reason. Then you won't be waiting all night."

"I'll send you a text."

"Oh, sure." She relayed her number to him and he typed it into his phone. Then she stared at hers, but the screen didn't light up. "Did you send it?"

"No, but I will when I get there. You should get home to your mum. I'll see you soon."

He did an about-face and headed west on Grand River Avenue toward the other end of the small business district. Walking into the sinking sun, he was lost to sight within seconds.

Esther slipped on her sunglasses and headed for her car, feeling bizarrely reckless at the idea of not going through the motions of her regular routine and being in bed by 10:00 p.m. Instead, she'd be discussing her favorite subject with someone who had equal interest and insight into the matter.

How divine.

Chapter

SEVEN

❖

Viviana dipped her brush, squared her shoulders, and laid a thin glaze of varnish over the corners. She covered the cobalt and zinc white porcelain vase, the drooping viridian fronds of rue, the blushing peonies with their citron centers. Then she moved out to the mummy brown table and the Mars red wall, the shadows heavy with manganese violet. She'd successfully avoided using black as Renaud had suggested, and she liked the result.

Though it had exasperated her employer, who preferred his models to remain silent as well as still, Viviana could not help asking questions when Renaud had asked her to sit for him in the days following her first modeling session. Before and after getting into position, she would peer at his canvas, pointing to various features and asking, "How?" His explanations were useless because of the language barrier, so he had begun to set aside time each day to show her a technique. After several weeks of this, he let her try them out herself with old supplies. Thus,

70

without ever meaning to, Renaud had found himself a student and Viviana had found herself a teacher.

Now she stepped back to admire how the varnish revitalized the colors of the dried oil paint, bringing each of them back to life after the fading of the past months. If only there were a similar tonic for human beings.

Viviana felt the loss of Monique Renaud more keenly than she thought she would. After all, she had only known the woman for six months before her illness erased her from this world. Perhaps it was because Monique was the only other woman in the house who had been kind to her. As Viviana had slowly emptied Monique's armoire and trunks of their beautiful dresses so that her husband could paint Viviana in them, she was given so much more than fine clothing. She was given companionship, friendship, and care. She was given language lessons through fine conversation with a woman who spoke slowly and clearly and filled Viviana's mind with wonderful and terrible things.

The frail woman in the voluminous bed had told her about growing up on the northern coast of France, of her grandfather who had fought for Napoleon Bonaparte, her mother who had died of cholera, her brother who ran a secret newspaper during the oppressive regime of Napoleon III. She had regaled Viviana with stories of Valentin's courtship of her and pricked her heart with the stories of her four miscarriages. She told her about the day she planted the peonies along the east side of the house, one for each of her lost children.

As Monique divulged both the beautiful and the broken parts of her life, Viviana did the same. She told Monique of the loss of her parents, her love for her brother, her fear of being left alone in the world. She told her of the civil unrest in Spain, of Ignasi's fierce loyalty to the church and her defenders, of his desire to join the fight. She even told her about her decision to go with him, to live like a man among men so that she would not be yet another woman left bereft because of war.

But she could not bring herself to tell Monique how Ignasi died. That she would never voice. Because to say it out loud would mean facing the unvarnished truth.

One thing she did tell Monique, though she debated on whether it was right to do so, whether she might cause problems between a husband and wife or even get herself dismissed, was what Vella had said about the arsenic in the wallpaper and how it was poisoning her. Viviana implored her to move to a different room. Monique merely chuckled and dismissed the notion that something so lovely could be deadly.

But it was. Monique was gone. And Vella, despite his promise to return within nine months at the most, still had not arrived after nearly ten. His sketches of people and places he encountered on his journeys had come weekly at first. Then monthly. Then not at all.

Viviana cleaned the varnish from the brush with mineral spirits and thanked the Lord once more for Renaud's willingness that she should learn the art of painting. If she did not have this outlet, even for the few hours a day she could snatch from her other duties, she might fall prey to despair.

She removed her smock and smoothed a hand over her hair, which was finally long enough to pin back into a small chignon, the volume of which Viviana could improve if she wanted to fuss with a foundation of felted wool. When Ignasi had cut off her hair, it was the first time it had ever felt the keen edge of a pair of shears. When she saw the dark river of hair that fell at his blade, she'd been too stunned to cry—there was so much of it. She'd had no notion of how long it would be gone. It was Renaud who had pointed out how often she touched it, as though she needed constant reassurance that things could return to how they were. But that would be like trying to scrape dried paint from a failed painting to get down to the clean canvas. Such a thing was impossible. The only thing to do was to paint over the flaws.

"Well?" she prompted Renaud, who was busy with his own painting in another corner of the studio.

He looked in her direction and squinted, then came out from behind his easel, rustling papers and sketches under his feet as he approached the small still life. "You've certainly captured the colors. The forms are better, as are the shadows and light. Why haven't you signed it? I showed you how to form the letters for your name."

"I have."

"Where?"

She pointed to a scratched-in *V* on the edge of the table holding the peonies.

"That? It looks like part of the table. And it's merely your first initial. Where is your surname? Don't you want your name to be known? Aren't you proud of what you create?"

"Of course I'm proud of what I create." But of course she did not want her name to be known. Not when it was associated with what she had done back in Spain.

"Then declare it!" said Renaud.

"I prefer to use just the *V*. For now. I am still learning, after all."

He was shaking his head. "At least paint it in boldly so someone can see it." He picked up her rigger brush, mixed some mineral spirits with the chrome yellow on her palette, and handed it to her.

"There. Isn't that much better?" Renaud said as he went back to his own work. "I do wish you'd chosen some other flower. Peonies are still a bit beyond your skill level."

"That's what was blooming at the time."

He offered a vague grunt in answer.

Though she liked hiding her signature within the painting, Viviana acquiesced and marked the corner of the still life with a graceful *V*.

"Anyway," she continued, her French far more confident than

it had been the year before, "I wanted to practice mixing colors for portraits, and the peonies are nearly the same color as a Frenchman's skin."

"A French woman perhaps." He regarded her, "Why paint a French person?"

"I am surrounded by French people. Who else would I paint?" Renaud came back out from behind his painting and began rummaging around in a trunk. He was at it so long, Viviana wondered if perhaps he'd forgotten what he was looking for. He seemed so much older since his wife died.

Finally, he emerged with a triumphant "Voilà!" He dragged a small prop table over to her work area, swept the objects off of it with a wave of his hand, breaking a figurine in the process, and perched a cracked mirror upon the scratched surface. "Paint her," he said.

Viviana looked at herself in the mirror. "I can't paint her."

"Why not?"

Because I cannot stand to look at her. "You paint her far better than I ever could."

For the past nine months, Renaud had painted her in gardens, in rooms, in gowns, in rags. He had even painted her mostly nude as Erato, the passionate muse of lyric poetry, though she would have preferred to represent Urania. Erato, Renaud had told her, was given in marriage to Malus, a word that in Latin meant unpleasant, wicked, unfavorable. When Viviana voiced her desire to instead represent the muse associated with astronomy and mathematics, he would not even consider it. Urania was always dressed in blue, and blue was expensive.

Viviana had consented to model in a state of undress only after Renaud brought in other models for his paintings, allowing her to practice life drawing at the same time. They were mostly men—though there was one woman—whom Renaud found on the streets of Toulouse. They were eager for the small fee he paid, the young because they had spent their rent money on cabarets and absinthe, the old because they were often infirm and out of work and had no one to care for them.

After her initial embarrassment to see another person completely disrobed and standing in the middle of the room as though such a thing were normal, Viviana relaxed and applied herself to transferring their three-dimensional forms to the two-dimensional medium of paper and charcoal. The discomfort faded quickly away, and the bodies before her became objects—the same as a vase of peonies—to be represented as truthfully as she could manage.

Her first attempts were terrible, and she did not want to show them to Renaud for fear he would count her a lost cause and send her back to the kitchen. When a curious model glanced at her sketch pad, she apologized over and over until Renaud ushered the man out of the house and returned to reprimand her.

"Never talk to the model," he'd said, "and never apologize. Never let on to others that you haven't drawn or painted precisely what you meant to. It is none of their business what your intentions were. Let them think you meant it to come out that way the whole time. They are not the artist. You are."

Now as she looked into the mirror, Viviana wondered who looked back at her. Was it indeed an artist? A scullery maid? An orphan? A soldier? A killer?

Who was she really, deep down inside? She was not the muse of lyric and erotic poetry. She couldn't even read poetry. She was not a queen, a nymph, a saint. She was not any of the women Renaud had painted her as. She was nothing. Just an obscure girl with no country who was not worth coming back for.

"Here," Renaud said, carefully removing the painting of the peonies from her easel and replacing it with a canvas larger than any she had attempted thus far. "You think too small. Assert yourself. Shamelessly proclaim your presence and your vision. And if you are going to fail, fail boldly. Just don't use any ultramarine as you do it."

Chapter

EIGHT

◆

MICHIGAN, PRESENT DAY

As it turned out, Esther was in and out of the house in just under forty minutes, which, after parking in the ramp behind Charlie Kang's restaurant and walking to the hotel, put her exiting the elevator on the top floor of the Graduate at just about the time the sun was kissing the horizon. The moment she entered the bar, Ian Perez was out of his seat and closing the distance between them.

"Oh, good," he said. "I was hoping you wouldn't miss the sunset."

From up here, the view to downtown Lansing, with its tight cluster of modest buildings flanking the white-domed capitol, was a rich and unobstructed carpet of dark green trees. South of downtown were Wynken, Blynken, and Nod, the three iconic smokestacks of the former power station. Closer to the hotel and just across Grand River Avenue were some of the oldest buildings at Michigan State University, all red brick and gray slate and copper oxidized to a cool lichen green. Just beyond them, she could see the Breslin Center and Spartan Stadium.

All was bathed in golden light that was giving way to the dioxazine purple blanket of night approaching from the east. It was almost worth painting.

"Beautiful," she said. "What a great view."

He motioned to the cushy leather stool behind her. "Drinks are on me."

She hung her purse from the under-bar hook after a couple unsuccessful blind tries and settled onto the stool. "No, I don't think so."

"I insist. I realized I never paid for admission to the museum, let alone a private tour."

"You didn't pay to get in?" That Kylie.

"I just asked the girl behind the desk if you were there and then she called you." He settled down on the stool to her right. "So this is all on me tonight."

"What can I get you?" the bartender said, handing her their list of specialty cocktails.

Esther rarely drank, though being in the art world, she had to know a little something about wine. A very little. Rather than branch out, she stuck with the familiar. "Pinot grigio?"

"And let's have an order of watermelon and feta skewers," Perez added.

The bartender pointed at his empty lowball glass. "Another?"

"Please."

Esther wondered what he'd been drinking before she got there. And what he'd been thinking. Was he coming up with a diplomatic way to say that Francisco Vella was about as famous as he deserved to be?

"Everything okay at home?" he ventured.

"Yes. Just fine."

"Excellent."

"It's a good thing too. You forgot to text me so I'd have your number."

He shook his head. "I didn't forget."

She frowned and started to fish around in her purse for her phone. "I never got one."

"Yes, well, I never sent one."

She stopped fishing.

"I didn't forget. I just didn't . . ." He seemed to be looking for the right way to say it.

"You didn't want me to be able to text you," she supplied. "To decline." She pursed her lips but couldn't keep from smiling a little. "That's quite clever for—" She stopped. She was going to say "for a man your age," but that was hardly polite.

Perez scratched his forehead at his receding hairline. "I thought so. There was just so much left to say."

The bartender set Esther's wine down in front of her, then switched Perez's empty glass for one with about an inch of liquid in it that was the same color as the glow in the western sky.

"Cheers," he said, holding up his glass.

"Cheers." She clinked hers against his and noted the lack of a wedding ring. Had he worn one back when she was in college? That was something she would never have bothered to notice about a professor. But she supposed it was far more likely that he had been married and was now divorced or widowed than that he'd never married. After all, he was a fine-looking man with a pleasant personality who made a decent living and could hold up his end of a conversation.

"So anyway," he said after a sip of his drink, "I've been thinking about Vella and what I saw today and what you asked back at the museum."

"And?"

"And I have a question for you."

She sipped her wine. "That hardly seems fair."

"Now hear me out. I want to know the answer to this."

"And I want to know the answer to *my* question."

"Yes, yes, yes. All in good time. But first answer this one for me: What are the marks of a major artist?"

She blew out a puff of air. "Off the top of my head . . . talent, training, skill, output, reception, whether any boundaries were being pushed, what price they command." She took a drink and waited for a response.

"Sure, yes, all of that," he agreed.

The watermelon and feta skewers arrived.

"Now, taking each of those one by one," he continued, "ask yourself if Vella exhibits the kind of training, skill, output, and so on one would need to have to be considered a major artist." He paused, picked up a skewer, and nudged the plate toward her. "I can start if you like. Talent. Sure, he was talented. Skilled? Yes. But uncommonly so?" He wiggled his hand noncommittally. "I'm not so sure. Training? Is anything known about his training? You didn't really mention it during the tour."

"Not much," Esther admitted. "He seems to have been largely self-taught. He did rub shoulders with a lot of other artists."

"Yet his style does not seem to be closely imitating any particular artist of his time, which might otherwise give us a clue of his greatest influences."

"But doesn't that speak to genius?" she asked. "To blaze one's own path rather than merely copy the style of someone with more name recognition?"

Perez smiled. "Such a delightfully American notion, trailblazing. But if he was painting in Europe in the late nineteenth century, that would not have won him many accolades."

"Monet went his own way, and no one with any taste liked what he was doing at the time." Esther set down her glass so her hands were free to emphasize her points. "And Pissarro and Cézanne and Sisley. The Salon wouldn't show most of their work because it wasn't in keeping with the established notions of what art was. They weren't receiving any accolades at first. Even the people who went to their independent exhibitions mostly slammed them in the press."

He acknowledged the points with a nod. "This is true, but

all the artists you mention were trained. Some at the academy, some by apprenticing under a master painter."

"And many Impressionists left their schools or were kicked out."

He smiled. "Sharp and argumentative as ever."

She laughed. "Don't try to change the subject when I'm clearly getting somewhere." She started to take a sip of wine only to realize her glass was empty.

As the skies all around them darkened and the bar filled up with other people having their own animated conversations, Esther lost herself in the spirited back-and-forth of two people at odds in the most congenial sense. Though her work at the museum had afforded her a number of opportunities to talk to people about art, she rarely felt that they were really talking about the same thing. Much of the time she got the feeling they were on the lookout for someone more important and influential they should be talking to. And she always went home exhausted and deflated and a little bit depressed.

This was different. This was stimulating. This was effortless.

This was . . . fun.

"Well, I can tell you this," she finally said when they had come to the end of what knowledge they had of Vella, "you cannot judge him truly because you have not seen his greatest work."

"I beg your pardon? The selection you had at the museum seemed rather extensive."

"Extensive, but not exhaustive. His finest painting is not in the museum."

He sat up straight on his stool. "Where is it? France? Spain? Switzerland?"

"It's at 1745 Chesterwood Parkway."

"And where is that?"

"Just a few blocks from here."

He set his empty glass down on the bar. "Don't tell me it's at your house?"

Esther raised her eyebrows but said nothing.

"Well, let's see it."

"You can't see it now. It's"—she looked at her watch—"oh my gosh, it's past eleven!"

"Will you turn into a pumpkin at midnight?"

"What? No. I just don't normally stay out this late." Esther grabbed her purse, stood up, and swayed.

"Oh, I don't think you should be going anywhere," Perez said.

"I've just been sitting too long. My leg fell asleep. I don't generally sit for hours at a stretch." She dug in her purse. "Are you sure I can't pay for my wine?"

"I'm sure," he said, standing.

She pulled out her phone. No texts. No missed calls. Everything was fine. Probably.

"Are you worried about your mum?" he said.

"I'm sure it's fine."

He motioned to the bartender to close the tab. "Let's get you an Uber."

"I only had one glass of wine."

"You had three glasses of wine."

"I did? No, I—"

"You did. And you didn't eat any of the appetizer."

The bartender handed him the check and his credit card. He added a tip and signed it, and before he could slip it back across the bar Esther looked at the total. Clearly she had had more than one drink. How stupid of her to stay out so late, and now she couldn't in good conscience drive home.

"I'll take the bus," she said.

"The bus?"

"Yes. There's a stop just outside the hotel and one not far from my street."

He was shaking his head. "I don't feel good about that."

She waved away his concern. "The bus is fine. I take it all the time."

81

"Why don't I just drive you home in your car?" He started steering her to the exit. "It's so annoying that men can walk wherever they want, whenever they want."

Esther sighed. "I'll drive you home and walk back."

"I agree," he said, then held out his hand, motioning for her to lead the way.

They passed the security guard at the entrance, and Perez pushed the button for the elevator. Three loud college bros tumbled out of the bar and into the hall behind them as the elevator arrived, then pressed in after them, pushing them into opposite corners of the box. One of them was talking in an outside voice about some kegger he'd been to the last night of school. Esther caught Perez's eyes then rolled hers. He tried and failed to suppress a laugh, which came out as a snort, earning him a glare from one of the guy's pals. The elevator doors opened on the first floor, and the guys loped off and around the corner. A moment of silence, then they both burst out laughing. The doors began to close.

"Oh!" Esther yelped and dove for the button. The doors opened. Feeling a little foolish, she pulled her purse farther up on her shoulder and walked out, Perez close behind.

They passed the closed coffee shop and strode across the lobby and through the revolving door. Outside the air had turned cool, almost chilly, and the streetlights lit the dark in warm yellow light. There was talk of switching them over to cold white LEDs, but Esther hoped it wouldn't come to that. There were just some things that should not be sacrificed on the altar of being "green," and atmosphere was one of them.

Esther led the way back to the parking ramp. As they headed into the alley behind Charlie Kang's, the easy camaraderie from the bar evaporated and Esther felt profoundly self-conscious. She rubbed her bare arms, wishing she'd thought to bring a sweater.

"Here," he said, stopping to slip off his jacket.

She put up a hand. "Oh, no. I'm fine."

"Nonsense, take it."

He propped it over her shoulders like he might put it on the back of a chair. The lining was warm from his body.

"How old are you?" she blurted.

"Sixty-five."

She started walking again and did some quick mental math. "So you were near my age now when I first had you freshman year?"

He gave it a moment of thought. "That sounds right."

She pulled at the sides of the jacket, tucking herself further into its warmth. "Huh."

"What?"

"It's just that professors seem so much older when you're a student, but really you weren't *that* old."

"And by that you really mean to say that *you* are not that old, right?" he teased.

"Yes. Of course that's what I was *thinking*. Though it's a little rude to say it out loud." Only that wasn't what she had been thinking. Not exactly.

He laughed and ran a hand over his thinning hair. "I'm a lot older than my students now. Every year they look younger, I feel like I'm teaching primary school sometimes."

They reached the parking ramp, and Dr. Perez held open the door to the stairwell.

"That's exactly what I'm talking about. Come September it will look like a daycare out here—mixed with an Urban Outfitters." Esther sighed. "I like living in a college town, but I think I'd feel better about myself if I didn't."

He let out another laugh, which echoed against the concrete walls. Then they were silent, walking in step across the parking area to her car. Esther handed her keys to him, and he opened the passenger side door for her.

"How long have you lived here?" Perez said as he turned onto

Grand River and almost immediately had to cross four lanes of traffic to take the left fork onto Michigan Avenue.

"All my life. The house used to be my grandfather's. Then it went to my mother when he died. I've lived there since I was two days old. It's a good thing too. I would never be able to afford it in today's market. The property taxes alone are like a mortgage payment."

They stopped at a light. "Why did you go all the way to Hope for school when MSU was literally just down the street? Surely they have an art history program."

As the light turned green, Esther took a deep breath. "Like everyone else, I wanted to get away from my mother." She thought he'd chuckle at that, but when she glanced his way his face was serious. Still, he didn't ask. And perhaps it was because he didn't that Esther found herself volunteering the information. "She suffers from schizophrenia."

There was no hint of judgment or even surprise in Perez's face. "When was she diagnosed?"

"Well, when she was a teenager she was diagnosed with hysteria, if you can believe that. It wasn't until she was in her late twenties, I think, that the right diagnosis was made." Esther pointed. "Turn up here, onto University Drive. It's one of the reasons they moved from Detroit to East Lansing. Harder to be mentally ill back then. Lots of talk and I would imagine a good deal of shunning in their social circles. Veer right. I think my grandfather wanted to start fresh. It was just him and her. No wife to help him manage it." She pointed again. "Turn left at that fire hydrant. She died when my mom was just four. He pulled her out of Cranbrook, away from her friends, took a job at MSU, hired a nurse, and opened the gallery. Here we are. That brick one with the half timbers on the second story."

Perez pulled up in front of the two-and-a-half-story Tudor Revival. They both got out of the car, and Esther came around to where Perez stood at the end of the walk. In the weak lamp-

84

light, the weedy gardens looked almost purposeful, though they had been sorely neglected since she'd stopped hiring out the landscaping work to save money. She slipped off Perez's jacket, held it out to him, and immediately felt her skin erupt in goose bumps. He took it from her but did not put it on.

"Do you worry about your mum?"

"What do you mean?"

"It seems you can't leave her alone for very long."

"Yes, well, if she's taking her medication properly, she's fairly stable. I used to worry about her more. About one in ten people with schizophrenia die by suicide, and she has made attempts in the past. But meds help with the paranoia and hallucinations and voices and such. Other aspects of it are harder to treat, but I think it's the positive symptoms—believe it or not, they call those *positive*—that might push people toward suicide. Just to make it all stop, you know?" He was looking at her with a potent mix of pity and concern, which she felt compelled to assuage. "So I went away to school. My mother had a live-in nurse at the time. It was . . ."

She drifted off to that golden time. Drunk on freedom from the need to be ever watchful, she'd blossomed into her own distinct person at Hope College. She'd basked in her anonymity, she'd made a couple real friends, and she'd focused entirely on her own thoughts, her own dreams, her own desires. Four precious years. That was all she'd had before her mother's nurse turned in her notice. Esther had moved back home, taken up the helm at the museum, and allowed her ambitions to fade like the once-bright carmine red pigment in J. M. W. Turner's painting of the *Fighting Temeraire*.

"Anyway," she said, "this is where I live. Thanks for getting me home."

"Thank you for trusting me with the information about your mum."

Esther felt a knot rising up in her throat.

85

He started to put a hand on her shoulder but let it drop back to his side. "Are you okay?"

She put on a fresh smile. "Of course."

He nodded. "Okay then. I better be off."

She rubbed her arm where his hand would have touched.

"You can take the bus. You'll want the bus stop across Michigan Avenue. Between Rather and Butterfield Hall."

"I can't imagine the hotel is more than a mile away." He slipped on his jacket. "I think I'll just walk. Though it's a good thing we all have GPS on our phones nowadays. Not sure I'd be able to find my way out of this labyrinth you've taken me down without satellites to guide me." He raised a hand in farewell and turned toward the way they'd come.

"Dr. Perez," Esther said, her words spinning him back around. "Thank you. I had a really nice time tonight. Discussing everything."

He smiled. "So did I. It's been an absolute joy to chat with you. And do call me Ian, won't you?"

That was all that needed to be said, but neither of them made a move to go. Esther knew why, despite the chill air, she did not want this night to end. For a few hours, she'd felt like she was back at school, back in that slice of her life when she'd felt most herself. She'd forgotten her mother and the museum's budget sheet and the clock of her life slowly spinning itself out within a five-mile radius from home, and had reveled in talking to someone who talked back with the same level of enthusiasm and interest in a subject she'd almost forgotten she was passionate about.

"Did you—want to come in and see the painting?" she said finally.

As soon as she said it, she realized how it sounded. For just a moment he looked like he was going to accept the invitation. Then she saw him change his mind.

"I'm sure it looks better in the light of day," he said.

Esther felt a strange mixture of relief and disappointment at his answer.

"Maybe I can stop by sometime tomorrow before I leave town," he said.

Esther nodded. "That might work."

"I'll text you."

She raised her eyebrows. "For real?"

He laughed. "Yes. For real."

"All right then." She stepped up onto the porch and unlocked the door. "Have a good night."

She slipped inside, threw the deadbolt, and kicked off her shoes. "What a good night," she whispered.

Chapter

NINE

◆

SOUTHERN FRANCE, 1880

I t was September when Vella finally turned up once more in
Toulouse. Viviana's hair now reached her clavicles, a word
she knew, along with all the other bones of the human body,
from studying a medical book Renaud kept in the studio and constantly irritating him with her requests to know what the labels
said. She could name all the organs and the major muscles. She
knew precisely what proportions of aureolin and cerulean and
alizarin made the best base color for skin. She could render silk
and stone and steel. And she had painted over her self-portrait
so many times that she thought she could see the ghosts of all
her failed attempts pushing up from beneath her latest. Perhaps
she needed to start all over.

Viviana had expected to feel a thrill upon seeing her old ad-
mirer after more than a year, but when Vella entered the studio
without so much as a knock and invaded the space behind her
in the mirror, her first emotion was exasperation. It was followed quickly by relief—that he was indeed alive and looked well

enough, though thinner than when she'd last seen him—and she hoped he had not noticed her first reaction.

"There she is," he said in Spanish, "the lady with the dark hair."

"There he is," she replied in French, "the man who disappeared."

His smile faltered. Recovered. "I see the painted has become the painter," he said in French.

Renaud approached from the other end of the room. "Indeed. She has come a long way from when you saw her last. Much to the displeasure of Madame Dorset and Mademoiselle Lisette."

Vella chuckled. "But I imagine that Madame Renaud must be pleased, kind as she is."

Viviana looked at the floor.

Renaud gathered himself. "Monique has died. We buried her nearly six months ago."

"Oh," Vella said, swallowing the word even as it left his mouth. "I am so sorry. I had not heard."

There was an awkward moment where no one knew the right thing to say. Viviana wished that Madame Dorset would come to the door in a huff about needing her in the kitchen, but the doorway remained empty.

"Well," Renaud finally said, "I believe you've come at just the right time, as always. I am sitting down to luncheon soon. You'll join me, of course."

Vella offered a nod of acceptance. "It would be my pleasure."

Renaud held his hand out to Viviana, and she placed the brush she'd been using into it. "Vivienne, let Madame Dorset know we'll have one more to lunch."

Viviana removed her smock and left the studio. She'd gotten rather used to it, this taking off of one identity and putting on another. In the studio, she was Viviana. But when it came time to do her real job, it was back to Vivienne. A few letters, an extra syllable—these painted the lines of demarcation between servant and student.

She relayed Renaud's message to Madame Dorset, who clearly resented the last-minute change. Lisette, on the other hand, was quite obviously pleased at the news of their guest, and Vivienne found herself wondering if Vella had ever flirted with Lisette as blatantly as he had with her.

As Lisette served lunch in the dining room, Vivienne settled down at the kitchen table as usual. But when Lisette came in to join her and Madame Dorset, she said with a disgusted sigh, "He wants you there."

Vivienne waited for more information. Who wanted whom?

Lisette glared at her. "Well?"

"Well, what?"

"You'd better be on your way," Madame Dorset said, not bothering to hide the contempt in her voice.

Vivienne stood and picked up her plate.

"Oh, for goodness' sake," Madame Dorset said. "Leave that here, Lisette will serve you in the dining room."

"I will not!"

"Yes, you will." Madame Dorset smacked her on the backside as she did Renaud's spaniels when they got underfoot.

Lisette stomped out of the kitchen, and Vivienne followed several steps behind. But once they entered the dining room, Lisette was all smiles and swooshing skirts. Vivienne caught a look pass between Lisette and Vella, she intent on reminding him of something, he intent on forgetting the same.

Vivienne sat across from Vella, Renaud at the head of the table to her left, and waited quietly as Lisette put a place setting in front of her—with a little more force, Vivienne thought, than necessary. She did not look up from her lap until Lisette had disappeared once more through the door, and she was sure Lisette was just on the other side of it, ear pressed up against the wood.

"There now," Vella said. "That's better."

So this was his doing. Of course. Renaud would have known

90

just what kind of domestic turmoil this would cause. Perhaps Vella did as well, but he was too selfish to care.

"Renaud was just telling me about your training in my absence. He says you're very talented."

Viviana ladled the bouillabaisse that Lisette should have served her into her bowl.

"I was telling him that he ought to send you to Paris, to the academy," Vella continued.

"And I was telling *him*," Renaud interjected, "that they have never accepted a female student since their founding nearly seventy years ago, and I very much doubt they will in another seventy." He turned to Vella. "Your impudence is unconscionable. You breeze in here once or twice a year to overcharge me on supplies, wreak havoc in my household, and then disappear with nary a word. I've humored you for your father's sake—God rest his soul—but I'm getting a bit tired of the whole routine."

Vella's smile had not dimmed. "A good teacher would want his student to surpass him. And she's not going to do that here."

"She's not going to do it in Paris either. The liberties I have afforded her in my studio—do you think those stuffed shirts would ever allow her to draw from life as I have? To paint anything but flowers and bowls of fruit?"

"From the paintings I saw in your studio just now, it seems perhaps you're more worried about losing a beautiful model than a promising student." Vella threw a look across the table. "Not that I blame you."

Viviana laid down her spoon. "I fail to see why I was needed for this conversation. The two of you can apparently talk about me as easily with me in the room as out of it."

Renaud cleared his throat. "You're right, Viviana. I'm sorry."

She saw Vella notice the use of her Catalan name. "Viviana? Vivienne? Which are you?"

Viviana ignored the question. "Why were you gone so long, anyway?"

Vella shifted in his seat. "I ran into some unforeseen complications."

"Where? Your pictures stopped after Genoa. I had been expecting sketches of Roman ruins and Moorish villas."

"Yes, I apologize for the oversight. I didn't actually make it to Rome or Tunisia this trip. I went straight from Genoa to Gibraltar."

"Oh," said Renaud, "family troubles?"

"After a fashion."

When he didn't elaborate, Renaud pressed him. "Is your mother well?"

"Yes, never better. The family is all fine. Bigger, in fact. I acquired two more cousins." He paused and Viviana could feel him looking at her, but when she glanced up at him, he looked at his saucer. "And I got married."

Viviana's grip on her spoon faltered, and it clinked against the edge of the bowl. She felt her jaw hanging slack and deliberately forced her mouth closed.

Renaud regarded him. "I didn't peg you as the marrying type. Someone from your home rock?"

"Paris, actually. We met when I was last there, after I left Toulouse last summer."

"And you married her? Just like that?"

"Well, no," Vella admitted. "I didn't marry her right then. I moved on along my planned route. We exchanged some letters. And after my quick stop home I traveled straight back to Paris for the ceremony."

They wrote letters? As he was sending Viviana his drawings of stately churches and beautiful valleys rimmed by mountains, he was writing to a girl in Paris?

Viviana stood up from the table. "I think I should help in the kitchen."

"Nonsense," Renaud said, still seated. "We haven't even finished the soup."

Viviana glanced at Vella, who'd stood as soon as she had. His eyes implored her to understand, but she couldn't. He had asked her to come with him, practically claimed it was God's will that they should be together, vowed to return, sent her beautiful drawings. Then he meets a woman in Paris and suddenly he's married?

She turned to Renaud. "Please be sure to buy plenty of Indian yellow and rose madder from Monsieur Vella. And if you like you may hold back some of my wages if it will get us enough blue to be less stingy about its use. I feel I would like very much to try my hand at a seascape."

She pushed through the door and nearly knocked over Lisette, who, as suspected, had been eavesdropping. Viviana brushed past her and headed for the basin full of pots that she knew awaited her.

VIVIANA SCRUBBED AND POLISHED the pots Madame Dorset had used to make lunch, then searched the cupboards for more objects she could make shine by sheer will and the application of the proper chemical. Sodium chloride for copper. Calcium carbonate for silver. Sodium bicarbonate for brass. Salt. Chalk. Baking soda. Inert white powders that would come alive and eat away the ugly tarnish that had spread across the once-bright vessels. As she scrubbed and buffed and polished, she imagined her hurt pride, her jealousy, her embarrassment being lifted off her own soul.

She was at it for so long, Madame Dorset finally told her to stop and put away the mess so she could make dinner.

Lisette smirked at her every chance she got, so Viviana decided to stop crossing her eyeline and go for a walk in the garden. Since Madame Renaud had fallen ill, the kitchen garden was the only one that was actively maintained. The rest of the grounds had been allowed to grow wild, which probably wasn't noticeable the first year. But now, three years on, the paths were narrowed by leggy perennials that were never cut back, and weeds shot impudently up out of the beds. Even the peonies Viviana had cut for her still life back in the spring were tangled with the die-off of last year's stems and leaves and, this late in the year, covered with powdery mildew.

Always some new insult, some other reminder that life was not as it should be. That if you let your guard down for even a moment, rot would creep in.

As she lost herself among the roses that were getting ready to bloom a second time, Viviana thought she heard a rustling behind her. Couldn't she be left alone for even a moment? Couldn't she have a little quiet to sort through her thoughts?

"Lisette, don't you have anything better to do than taunt and torment?"

There was no answer. The rustling had stopped. Viviana was just about to walk on when all at once a terrified brown rabbit tore past her, practically at her feet, and two creatures came tumbling down the path in pursuit, a churning mass of brown and white. Graciosa and Percinet. The spaniels bounded by her and disappeared behind an overgrown laurel hedge.

Viviana closed her eyes and took two slow breaths to calm her pounding heart. When she opened her eyes, Vella was there, standing not ten feet away. She set her jaw and walked in the other direction.

"Vivienne! Viviana!" He caught up to her. "Wait."

"I have nothing to say to you," she said.

He caught her arm. "Maybe, but I have something to say to you."

She stopped but did not look at him.

"I know this all comes as a shock."

"What?" she said. "That you married the first girl you laid eyes on in Paris? I had been under the impression that you desired to know me better, but perhaps you just wanted to know *someone* better and it didn't much matter who."

94

He pressed his lips into a line and breathed out of his nose. "I got a telegram when I was in Genoa. She was pregnant. I was going to just send her money. But she needed to be married, and quickly. Her family is very religious. So I went back for her. Do you understand? I didn't mean for it to happen."

Viviana crossed her arms. "I can think of something you could have done differently so as to avoid it."

His face fell. "If you had come with me—"

"No. No, this is not my fault. There are things in this life that I deeply regret that were my fault, but this is not one of them."

He met her eyes. "Yes. I know. I'm sorry."

"How could you just not tell me? How could you let me go on thinking that you cared at all?"

"I would have written to you if you could read."

"You couldn't have written to Monsieur Renaud and asked him to read it to me?"

He took a step toward her. "She just needed to have a husband on paper and financial support for the child, and I've seen to that. She will continue to live with her family in Paris, and I will continue to work abroad and visit once or twice a year when I'm in the city. And no one will look askance at it."

Viviana knit her brow, trying to follow his line of thought. "So?"

"So it doesn't prevent you from coming with me this time."

Once more that day she felt her jaw dropping at something he'd said. "Are you out of your right mind? That you could believe I might possibly consider accompanying you now when I wouldn't last year when you were unattached—"

"But you see, that's the genius of it. I'm a married man. It would not be improper. I'll simply tell people you are my sister. No one would question it. We'd take separate rooms. It would be fine."

"It would not be fine. Your Paris bride has a religious family? Did it ever occur to you that I might be religious myself? That

I might live by any particular moral code that would preclude me traveling around with any man not my husband, even if he was married?"

"You lived as a boy and served in an army! Surely that's worse than pretending to be my sister."

She was shaking her head. "That's not the point. That's not it at all." She looked at him hard in the eyes. "What makes you think we could travel the world together and not make the kind of mistake you made in Paris? Are you really so naïve? Or is that a 'mistake' you were planning to make all along?"

Vella's expression gave her the answer he would not voice.

"Last year you told me that you thought God brought us together in that studio for a reason. I think you're right. I think it was a test—one that I passed."

Viviana turned and headed back to the house. Lisette was waiting for her in the kitchen doorway when she arrived.

"Well, well, well," Lisette purred. "There are all sorts of secrets coming to light today."

"What does that mean?"

"Oh, you know. Francisco's secret wife . . . your secret crime."

Viviana stopped short. Had Lisette followed her into the garden after all? Had she overheard? Yes, technically, pretending to be a man and joining the army was probably a crime, but so what? Would anyone in France believe the story? Or care?

"Lisette, I don't know what you're talking about."

It was then that Viviana saw the telegram Lisette was slowly waving back and forth.

"Madame Dorset received this from a messenger just a few moments ago. She's off telling Monsieur Renaud right now."

Viviana schooled her features. "Telling him what? There is nothing to tell."

"Isn't there?"

Viviana shook her head, but her heart began to thump wildly in her chest.

Lisette handed her the telegram, then snatched it back. "Oh, right, you're illiterate to boot. Here, I'll read it to you. 'Madame Dorset, Capitán Hugo Gras injured, Ignasi Torrens killed by brother Vincenç Torrens at Seu d'Urgell. Later confirmed to be sister Viviana. If you have knowledge of her location it is requested that you contact the Spanish embassy immediately.' Signed by Inspector Pascual Marco of Barcelona."

How? How was this possible? How could Madame Dorset know anything at all about her past?

"I knew there was something wrong with you the moment you crawled out of the gutter and showed up looking for a job." Lisette shrugged. "I guess you shouldn't have been so chatty with Madame Renaud."

"Monique?" Monique had told on her?

"Yes, well, she never asked me to call her that," Lisette said. "The two of you were awfully chummy in there. I was hoping you'd be in her room long enough to get sick too, but—"

"You were spying on me?"

Lisette feigned innocence. "It's not my fault you weren't more careful about what you said. Murderer."

Viviana's vision dimmed around the edges. She touched the scar at her throat, then felt the world around her begin to spin. Then she was falling, Lisette's face disappeared, and in its place an ultramarine sky fading to Prussian blue. Before it could go black, she felt strong arms beneath hers and heard Vella whisper in Spanish close to her ear, "Viviana, what is wrong?"

Everything, she wanted to say.

Everything.

THE PLANS WERE LAID that very evening in the studio while dinner grew cold in the dining room, but Viviana had little to do with them. As Renaud and Vella decided a better fate for her than to be arrested and sent back to Spain to stand trial for the death of her brother and the attack on her captain—The man had survived? He was out there, looking for her?—she sat on the same threadbare settee she had when she first met these men who now held her freedom and possibly her life in their hands.

She looked around the room she had grown to love more than any other and cataloged all that she would leave behind. The finished canvases leaning against the walls, the record of her growing skill. The jars of brushes that had become extensions of her own fingers. The oils and pigments and solvents that Renaud still mixed himself and stored in pigs' bladders, though Vella had been pushing him to try more of the premade colors in tin tubes that were popular with the younger artists. The jumble of arbitrary and anachronistic props Renaud loved to stuff into the backgrounds of his sentimental scenes.

How could she leave this place? How could Madame Dorset and Lisette dislike her so much that they would try to get her deported? That they would send her back to Spain where she would certainly face a firing squad?

"Viviana."

Wouldn't the magistrate or the tribunal or whatever it was she would face listen to reason? To her side of the story?

"Viviana?"

If she sought sanctuary in a convent, would they allow her to continue to paint?

"Viviana!"

The men were looking at her. "Yes?"

Vella reached down and pulled her to her feet. "You need to pack."

She was shaking her head. "I can't."

"I'm afraid you must," Renaud said, kindness and sorrow tinging his voice. "You may take as many of Madame Renaud's things as you need and Vella can accommodate. The two of you go and do that now, and I will try once more to talk some sense into Madame Dorset."

"You should dismiss her and that conniving girl," Vella said.

"It wouldn't do any good," Renaud said. "In fact, it may be worse. They just want her gone. If she leaves, they will be satiated. If they were out of their jobs, they would surely pursue justice in Viviana's case out of revenge."

"Yes, I suppose there is sense in that," Vella said. "Come, Viviana. We must hurry. We don't want to miss the last train."

"Take the trunk from Monique's room," Renaud said. "You may have anything of hers that you fancy. But I advise leaving the bustles and such here. They'll take up too much room. You'll just have to get what you need in that department when you get to Paris."

Paris. It had not fully hit her until that moment that she was going to Paris. A city of artists. A city in which one might start over. Again. With a new name, a new profession, a new identity altogether.

Perhaps she could not stay where she was, but neither was she bound to follow Francisco Vella the rest of her life like a concubine, dependent on his largesse for food and shelter and subject to his whims and wants. She had found her own way through the Pyrenees Mountains to Toulouse. She could find her way in Paris. She had lived as an unwanted child, an orphan, a soldier, a deserter, a scullery maid, a model, a student. Surely she could live as an artist.

All she had to do was change her name.

Chapter

TEN

◆

MICHIGAN, PRESENT DAY

Esther woke to the sound of breaking glass. She rushed downstairs to the kitchen to find her mother standing barefoot on the white tile floor surrounded by what used to be the coffee carafe and its contents.

"Don't move," Esther commanded. She slipped into her Wellies at the back door and grabbed a broom. "What happened?" she said, sweeping away the glass that was closest to her mother's bare feet.

"It slipped."

"It's everywhere."

As she dragged the glass and the coffee into a sloppy pile, she imagined what it would be like to live alone. No feeding another person, worrying about another person, cleaning up another person's messes, her schedule never tied to someone else's needs. She could put anything she wanted on the walls. She could leave town whenever the urge presented itself and come back whenever she desired. She could go out with friends. She'd have friends.

Yet here she was, forty-four, single, childless, and taking care of a woman who never thanked her for her efforts, to whom it never seemed to occur that her daughter had given up her life for her. Whose condition, Esther knew, left her little capacity or motivation to express gratitude. Still, sometimes it hurt.

When the floor was cleared of glass, Esther led her mother to the dining room table to sit down.

"I know what's going on here," her mother said.

"Oh?"

"Yes," Lorena said. "I know exactly what's going on here."

Esther got out the mop as Lorena launched into her theory of what was going on here. Such talk was white noise for Esther at this point, though as a child she had taken everything her mother said at face value. Lorena's paranoia became Esther's reality. Teachers tried to correct her when those weird theories leaked into class discussions or writing assignments. For years Esther pushed back; it was hard to come to terms with the fact that most of what your parent had told you was not true. It wasn't until she was away at college that she accepted the extent to which she was wrong about many things. And then when she moved back home, that realization made living with Lorena far more frustrating than it had been before.

Ten minutes later, Esther was reasonably sure she'd corralled every tiny shard of glass and every drop of coffee. Then she saw the splatters on the lower cupboards. She cleaned those off with a damp sponge and turned to her mother, who was still talking.

"Do you want some coffee, Mom?"

"Yes. That's why I made coffee."

Esther dropped the sponge in the sink. "Do you want to go out?" She tried this question out on her mother every so often, despite knowing the answer would be no. It might be futile, but it did add just a little bit of variety to their conversations.

Lorena narrowed her eyes slightly. "Sure."

Esther tried not to let utter shock show on her face. She had to be careful not to make this seem like a big deal or Lorena might get suspicious. "Okay, let's get dressed, then we'll go to B—" She stopped. Their old Biggby location was gone, wasn't it? Had been for years now, but she so seldom went out for coffee it had almost slipped her mind. What else was nearby? There was a Starbucks—meh. There was a Dunkin'—yuck. There were other Biggby locations farther afield.

And there was a coffee shop in the lobby of the Graduate hotel.

"Would you like to try something new? And maybe a short walk as well? We could both use the exercise."

Her mother's eyes narrowed even more. "Fine."

They were out the door five minutes later, slowly heading east on Michigan Avenue to where it met up with Grand River. When they crossed the street by Peoples Church, Lorena grasped Esther's hand and kept holding on to it after they reached the sidewalk again. Esther wasn't sure if it was out of some latent motherly instinct or because her mother was nervous being out of the house. Either way it was nice.

Inside the hotel, the lobby was bright and busy, but the line at the coffee counter was short. Within a few minutes the women were seated at a small table, Esther with an Americano with just a little cream, her mother with plain black coffee. They sipped in silence, taking in the two-story gallery wall near the contemporary, open stairs to the second floor. It was an eclectic assortment of paintings, sketches, and prints, but whoever had arranged the pieces—there had to be over a hundred of them—had a good eye, and the overall impression was one of harmony and a bit of whimsy.

"There are some interesting pieces in there," Esther said. Lorena's eyes darted across the wall. "One of my early ones is up there," she said with not a wisp of surprise lacing her tone.

"Really?" Esther craned her neck. "Where?"

Lorena pointed. "There. Toward the right, just a little above the one with the wide green matting. It's a nude study in charcoal."

Esther rose to her feet and walked over to get a better look. Indeed there was a charcoal nude on the wall. But there were lots of charcoal nudes in the world. It seemed highly unlikely this was her mother's. She walked about a third of the way up the stairs to read the signature. And there it was, in the bottom left-hand corner—L. Vella. Lorena had always signed her pieces with Vella, though her legal name was Markstrom. She'd refused to take her husband's name when they married, and when he left she'd legally changed Esther's name to Markstrom as well.

"We're only Markstroms because your grandmother had to go and change her name when she got married," she'd said when Esther asked her about it many years ago. "It's an antiquated tradition that has no place in our modern world."

"Then why don't you change your name to Vella for real?" Esther had asked.

"I plan to. And we can change yours too."

Only she never did. And neither did Esther. They were Markstroms, a name that meant something to people of a certain age in their town. And changing took initiative, something Lorena had less and less of, something Esther was too busy for.

She returned to the table. "You didn't tell me you sold something to a hotel."

"I didn't," Lorena said. "I gave it to the model in lieu of payment almost forty years ago. She was going to give it to her new husband as a wedding gift."

Esther sipped her Americano. "I wonder how it ended up here."

Her mother shrugged. "Probably got divorced."

"Who do you think got the drawing? Him or her?" Esther spied a hotel employee near the front desk. "Hold that thought." She got up from the table, taking her coffee with her this time.

As she approached the man near the desk, he produced a friendly smile and said, "What can I help you with this morning?"

She glanced back to the table to make sure her mother was still there, then turned her attention to him. "I was just wondering where all the artwork in here came from."

"Ah! Yes." He clapped his hands together and started walking her toward the gallery wall. Clearly this was something he enjoyed talking about. "These pieces—and the pieces you'll find all over the hotel—were locally sourced. They came from estates and antique shops and flea markets around the Lansing area, and on out to cities like Laingsburg and Owosso and St. Johns. All around mid-Michigan."

Another glance at the table. Lorena was frowning.

"But you didn't buy from the artists themselves?"

"I don't think so, no. My understanding is that they were just sort of gathered from estate sales and such."

"Hmm. And nothing bought from local galleries?"

He seemed to sense the touch of combativeness Esther couldn't keep out of her tone. His smile faltered and his eyes got that apologetic tilt to them that everyone hates to receive but no one can help giving in awkward situations, such as the one she'd just put this poor guy into.

"I'm not one hundred percent sure. I think they were looking for things that looked old rather than things that had just been made. But not too old, you know? Just kind of that vintage sweet spot."

Esther smiled at him. "Thanks." He seemed relieved to have been released from her line of questioning, and she was rather confident that by evening she'd be the subject of a story that began with the words "There was this annoying woman at work today . . ."

She sat back down at the table with her mother.

"Who was that?" Lorena demanded.

"Just someone who works here. I was asking about—"

"I know what you were talking about," Lorena all but shouted.

Conversations around them ceased and heads swiveled their way. People who had been walking across the lobby with purpose, roller bags in tow, stopped altogether and stared. The man Esther had been talking to put his hand on a small walkie-talkie on his belt. She caught his eye and lifted a hand to say *everything's fine* even though it might not be, depending on how she handled things.

"No," Esther said calmly, "you do not know what we were talking about, but I will tell you if you will give me a chance."

Lorena narrowed her eyes but said nothing. As the gawkers returned to their own business, Esther relayed the conversation, and her mother seemed to relax just a bit.

"That was a clever idea," Lorena said, not seeming the least bit bothered that no one at the hotel's management company had thought to support living artists with their purchases. No one bought Lorena's paintings now anyway because they never left the house. Then the suspicion crept back into her voice. "Why did you want to come here for coffee?"

"Our Biggby is gone," Esther said. "This is close to where it was. And it was a nice morning to walk somewhere. You know you need to get more exercise."

Esther could feel her mother looking at her.

"Isn't this where you said you were going last night?"

"Yes, that's how I knew about it."

Esther took a sip of her coffee, then almost dropped the cup. Her mother was smiling. Granted, it was a small smile, just the slightest upward turn at the edges of her lips. To anyone else, it might not even register as a smile. But Esther noticed it. It was the first time she'd seen Lorena smile in at least six months.

"Are you hoping to run into him?"

Heat rushed to Esther's face. "What?"

"That man you were meeting."

"No. He said he was going to be out at bookshops and maybe at the Broad."

Lorena let out a sarcastic snort.

"Mother, please," Esther said. "It's not like that. He's practically your age."

Her mother gave a little nod, but Esther could tell she didn't believe her.

"Anyway, I don't have to run into him here. He's coming by later to see *La Dama del Cabello Oscuro*."

"Oh?" Lorena raised her eyebrows.

"Stop that."

"When?"

She shook her head. "I don't know exactly when. He said he'd text me. But I'd appreciate it if you could keep your clothes on your body today."

Lorena shrugged. "Why bother? There's not a room in the house that doesn't display it."

"Yes, well, it's much nicer to see a painting of a woman's naked body than to have her slouching in a chair with no shirt on when you meet her."

Lorena sighed. "I suppose. And I don't look my best lately." She seemed to think for a moment. "Keep him in the living room. I get older and fatter the further you get into the house."

Esther considered her mother. She had once been very striking, but years on antipsychotics had taken a toll on her physique, one of the main side effects being weight gain. Despite doctors' orders to the contrary, her mother continued to smoke cigarettes. And Esther was fairly sure the girls at the sorority over the back fence were slipping her marijuana with greater frequency now that it was legal. All these things made her mother feel good in the moment, but they had serious long-term negative effects on her physical and mental health and her appearance.

"Why do you continue to paint yourself each year if you don't like the way you look?" Esther asked.

Her mother was quiet a moment. And then she was quiet for so long Esther feared she'd hurt her feelings.

Finally, she answered. "I want to be seen." A pause. "Even if it's just me who sees me."

Esther swallowed down a gray slurry of guilt and resentment before reaching out and touching her mother's arm where it sat on the table. "I see you."

Her phone dinged in her purse. She didn't move to retrieve it. Even so, her mother looked away and sat back with her coffee cup.

"You should get that."

Esther felt a little hollow at the lost connection. She dug her phone out of her purse and tapped on the text notification. It was from an unfamiliar number with a 616 area code.

Ian here. Up for lunch later?

Chapter

ELEVEN

✦

PARIS, 1880

P aris was filled with ghosts. The ghosts of those who had died during the long siege of the war with Prussia and the short reign of the Paris Commune. The ghosts of buildings long empty after arson gutted them. The ghost of the trust Parisians once had in one another, torn asunder after the troubles of the past decade. There was a palpable tension flickering between the people at the train station, running from one person to another like rats skittering between the piles of rubble that still lined the edges of some streets. The government may have returned from Versailles where it had ridden out the storm, but any sense of normalcy that might engender was little more than a veneer.

This was not the city Veronica Vella had been expecting as she stepped down from the carriage onto a narrow, dirty street, moments away from meeting her fake sister-in-law, Dolorés, for the first time. She had not pressed Vella for details of his new bride on the train, preferring instead to memorize facts about her own adopted ancestors. Veronica's new extended family had

108

arrived at various times on Gibraltar from Genoa, Spain, Malta, and even England and Scotland, all the way back to before the Treaty of Utrecht in 1713, when Spain signed away all claim over the peninsula to Britain forever. Vella's tales of their exploits as smugglers and traders might have been entertaining under other circumstances, but for now they were simply the colors with which Veronica would paint a new self-portrait.

She was no longer the sister of a fearless Catalan soldier but of a weak-willed Gibraltarian merchant. She no longer spoke the French she had labored to learn. Instead she would pretend not to understand the people around her, and her worldly brother would translate. After all, what opportunity would she have had to learn French while growing up in a household that spoke Spanish? Her invented past as a laundress for the family of a British officer didn't allow for French.

For as long as they were in Paris, she was to stay in her sister-in-law's household, where she would not speak to anyone. In the train this restriction had felt unfair, but now as she was invited courteously—but not, she noted, with much enthusiasm—into the cramped home of Vella's new in-laws, she was relieved that she would not have to make polite conversation with the woman who had made him forget her so quickly.

Introductions were made, and Veronica said in affected, halting French, "I am so pleased to meet you," then fell silent as Monsieur and Madame Tribolet parted, revealing a young woman seated in a rocking chair and cradling an infant in her arms. She was not particularly beautiful. Her eyes were small and unremarkable, her lips thin and unsmiling, her nose slightly turned up. Her hair was an ashy hue, neither blond nor brown, and looked brittle from overstyling. But far more remarkable than the fact that someone as handsome and charming as Francisco Vella would be tempted by such a plain creature was the fact that the child in her arms looked nothing like him.

Veronica studied the baby. It was pink-cheeked and blue-eyed, with a tuft of strawberry-blond hair poking out from underneath the white bonnet on its head. She looked at the man who was supposed to be her brother, watching as the bright light of shock on his face was slowly veiled by a curtain of understanding before it hardened into a wall of anger.

"Dolorés?" he said quietly. "Whose child is this?"

She would not look at him.

"Dolorés," he said again, "what is the meaning of this?" The child stirred and whimpered, and his mother repositioned him. "Émile would not answer my letters," she whispered. "I had no other choice."

Veronica looked at Monsieur and Madame Tribolet, who stood stone-faced by the door. Whoever and wherever Émile may be, they were stuck with Francisco. And he was stuck with them. Vella cleared his throat. "Perhaps we should get settled," he said in French.

"We are not actually staying here, are we?" Veronica said in Spanish.

"Where else?" he replied. "This was the arrangement. We will stay through Christmas and the new year."

"She tricked you."

"I'm sorry," he said in French to the rest of the room. "Veronica does not realize how rude it is to speak Spanish in front of you. We were just discussing the luggage. If you'll show us where we're sleeping, I will get it situated."

Madame Tribolet stepped forward, touched Veronica's arm, and beckoned her to follow. She led her up a staircase, around a bend, and then up another stairway, narrower than the first. She opened a door to the right and stooped to walk through it into a dark chamber with a ceiling that slanted under the roofline and a single dormer window the size of a small canvas.

"Merci," Veronica said.

The lady of the house gave her an appraising look. "You're not really his sister, are you?"

Veronica wanted to say no, wanted to tell this woman the truth, wanted to point out that her daughter had no claim over Vella, that she had deceived him. Instead she smiled and shrugged and said to her in Spanish, "Your daughter has brought shame upon your house, and you have compounded her shame by allowing this farce to continue."

Madame Tribolet narrowed her eyes, and for a moment Veronica worried that she may have understood her. Then the woman turned and descended the stairs.

Veronica looked around the room and sighed. It was cold and damp and dismal, and she could not imagine staying even one night here, let alone a month. She heard footsteps behind her, and a moment later Vella and the carriage footman eased Madame Renaud's trunk through the door. Vella placed a coin into the young man's hand and sent him on his way.

When they were finally alone, he sat down on the trunk, put his chin in his hands, and said in a muffled voice, "I can't believe this is happening."

Viviana scoffed. "You? This is your mess, and here I am forced to live in it."

He looked up at her, brow knit, the corners of his mouth reaching for the floor. "Yes, this particular situation is my mess, but the only reason you are forced to live with it is because of a mess you created for yourself back in Catalonia. If you had not—"

He stopped short of saying it, so she said it for him. "If I had not killed my brother. My real brother."

He lifted his hand as if to say yes.

She sat down across from him on the narrow cot that was to be her bed. How like a cell this room was. How much more than she deserved.

Vella caught her eye and said quietly, "Viviana, we have both sinned. I succumbed to a moment of weakness. I did not mean to. For all the people I meet along the way, this is a very lonely life. I just did not want to be alone anymore." He reached out and took one of her hands in his. "I am sure that you did not mean to harm your brother."

Her eyes pricked with tears. No, she had not meant to harm her brother. She had meant to protect him. She had meant to watch over him, to keep him out of trouble.

"We cannot change these things," he went on. "But maybe we can help each other carry the burdens they have laid upon our backs. Because the way I see it, we both need a friend right now."

A friend would be nice. It had been a very long time since she had had a friend.

Viviana looked at her hand in his and pulled it gently away.

"Are you going to seek an annulment?"

"I haven't had time to think about that yet."

"It seems the only logical thing to do."

"Perhaps." He stood. "I need to talk to Dolorés first. Get the entire story. Find out who Émile is. And where."

Vella left the room, closing the door behind him, and Viviana listened to his footsteps recede down the creaking stairs. She took another hopeless look around the cave of a room and almost started crying.

She had once slept in an actual cave in the Pyrenees Mountains as she made her way away from one lost cause to what turned out to be another. Exhausted, hungry, and cold, she'd gathered enough dry brush to start a fire that might keep her just warm enough during the night so that she would not freeze to death. As she settled down on her tattered and filthy blanket and looked up to pray to the God she feared did not hear her anymore, her eyes were filled with visions of deer and horses and bison racing along the arched ceiling. Startled, she stood, retrieved a burning stick from the fire, and held it up to the stone. In black and red pigments—which, thanks to Renaud, Viviana now knew to be charcoal and iron oxide—some sojourner of old had painted dozens of beautiful, fat creatures he depended on for food. Probably life wasn't easy for him either. Probably he'd made a fire to keep warm through the long night. Probably he knew hunger and war and fear, just as she did. And yet, he'd been an artist. He'd made his mark on this world against all odds.

Viviana unlocked the trunk and began putting away her things in drawers and on hooks. If she was indeed going to live in this room for a month or more, she may as well make the best of it just as that ancient hunter had. When she hung up the last of Madame Renaud's dresses, she saw something in the bottom of the trunk that she had not put there. It was her many-layered self-portrait, removed from its stretchers, wrapped around her smock and her brushes.

Her heart wanted to sing and cry at the same moment. Dear old Monsieur Renaud, who had been so intimidating and in-comprehensible at first, but who had transformed into a kind yet challenging teacher when his model began asking questions about how he could make his hands replicate what his eyes saw, and even make it better. If Lisette had bothered to ask questions when she represented Terpsichore dancing in a wooded glen, would she have been his student rather than Viviana? And who might be next? Who might be his next muse up on the wall? Who would ever be worthy of all that ultramarine blue?

She would miss him, both the man and his instruction. If she was to be stuck in this dark garret, in this inhospitable house, in this ruined and rainy city for a month, she must find a way to paint. She must make her own mark, even if she had to gather up the remains of the fire in the hearth in order to have the materials to do it.

But what was she thinking? Her new brother was a colorman. She had every pigment in the world available to her. She had her brushes. She could not hope to enter into any kind of formal school. But perhaps she could find another Renaud. Another old man who needed a model who might be willing to pay her in instruction rather than francs.

She did not know any artists in Paris. But Vella did.

Chapter

TWELVE

✦

MICHIGAN, PRESENT DAY

Esther climbed the stairs at El Azteco, stepped out onto the rooftop terrace, and scanned the tables.

"Meeting someone?" the hostess said.

"I don't think he's here yet."

"Yes." She had invited her mother to join them, if only to dispel the crazy notion that Esther was somehow interested in her former professor, but after the stress of coffee out, Lorena was antsy to get back into the house and back to her painting.

The hostess grabbed silverware and indicated a booth partly enclosed by wooden lattices. "Here okay?"

Esther pointed toward the narrow table that stretched along the edge of the roof, facing the street below. "Maybe there?" Perhaps her mother wanted someone to really see her, but after Lorena's insinuations, Esther wanted there to be plenty of other things for Ian Perez to look at. He may be a lonely old guy—and she may be a lonely and getting-older woman—but that was not what this lunch was about.

114

The hostess led her to the table and set down the silverware. "Your server will be right over."

Almost immediately, a girl who looked just like the hostess but was, in fact, a different person set two waters on the table and announced herself as Chelsea. "We waiting on someone?"

"Yep."

"No problem," Chelsea said. "I'll just keep an eye on you and be back when your second arrives."

Esther sipped her water and looked out over the edge of the patio. Part of the street below had been closed to cars for the summer and covered with café tables, Adirondack chairs, and hammocks, a practice that had started during the pandemic and continued because it was just an all-around good idea. Children made chalk drawings and hopscotch courses. Couples held hands or pulled small dogs in wagons. A woman with short hair and a prosthetic leg walked in perfect step with a man with wavy brown hair and a beard. College students who'd stayed for the summer roamed about in groups, sliding along the spectrum between self-conscious persona projection and complete obliviousness that anyone else in the world actually existed.

It was amusing to watch the young people try so hard to impress each other while simultaneously maintaining the facade that they couldn't be bothered with other people's opinions of them. And there was something nice about the couples, even if she did ultimately dismiss them as representatives of some unattainable future.

It wasn't that she didn't want to find someone who shared her interests and challenged her intellect and treated her kindly and was genuinely engrossed in what she had to say. Everyone wanted that. It was just that her life, simple as it was, was complicated, and most people, whether looking for friendship or for something more, were looking for easy.

Lorena wasn't always a chore, but she wasn't easy. She needed supervision. Would always need it. Esther was all her mother had. If she didn't take care of her, who would?

It was best to keep relationships superficial. Whatever personal boundaries she had come up against last night after three glasses of wine and accepting a man's jacket and allowing him to accompany her home in the dark needed shoring up. Though, as she glanced at her watch and noticed it was six minutes after they'd agreed to meet, Esther thought perhaps she wouldn't have to worry about it anyway. Maybe he'd blow her off. Maybe he'd forget. Maybe she'd be eating alone.

Then she spied a figure with thinning hair in khakis and a dark-blue short-sleeve button-down striding toward the building with his phone in his hand. Her phone dinged.

She tapped out a response.

I'm on the roof.

She liked that he used a period despite the sentence fragment.

A moment later, Dr. Perez was walking toward her, taking off his sunglasses as he did. She stood and held out her hand to him and fought the smile that seeing him induced.

"Hallo again," he said in the most charmingly British way possible, fumbling a bit to get his sunglasses and his phone into his left hand in order to free up his right.

A quick shake and they both sat down.

"And how was the Broad?" she asked.

"I haven't been. I was lost in Curious Books all morning." He scanned the QR code for the menu. "Rabbit holes. So many rabbit holes."

"On the contrary, I found too much worth buying. I left there with a box of books, dropped them off at the hotel, then came

"No bags, though," she pointed out. "You didn't find anything actually worth buying?"

116

here. Though I had to change my clothes first—the box was less than pristine and soiled the shirt I was wearing. That's why I'm late. I'm sorry. I should have let you know."

Esther was about to object to the idea that he owed her any special consideration for being less than ten minutes late when Chelsea circled back to the table to drop off some chips and salsa and get their drink orders. Perez motioned for her to go first.

"I'm fine with just water," she said.

"Same."

"We'll barely see her now," Esther said after Chelsea walked back toward the kitchen.

"Oh?"

"No alcohol equals lower bill equals lower tip, right? She'll focus on that table." Esther nodded toward a raucous group of eight people. Four men with beers, four women with margaritas.

"Ah well," he said. "Fewer interruptions."

They dove into the menu, made their selections, then waited for Chelsea to remember they existed. Perez filled the time explaining the books he'd bought to fill in some gaps in his research before a planned trip to Alsace-Lorraine for some hands-on investigative work.

"So you're researching art stolen by the Nazis?" Esther asked after they'd finally ordered.

"Some stolen. Some hidden away and then lost to history."

"When was the last time any of it was found?"

"Oh, they found quite a bit—hundreds of pieces—in 2012 in Munich, in the home of the son of one of Goering's authorized dealers of so-called 'degenerate art.'"

She rolled her eyes. "So degenerate he kept it for himself."

"Precisely. That collection is now in a museum in Switzerland."

"Not back with the families that originally owned them?"

"Not most of it, unfortunately. Six pieces were confirmed to be looted and returned to their rightful owners—or rather, their

117

descendants—but many more are still under investigation. It's difficult to establish provenance. So many families were simply wiped off the face of the earth and so many records were destroyed."

Esther dipped a chip into the salsa and thought of her family's collection. How terrible to imagine it being stolen and to be helpless to reclaim it. "I wonder how many people are out there in museums on a given day looking at a piece of artwork they know is rightfully theirs, and yet they can do nothing about it." She popped the chip into her mouth and chewed thoughtfully. "It's a wonder any of it is found anymore. The Munich discovery was in 2012? That at least offers some hope. I would have thought if it hadn't been found in the twentieth century it was gone for good."

"Well, of course there's always hope," Perez said. "That's what art is, after all, is it not? The expression of the human spirit."

Esther thought of all the dark and violent and melancholy paintings she'd seen over the years. Of her mother's increasingly expressionless self-portraits lining the walls of the house. "The human spirit does not always express hope, though, does it?" she said. "Not all art is pretty."

"True enough. But the fact that someone puts a brush to canvas means that they have some sort of hope—that someone will see it, and that the viewer will see them through it. That they'll make a true connection with another person so they can make them see the worth in what they see." He caught her eye. "Did I get that right?"

She fought back a smile. "Nearly."

Their food arrived, and for the next half hour Esther peppered Perez with questions about his research, all the while trying to push down the jealousy she felt bubbling up within. Why couldn't she travel? Why couldn't she meet new people in new places? Why couldn't she see what was beyond the horizon? She kept him doing most of the talking and, as such, finished her enchiladas long before he got to the halfway point of his burrito.

Finally, he waved his fork in the air. "It's my turn to ask you a question. One that will take you a while to answer so I can catch up. How about this: tell me everything you know about the artist who painted that summer landscape I was so taken with at the gallery."

Esther cracked the point off a tortilla chip and tossed it to a house sparrow that had hopped up on the empty table next to them. "What makes you think I know anything about her?"

"You knew it was a she."

"True. That's easy enough to know, even today."

"Does she show at your gallery often? Was this her first time? Is she a student? A professional? Is she old, young, Black, White? Does she carry a small dog in a big purse? Just tell me about her."

"She's rather private," Esther said.

When she didn't say any more, Perez took another bite and gesticulated pointedly with his fork between his plate and his mouth.

Esther sighed. "Okay, let's see what I actually know about her. She's not a student, but she's not a professional. She's . . . a dabbler. Middle-aged. Has another job. Paints when she can fit it in. She's shown at the gallery before. And sold."

"Do her paintings sell quickly?"

"Are you wondering if the one you like will be available?"

"I am."

She considered this. "I think since it's so small and will therefore likely be priced on the low end of what's there, yes, it has the potential to sell. Especially to someone just starting their collection."

"Then I'd like to buy it. Before I leave. You could still have it in the exhibit. I could simply pick it up at a later time."

"I could ship it to you, if that's more convenient."

119

"Convenience doesn't concern me as much as it seems to other people. I'd rather have another excuse to visit."

"Why? Were you hoping to meet her?"

"I feel like I already have."

Esther narrowed her eyes. "Well, yes, you can certainly tell a lot about an artist from her work."

He smiled. "Indeed you can."

"So, what do *you* know about her, from that one painting?"

He put down his fork and wiped his lips with his napkin. "I guess I don't want to presume—"

"Fair enough. What do you *imagine* about her?"

He took a sip of water. "I think—from that one painting, mind you—that she is someone who feels deeply but has few opportunities to show that depth of feeling. She's someone who loves nature but does not get out in it enough to feel comfortable representing it on a grand scale. She's unsure of her talent, so she paints small. A smaller canvas will mean smaller mistakes. Harder to see." He paused. "She doesn't feel like she can truly be herself."

Esther realized she was clenching her jaw. "Well, that's an awful lot from one little painting."

He tipped his head to the side. "Am I close?"

"I guess you'd have to ask her."

For a moment she looked like he was going to say something else. Then he leaned back in his seat and flagged down a waitress. "We're ready for the check."

"That's not our waitress," Esther said.

"Isn't it?"

A moment later the right girl came back around and Esther started pulling out her wallet, but Perez was already pressing his credit card into Chelsea's hand.

"Now wait a minute, you bought last night," she said.

"So?"

"So at least split it."

120

He pretended to try to call Chelsea back, then shrugged. "I'm afraid it's too late."

She sighed.

"I'll tell you what," he said. "You do me the favor of showing me this fabulous painting I keep hearing about and we'll call it even."

"I was going to do that anyway."

"Okay, ah, here we go—take a walk with me. We'll take the long way to your house through campus—"

"You mean the *very* long way, *away* from my house, and then eventually back to it."

"That's the way," he agreed. "I really would appreciate it. I'm leaving this evening and I'm afraid it will be our last chance to chat. I haven't quite overstayed my welcome, have I?"

She pressed her lips together but smiled nonetheless. "Not quite."

121

Chapter

THIRTEEN

✦

Veronica stood behind Vella, doing her best not to appear too eager as a trim woman with a round face opened the door at 19 Rue Laval. The studio was just south of Montmartre, the area of Paris that Vella had said was fashionable with artists, writers, and composers that he assured her were important despite the fact she had not heard of them. The woman before her, however, apparently did not spend a lot of time there. "It is not appropriate for women," Vella had explained along the way. "People would talk."

Mary Cassatt welcomed them inside, speaking fluent French, though she was by birth an American. Her studio was a short walk from the studio of her friend Edgar Degas, which was the next stop Vella intended to make. They had already visited various shops that supplied Paris artists with paint, but Vella maintained close personal ties with several artists throughout the city who trusted that his products were unadulterated and would not react in surprising ways when applied to their canvases.

After introductions, the three of them sat down to tea, during

122

which there was much pointless translating between French and Spanish and back again in order to include Veronica in the conversation. As Vella explained his new products to Cassatt, Veronica took in the room as discreetly as possible, noting the many paintings, a pretty vase, the fine carpet. She was surprised but pleased to see creases in the white tablecloth, telegraphing where the folds had been. The fact that Cassatt hadn't bothered to iron it was in some strange way rather delightful and invited some speculation. Did she never iron her tablecloths? Was it because she was American? Had she set the table in a hurry? Was it an oversight? Or a deliberate statement about what she thought of Vella?

Eventually, the tea was drunk, the fruits and sweet breads were consumed, and Cassatt made her purchases.

As Vella prepared to leave, Veronica asked him if perhaps she could stay behind with Señorita Cassatt while he made his next stop. "I have never met a woman artist and I would like to see what she paints."

Vella translated the request, explaining that his sister was learning to paint, and Veronica received an enthusiastic invitation to stay for the afternoon.

"You don't speak French," he reminded her as he took his leave. "Just point and smile and nod."

Once he had gone, the ladies settled back into their chairs.

"I'm afraid I don't speak Spanish," Cassatt said. "And you speak no French?"

Veronica pretended confusion.

"Do you speak English?" the artist tried.

Veronica shrugged.

"And I don't suppose you speak German."

At the same time, both women sighed. They met each other's eyes and laughed.

"Well, I suppose that expression at least is the same in every language," Cassatt said.

This was ridiculous. The only restriction on their conversation was a false one. How silly to pretend not to understand her hostess. Surely there could be no harm in letting one person in on her ruse.

"Can you keep a secret?" Veronica said in French.

Cassatt looked momentarily surprised, then smiled and said, "Of course."

"I do speak French."

"Yes, I can see that." The artist regarded her with a tilt of her head. "Your brother doesn't know?"

"No," she said, but stopped short of divulging anything else about her situation. It was liberating to tell even that small portion of the truth.

"I see," Cassatt said. "I suppose what men do not know does not hurt them, eh?"

Veronica considered Dolorés's deception and wondered how true that really was.

"Now then," Cassatt continued, "since we can both understand each other, what is it you would like to talk about?"

"I would very much like to see your work. I have been studying painting—" She stopped short. She could not reveal her association with Valentin Renaud without undermining Vella's fiction and possibly her own safety. "But I think I would fare better if I had a teacher."

"Oh, my dear, I'm afraid I don't have any intention of taking on a pupil at this time."

Veronica tried to hide her disappointment behind a smile.

"Of course, I understand. And I don't even know how long we will be in Paris. I was only hoping I could see some of your work and perhaps get some advice."

Cassatt stood. "Certainly. Follow me and I will show you some of what I have been working on."

They walked to the main studio room, where Veronica had to catch her breath. From every direction came the most exquisitely joyful colors—pale pink, incandescent yellow, creamy peach—forming an array of women and children in soft dresses against backdrops of parks and theatres and sitting rooms. Unlike Renaud's paintings, which were dark and rich and crowded with detail, Cassatt's work was light itself. Where Renaud gave the viewer many things to look at, stuffing every corner with furniture, statuary, and knickknacks, as though he was afraid the viewer might get bored with the actual subject, Cassatt's confidence that her simple subject and her treatment of it was more than enough showed in every bold brushstroke.

Veronica made her way slowly around the room, drinking in Cassatt's way of viewing the world, then stopped at a very large painting that nearly knocked her back a step. It was so . . . blue. Four enormous, overstuffed blue armchairs, upon one of which a tremendously bored child slumped, her white pinafore trimmed with lace, her oversized hair bow, sash, and socks rendered in green and blue and red plaid. In the chair next to her, a scruffy brown and black dog slept contentedly.

"This one I showed at last year's exhibition of Impressionist artists, after it was rejected for the American section of the World's Fair in 1878."

Veronica detected a bitter note along the edge of Cassatt's voice, and the expression on her hostess's face was suddenly remarkably like the impatient child in the chair. Veronica took a step closer to the painting, leaned in. She was struck by how sloppy the whole thing looked up close. Thick paint, visible brushstrokes, one tone of blue laid on top of or next to another rather than blended seamlessly together. If she had painted like that back in Toulouse, Monsieur Renaud would have made her start over. It was less than amateur looking—it was infantile. But when you stood back a little . . .

"It's beautiful," Veronica said.

"You think so? I suppose it fared well overall—the critics are rather ruthless. They were especially thorny this year, though

125

to be fair, this spring's exhibition was rather a hodgepodge." She pointed at the painting. "The little girl there belongs to a friend of Edgar's. And I guess a bit of this painting belongs to Edgar himself."

She let out a kind of half sigh, half laugh, and Veronica looked at her expectantly.

"Oh, nothing," she said, placing her hand on her hip. "Just . . . I'm sure you must know what it's like. You ask a man for some advice and he goes and takes over." She pointed at the background of the painting. "Some of this is his work. Same thing happened to Berthe Morisot— Oh, I should arrange for you to meet her while you're in Paris, though she's terribly caught up now in motherhood and has less time for her friends. She and Édouard Manet worked together for years. She asked his opinion on a cloak her mother was wearing in one of her paintings, and he took the brush right from her hand. Before she knew it, he'd claimed a quarter of that painting as his own. She was very upset, though she has the good manners not to show it outside of a very small circle."

Veronica nodded her understanding. Renaud had once done the same, when she was having trouble getting her head around the reflections of lemons on a silver teapot. He began to show her how to do it, got lost in the act of painting, and was still at it twenty minutes later, though he'd moved from the teapot to other parts of the picture. She said nothing, simply walked over to his work in progress and began making her own adjustments. When he finally noticed what she was doing, he rushed over, silently took his brush from her hand, and returned hers. They went on working on their own canvases as though nothing had happened. He never reworked any of her paintings after that.

How badly she wanted to tell Mary Cassatt this story. To share in this experience of being corrected by a man, even a well-meaning one. To laugh over it and roll her eyes and thus tighten the bond that might exist between them. But she could not. Just as the painting of the girl in the enormous blue armchair was not entirely Cassatt's own, Veronica's life was not entirely her own. Her past had been erased, her present was being written by someone else, and her future was a complete mystery. Was there any part of her life over which she could claim dominion?

Cassatt crossed her arms over her chest. "So what is it you want to paint, Veronica? What captures your imagination?"

Veronica considered this. Cassatt's paintings of women at the opera were quite fetching, though Veronica couldn't imagine ever having the funds and friends needed to sustain a life that included going to the opera. Cassatt's renderings of mothers and children were nice, but that kind of domestic life was entirely foreign to Veronica. She hadn't grown up in a close and loving home. She certainly didn't live in one at the moment, even if there was a mother and child in it.

What captured her imagination? The people and places Vella had dangled in front of her when he'd first asked her to accompany him on his travels. The thought that there were even more places he had never seen, places that could be entirely her own. Oh, why hadn't she just gone with him when he'd first asked? If she had, she might even now be in Venice or Rome or North Africa. Instead, she had said no. Out of propriety. Out of piety. Out of what people might say. She could have said yes. She could have chosen a future rather than being dragged into one.

"I want to paint the world," she finally said. "I want to see the world and paint what I see."

Cassatt gave her a sad smile. "Don't we all."

Veronica felt her heart fall like a stone dropping into a dark pond. If Mary Cassatt—this independent, unmarried woman living out her vocation an ocean away from where she was born—felt trapped, what hope was there for someone like her?

"I suppose you'll see a good deal of the world as long as you remain with your brother," Cassatt said.

Yes. This was still true. If she had gone with Vella to begin with, it might have been much the same as it was now, the only difference being that she would not have to lie about who she was. Lisette would not have heard her frank conversations with Monique Renaud and conspired with Madame Dorset to rid their household of her. She would not be running from anyone.

"But if you marry and have children," Cassatt continued, "you can bid farewell to the itinerant life. Especially if you settle in France. A woman can't go anywhere here without a chaperone. And there are some places she can't even go with one."

"You're not married. Who serves as your chaperone?"

"My parents, mostly."

Veronica studied her hostess. She had to be in her mid-thirties. Yet she must be accompanied by her parents?

"As long as you have your brother," Cassatt said, "you will always have greater freedom of movement."

Veronica bristled a little. "But if I must always follow him wherever he wants to go, will I ever be truly free?"

"Of course not," Cassatt said plainly. "The only way a woman can call her life and her time her own is by remaining unmarried and not having children. But even then, she is not free to do what she wants as a man is."

Veronica sighed. "I don't understand why."

Cassatt placed a hand on her arm. "Neither do I. But take heart. There is still much that a woman can do if she puts her mind to it and straightens her spine a little. Men and women are different for a reason. You see things your brother will never see. The things you both see, you see from different angles, in different light. Both ways of seeing are necessary to get the whole picture. Man is one eye and woman is the other. Without both eyes functioning, the world would appear rather flat."

"Hello, ladies," came Vella's voice from the hall. He switched to Spanish. "I trust you've had enough time to look through the collection?"

"Yes," Veronica said in Spanish. "Please tell Señorita Cassatt that I appreciate the opportunity."

Vella relayed the message in French.

Cassatt replied to him but looked at Veronica. "Please tell your sister she may visit me again. Perhaps I can also get Berthe to take her eyes off her precious Julie long enough to take a caller some afternoon as well."

"Very good," Vella said. "Though we may not be in Paris long. Just through the holidays, then I believe we will be off again."

"Then I will be sure my invitation to return is prompt. In fact, I'll give it right now. I'd like Veronica to come back next week, around the same time?"

Vella nodded. "I'm sure that can be arranged."

Cassatt smiled. "Lovely." When Vella turned toward the door, she sent a wink Veronica's way.

Chapter

FOURTEEN

✦

MICHIGAN, PRESENT DAY

The route Esther chose took her and Perez past the Alice B. Cowles House, the oldest extant building at Michigan State. They ambled through the botanical garden, crossed the Red Cedar River at Beal Street, and stopped at the statue of the Spartan. Then they followed the MSU River Trail until it spit them out by the Kellogg Center. Along the way, they alternated between discussions of Perez's research and a companionable silence. They laughed at this and commiserated over that and truly enjoyed one another's company. The only thing that marred the time together was the fact that Esther felt she had already run out of stuff to talk about when it came to her own life. He'd seen the museum. What more was there?

It was two o'clock on the nose when they reached Esther's front door. In the forgiving darkness of the evening before, the house had looked rather enchanting, with its soft yellow lights and the ghostly forms of the giant hosta leaves and frilly bearded irises, riddled with weeds as they were. In the midday light, however, even the shadows cast by the huge oak and maple trees could not hide its general shabbiness.

In the space of three seconds, Esther saw every flaw—the faded address on the molding, the cracks in the walk, the bare patches in the scraggly lawn, that weed tree she'd let go too long that would now be impossible to remove without some piece of equipment she most certainly did not possess. Each imperfection a mark on her record as a "together" type of person, which was something she always strived to be—because she always had to be.

She climbed the steps to the front porch, feeling Perez right behind her, then turned and said, "Just give me a minute to let Mom know we have a guest."

He took a step back. "Of course."

Though leaving him out there alone would afford him more time to catalog the shortcomings of the house and yard, Esther couldn't risk them walking in on her mother in the nude. She unlocked the door and slipped in, closing it behind her.

As she glanced through the living room, the dining room, and the kitchen, she felt a surge of self-consciousness. The eyes from dozens of portraits of her mother followed her from room to room—looking. Looking at the clothes she'd picked out more carefully than normal. Looking at the flush on her face that she couldn't entirely chalk up to the brisk walk. Seeing through her attempts to convince herself that Ian Perez had not been flirting with her, just a little bit, every time they'd been together. That even if he had laid on an extra layer of charm, Esther had not made any effort to be charming in return.

Had she? It was hard to say when one so rarely spent time being sociable.

Esther went upstairs, knocked lightly on her mother's studio door, and opened it a crack. Lorena was curled up under a blanket on the small antique settee. Esther crept back out of the room and down the stairs to the front door.

"My mother is asleep," she said, ushering Perez into the foyer. "We'll just need to keep our voices down."

"If this is inconvenient . . ." he said as he walked into the house.

Esther was glad he was so keen. She did want him to see Francisco Vella's beautiful painting of the lady with the dark hair. It might not change his mind about whether her ancestor was a major artist or a minor one, but it would, she was sure, raise his estimation of Vella's talent. And, by extension, her eye.

"Now," she said, her body blocking the way out of the foyer, "I should warn you that there are a lot of paintings in this room. But only one is by Francisco Vella."

He rubbed his hands together. "Ooh, shall I guess?"

She stepped aside. "It will be obvious."

Perez walked slowly into the room, taking it all in. Esther followed at a respectful distance, giving him space to absorb and interpret. This was something she strove to accomplish at the museum, whether she was giving a tour or simply lurking in a dark corner in case someone had questions. Some people did want to be told what to think about a painting. They wanted the facts. Who painted it? When? Where? For what purpose? What did it all mean? But most people who bothered to come to a museum of their own accord came because they wanted to have a personal experience—an exchange between artist, no matter how dead, and self, no matter how lost or confused or lonely or sick in love. Esther held back, gave them space to make their own connection, and had the privilege, on occasion, to see someone long dead or far away touch someone right before her eyes.

From her current vantage point, Esther pinpointed the moment when Dr. Perez saw *La Dama del Cabello Oscuro*. She saw him stop, look, appreciate. But then he looked away, letting his eyes travel across painting after painting after painting of Lorena Markstrom. Age nineteen, age twenty, age twenty-one. The hair getting longer. Shorter. Longer again. The posture slouching here, straight there. Just the head and neck, then add the shoulders, perhaps the torso, then a full-length nude. The eyes ever looking straight out at the viewer, penetrating, challenging.

Perez drifted into the dining room, into Lorena's thirties and forties. Into her development of crow's-feet and gray hairs, into her slow weight gain.

It had been a while since Esther had really looked closely at the self-portraits her mother had produced over her lifetime. As a child she'd examined them daily, marveling at the way an artist could take a mess of colors, many of which seemed to have no business representing skin, and arrange them in such a way that Esther could actually recognize her mother's face, her feet, and all that came between. How what looked like arbitrary dabbing when you stood right up close to a painting could actually look real and three-dimensional when you stood back.

It was magic.

Among the dozens of Lorenas in the house, one could find a representation of almost any major art movement. In her search to accurately reflect her full self, Lorena had employed the techniques and sensibilities of the Italian Renaissance, the Rococo period, Romanticism, Realism, Impressionism, post-Impressionism, Surrealism, Abstract Expressionism. And somehow even those paintings that were on the abstract side of the spectrum seemed to represent her truthfully.

Though her condition had rendered Lorena unable to experience much pleasure or express many emotions as intensely as other people could, Esther did believe that her mother was in there, somewhere, and was slowly and persistently making herself known through her paintings.

At the door of the kitchen, Dr. Perez turned to face her. "This is phenomenal." He leaned in toward the bottom left-hand corner of one of the canvases. "Who is L. Vella? This can't be his wife?"

"It's my mother's work. She paints a self-portrait every year."

"Extraordinary."

He studied one of the smaller portraits—one that had always been among Esther's favorites. It was the first one where her mother had actually looked calm and relatively happy. Those that came before it in time all had a kind of manic edge, a touch of fear. And then she started her first antipsychotic medication. For a small space of about three or four years, her portraits were rather pleasant. After that, her expression had turned frighteningly blank.

"They are in nearly every room in the house," Esther said. "Except mine. That's why I don't like to be away from home too long. I'm afraid I'll get back and she'll have taken over my walls as well."

"In all our chatting, you never mentioned she was also an artist. Come to think of it, I don't recall you ever mentioning that back when you were a student either."

Esther knit her brow. "I'm sure I did." But was she? During those years, she had worked to distance herself from her mother, in every sense of the word.

"I think I would have remembered that," he said. "Anyway, it really is remarkable that you have so many artists in the family. Vella, your mother, you. Did anyone else paint?"

"I don't believe so, no. Actually, I think there were a lot more businessmen in our family tree than artists." She stepped into the middle of the room. "Anyway, we're not here so you can see my mother's self-obsession. We're here so you can see *La Dama del Cabello Oscuro*, the only painting on this floor *not* produced by my mother."

He joined her in the middle of the room, and she directed his attention above the fireplace. For as long as Esther could remember, *La Dama del Cabello Oscuro* had hung there like a religious icon above an altar. The painting was large, and its elaborately carved gilt frame made it loom even larger. As a child Esther had concocted various scenarios in her mind about the woman depicted in the painting. Sometimes she was the Virgin Mary, sometimes she was Saint Catherine of Bologna, sometimes the biblical queen whose name Esther shared. She was by turns demure or stubborn, meek or cunning, pious or sensual, regal or rustic. Whatever Esther had needed her to be. And she was clothed in lustrous, ethereal blue.

Though Vella had been a contemporary of the Impressionists, he had not been part of their exhibitions. His name was rarely mentioned in their correspondence, and when it was, it was only in relation to his role as a man who sold paints and pigments or brokered art sales. And while many of the paintings in the museum were more in line with the Impressionist style, *La Dama* was painted in a more formal style that hearkened back to the works of Caravaggio and Artemisia Gentileschi. Deep shadows, rich fabrics, supple skin, a single, strong source of light.

There was nothing breezy about this painting. It was painted in a studio, not en plein air. The lady was exquisitely physical, corporeal, present. A living, breathing being, not simply the idea of one. It felt like it was from an earlier epoch of human history, and yet there was something incredibly modern about it.

La Dama's long dark hair flowed in shining waves over her shoulders—thrilling in an age when women wore their hair up for portraits. A gossamer collar tucked into that blue satin gown shrouded her chest but did not quite obscure a scar on her throat. The scar had fascinated Esther over the years. What had happened to the woman? Had she been wounded in some innocent childhood accident? Was she a farm worker injured on the job? Had some rake grabbed her and threatened her life with a knife to her throat, and in the struggle she'd been cut? Had she been a prostitute, abused and forgotten?

Yet something in her eyes precluded all of that. She was

confident, bold, even challenging. She looked out at the world as someone who knew exactly who she was and what she was capable of—an expression that pointed toward a movement that hadn't even faces in her mother's self-portraits. Or her own.

And yet, despite its classical feel, there was one bizarre design element that pointed toward a movement that hadn't even started when the work was most likely completed. From the chest down, cut into the flesh and the dress as though with a pickaxe, were the tunnels and caverns of a complex cave system. Empty pools of dark water filled rock-hewn basins. Stalactites dripped with moisture. Bats fluttered or tucked themselves in crevices. It was disturbing and haunting and always made Esther's heart ache if she dwelled on it too long.

"So," Esther said after Perez had viewed the painting in silence for a few minutes, "what do you think?"

"It's very well executed," he said.

Esther deflated a bit. Well executed? It was more than that. It was exquisite.

Her former professor seemed to sense her disappointment with his answer. "It shows a tremendous control of one's technique, a good deal of talent, a clear understanding of color theory, good lines. And the caverns twisting inside of the figure—they're fascinating and haunting and beautiful. But . . ." He trailed off.

"What don't you like about it?"

He made a pained face. "I'm not an expert on Vella, and you certainly know far more than I, but . . . I don't know. At first blush I'd say it doesn't seem to fit snugly with what I saw at the museum." He paused as though trying to weigh the consequences of what he might say next. "Are you sure it's his?"

PARIS, 1880

Two days after meeting Mary Cassatt, Veronica found herself in the parlor with Madame Tribolet, Dolorés, and the baby, Didier. She did not want to be there, but Vella was out and it would have been rude to shut herself up in her room—to say nothing of dark and depressing. Madame Tribolet was sewing lace onto the edge of a baby bonnet while her daughter embroidered a small pillow. In an attempt to include her houseguest in the activities, Madame Tribolet had handed Veronica a basket of stockings that needed mending.

The fake past Vella had cooked up for her—a laundress in the household of an English officer—would certainly have given Madame Tribolet every reason to think this would be a useful way for *Veronica* to pass the time. The only trouble was that *Viviana* didn't know anything at all about sewing or mending. During her time in her aunt's household, her chores were washing the dishes and sweeping the floor. At the orphanage, she worked in the kitchen peeling and chopping vegetables and kneading bread. In the army, she cleaned and maintained her weapon and took part in drills and shot enemy soldiers. If her uniform lost a button, Ignasi sewed it back on.

Veronica rooted around in the basket a bit and, after several tries, threaded a needle the way she'd seen Ignasi do it before realizing there was no way she could fake this without arousing more suspicion about herself. Instead, she thought a moment and then stood.

"Imagen?" she said in Spanish, which she knew sounded enough like the French word *image* that they would understand she was talking about a picture. She motioned toward the tableau of three generations of Tribolets before her and repeated, "Imagen?" Then she made a painting motion with her hand in the air.

Dolorés looked at her scornfully, but Madame Tribolet's face was bright. "Oui. Très bien." Then she followed up very loudly with "Sí," which sounded more like a command than an affirmation.

Veronica headed quickly up the two flights of stairs to her small room, excited by the prospect of painting, even if it would be a tremendously domestic and sentimental portrait of two women she didn't much care for and a baby she had no interest in. It would give her a chance to try out some of the techniques she had seen in Mary Cassatt's studio, which seemed far more forgiving when it came to portraiture than anything Renaud had taught her. If she liked the result, she might try painting her own portrait once more in that expressive and spontaneous style.

In a few moments, she was back in the parlor, situating herself in a corner that allowed her to see her subjects. She did not have an easel, but she did have a thin oak panel that she'd already prepped. This she positioned on her lap. Her paints and palette she set upon a small side table that she covered with a cloth. Madame Tribolet and her daughter sat on either end of a settee, angled toward one another. Behind them, a large window lit the scene so that the far sides of their faces were bright white, almost lost in the light. The edges of their hair shone like halos, and shafts of light cut past them, illuminating their handwork but leaving the near sides of their faces in shadow. Between them, on the low table in a shallow basket lined with blankets, was the baby, his pink cheeks shining like rose petals, his little fists like naked baby birds. The tableau looked like an icon she had once seen of Saint Anne, the Blessed Virgin, and the baby Jesus, and it pleased her that this scene might represent a modern—though perhaps ironic—take on the ancient holy family.

Fighting against the process Renaud had drilled into her—which included value sketches, mixing up a whole rainbow of colors and tones with a palette knife, and creating a small color-reference painting, before finally underpainting and meticulously drawing out the picture with thinned paint—she got to work immediately. She hastily mixed three shades of dark, medium, and light and blocked in the basic shapes. Then she started trying to capture the color and feel of the light in the room. She resisted blending anything on the canvas, tapping and dragging and pushing unthinned paint into place in curious combinations, relying on her knowledge of color theory and her own observation of the light to guide her rather than Renaud's voice in her head.

Thus passed a pleasant and even exciting hour of silent creation. Madame Tribolet and Dolorés occasionally talked to one another, but Veronica tuned them out completely, such that it actually did seem like she did not understand the French language. She didn't even catch an occasional word like she used to with Lisette. Their voices were like the sound of waves on the shore. Veronica began to feel as though she was not actually in the room, but that she was somehow outside of this interior space in some other realm of existence, somewhere between earth and heaven, not quite human and yet not quite divine.

She had never felt such in Renaud's studio. She had never felt this way at all.

She was so fully immersed in this liminal state of mind that she did not notice Vella had entered the room until he stood over her, squinting down at the painting.

"Oh dear, not another one," he said in Spanish.

"Another what?" Veronica said.

He spoke in French. "Another innovator, another intransigent, another Impressionist." He switched back to Spanish.

"Señor Renaud would be appalled."

Madame Tribolet rose at his assessment and came to inspect the painting. Veronica braced herself for a string of criticisms, but the woman said simply, "Perhaps your sister should stick to laundry." Then she went into the kitchen to see about the evening meal.

Dolorés showed very little interest in seeing what her mother and husband were commenting on, preferring instead to redirect the room's remaining occupants to the little cherub in the basket, who was beginning to fuss and whine. "Oh, my angel, my little angel," she cooed, "do you suspect your so-called aunt is a talentless harlot as I do?"

"Dolorés," Vella warned.

"What? She cannot understand anyway."

"But why say she is a harlot?"

While Veronica appreciated Vella coming to her defense, she would have far preferred he protect her artistic reputation than her honor. She knew that she was a virtuous woman. But as with so many artists, she had serious doubts about her work. Though moments ago she'd been enthralled with the picture she was laying down on the oak panel, now she looked at it more critically. This did not look like what Mary Cassatt produced. This was a bit of a mess.

"I say she is a harlot because she is not your sister," Dolorés said.

"So you keep insisting, but I might point out that this"—he indicated the baby in the basket, who was on the cusp of real crying now—"is not my son, and yet I do not call you a harlot, which I might easily and justifiably do."

Veronica thought about how someone should really pick up that baby and get it to stop making that noise. Where was Madame Tribolet? Surely she could hear this from the kitchen.

"How dare you?" Dolorés said. "Would you say such a thing were my father around?"

"If your father was around more, you might not be such a dishonorable woman!"

All Veronica wanted was to slink out of the room, perhaps go outside, but she was sure she would still hear the baby crying—it was practically wailing—even if she walked down the dirty street.

Dolorés was on her feet now, jabbing a finger into Vella's chest. "Dishonorable? You speak of dishonor? If you had not been so drunk that night, this never would have happened!"

"Me?" Vella practically yelled.

Veronica could not stand it even one more second. As the two equally-to-blame people continued their argument, she stood, set the painting on the chair she'd just vacated, and scooped the baby out of the basket. Then she marched out of the parlor and up the stairs, not stopping until she reached her room on the third floor. By the time she shut the door, the baby's cries had subsided to an occasional gurgle. She supposed it was the bouncing and rocking motion of going up the many steps that had soothed him, so she kept moving and bouncing gently to keep the pacification going.

"Oh, Didier," she sighed, "I'm afraid you will have a very difficult childhood." She spoke in Catalan, a language she had not used in nearly two years, a language that had been replaced with French in her thoughts and even in her dreams. "Your mother is a suspicious and conniving liar who seems only to value your ability to obligate a man to support her. Your real father does not care about you enough to even inquire after you, let alone support you. And your replacement father plans to leave you behind and continue his vagabond lifestyle." She sat down on the narrow bed and looked into the cherry-cheeked creature's blue eyes. "Does no one want you?"

Didier looked back at her as though hoping this stranger holding him would be able to answer the question, would be able to tell him that someone, somewhere, really loved him.

"I know what it is like to be inconvenient and unwanted," she whispered. "I know how it feels to be alone, unseen, unheard even when you are crying out at the top of your lungs." She blinked hard. "Perhaps—"

Before she could give the little creature some sliver of hope for the future, Dolorés swung open the door and took the baby from Veronica's arms as Vella came in behind her. "Tell your 'sister' that the next time she touches my baby I'll see her out on the street before she even knows what's happening." Then she was tromping down the steps, which started Didier crying all over again.

Vella shut the door behind his bride. It was only then that Viviana noticed he was carrying her painting. He held it out and said in Spanish, "Perhaps you can fix it."

Across the picture, Dolorés had left the evidence of her disapproval in an angry arc of smeared paint.

"No," Viviana said. "I like it better this way."

Vella set it on a small table, sat on the single hard wooden chair, and laced his fingers together. "We don't have to stay much longer. Just until the new year."

"Why stay even that long?" Viviana said. "It is quite clear that no one wants us here. I may bear the brunt of the disdain because I am stuck in this house with these women most of the time, but I hear what they say about you when you are gone, and there will be no tears shed when you leave."

"That may be, but my plans were to stay until the end of the month, and I have no place for us before then. The winter holidays are a difficult time to find accommodations in Paris."

"But you know so many people. Is there no one who would have us for even a few days?"

"These are not my friends, Viviana. They're clients. I never stayed with the Renauds. Occasionally I was invited to eat a meal there because Monsieur Renaud and my father had been friends, but I rented a room in Toulouse."

Viviana sighed and thought wistfully of Mary Cassatt's home and studio. Surely there were rooms there. But she'd just met the woman. She certainly could not invite herself to become a houseguest. She would just have to stick it out here.

"Did you talk to her?" she asked.

"Who?"

"Dolorés, of course. You said you were going to talk to her, to get the whole story of what happened between her and Émile and find out where he is. He might be in the city even now. Couldn't you get the authorities involved? Couldn't he be ordered to claim the boy as his own and support him?"

"There is no need to get the authorities involved." Vella sat back. "Émile is dead."

"Dead? Does Dolorés know this?"

"Not yet. At the moment, I am the only one who knows. And now you."

Viviana's breath hitched and she waited for an explanation, hoping for one that did not involve manslaughter, though that was the plainest reason only Vella would know about the man's demise.

"I asked around the places near where I met Dolorés in Montmartre. It didn't take long to find him—half-drunk at nine in the morning, pounding on a piano in an empty cabaret. He was still there from the night before and the owner wanted him out, so I gave him a hand. Took him around the corner to an alley and started asking him about Dolorés."

"Did he know about the baby?"

"Oh, yes. He'd gotten her letters. He'd gotten a number of such letters over the years from a number of girls. He said he wasn't interested in being a husband or a father." He scowled. "Dolorés was a good time, nothing more."

Viviana could not keep herself from letting out a laugh. "Isn't that what she was to you?"

Vella's face hardened. "If that was all she was, why would I be here now?"

Viviana shrugged. "Guilt? You don't love her. You said yourself you'd just been lonely."

"I thought I had a child. My child. I was not going to leave that child without some kind of father."

"An absent father. A letter writer who sends money for new shoes and brings an exotic trinket or two home each Christmas."

"Isn't that better than nothing?"

Viviana softened her tone. "Yes, perhaps it is. I would have wanted to see my father each Christmas if I could have."

Vella seemed to relax the muscles in his shoulders. "I know it is not ideal. For anyone. But money is all she wants. I can give her that."

Viviana nodded and tried to accept that this was not really any of her business anyway. "So what happened to Émile?"

Vella took a deep breath. "Yes . . . Émile." He paused as though trying to decide how much to reveal. "He did not care for my line of questioning. Things got heated, then he picked up a brick from a pile that was in the alley and threw it at me. I dodged it, of course—it's not hard to outmaneuver a drunk man—but you know, it still made me angry, to have someone attempt to hit me in the head with a brick. So I punched him, just thinking to hurt him a bit, give him something to remember me by. But he stumbled back and fell and his head connected—hard—with that same pile of bricks. He was bleeding all over, and I went back inside to tell the cabaret owner so he could find a doctor, but he wouldn't do anything about it. He said Émile wasn't worth the trouble and all of France would be better off without him. I couldn't disagree. But I thought I'd just go back out to check on him anyway. And he was dead."

Viviana tried to feel pity for this man she didn't know. It was more difficult than it should be. She wondered briefly if most people would feel any pity for her if they knew her story. The whole story, anyway. It was easy to pity an orphan. Perhaps less so a murderer.

She did pity Didier, however—pitied his entire sorry existence. Right then she resolved to pray for him. She would pray that he'd grow up a strong and honorable man, that he might someday meet a worthy woman and be to her a faithful and loving husband, and that he would not only find satisfaction in whatever he put his hand to, but that he would encourage his wife and any daughters he might have to find satisfaction as well. She would pray that he be spared the horror of war, that he would keep himself unstained by worldliness, that he would be nothing like his real father.

She glanced up, startled to find herself caught in Vella's steady gaze. "What is it?" she asked.

He blinked once, perhaps realizing that he'd been staring. "I was thinking of what my face might have looked like if Émile had had better aim. It made me wonder . . . what happened to you? How did you get that scar?"

She forced her hand to remain on her lap rather than cover the scar. "I don't care to talk about it."

She stood to leave—to go where, she had no idea—but he stopped her with the back of his finger against the back of her hand.

"Please. Tell me. I promise, whatever the circumstance, I will have nothing but compassion for you. I just want to know you. I want to know who I will be traveling with, who will be sitting across from me at the table. I just want . . . a friend."

145

"I can be your friend without telling you about this."

"A friend does not hold back the ugly parts of life."

She put her hands on her hips. "Is that so? Then why don't you tell me something ugly about yourself?"

He opened his hands in a gesture of vulnerability. "Certainly. I have a scar of my own." He rolled up his pant leg past his calf. There, just below his knee on the outside, ran a ragged pink and white scar that reminded Viviana of a strip of fried pork fat. He turned his leg, revealing a similar scar on the inside. "When I was fifteen, I fell off my uncle's boat when we were fishing just off the coast near the Torre Nueva watchtower. I was waiting for him to toss me a line and pull me back in when I was bitten by a shark. It was shaking me and pulling me under. My uncle speared it and pulled us both into the boat. There was so much blood I passed out. Next thing I knew I was in my own bed, delirious with fever. The cut was not clean. It became infected and I nearly lost the leg." He rolled the pant leg back down and looked expectantly at her.

"I'm sorry that happened to you. That must have been terrifying." She smiled weakly. "Unfortunately, hearing your story does not make it easier to tell my own, because you are the victim in that story. We may both have scars, but in my story, I am not the victim."

Vella waited, silent and unmoving. So like Ignasi had been that day, crouched behind a broken-down wall, waiting for cover fire in order to get back to the fortress of Seu d'Urgell after his daring reconnaissance mission, his head full of important information about the enemy's position and weaknesses. Viviana knew it was him. She could tell by the way he had moved, darting between stunted trees and piles of rubble and dead horses. But the captain hadn't recognized him at that distance.

She tucked her ever-lengthening hair behind her ear and sat back down. "I received this scar," she said slowly, "as a reminder." She allowed her fingers to drift down to the ridge of flesh and swallowed, feeling her throat move beneath it like the roll of an earthquake under a mountain range.

"A reminder of what?" Vella all but whispered.

"The chain of command. My duty. My place." She deliberately folded her hands and turned her neck toward Vella. May as well give him a good enough view that he did not have to steal glances anymore. "My captain at Seu d'Urgell ordered me to shoot an enemy combatant, and I did not comply immediately."

Viviana caught a look pass over Vella's face.

"It's not what you think. It was not because I, as a woman, could not pull the trigger, could not kill a man. I had already killed many men. It was because he was wrong. Because I knew that the figure I had been watching was not an enemy. It was my brother, Ignasi, coming back from a mission."

Vella frowned. "Did you tell your captain this?"

"He did not give me time to tell him at first. He grabbed the front of my shirt and pulled me to my feet, then he put his knife to my neck. 'If you have forgotten how to follow orders, Torrens, I can refresh your memory easily,' I answered him, saying that I could follow orders that were sensible, but I would not shoot one of our own soldiers. He spun me around so that I was facing the spot where the target was hiding, keeping the knife against my neck. 'Either obey my command,' he said, 'or I will relieve you of your duty and your life.'"

Viviana paused, feeling the monstrous anxiety creeping out from her heart into her fingers and toes. She didn't speak for a long time.

"What did you do?" Vella prompted softly.

She swallowed, pushing the past down into her stomach like a bite of food insufficiently chewed. "I aimed at the edge of the wall near where Ignasi was hiding—to warn him, not to kill. But just before I pulled the trigger, I felt my captain stiffen against me. He started to turn me around just as I pulled the trigger. Instead of hitting the wall, the shot went into the open space left by cannon fire—at the same time Ignasi decided to leave his hiding place."

"He was hit," Vella stated.

Viviana nodded. "I didn't see it, only heard him yell out in pain."

"So you took the shot . . . and he cut your throat anyway?" Viviana took a long, slow breath. "No. Not then."

Vella leaned in.

"I think he had realized at the last moment that I was right. Why else would he turn me around?"

"Why wouldn't he just say 'Don't fire' or 'Hold' or put his hand on your rifle to lower it?"

"I don't know. Perhaps he didn't have time to think. We rushed down from the post and crept out to where Ignasi lay. He was still alive, shot in the thigh, blood everywhere. I removed my shirt to tie around the wound to stop the bleeding."

Vella winced.

Viviana gave a little shrug. "He was my brother. I didn't even think about it."

He nodded. "Of course you didn't."

"It took me a moment to realize that the captain was staring at me, and at first I didn't know why. It only dawned on me as we carried Ignasi to a nearby cave where the army stored some food and medical supplies. But I was so focused on helping my brother, I didn't think about anything else. I wasn't worried I'd been found out. I was only worried about Ignasi. I thought we could save him."

Vella reached out and put a hand on hers. She had not realized her hands were shaking. She pulled them back.

"We put him down in the cave, and the captain sent the guards away. I didn't understand why he did that. They could have helped us. I told myself they must be going for more help. For the medic. Then the captain grabbed my wrist and pulled me to my feet and cut the strips of cloth that were binding my chest with his knife."

Viviana stood and paced a few steps across the small room. She had not had to face the priest to whom she had confessed these things after her escape to France. She could not face Vella now. She looked instead at the ruined painting of the Tribolet women.

"He pushed me further into the cave, yelling at me about being lied to, saying that we'd made a fool of him. I kept looking at Ignasi, aching to get into the supplies and find something that would help him. The shirt around his leg was saturated with blood and his face was gray. He was all I could think about. I had no idea that—" Her voice caught. "Then the captain—" She tried again. "He knocked me down and put the knife back to my throat, and I realized in that moment what was happening. He would have done something truly terrible. But I had my own knife. In my boot." From the corner of her eye she could see Vella watching her. "I reached down, grabbed my knife, and plunged it into his thigh, then his side. His knife cut my neck as he fell on top of me. I had to push him off—he was so heavy and my hands were slippery with blood. He was yelling out for the guards, so I hit him with the butt of my rifle—many times—until he stopped. Then I went to Ignasi . . ." She took a deep breath. "He was already gone."

Viviana heard a slow breath escape Vella's lips. She smoothed her skirts. "I quickly gathered some supplies—the guards could return at any moment. I wiped as much blood off myself as I could with a rag, took Ignasi's shirt for myself, and wrapped my neck with a strip of cloth I tore from the bottom of the captain's shirt. Then I ran. I hid in the hills that night. There were people searching. They came very close to me but did not see me."

"Perhaps God was protecting you," Vella said.

She scoffed. "Why would God protect me? A liar and a thief and a murderer. Why allow me to escape then, only to be hunted down later? I should have stayed and been shot. It would have been just."

"And the captain? What would have happened to him for attacking you?" He didn't wait for her to answer. "Nothing. Nothing would have happened."

Viviana knew this was true. But knowing that the scales of justice were out of balance did nothing to assuage her guilt over what she'd done to Ignasi.

"One thing I don't understand," Vella said. "The telegram indicated the inspector knew your real name."

"I suspect after some digging he found the orphanage. Ignasi always used his real name. It had only ever seemed important to hide my true identity, not his." Viviana felt a wave of weariness overtake her. "Whatever happened, it cannot be changed. Just as I cannot erase this scar from my neck—or the image of my dead brother from my mind. They will always haunt me."

And the Spanish authorities, she realized, would always hunt her.

Chapter

SIXTEEN

MICHIGAN, PRESENT DAY

Esther felt like she'd just had the wind knocked out of her. What did Perez mean, "Are you sure it's his?" Who did this guy think he was? Who was the expert here? Who had made this artist her life's work? Who was his descendant, for crying out loud?

She took a moment to compose herself before saying, "It's in a different style, yes."

"A very different style."

"But it's definitely a Vella."

He looked again at the painting, moving closer, picking out the details. "Well, there's a signature, such as it is."

"They are all like that."

"And I assume you've matched this one to the pieces at the museum."

"Of course. Not only does the form match, but the pigments match. Every signature is done in chrome yellow, which would have been brilliantly saturated when first applied, but of course

151

it ages terribly, and that's why they are all far more brown now and often get lost in the scene."

She was waving her hands around in her passion to defend her position. She clasped them together in front of her now. No good seeming hysterical. Volume did not win arguments. Logic did.

"Of course," she continued in a more measured tone, "that's just a visual assessment. There's never been enough interest in his work to warrant chemical testing or X-rays or anything. I wrote to the Detroit Institute of Arts about the collection a couple of times, but nothing came of it. Beyond that, the pigments in the paintings themselves appear consistent from work to work, though it seems that as his technique develops and his personal style settles in, he removes certain pigments from his palette. So where an early piece may have a dozen or more pigments represented, later pieces have perhaps three or four, plus white."

"So either he was falling on hard times and couldn't afford more, or he didn't have access to more, or he just chose to simplify his palette."

"I think the last is the only good explanation. As I said in the tour, he was a merchant who dealt in pigments, so he would always have had access. And this blue, it seems to me, is ultramarine, which would have been very expensive."

Perez stroked his chin. "Where did it come from, if you don't mind me asking?"

"The provenance of this painting has never been in question. My grandfather bought it in 1949 from the estate of Valentin Renaud in Toulouse. Besides being a colorman, Vella sold paint to a number of artists in France, including Renaud, and later became an art dealer as well. Renaud had no children, but his holdings were transferred to his nephew, Henri. Much of his work was lost in a fire, and more was lost during the German occupation in the latter part of World War II once they'd taken

Vichy France. Apparently the house was taken over by German officers for about a year. This was one of only a handful of works the family retained. It must have been an especially prized piece and hidden away. I don't think the Germans would have cared for it. Without the cave element, perhaps. But that's rather surreal for their tastes. Regardless, it did survive until the family reoccupied the house. They were hard up for cash after the war, as most probably were. This painting was purchased directly from them. We have the paperwork to prove it."

He shook his head. "No need to prove anything. I'm not saying it's *not* his. I'm just bringing up a basic question which I'm sure you'll remember from classes. After all, history is littered with copies and fakes with a convincing signature on them."

"Is it just the style of the painting that's bothering you? Because something else I learned from your classes is that many artists started out in one style—often the conventional style of their day or the style of the person they were apprenticing—before developing their own unique expression of their gift. Monet. Picasso. Van Gogh. They all show a distinct shift from one style and palette to another. Look around you. My own mother has dabbled in every style out there. She still painted every single one of these."

He gestured to the painting above the fireplace. "And which is this, do you suppose? The work of a talented young copyist or an independent and mature artist with a clear vision?"

She crossed her arms. "I believe this is Vella at the height of his talent. He's clearly anticipating a later movement in the art world."

Perez dipped his head to concede her point. "Perhaps. But it's a big leap from the pieces at the museum. They are far more Impressionistic. Are there any transitional pieces out there to bridge the gap?"

She shook her head. "There may be. I don't know. There are some catalog descriptions of a few paintings we don't have. Some things that must be in other private collections, probably in

Europe. But I don't need any bridge pieces to convince me. The most obvious clue is staring you right in the face."

"Is it?"

She gestured to the painting. "Isn't it?"

Perez looked at the painting. At her. Back to the painting.

She laughed. "I can't believe you would miss this. Look at that woman's face. It's the same as the woman's face in so many of his other paintings. The same model. Which some say must have been his wife. More cynical people suggest it may have been a mistress. But no matter who it is, it's always the same woman. Of course his biggest and most impressive portrait would be of her."

Perez looked unconvinced, but he wisely said no more.

"Well," Esther said, "you must be wanting to get on the road."

At the shadow of hurt she saw cross his face, she felt a pang of conscience. Why was she taking this so personally? The poor man was just doing what came naturally to an art history professor and scholar. For goodness' sake, his research was all about telling a painting's true story.

"I'm sorry," she said. "I'm being defensive."

He shook his head. "Passionate."

She laughed lightly. "Yeah."

"You're right, though," he said. "I should think about getting back to my car and getting on the road. There's just one more piece of unfinished business."

"Oh?"

"The painting."

She looked around the room. "You'll have to be more specific."

He laughed. "The landscape at the gallery. The little one. I still want to purchase it. How do I go about that?"

"Oh, I'd forgotten." She glanced toward the stairs that led to the second floor. "I can't take a credit card here. And I shouldn't take cash unless I can put it right in the till."

"Back to the museum then?"

"Well . . ." She hesitated. "Just let me check on my mother first."

"Of course."

Esther trotted up the stairs to her mother's studio and again knocked lightly before walking in. Lorena was still curled up on the settee.

"Still sleeping," she said to answer Perez's raised eyebrows when she got back downstairs. "Why don't I drive us to the— Oh. I *drove* to El Azteco for lunch. Then we walked here." The heel of her hand connected with her head.

Perez was laughing. "Then I imagine my car is closer. We can just walk to the hotel and the valet can grab it. I can drive us to the museum, I'll make my purchase, you can keep the painting there for now, and then I'll drop you off at your car."

It would take so much longer than if she just had her car. But what choice did she have?

"Okay. Let me write a note to leave for my mom first."

She scribbled off her plans, ran back upstairs, and stuck the note on her mother's easel where she would see it.

THE WALK TO THE HOTEL did not take long with no detours. Esther set the pace—quick—and Perez followed a step behind. Not much was said, and Esther's brain used the quiet time to run again and again through the evidence that supported her claim that Francisco Vella was indeed the person who had painted *La Dama del Cabello Oscuro*. By the time Michigan Avenue met up with Grand River near Peoples Church, she was convinced that Dr. Perez was simply wrong. The only piece of information—she wouldn't even call it evidence—he had was that of the difference in styles. But that was easily explained, and she had already done so.

When they reached the front of the hotel, he gave a card to the valet. "I still have to check out," he said to Esther. "Do you want to wait out here?"

"Sure, that's fine."

"I'll be right back."

Esther sat down at a café table on the sidewalk and pulled out her phone to see if there were any messages from her mother. Nothing. Which wasn't odd. What was odd was that Esther kept looking for one. And not being able to stop made her uneasy about the whole thing.

Just then the valet pulled up in a silver hybrid Toyota High-lander, got out, and opened the passenger side door. "Ma'am?" Esther realized he was talking to her and silently mourned the days when a stranger might address her as "miss."

"This is you, right?" he queried.

"Um . . . maybe."

"You're with the guy with the glasses in the khakis and the blue shirt, right?"

"Oh, yes." She stood up and tried to catch Perez's eye through the lobby windows, but he was talking to someone at the front desk. She got into the car, moving a sketchbook off the passenger seat to do so, and the valet shut the door after her.

Except for the sketchbook she held, the interior of the car was spotless. No travel mug in the cupholder, no sunglasses sitting on the dash, no stray receipts or straw wrappers or even any crumbs. Not a single flaw. It was like it had just hit the show-room floor. Only the Hope College parking pass sticker on the windshield indicated it had an owner.

And the sketchbook.

Esther glanced back at the hotel, then opened the sketchbook. She flipped through pages of drawings of familiar landmarks from her student days—the beautiful stone library, the soaring chapel, the enormous anchor surrounded by tulips. There were sketches of birds and plants and mushrooms. There were figural drawings too. Students on campus. A man on a bench. A man walking a dog. A woman seated at a bar. A woman standing before a window—or was it a painting?

She shut the book and placed it on the driver's seat. A moment later, the driver's side door opened.

"Sorry that took so long," Perez said, noticing the book and tossing it into the back seat.

"No problem," she said. "Do you know how to get to the museum?"

He got in and buckled his seat belt. "It's just down the street, right?"

Perez pulled out into traffic, did a Michigan left, then headed east on Grand River. In a couple minutes, they were there, pulling into a parking spot behind the building. Esther unlocked the back door and led the way through the dark hall and into the gallery where she'd found Perez the day before.

"There it is," he said, as though pleased to see it hadn't moved in the eighteen hours since he'd first seen it. "But we never discussed price and there's not one listed."

"I have the information in my office. I'll be back in a minute."

Esther went back down the hall, unlocked her office, slipped inside, and closed the door. She stood there for a moment, staring at nothing. In her mind she envisioned herself going to her desk, opening a drawer, pulling out a ledger, flipping through the pages, running her finger down lines of text. In actuality, artists simply emailed or texted her information like this. But she didn't have to look for anything anyway. She knew how much to charge for that painting. She had painted it.

When she thought enough time had passed, she left the office and reentered the gallery. Perez had not moved from his spot in front of the painting.

"So?" he said.

"$750." She'd originally planned to charge $500—the painting was so small—but in the course of the afternoon she realized that she wasn't sure she wanted her former professor to have it. She couldn't say exactly why, though pettiness came to mind.

But Perez didn't flinch. "Sold." He pulled out his wallet. "How do you want to do this? Cash or card?"

Cash? The man just walked around with that much cash on him? *After* a trip to Curious Books? No wonder her education had been so expensive.

"It doesn't matter. Either way I'll have to boot up the computer system. Have to put certain information into the artist's profile with us."

Perez counted out the bills. "Even if I'm paying the artist directly?"

She wagged her head at him. "You seem to have an awful lot of trouble with this sort of thing, don't you? You assign the execution of an unsigned piece incorrectly and you fail to accept the obvious execution of a signed piece." She clucked her tongue. "Perhaps too much time in your ivory tower has dulled your instincts."

He was wearing a full smile now. "We'll see about that. Now, if I'm going to pay $750 for that little painting, I think I warrant a few more clues to the artist's identity if indeed I have gotten it so wrong—which I doubt."

She turned and walked to the front desk. "I can't tell you much. Only that she lives in the area."

He followed close behind and leaned his crossed arms on the countertop as she turned on the computer. "Does she mostly do landscapes?"

"She does do a lot of landscapes."

"Are they mostly from around here?"

"She does a lot of scenes that are close to home."

"Not a big traveler?"

She smiled sweetly up at him. "I couldn't say."

"Tell me," he said, "was any of my assessment of her at lunch in the least bit accurate?"

"I don't even remember what you said," Esther replied. Though she did. She remembered every word of it. And every word was true. She was someone who felt deeply but had few opportunities to show it. She did like spending time in nature when she could manage it—but she never visited anywhere truly wild. She settled for Fenner Nature Center and an occasional walk down the Lansing River Trail. She did paint small because it felt risky to paint big. Most of all, she never felt wholly like herself. She often felt like she was living a tamer version of life than the one she was truly meant to live.

Rather than repeat his assessment, Perez silently held out the $750. "Well, whatever it is you have to do to keep this all on the up-and-up."

She took the money from him and set it on the counter. A few minutes of typing things up—piece name, artist code, buyer name, agreed-upon price, date paid—and they were almost done.

"I just need your address so we can ship it out to you after the exhibition closes," Esther said.

"I told you, I'll come pick it up. When does the show end?"

"Not until August, I'm afraid. Then we'll clear it all out to make room for student work during the fall semester."

"Perfect," he said. "I'll consider taking possession of it as my reward for finishing the research for my book. I need a hard deadline. Something to work toward. And I'll be back from France by then."

Esther put the money in the cash drawer of the register, shut down the computer, and stood. "I guess that about does it."

"Then let's get you to your car."

It was less than a three-minute drive to the Charles Street ramp, but Esther let Perez drive her there rather than walk, which would have taken closer to ten. He pulled into a street parking spot across the road from the ramp, and she reached for the door handle.

"Once again," Perez said, "thank you for such marvelous conversation. It's truly been a pleasure to reconnect."

"Same to you," she said. "Now I guess you better get to work."

He smiled. "Yes, indeed. Don't want you to have to find a place to store that painting for me. I assure you I will be more than ready to pick it up the moment the show closes. Just let me know when the time comes what's most convenient for you."

"Of course." She got out of the car, shut the door, and jaywalked across the street. At the entrance to the parking ramp stairwell, she turned and gave a little wave, then pulled open the metal door.

Twelve minutes later, Esther was back home, dropping her purse on the table in the foyer. "Mom, I'm home!"

She went into the kitchen to start some water boiling for tea, then tromped up the stairs to Lorena's studio. She knocked. "Mom?"

Nothing.

She peeked into the room. Lorena still had not moved. Concerned now, Esther came all the way into the room and touched her shoulder lightly. A string of white foam stretched from Lorena's mouth down to the cushion, and beneath the blanket her fingers clutched a small orange cylinder.

"Mom!" Esther shouted. Then she ran back down to her purse in the foyer, dug out her phone, and dialed 911.

Chapter

SEVENTEEN

✦

PARIS, 1880

Where are we going?" Veronica asked for the third time as the carriage eked its way along the busy street.

"You are so impatient!" Mary Cassatt laughed. "You'll see soon enough."

It wasn't exactly that she was impatient, she didn't think. It was that she felt unprepared. When Cassatt had surprised her with an outing, she'd thought it would be to go somewhere to paint en plein air, as she'd heard the so-called Impressionists usually did. But she had not brought along any supplies, and she couldn't see that Cassatt had brought any either, unless they were in a trunk strapped to the back of the carriage.

She supposed that it was better if they were not going somewhere to paint, after all, since she was wearing one of Monique Renaud's nicer dresses—dark blue with a tiered skirt and an even darker velvet jacket trimmed with lace. The dress was five years out of date, flouncier than the newest styles, but it was one of her favorites.

Soon enough, indeed, they arrived at 9 Avenue d'Eylau and entered a well-appointed apartment with light streaming in through the tall windows and the doors that led to the balcony.

"Veronica Vella," Cassatt said, indicating a thin woman with a regal bearing and striking dark eyes, "this is my friend, the painter Berthe Morisot." Standing just behind the lady of the house was another woman, her dark hair piled atop her head, her eyes tired beneath heavy brows. "And this is our mutual friend, Marie Bracquemond. Also a painter."

Veronica curtsied to each of them in turn and tried to keep from smiling too broadly. God had already blessed her with meeting one female painter. Now here were two more?

"Ladies, this is Francisco Vella's sister, Veronica." Cassatt held up a finger. "Now, I must warn you straightaway that Veronica's brother does not know that she speaks French, so please use discretion if the subject ever comes up in your dealings with him."

"I have no dealings with him anymore," Morisot said. "Eugène takes care of all that."

Veronica wondered if Morisot was relieved not to have to deal with her fake brother—her faux frère, as she had come to think of him—or if the woman's husband had usurped a responsibility that she had actually enjoyed. It was hard to say. Morisot's voice did not betray her true opinion as easily as Cassatt's did. Perhaps this was because Morisot was French by birth while Cassatt had been transplanted as an adult. Perhaps Americans were not as artful as the French. Or perhaps they just did not cultivate artifice with the kind of cunning the French seemed to enjoy. Perhaps Veronica would like America.

"This is a beautiful room," she said to her hostess.

"Thank you," Morisot said. "We have enjoyed living here, but it is getting a bit small for us now that we have a two-year-old girl. We've been talking of moving outside of the city and building a house."

"Is your daughter here?" Veronica said. "I would love to meet her." This was not true—she had no special affinity for children just as she had no special affinity for dogs—but it was, after all, a thing that seemed appropriate to say. From Morisot's radiant smile, clearly she'd said the right thing.

"Julie is on an outing with the nurse this afternoon. But perhaps another time."

Veronica thought she caught a wry smile brush across Cassatt's face, but it was gone before she could be sure. She was certainly relieved not to have to fawn over the child herself. She did enough pretending in that department with baby Didier. It was not that she especially disliked children. It was simply that the worshipful reverence with which so many women regarded children—dressing them like dolls, fussing over every incoherent sound they made—was completely foreign to her. She could remember no moment of being the object of such affection.

After some small talk and some discussion about various pieces of art and furniture about the room, the women settled down to tea. Though they were at Morisot's table, Cassatt set the course of the conversation, informing her friends of Veronica's situation and inviting their advice for her on how to move forward.

"Your brother won't stay with his new wife in Paris?" Morisot asked.

"I do not think so, no," Veronica said, wondering whether to say more. She decided against it. She did not want to harm Vella's business. Not when her livelihood was now attached to his.

"And she will not travel with him?" Morisot pressed. "I mean, when the baby is older and stronger?"

"There seems to be no indication that she will. She does not strike me as someone who would travel well. And anyway, it seems her parents do not want to part with her."

"I don't blame them for being cautious," Cassatt said. "When I wanted to come to Paris, my parents came with me rather than leaving me to my own devices."

"Yes, but you weren't married," Morisot said. "Vella's wife wouldn't be left to her own devices. And I am sure Veronica would love to have another woman along, to say nothing of a sweet little niece or nephew." She turned to Veronica. "Is it a boy or a girl?"

"A boy."

"I think she is lucky," Bracquemond spoke up. "His wife, I mean."

There was a palpable silence.

"With him gone so much of the time, she is free to do as she pleases," Bracquemond continued. "Like you, Mary. Or like Rosa Bonheur."

Morisot clucked her tongue.

"Who is Rosa Bonheur?" Veronica said. "Is she also an artist?"

"A confused old woman is what she is," Morisot said. Cassatt leaned in. "She is an artist. A very fine artist of animals and of rural life. Her bulls practically charge off the canvas, they are so lifelike."

"Why is she confused?"

The women looked at one another to see who was going to answer Veronica's question.

"She lives as a man," Bracquemond finally said.

"She dresses as a man," Cassatt corrected. "In order to be less obtrusive in the places she paints. She has a special license from the police."

"To dress as a man?" Veronica said. "You need a license for that?"

"In Paris you do."

Morisot looked like she had caught a whiff of turned milk. "A woman in trousers is too modern for my tastes."

Cassatt caught Veronica's eye. "I think you'll find that between us, we have differing opinions on such things. Suffrage, marriage, family, men. Certainly our experiences have some similarities"—she looked at Bracquemond—"and some differences."

Veronica wished she could know what difference there had been in Bracquemond's experience. Perhaps it might help her in her own situation.

"It would be easier if men simply treated us as they treat other men," Veronica said, remembering the camaraderie of the battalion in which she had served. She could not fault Rosa Bonheur for her masculine manner of dress. She had never felt as much support and love and friendship from her fellow man as when she had lived as one. Men were so good to each other. Could they not extend that warmth of feeling to the women in their midst? Did one have to be like a man to have a man's respect?

"I don't know that I would want things to go that far," Morisot said. "I enjoy being treated like a lady. We are not men, after all. Nor would I want to be."

"I would be content with courtesy and respect," Bracquemond said. "Perhaps a simple acknowledgment of one's talent."

Veronica wanted to say that Monsieur Renaud had been courteous to her. That he had encouraged her, taught her to draw and paint, allowed her to draw from life, supplied her with materials. That he had sent her away when he did not want to in order to preserve her freedom and possibly her life. That he had made sure to send along the brushes he had given her and the self-portrait he had encouraged her to paint. She didn't know if he respected her, but he had been courteous.

But she could not say any of this. Her newly fabricated life story did not include her tutelage in Toulouse. It did not include anything she had been through, anyone she had loved.

"You cannot seek men's sanction on your activities or approval of your ambitions," Cassatt said. "For even if you get it, you will find that it is not enough."

Veronica turned back to her. "Why do you say that?"

"Because," Morisot said, "there has never been a man—even the best of men—who ever treated a woman as his equal."

Cassatt nodded. "Precisely. Planted within every compliment

is a seed of insult. Your work will be called 'charming,' 'delicate,' 'pretty'—words that seem fine praise until you realize that they are but the verbal equivalent of patting a child on the head. What you truly want to hear is something else entirely. That your work is moving, powerful, striking, devastatingly true. These little condescensions and slights will grow thorny and poisonous in the rich soil of your mind—which, after all, is not so simple and blank as they assume. This desire for legitimacy in their eyes, will grow to overtake you. It will choke out the confidence you once had in your own ability, your own worth. It will siphon off all the resources meant for the flowers you intended to grow." She paused and looked directly at Bracquemond. "The talent and passion you once had for your art will dry up and wither for lack of nourishment. Then what will you be left with? Only the thistles, which will continue to prick and draw blood even as you tend to their every need and want."

Morisot leaned toward Veronica. "You must decide straightaway whom your garden is meant to please—others or yourself? For your sake, I hope you choose yourself. There is nothing so beautiful as a work of art that pleases its artist."

All this time, Bracquemond had remained silent, restrained, like a held breath. Veronica sought to release her. "Do you agree, Madame Bracquemond?"

The dark-haired beauty looked at her from beneath heavy black brows, her eyes sparkling with some unspent emotion.

"Yes," she all but whispered. "Yes."

LATER THAT AFTERNOON, as Viviana and Vella rode back from Cassatt's house to the Tribolet residence, she asked him what he knew of Marie Bracquemond.

"Not much," he said. "She is the wife of Félix Bracquemond, a printmaker. He's also in ceramics production. She does charming designs for some of the ceramics. Quite delicate ones, if

I'm not mistaken. And she paints a pretty picture. Why do you ask?"

Viviana couldn't answer for a moment. Had he really used all three of those words in just three short sentences? Charming. Delicate. Pretty.

"She seems rather unhappy to me," she said.

"Goodness! You spent only a few hours with her and you can see that?"

"Well, perhaps I was imagining it."

"No, I don't think you were." He shifted in his seat across from her and leaned in as though the driver outside might hear. "Félix is not the easiest man to get along with. He has the unfortunate quality of always having to be right, which means any discussion on any subject can, and often does, turn into an argument. I've had my own arguments with him, and I've heard how he treats his friends. I can't imagine it's much easier to be his wife."

Viviana considered this. "Does he support his wife's art as Eugène Manet seems to support Madame Morisot's?"

"I should say not. From what I've heard, he barely lets her out of the house. I'm surprised she was even allowed to go to tea this afternoon."

She was quiet a moment. Then, "What are you going to do about Dolorés?"

Vella sighed and picked at his thumbnail. "Yes, that does need a final decision, doesn't it?"

She raised her eyebrows expectantly and waited for him to tell her what that final decision was. But he only looked out the window of the carriage as though the answer were somewhere out there on the broken streets of Paris.

AS SHE LAY IN THE NARROW BED in the garret room that evening, Viviana considered the three women with whom she'd spent the afternoon.

From what Vella said and from reading between the lines of the conversation at tea, Marie Bracquemond was apparently married to a man who did not encourage her, respect her, or even behave courteously toward her. He stifled her ambition, preferring her to paint charming and delicate designs for his ceramics business rather than spend her time and talent on her own artwork. He even curtailed her movement.

Berthe Morisot, an established and respectable artist, seemed to be quite contentedly married to a man whom people spoke well of, and she, along with Cassatt, was a successful member of a group of artists that was otherwise almost exclusively male. She lived a settled life, one that would be even more settled once her new house was built, and she clearly doted on her daughter, who was already the subject of numerous paintings. So a woman could be married and happy and work on her art, if she wanted to remain in one place and paint only in the garden and the park.

Then there was Mary Cassatt, unmarried, intrepid, a little feisty. She had guests when she wanted, visited friends when she wanted, painted when she wanted. She was the freest of all of them, but even she had to have chaperones, people to watch over her, to vouch for her good behavior. She had to bow to convention as much as any other woman in France did.

Were all places in the world like this? Was there anywhere a woman could go where she could be her whole self, with no apology or accommodation for the whims and wishes of others? Somewhere she could do the work she was called to, unencumbered? Or was there a man waiting on every train platform, on every dock, in every room, to whom she would be expected to defer? Whose dreams and desires she would be expected to put first?

The only way for Viviana to find out would be to leave Paris. To follow Vella across Europe and Africa, his doting sister always a few steps behind.

At least she would not be standing still.

PART

TWO

Chapter

EIGHTEEN

◆

TUNISIA, 1881

Viviana stood on the shore of the Gulf of Tunis and closed her eyes. The smell of the surf, the taste of salt in the air, the heat of the just-risen sun, the sound of waves and seabirds and the busy fishing docks down the shore—she drank it in, allowed herself to visualize it all in her mind's eye until she could see it clearly. Then she opened her eyes and began mixing colors on her palette.

Today it was vermillion red, cadmium yellow, and cerulean blue. Other days it might be red lake, Naples yellow, and Prussian blue. Or alizarin crimson, chrome yellow, and cobalt blue. Whatever the particulars on a given day, her plein air palettes were simple, limited to the primaries, from which she could create any shade, toned up or down with lead white or lamp black, though the latter she used as sparingly as possible. Even deep shadows were the haunt of color.

It had taken time to get to this point. She had never depended on premixed oranges, and violets were fairly straightforward to make. She had all of this well in hand before they'd reached Munich. But it wasn't until they'd made their way from Vienna south of the Alps and come down into Venice that she'd figured out which blues and yellows made which greens. By Naples she was feeling competent with everything but the browns. Those had been the hardest of Vella's premade hues to remove from her repertoire. Yet now, on this ancient continent that showcased every shade of brown in both the people and their environment, she had finally released them, preferring to find them within the bright primary colors from which all other colors were made.

Just in time. Mummy brown had been her favorite shade, and mummies were harder and harder to come by. Vella had been hoping to bring one home to Gibraltar to restock his supply, but all he'd managed to find for sale from his usual source in Tunisia was an assortment of limbs of questionable age and dubious authenticity. He doubted they had even come from Egypt. And now that this outpost of the Ottoman Empire had become a French protectorate, it was unclear if the kind of back-alley dealings Vella depended on would continue to be tolerated.

In fact, Vella had meant to come to Tunis earlier in the year when it was not so hot, but the French troops amassing on the border between Algeria and Tunisia in the spring had him refiguring his timetable and tarrying in southern Europe for months as the French secured their hold. So Viviana's first experience of Northern Africa was at the height of summer, the streets teeming with French soldiers and a newly conquered populace that, from what she could see, seemed to be taking it rather well. Business was continuing as usual, and the pockets of resistance in the hill country beyond the city had all but been squelched.

Viviana did not mind the weather. Paris and Munich and Vienna had had their own kind of beauty, but she missed the intense heat and sun of the Catalonia of her youth. In northern climes she had often felt antagonistic toward her surroundings. Bracing against a biting wind. Hiding from cold rain under an umbrella. Here she could hardly tell where her own body ended and the sun-soaked world began. And yet, despite that comfort, the military presence was disconcerting. It reminded her too much of things she'd rather forget.

In the end, Vella had not bought any mummies, in whole or in part, genuine or otherwise. Viviana was relieved. Since she'd learned that the paint was called mummy brown not because of its resemblance to the hue of mummified human remains but because it was those very remains, ground into a fine powder, that gave the paint its color, she'd felt uncomfortable using it. There was a bit left in a tube in her larger stock of paints, but she could no longer bring herself to squeeze it out onto a palette to be applied to a canvas. Neither could she throw it away, knowing that part of a human being was bound up inside of it, suspended in oil, encased in a flexible tin sarcophagus. So the tube rattled around and slipped through her fingers as she dug for other colors until it worked its way down to the bottom of the box and was left in relative peace.

Unlike Viviana herself. She had thought that she'd feel happier about this itinerant life, visiting all the magical places Vella had described to her the first time they met, painting colorful markets and busy plazas, interesting people and exotic foods. It was what she had told Mary Cassatt she wanted to do. But now that she had what she wanted, she couldn't help wanting something more. Something that was hers. A life of her own. A life where she could make her own decisions about where to go next, what to do there, and how long to stay. A life where she could be herself.

If playing pretend was wearing on her, it did not seem to bother Vella at all. The farther they got from Paris, the more he seemed to forget Dolorés and Didier existed. With each border they crossed, Vella sat just a little closer, looked at Viviana a little longer, talked with a little more familiarity. If she objected, he laughed it off as simply part of the ruse of being her brother—

they must convince people they had spent their lives together, after all. But Viviana had had a brother, and the way Vella looked at her was not the way Ignasi had.

She could feel his eyes on her even now as he lay on a blanket just beyond her peripheral vision, propped on one elbow, ostensibly writing in his journal. Beyond the pages of handwriting that Viviana could not read, the journal was where Vella sketched scenes from his travels, many of which now seemed to feature her more prominently than they did the buildings and monuments and landscapes surrounding them. He made less and less effort to hide this, once even asking her to turn her head back toward the window when they were on the train between Venice and Milan so he could finish a drawing.

Viviana tried to ignore her discomfort at her situation. But it was abundantly clear that the space she inhabited was a kind of no-man's-land. She was not one thing or another—neither wife nor mistress, neither sister nor stranger, neither self nor someone else. She was bound to Vella by circumstance but not by law—or even by love, she realized. When she had first met him in Toulouse, he had charmed her with his entertaining stories and his attentions. She'd been astonished when he'd asked her to come with him on his travels, but not truly angry. There was righteous indignation at his presumption, certainly. But hadn't she also been flattered? That someone could fall in love with her after only a few hours' conversation.

But that feeling in Monsieur Renaud's studio was not love—neither what she'd felt toward him nor what he'd felt toward her. Instead, they had been willing victims of two common vices: pride on her part, lust on his. Nothing more. And now, having spent eight months with Vella, Viviana could see clearly that he was just a man. A charming man, perhaps, but utterly ordinary. And having seen beautiful women in every important city in Europe, she could see clearly that she was an utterly ordinary woman. It had merely been their circumstances—thrown close together in a room she shouldn't even have been in, wearing a yellow dress that wasn't hers—that had cast their first meetings in a romantic light.

Just as the rising sun cast the harbor before her in such a glow. There was nothing truly special about these boats, these docks, these men bringing in the morning's catch. They were ordinary, and similar ordinary scenes were being played out at harbors all around the Mediterranean, that morning and every morning. It was only the angle of the light that made it romantic. Simply the way the sun and the earth aligned at that moment. Very soon, the sun would rise higher in the sky. The light would change and the spell would be broken.

The spell with Vella had cracked the moment Viviana had learned about Dolorés, but it hadn't completely broken until he told her that he did not intend to seek an annulment. He tried to frame it as chivalry, but to Viviana it stunk of cowardice. To end the marriage would mean explaining to people what had actually happened. And it would mean acknowledging to himself that he had been made an utter fool. It was less a blow to Vella's pride to continue the farce than to admit he'd been tricked by a woman who'd valued her own person and her own integrity so little that she'd slept with multiple men outside the bonds of marriage with seemingly no thought to the consequences. Was this sort of thing the reason women needed chaperones? Where had Dolorés's been?

"Are you nearly finished?" Vella said, closer than she had expected. He'd vacated his spot on the ground and was now just a couple feet behind her.

She kept her attention on her easel, procured before they left Paris in January. "Are you bored?"

"Never when I'm with you," he said. "But I am getting hungry."

"There are dried figs and pistachios in my satchel."

"I was thinking of something more substantial."

"I told you to eat before we left the hotel."

"I wasn't hungry then." He sighed. "When you're finished, we'll eat a real meal."

"I don't know when I'll be finished," she said. "Eat some figs. You'll feel better." He said nothing, and Viviana could feel him behind her, not moving, certainly not eating figs. Finally she turned around. "What is it?"

His smile momentarily disarmed her, which irritated her. A couple days ago he had shaved off the beard he'd let grow during their sojourn in Italy, and the stubbled growth that had already appeared gave his face the carefree, rakish appearance it had when she first met him.

"I was just watching you work," he said.

"Well, stop. Or at least don't watch so closely. It's distracting to have someone right behind you, breathing down your neck." She turned back to her painting and tried to focus, but still he did not move.

"Why don't you paint more people?" he said.

"What are you talking about? There are people in nearly all of my paintings."

"But those are scenes. I mean portraits. Commissions. There's good money in that."

She dabbed in some bright reflections of the sun on the water.

"A portrait takes a long time."

He came up beside her and motioned to the board on her easel. "You paint an entire harbor in a morning. How long can a person take?"

"This is merely a study. To practice. To capture the light and the colors. These are for me to use later as references for studio paintings."

"And yet you've been leaving them in cities all across Europe." She looked around. "Where is my studio? Where is my home? Anyway, there is no room to keep them. At every port you pick up more merchandise. The crates and trunks and valises are always full, no matter how much you sell. Where would I store them as they dry?"

"I could make room. We only have a few more stops before Gibraltar. You should at least start keeping them now."

"Surely there will be no space there."

"Why do you say that?"

"What do you mean? You've said it is a very small place and you have a large family all living on top of each other. I don't even know where I will sleep there. Or who I will be. I cannot be your sister Veronica. I think perhaps your mother will know that she did not give birth to me."

He smiled at that. "No, you will not be my sister."

"Then who? What is my story this time?"

Vella put his hands on his hips. "You think I have not given this any thought."

"You've given me little indication that you think much about my situation. My impossible situation."

He turned serious then. "Is that truly what you think? That I'm unconcerned with your welfare? Your future? That I haven't spent nights awake, trying to sort out what to do with you?"

"What to do with me? You speak as if I'm some stray you picked up along the way."

"Aren't you?"

The twinkle in his eyes showed clearly that he'd meant it as a joke, to make her laugh, to break the tension. But the truth of it stung.

He saw his mistake immediately and took her hand. "Viviana, I have agonized over you. These past eight months—every time you have smiled as I introduced you to a client, every cup of tea you've tipped to your mouth, every time I handed you a key to the room next to mine, every beautiful painting that has appeared at the end of your brush—I have fallen more and more in love with you. Can't you see that? I feel like I'm up to my neck in quicksand. I feel like I'm losing my mind. All I want to do when we arrive in Gibraltar is introduce you to my mother as the woman I love, the woman I intend to marry."

Viviana rolled her eyes. "Then why didn't you seek an annulment from Dolorés? It seems obvious that that is the solution to your problem."

"Is it, though?" he asked.

"What do you mean? Of course it is."

"So if the marriage to Dolorés was annulled, you would marry me?"

Viviana swallowed and gently pulled her hand from his. "No. I would not marry you." The slight hope she'd seen on his face when he asked the question vanished. "It's not that I don't want you in particular," she rushed on. "I don't want to marry anyone."

He took a long, slow breath and let it out. "I thought not."

Her heart collapsed in on itself as the sadness in his eyes washed over her. She did care for him, and she had not wanted to hurt him. He truly was a good friend to her. Her only friend.

"I'm sorry, Francisco. I'm so very sorry." It was the first time she'd used his first name when she wasn't pretending to be his sister, and the intimacy of it shocked her. For a moment, she wondered if perhaps what she felt toward him was indeed love. But she checked the feeling and stood firm. "It's just—"

"It's fine." Vella gathered himself and rubbed his hands together. "And to answer your earlier question, you could be yourself when we reach Gibraltar. Viviana Torrens, freedom fighter turned painter. A fine backstory if I ever heard one. The British would never turn you over to the Spanish."

Viviana considered this. "What are they like?"

"The British?"

She nodded. "In all my life among the Spanish and the French, I never heard a good word spoken about them."

"They have their faults—too many to count, really. For all their pomp and pageantry, they are as shabby and depraved as they would accuse all other races to be. Off-duty soldiers are

ERIN BARTELS

always drunk. They all look down their sunburned noses at us. Call us lazy, aimless, careless. To them we are rock scorpions or apes, derided for our Spanishness, mocked for any attempt to seem English."

"It sounds like a terrible way to live, surrounded by people who wish you weren't there."

"Oh, but they need us." He smiled. "Need us to cook and clean and care for the things they'd rather not be bothered with. And, most importantly, they don't care about smuggling, which makes many a Gibraltarian a decent living. In fact, the guns at the garrison will fire at Spanish ships if they enter British waters while trying to intercept smugglers. Some have even been sunk."

Viviana knit her brow. "Are there a lot of soldiers there?"

"Six thousand. Maybe more. Fully one-third of the population."

She felt her frown deepen. Were there soldiers everywhere a person went?

Perhaps sensing her discomfort, Vella added, "I can tell you the places to avoid."

"I am beginning to feel I'd like to avoid the place entirely."

"I'm afraid that's impossible. I have much to do to prepare for our next trip. I'm sure you'll find it a fine and diverting place when you get there. So many different types of people of every hue and manner of dress to paint. It is a truly cosmopolitan city."

Viviana sighed and felt a deep longing for the studio in Toulouse. For a short time at least, her life had felt relatively stable. She'd been able to be herself with Monsieur Renaud, had been able to let go of her cares for a while, to focus on learning to paint. If only Monique had not died. If only Madame Dorset and Lisette had not hated her so.

"What will your family think of me?" she said.

"They'll love you," Vella said. "They will be so thrilled you're there."

"Won't they wonder why I am with you rather than your wife?"

179

Vella glanced off to the side, then met her gaze again. "They don't know about her."

Viviana's eyes widened. "They don't know you're married? That there's a child?"

He waved his hand dismissively. "It seemed unnecessary to burden my mother with such information. As you can imagine, she'd be very disappointed in me. And she doesn't care for the French. She does, however, have a high opinion of the Catalan people, so she will like you. Perhaps she will want you to paint her when she finds out you're an artist."

She scoffed. "She won't like me very much after it comes out looking nothing like her."

"What do you mean? You paint fine people."

"I can paint people, yes. But not a *person*. I always get something wrong. I cannot even manage to get a true likeness of myself after many tries."

"Don't be ridiculous. Your self-portrait looks just like you. You're so beautiful in that yellow dress. And I've seen the figures you've based on yourself in your paintings, and I think they look quite accurate. Apart from the fact that they don't have the scar."

"I've never put myself in my paintings," she said.

Vella looked at her like she was delusional. "What are you talking about? You're in all of them."

"I am not. Where on earth do you get this accusation?"

"It's not an accusation. It's an observation. In every scene where you can see a woman's face, she looks like you."

Surely that could not be true. "How self-obsessed do you think I am?"

"You really don't believe me," he said. "And now you've given them all away, so I'll never be able to prove it to you. Unless we find them again on our next grand tour of Europe. That could be a fun game, couldn't it? To search them all out."

"Impossible. And pointless."

ERIN BARTELS

He thought a moment. "You know, I could draw you from memory."

She did not doubt that. Anyone with any talent at drawing who spent as much time looking at her as Vella did would find reproducing her likeness rather simple. And he did have tremendous talent, which she was sure to never say to him.

"Well, I am not you," she said. "I'd have to study a person's face for some time, and we're never anywhere long enough for me to do so. I couldn't very well ask someone I'd just met to sit for hours and hours for a portrait that wouldn't turn out to be a true likeness. I certainly could not charge anyone for such a thing."

"You cannot improve a skill you never practice." He swept into action, snatching the painting of the harbor from her easel and slipping it into an open slot in her wet canvas carrying case.

"Stop. Vella, stop."

But he was already placing a new oak panel on the easel. "There."

She sighed and decided that the kindest thing to do would be to indulge him. After all, she had broken his heart mere moments ago. "And who am I to paint?"

He repositioned her easel then situated himself against a rock, journal in hand, looking for all the world like she had just happened upon him in his usual thinking spot.

"Fine. I shall paint you," she said. "But I warn you that it will take me all afternoon. We'll be baked alive and you'll have to skip your precious lunch."

He pulled out his pocket watch. "Nonsense. You have one hour."

181

Chapter

NINETEEN

Michigan, Present Day

Esther smoothed her mother's gray hair as best she could and spritzed it lightly with hairspray. She'd never been particularly good at doing hair, whether hers or someone else's, but she had managed to retain the ability to do a rather poor French twist from living through her college roommate's obsession with Audrey Hepburn. It was Lorena's first meal out since she'd come back from the hospital two months prior, and Esther wanted her to feel as beautiful and confident as possible.

It would also likely be their last chance for a nice dinner out before the students began arriving for the fall semester. Move-in week, with its heavy traffic and crowds, always sent Lorena into fits of paranoia. Esther typically left the museum closed from August 20th or so through Labor Day so she could stay home with her mother, even though she might expect more patrons as freshmen and their parents roamed the streets and familiarized themselves with the place where they'd be spending so much time and money for the next four years.

But as it was only August 6th, they were going out. Lorena's psy-

182

chiatrist, Dr. Wu, had suggested she needed more social interaction, not less, if she was going to learn to cope with her fears rather than let them overwhelm her as she had back in June. Lorena had insisted it wasn't fear that had led to her overdose, but she also would not tell Dr. Wu what had. At home, Esther kept trying to pry the answer out of her, finally threatening to take away her painting supplies if she didn't fess up. At that point, Lorena admitted it had something to do with Esther talking to "that man at the hotel."

"What hotel?"

"The one with the coffee."

"The Graduate?"

"Yes."

"The man I talked to about the artwork?"

"Yes."

Despite her mother nearly making a scene there, this made little sense to Esther. Lorena was often suspicious when she saw Esther talk to other people—nurses, doctors, the mail carrier—but that had never before driven her to such paranoia that she'd attempted suicide. At least, not on Esther's watch. The earlier attempts had occurred when Lorena was under the care of her father and her ex-husband.

Esther discussed her mother's medications and dosage with Dr. Wu, who agreed that perhaps there was a chance the current regimen was no longer effective and they might try something else.

But then, on the Fourth of July, as Esther distracted her mother from the sound of fireworks outside with a night of listening to her favorite records using noise-canceling headphones, Lorena suddenly sat up straight, took off the headphones, and said, "Do you wish I was dead?"

"No," Esther said, hurt by the question. "Of course not."

"I thought maybe if I was dead, you could go off with that man."

"What man? What are you talking about?"

"The man at the hotel."

It took Esther a moment to pull the man's face from her

memory. "That guy? That smarmy guy who told me where they'd gotten the artwork on the walls? Why on earth would you think I was interested in him?"

"No," Lorena said. "Not that guy. The other guy. The professor. The one you invited over to look at *La Dama del Cabello Oscuro*."

In a flash of supreme clarity like fireworks lighting up her brain, Esther understood. She moved from the chair to the couch next to her mother. "Mom, I told you that I wasn't interested in him in that way. He was in town to see the museum and to get some books for his research. We talked about Vella and *La Dama*—and your work, actually—and then he left for a research trip to France. I haven't spoken to him all summer."

"But I saw you. Talking about *La Dama*. I heard you talking in the living room and came down to say hello."

She paused, and Esther gave her time to organize her thoughts.

"You were enjoying yourself."

Esther snickered. "You must have come down early in the conversation. We actually had a bit of an argument."

"No. I saw the argument. You loved it." Esther was about to protest when Lorena added, "You were so alive in those moments. And then you left with him and I realized . . ." She trailed off.

"Realized what?" Esther said.

"That your life would be better without me."

Esther turned off the stereo and took the headphones from her mother's hands. "No. It would be different. Maybe. In some ways. But it wouldn't be better. It would be boring."

Lorena chewed on this a moment, gave a little nod. "Our lives are rather boring now, though, aren't they? We should go out more. Like Dr. Wu said."

And so they had, testing the waters with familiar places. Esther brought Lorena with her to the museum a few days, where she talked Eddie's ear off reminiscing about old times. They looked through the offerings at Curious Books, took a walk through the horticultural gardens at MSU. Then they decided to try dinner.

Esther had reserved a table for two at the State Room less than half a mile away at the edge of campus. In their more illustrious past, the Markstroms had taken artists and potential donors there, and there were still a handful of people on staff who knew Lorena and understood how to make her comfortable. They also didn't take it personally if she was cold toward them, which would make Esther's night easier. Rhoda, the oldest waitress there, had actually served at Lorena's wedding reception.

Esther pulled up to the front of the Kellogg Center, turned over her keys to the valet, and took her mother's arm to lead her inside. She could have saved a few bucks by self-parking in the ramp, but the low ceilings and dark corners and much longer walk through the hotel down to the restaurant seemed to Esther like unnecessary complications. They were seated immediately in a quiet corner and attended to by Rhoda, who wasn't originally supposed to work that night but had traded shifts with another server to accommodate.

Lorena perused the menu, voiced her disappointment that her favorite dish—morel mushroom risotto—was not represented there, and reluctantly ordered something else. Rhoda gave Esther a wink before taking their orders back to the kitchen. Twenty minutes and one water glass refill later, she reemerged with morel mushroom risotto on her tray, despite the fact that morel season had ended almost three months ago. Rhoda must have gone through a lot of trouble to find dried morels after Esther had made their reservation, knowing what her old friend would want.

Conversation was sparse but cordial. Esther could tell that Lorena stopped herself from saying something a few times, putting into practice Dr. Wu's advice to think about what she was about to say, decide if it was true, kind, or helpful, and then simply not say it if it didn't fit those parameters. There were no narrowed eyes, no knowing looks, no accusations of conspiracy or subterfuge, and by the time the crème brûlée came, Esther had actually relaxed. So much so that when she asked for the check, she wasn't prepared for Rhoda to tell her it had been taken care of.

Esther sat up straight and looked around. "By whom?"

Rhoda motioned to the bar. "Oh, he was there a minute ago. Older man. Thinning hair. Glasses."

"Did he have an accent?"

"Excuse me?"

"An accent, like a British accent?"

"I didn't speak to him. He told the bartender."

Esther put her hand on her mother's. "Just a minute, Mom." She rose from her seat and made her way to the bar. "Excuse me," she said, flagging down the young man behind the bar. "The man who paid for our meal, did he have a British accent?"

The bartender stuck out his chin and shook his head. "No, no accent. Older guy, thinning hair, glasses."

"But no accent?"

"No."

"Had you seen him before? Is he staying here?"

He gave a little shrug. "Sorry, ma'am. I don't know."

She went back to the table. Rhoda had sat in the seat she'd vacated and had Lorena laughing at something. Nothing Esther said to her mother ever made her laugh.

"Any luck?" Rhoda said, rising from the table.

"No."

"Did he have an accent?"

Esther thought she caught a look pass between Lorena and Rhoda. "No. I have no idea who it could have been."

Rhoda picked up Lorena's empty dessert dish. "Just one of Lorena's many admirers, I'm sure."

After saying their goodbyes, they waited out front for the valet to bring the car around. Esther studied the side of her mother's face. She was still smiling.

"So, do you have any idea who might have paid for our dinner?" Esther asked.

"No. But I did find it telling that you jumped to the conclusion that it must have been the professor you're not interested in."

Esther sighed. "He's just the last person who paid for something for me, and he said he would be back in town at the end of the summer to pick up the painting he bought back in June."

Lorena raised her eyebrows. "Mm."

The valet pulled up the car and opened the doors for them. Esther tipped him as she got in and drove them home, attempting all the way to ignore the fact that she had been a little disappointed when the bartender told her their mystery benefactor had no accent.

TWO DAYS LATER, Esther was filling two glasses of water when she received a text from Ian Perez.

Esther! I am back in the States, only partly recovered from jet lag, and bursting with news to share with you. If you have time this weekend, I'd like to stop by East Lansing to pick up my painting (perhaps a little earlier than you'd like, but I'm pressed for time the rest of the month—syllabi to write, etc.) and to tell you about my brief sojourn in Alsace-Lorraine and my even more brief side trip to Gib. There are two items in particular that I think you'll find quite interesting.

Though her immediate reflex was to tap out a response in the affirmative, one peppered with question marks and exclamation points that might draw out more information, she instead closed the messaging app, put her phone on the kitchen counter, and headed upstairs.

In Lorena's studio, she placed one of the glasses on a small table near her mother's easel and the other next to a chair. Esther sat in the chair, adjusted her posture, and tilted her head. "More to the right," Lorena said.

Esther turned slightly toward the window.

"A little more."

Another inch.

"Up."

Esther very slowly tilted her face up toward the ceiling.

"There. Stop. Perfect. Don't move."

Esther held the position for some time—she didn't know how long—until a dull ache formed in her neck, then ran down through her back and into her tailbone. Then she held it some more. The ache sharpened slowly, like cold water coming to a boil on the stove, until she couldn't bear it any longer. Then she silently counted to one hundred.

"Break?" she finally said.

"One moment," Lorena replied.

The moment lasted for an eternity, but then Lorena finally let out a big breath and said, "Break."

Immediately Esther released the pose, tucked her chin to her chest, and pulled at her shoulder muscles. It was only then she felt the painful tingling in her left leg, and she realized she'd had her toe pointed the entire time instead of resting her foot flat on the floor.

"How much longer?" she asked.

Lorena swished a brush through the thinner. "How should I know?"

"Can I see it?"

"Not yet."

It was after they'd returned home from dinner that Lorena suggested Esther should be her next subject. Though Esther didn't think a painting of herself would be especially desirable to anyone, nor especially beautiful, even in Lorena's hands, she had agreed. She'd thought it might give them more opportunity to talk, not remembering her mother's strict rules about models remaining silent. "This isn't the hairdresser's," Lorena had said the first time Esther tried to make conversation by speculating again about the identity of the man who'd paid for their dinner.

And so that was that. Esther was stuck holding an uncomfortable position for as long as Lorena required her, and she didn't even get a little conversation out of the deal. Instead, she held the conversation in her head, both posing and answering the questions but getting no closer to a conclusion because no new information was ever added. An old guy with thinning hair and glasses who did not have an accent. The only thing she knew for sure was that it was not her former professor.

What had he found in France, anyway? When he came to town, would he ask her again about the identity of the artist who'd executed the small painting he'd purchased for $750? Would she tell him? If so, why? To satisfy her ego? If not, why not? Simply because withholding information allowed her to maintain some illusion of authority and power?

These thoughts and more had occupied her mind during each sitting until her body screamed for primacy, at which point that was all she could think about. She felt every muscle, every bone, every joint. It was strange how staying stationary could be so incredibly painful. How an otherwise comfortable position became intolerable if one was not allowed to move at all. How what felt tortuous to the model would appear sublime and contented to onlookers.

The human body was meant for movement, as was the human life. That was Esther's problem, wasn't it? That nothing ever changed. That no ground was gained. That she'd lived in the same town in the same house since birth. That she'd worked in the same job in the same building for over twenty years, talking about the same collection of old paintings. That the gallery downstairs housed an unending and ever-changing stream of the human experience captured in color upon canvas, while she experienced only shadows of it.

"I'll be right back," she told her mother and headed straight for the kitchen. She picked up her phone, tapped out a response to Ian Perez, and waited impatiently for him to respond.

TWENTY

MOROCCO, 1881

From Tunisia, they sailed to Algiers and then to Oran, a French protectorate at the far western end of Algeria.

There Vellà transferred their trunks to a small vessel with an unusually large crew of rough-looking men. The boat was already heavily laden—Viviana knew not with what—and bound for Tétouan in Morocco. After loading more cargo in that city, they would sail to Gibraltar, giving wide berth to the Spanish port at Ceuta on the African side of the straits.

Viviana found it strange how many little parcels of land were carved away from one country by another in the name of military or commercial advantage. Why should Spain or France have any part of Africa? Why should England have a piece of the Iberian Peninsula, let alone all the other places across the globe they had wrenched from their rightful inhabitants? Why should Castille control Catalonia? Why was enough never enough?

As she lay down in yet another bed that was not hers, Viviana wondered at the point of it all. Such struggle and strife and bloodshed, and for what? A little more gold, a little more power, a little more prestige. How many men had experienced a lifetime of grasping and clutching, trying to hold on to what they had gained—only to die and lose it all anyway? How many lives had been wasted in pursuit of such fleeting rewards? How could that be what life was about?

And then, what was she living for? What did she hope to gain from her own efforts? She had never earned a single coin from her art. What was the reason to spend the time and effort she did to paint? What was she after? What were Mary Cassatt and Berthe Morisot and Marie Bracquemond after? Were they not also capturing things? Capturing light. Capturing color. Capturing moments in time and placing them thoughtfully on canvas so that they would not disappear entirely.

She thought of the antelope and bison racing across the ceiling of that cave in the Pyrenees. How much more permanent art was than power. How much more constant it was than a kingdom. How much more expansive than an empire.

That night she dreamed she was in a cavernous hall lined with paintings that came alive as she passed them. The muses on Valentin Renaud's wall, the operagoers in Mary Cassatt's studio, the mother and child in Berthe Morisot's sitting room. And her own many-layered self-portrait, shifting before her eyes—her hair lengthening, her clothes transforming from one costume to another, her eyes darting about, her fingers reaching for the bottom of the canvas.

Just as she was about to attempt to climb out of the painting, Viviana woke with a start. Her hair was plastered to her face, the space between her breasts dripping with sweat.

Vella burst through the door, bare-chested and wild-eyed, and rushed to her side. "What is it? What's wrong?" he said, grasping her hand.

She sat up, confused. "Nothing, nothing at all."

The Lady with the Dark Hair

"You were screaming. And you're drenched with sweat," he continued, wiping the wet hair from her cheek and her forehead. Weak gray light riding a cool sea breeze filtered in through the open window and seemed to whisk away what remained of her nocturnal visions.

"I must have been having a bad dream." But even as she said it, she knew it couldn't be true. It had been a good dream. Hadn't it?

Vella stood, still holding her hand. "That's a relief. I thought you were being attacked or had awakened to a cobra in your bed."

Viviana pulled her hand away and ran her fingers through her damp hair. "I don't suppose I'll have time to bathe before we must leave?"

"I'm afraid not." He motioned to the basin of water on the chest of drawers across the small room. "That will have to do. Perhaps there will be time for a swim before we land at Tétouan."

"I don't know how to swim."

"Is that so? Well, we shall have to teach you."

THEY WERE AT THE DOCK with the rising sun and pushed off as the night fishermen arrived home with the day's catch. The boat was cramped, the sailors heavily armed but jovial. Viviana sat at the starboard rail, looking out over the vast expanse of blue that was the Mediterranean. This was the "marine" in ultramarine blue. The blue from "beyond the sea." The pigment was ground from lapis lazuli rock found in the mountains of Afghanistan. Vella had procured a fair amount from a trader in Tunisia and had kept it on his person in bags hidden beneath his clothing until they had loaded their things onto this vessel. At that time, he entrusted it all to the weather-beaten men who now milled about both above and belowdecks.

"Why is it you trust these men with the ultramarine?" she asked when Vella finished his cigarillo and sat down beside her. "Aren't you afraid they'll steal it?"

"I've known most of these men most of my life. We've put our very lives in each other's hands countless times. So it is no great sacrifice to put our goods there as well."

"Did you serve in the military together?"

Vella let out a laugh. "No. Nothing like that. Though we've certainly had our share of brushes with the big guns out here."

"I'm not sure I understand."

"We're all merchants. Of a sort."

Viviana glanced around the boat at the barrels and sacks and bundles. "And what is this merchandise?"

Vella leaned back. "It varies. Today it would appear that we're dealing in cotton, coffee, palm oil, and tobacco. Perhaps a smattering of other items. Most will end up in Spain, though not by the regular shipping routes. One of the reasons—besides you, my dear—that we are avoiding Puerto de Ceuta."

"Do you mean to say these men are smugglers?"

"I would have thought that was obvious by the way the boat is outfitted," he said, "but perhaps not so obvious to a woman."

Viviana bristled. "What does that mean?"

He lifted his hands. "Well, for all your misspent youth, you are rather uneducated in the ways of the world, Viviana."

She was quiet a moment, gathering her irritation at his condescension and channeling it into a response. "Am I?"

Vella opened his mouth to speak, but she cut him off.

"How many men have you killed, Vella?" she said. "How many miles of wilderness have you crossed completely alone, scraping and scrounging for enough wild plants and insect larvae to keep alive, fending off wolves and feeding fires through the night to keep from freezing to death? How many times have you had to reinvent yourself, to lie about who you are, just to survive the brutality of men who count your life as nothing?" She stood. "But please, tell me how naive I am, how utterly helpless and unfit and in need of your protection and education to survive in this cruel and complicated world."

193

Without waiting for him to respond, Viviana walked to the other side of the boat, trading her view of the Mediterranean for a view of the Moroccan shoreline. She found herself standing next to two men who were looking at her with curiosity. How loudly had she been speaking? What might the others on board have heard? She fought the feminine instinct to look away and pretend she hadn't noticed them staring. Instead, she met their gaze boldly. So what if they'd heard her? These men were not law-abiding citizens who might be scandalized or incensed. These were men who flaunted their ability to outrun the law.

After the briefest moment, the younger of the two men looked away from her intense gaze, but the older man held out a tin of small cigars.

"Cigarillo, señorita?"

She softened her features and took one of the thin brown cylinders from the tin. "Moltes gràcies," she said, not attempting to hide her Catalan origins. Perhaps she would indeed be herself from here on out. If she did not do it now, how long would it be until the real Viviana was lost forever?

Chapter

TWENTY-ONE

◆

Michigan, Present Day

Esther was beginning to regret suggesting Ian Perez simply come over to the house rather than meeting up at a restaurant. She'd been reluctant to leave Lorena and had actually thought that if her mother could meet him in person, she might stop speculating about Esther's so-called feelings for him. But now, as she let Dr. Perez inside and felt Lorena hovering over her shoulder, Esther could see all the ways this could go wrong.

She made introductions and ushered Perez into the living room.

"Why don't the two of you sit," Lorena said, "and I'll make some coffee. We have a fancy new coffeemaker."

"Espresso machine," Esther corrected. "Which you don't know how to use. So you two sit and I'll make us some cappuccinos."

Esther sped through the process as quickly as the machine would allow, which was not quick at all. She strained to hear the conversation between her mother and her professor over the hissing and gurgling, but she could only make out a disembodied word here and there, and one loud burst of combined male and female laughter. When she walked into the room with a tray full of coffee cups and a plate of cookies, all conversation ceased.

"What did I miss?" she asked, not sure she wanted the answer.

"I was just telling your mother how incredible I think her collection of self-portraits is," Perez said.

"And I was telling your friend how it was a good thing the more recent ones were upstairs or he might not think they were so incredible after all," Lorena said.

"I don't know how that could be true," he said. "It seems a shame that they are all here and not in the gallery." He turned toward Esther. "Did you ever think of doing a show of your mother's work?"

She waited for her mother's standard response to the suggestion that Esther had made many times before: *Oh, pet, no one wants to see that.*

Instead, Lorena said emphatically, "I have thought of it." She indicated Esther. "But this one's a bit territorial."

"I beg your pardon?" Esther said. "I've told you you should do a show for years. You never wanted to."

Lorena looked at Perez and shook her head.

Esther suppressed a sigh. "Anyway, that's not what Dr. Perez came here to talk to me about."

"Actually, I wanted to talk to both of you," he said. "I think you'll both be very interested in a couple discoveries I made this summer." He took a sip of cappuccino and nodded appreciatively at Esther. "This is excellent. Though not, perhaps, as excellent as what I found in Colmar." He put the cup down. "By way of setting the scene for you, Colmar is a village in Alsace-Lorraine."

"Where the Colmar Treasure was found," Esther said.

"Correct!" Perez said.

Esther pointed at herself. "Art history major, remember? You probably taught me that."

196

"Yes, yes." Perez chuckled. To Lorena, "Do you know what the Colmar Treasure is?" When she shook her head, he continued. "It was a hoard of precious items hidden during the persecution of the Jews during the mid-1300s. They were falsely accused of spreading the black death. All over the Holy Roman Empire, from Flanders to Catalonia to Frankfurt, Jews were accused of poisoning wells and were tortured to get confessions from them. Many were killed, and their homes and businesses were ransacked. In Colmar, it seems one family hid many gold and silver items—jewelry and table service and such—in the walls of a house. It wasn't found for five centuries. I actually saw a few trinkets at the Unterlinden Museum while I was there, but it is believed that the people who first found the items in 1863 probably sold off a number of them before officially reporting the find."

Perez pulled out his phone and swiped at the screen for several seconds.

"It turns out that Colmar is still a very good place to hide your treasures. Not only did some of those medieval buildings survive to the nineteenth century, they survived two World Wars as well. An old university chum of mine from my time in London teaches in Munich now, and he was doing some work in the area when he came across an older woman who claimed she had a treasure of her own, and he invited me to join him there because he knew of my own research." He finally turned the phone toward Esther. "This was among the works we examined."

She took the phone from his hand and looked closely at the image. It was an unfinished painting of a young woman at an easel. "Watercolor or gouache?"

"Watercolor, I think," he said.

Lorena came around to look over Esther's shoulder. "Late 1800s?"

"Indeed," he said. "If you'll zoom in a bit, you can see there's a signature."

197

Esther focused in on the bottom right-hand corner. "Cassatt? As in Mary Cassatt?"

Perez smiled. "The very same."

"Were there other Impressionist works?" she asked, mind reeling at the possibility of lost paintings coming to light.

"There were a few other pieces worth mentioning, but I think this will be the one of greatest interest to you."

"Why?"

"Take a closer look at the subject."

Esther zoomed in on the subject's face. Though most of the painting was not particularly detailed—a mere sketch in places—the face was fully realized, and it was a face she recognized.

"Oh my word."

Lorena spoke up. "It looks like *La Dama*."

Esther looked from the phone to the painting above the mantle and then back to the phone. It did indeed look remarkably like the same woman. She zoomed in further, and there was all the proof she needed. The scar poking out from the collar.

"But—" she started. "So—Mary Cassatt knew Vella's mystery woman?"

Perez swiped at the phone in Esther's hand, bringing up the next picture. "Maybe she's not a mystery after all. This is the back."

Esther zoomed in on the writing at the top left of the image. There, in pencil, Mary Cassatt had identified her subject. *Veronica Vella*.

"Veronica?" Lorena said. "Who was she?"

"I was hoping you would know!" Perez said. "A wife, a sister, a cousin?"

"She had to be his wife," Esther said. "Otherwise, why would she be with him in Paris?"

"Don't jump to conclusions." Perez sipped at his cappuccino. "There's still much work to be done to figure out just who she was. But I thought you might like being able to put a name to a face you see all the time."

Esther swiped back to the previous picture and compared it again with *La Dama*. Her lady had a name now. Her name was Veronica. Veronica, the lady with the dark hair. "This is incredible," Esther whispered. "Just incredible."

"Where is this painting now?" Lorena said.

"The works have been turned over to the state—much to the old woman's irritation," Perez said. "I think she had an idea to sell them and that we would help her appraise their value. But they're not hers to sell. There is still much more research needed to discover who actually owned them, who hid them, who they truly belong to."

"If your grandfather were alive, he would certainly try to make some sort of claim over that watercolor," Lorena said to Esther. "He would be on a plane to France right now."

"I don't even have a passport," Esther mumbled.

"You may want to take care of that," Perez said, eyes twinkling. "Because that is just my first surprise."

Chapter

TWENTY-TWO

◆

GIBRALTAR, 1881

They approached Gibraltar from the south. Squinting against the brilliance of the sparkling Mediterranean, Viviana could make out layers of white fortress walls and white cliffs, then the steep climb up the Rock into the thin blue sky. The whole place seemed to be leaning away from the Spanish side of the Bay of Algeciras, as though centuries of cannon fire had put the peninsula's face into a permanent flinch. The vertical eastern side of the Rock was pale gray and pockmarked with caves. The sloping western side was green where there were no buildings, white and peach and tan down by the water where the Rock's cramped populace eked out an existence.

Their vessel traced the coastline a couple hundred feet out but still within British waters, or so said Dario, the sailor who had offered her the cigarillo. Viviana had stayed near him for much of the crossing, preferring to watch him work and ask him questions—*Where do you get the tobacco? What will you do with the cotton? Where did you get that Italian Vetterli rifle, and is it the old*

200

single shot model or the repeating model?—rather than talk with Vella any longer, though he could probably have answered her questions just as easily.

Dario seemed intrigued by her knowledge of his firearm and generally amused by her inquisitiveness (and perhaps just a little flattered at a young woman taking such interest in his work). He pointed out features along the shoreline as they covered nearly the whole length of the peninsula on their way to the wharf just north of the Old Mole. There's Europa Bay and Devil's Bowling Green. There's the military hospital, the barracks, the vast British fleet. There are the Alameda Gardens, the Grand Parade, the Moorish Wall. Then the main part of town, with the cathedral, the convent, the many shops and taverns. From afar it all looked rather pleasant. But a closer look at the garrison walls revealed hundreds of cannons, all pointed straight at them. Well, not them exactly, but at the bay behind them where the military might of kingdoms and caliphates had fought for supremacy for a thousand years.

When they docked at the wharf, Dario helped Viviana out of the boat and brought over her own trunk before returning to unload the cargo. She sat on it and watched the people come and go as Vella tended to his own trunks and boxes. There were Royal Marines, of course, in white pants and short red coats crossed with a white X, looking for all the world like a fine target. There were sailors in blue trousers and white shirts. Spaniards in black and red, every man with a cigarillo, every woman holding a fan. Moors in their white turbans and long, loose blue and white robes over knee-length white pants, their lower legs dark and bare, their feet clad in slippers the color of rhubarb.

All of these people mixed and mingled near the docks, but the farther inland they traveled, the more they branched off into their own groups, like with like. Dario had told her that though they were all Gibraltarians, each had their specialty. The Moors were porters or kept shops of "curiosities" to sell to tourists—

round velvet cushions, necklaces and bracelets of tinkling gold coins or shells, elaborate knives, yellow and blue slippers. The Maltese were sailors and fishermen and smugglers. The Spaniards were servants in English households or waiters or cigar rollers. The Jews kept shops and acted as interpreters for visitors because they knew so many languages.

"And the English?" Viviana had asked. "Are they all soldiers?"

"The girls? For the most part. Different ranks and divisions, so you'll see some in blue uniforms, some in red, some manning guns on ships, some manning guns on land, all of them manning stools in the pubs and taverns any chance they get. But the women . . . well, I suppose they don't do very much at all. Host other Englishwomen, mostly. Look down their noses at us."

"Are there any museums?"

"There are no museums," he'd said. "There's a library at the garrison, but only British officers are allowed to use it."

Now as she drank in all the sights around her, Viviana thought perhaps she didn't much care that there were no museums. There was plenty here for a woman with an artistic bent to put to her own use. The place hummed with human interest in every direction.

When Vella had finally loaded up a donkey cart with their things, he beckoned Viviana to follow him down Waterport Street, past Irish Town, and into the Spanish quarter where she would meet his family and see where she would be staying for the foreseeable future. Vella had said he would stop over for a month at least before resuming his circuitous trading route through France, Germany, Austria, Italy, and Northern Africa.

It was slow going up the winding roads to the Vella family home. Despite her sore feet, Viviana did not mind at first, as it allowed her to closely observe her surroundings. There were so many interesting people, so many quaint shops and stands. Occasionally they would pass a few Spanish men smoking outside a tavern, their appreciative "Que hermosa" or "Que bonita" loud enough for her to hear from her spot by the side of the cart but not loud enough for Vella up at the donkey's head, urging the tired beast on.

But the farther into town they went, the hotter and more oppressive it got. Buildings blocked the sea breeze. There were too many people in too small a space. Rank odors emanated from alleys. A scuffle between two drunken British soldiers would have sent Viviana into the cart had Vella not pulled her out of the way.

After what felt like forever, they reached the upper part of town where Gibraltar's oldest families lived.

"Here we are," Vella said. "La Buena Vista."

The name and the neighborhood were in direct opposition. The buildings were not grand old homes befitting long-established families but shabby tenements that looked for all the world like they might better serve prisoners than the women and children who went in and out of the dark doorways. The view was not of the blue waters of the bay or the straits but of other similarly dilapidated buildings. Vella had told her that not only did his mother live here but his three sisters and their families did as well.

She was trying to formulate the right thing to say to him when a small, grubby boy shouted, "Tío Francisco!" and came running, a kid goat in tow.

Vella scooped the boy up. "Cosmito! You're so much bigger than when I saw you last. I'll have to start calling you Cosmo now, eh?"

"Yes," the boy said, "especially because I'm not the youngest in my family anymore."

"What?"

"Mama had another baby last month. Her name is Josefina. I don't like her at all."

Vella tousled the boy's hair then pushed away the goat, which had started eating one of his bootlaces. "Why don't you like your new baby sister?"

"She's loud and boring and everyone thinks she's great."

203

Vella laughed. By now several other children had gathered round, shouting their greetings. Then a beautiful young woman with Vella's eyes and smile was striding toward him, her black skirt swishing, her black hair done up in braids all coiled around her head.

"Francisco!"

They embraced and began speaking rapidly to one another, switching from Spanish to English seemingly at random. Viviana could catch only part of what was being said but gathered that the woman was one of Vella's sisters—though not the mother of the loud and boring Josefina—and was filling her brother in on what he had missed. A sudden, stabbing pain shot through Viviana's heart as she could not keep from thinking of how she would never have such a reunion with Ignasi. Not this side of heaven.

Vella seemed to remember Viviana's existence. "Madalena, this is . . ." He trailed off, allowing Viviana to fill in whatever name and backstory she might choose.

"Viviana Torrens of Catalonia," she said. "I met your brother in France."

After a moment's hesitation, Madalena greeted her warmly in Spanish. "Have you been traveling with him on his route?"

"I have."

Madalena raised her eyebrow. "I have to say I am surprised that Francisco never mentioned you in his letters." She fixed her brother with a look. "But perhaps he didn't want our mother to get wind of you."

"I beg your pardon?" Viviana said.

"Now, Madalena—"

"I don't mean to be rude, Viviana," she said. "I just . . . well, our mother is very devout. I don't know how she will feel about her only son traveling with a woman when he is not married."

Viviana grinned. "Ah, but he *is* married."

Madalena looked quickly between the both of them. "Francisco, is this true? Are you married?"

Viviana prompted him with her eyes. *Aren't you?*

"Yes," he said slowly. "I was married in France."

Madalena covered her mouth with her hands. "I can't believe it! Mama is going to be so happy!" She swatted her brother in the arm. "And so, so angry with you, Francisco. How could you? You should have been married here in the new cathedral! Mama will never forgive you." Madalena grasped Viviana's hand. "Come. I will introduce you to everyone." Over her shoulder she added, "Cosmito, you and Juan and Domingo help Tío Francisco with all the baggage."

THERE WAS NO WAY she could remember them all, let alone remember which people belonged to which family. There was the matriarch, Consuela Vella, widow of Zaran Vella, whose seafaring ancestors had hailed from Malta and supplied the British with meat and citrus fruits during the Great Siege of 1779–1783. There were the three daughters, Paulina, Teresa, and Madalena, and their husbands, Gasparo, Manual, and Teodoro, and seemingly endless children, mostly rambunctious boys aside from the baby Josefina and a sullen-looking older girl named Emilia.

Madalena had brought Viviana first to Señora Vella, who was kind and welcoming and then sent her away to speak to her son alone. They left Francisco to his fate and made the rounds, from room to cramped room around a small inner courtyard crisscrossed by clotheslines that sagged low beneath wet linens, under which various troughs and buckets collected any dripping water to be reused later. According to Madalena, there was no more precious commodity on the Rock than water, especially at the height of summer when the rain collection tanks were running low. Bathing, if it happened at all, happened at the seashore, and no water could be spared to flush out the sewer system.

205

"You get used to it," she said of the smell.

The courtyard also served as a storage space for an assortment of odd items, a playground for the children, and a paddock for the animals, which included some ducks and chickens, a nanny goat and her two kids, and one mournful dog that never ceased its high-pitched whining as far as Viviana could tell.

"How many people live in this building?" Viviana asked after Madalena showed her the necessary—a hole in the ground inside a closet, out of which rank odors rose continuously.

"Let's see. Our family occupies the first-floor rooms, and we're"—she did some quick calculations—"well, twenty-three now that you're here. Upstairs there are the Bretans, the Laderos, and the Tagliaferos. Altogether they make about twenty more at least." Madalena put a hand on her arm. "I hope Francisco prepared you for this."

He had not. Perhaps he had tried—he had said there were tens of thousands of people squeezed into about a square mile of livable space, but somehow Viviana had not imagined that to be true. Surely he'd miscalculated. Anyway, with so many of that number being soldiers, she figured most of those people would be filed away on bunks in the barracks and didn't really count toward the total. And Vella had certainly not given her details about what such a population density meant for day-to-day living conditions. This made the siege at Seu d'Urgell feel luxurious.

The only answer Viviana could make to Madalena's comment was a thin smile.

Madalena patted her hand, then kept holding it. "Lucky for you, you'll be able to continue to travel with Francisco. At least until the children start coming."

Viviana bit her tongue.

They finally made their way back around to where Vella still stood in front of his mother. If he had just been chastised, he didn't show it. He took leave of his mother and gripped Viviana's elbow, hard, leading her out of the room and then back to the street.

"Why did you tell her we were married?"

"I didn't," Viviana said, yanking her arm from his grip. "I told her *you* were married, and you are. I thought I'd give you a chance to come clean to your family about Dolorés, a chance which you clearly squandered. But that is not my fault."

"You do realize that thanks to your strategic omission of vital information—that being the identity of my bride—you'll be expected to sleep in the bed with me."

She let out a light laugh. "First of all, my omission could have easily been filled in with the truth if you had an ounce of courage. Secondly, I'm sure a simple solution can be found. You take the bedroom and I will sleep in the sitting room."

"No, it is not simple. On your grand tour with Madalena, did she show you my rooms?"

Viviana thought back. "No."

"That's because I don't *have* my own rooms. I don't even have a room. When I'm here I sleep in the same room my mother sleeps in. My sisters and their husbands? They each sleep in the same room as all their children. There's no space for privacy here. No space for secrets. If my mother believes we are married, that means we will be sleeping in her bed now and she will move to the cot."

Viviana allowed this new reality to wash over her like the thin coat of umber she always used to tone her canvases. The impulsive statement by which she'd meant to push him into dealing with one sham marriage had created another—one she now seemed stuck with for as long as she was stuck on this rock.

Chapter

TWENTY-THREE

❖

MICHIGAN, PRESENT DAY

Esther was beginning to feel a little sick to her stomach. The idea of needing a passport was simultaneously thrilling and disappointing. She'd love a reason to travel abroad. But she knew already that it couldn't happen. She couldn't leave her mother. And she couldn't imagine taking her with her.

"I mentioned that I was stopping over at Gib since I was already in Europe," Perez was saying. "I have a cousin there who's a bit of an amateur historian on all things Gibraltar, and I had him look into the surname Vella. Neither of us knew anyone of that name, and it's such a small place we suspected the name may have died out there, as so many of the old names have. But my cousin, Adam, was able to find the Vella surname in a few lists of victims of epidemics." He consulted his phone. "It shows up in 1804 when there was a yellow fever outbreak, in 1821 with scarlet fever . . . 1832, cholera . . . and 1871, smallpox. With a little searching, Adam found that the smallpox victim, Zaran

Vella, was actually Francisco Vella's father. He was listed as a merchant on an earlier census, which I believe you said was the trade Francisco was also involved in. It's possible Zaran was on a trip and not in Gibraltar when they vaccinated people for smallpox, so that when he returned he was among the victims. There were only nine adults who died, most quite a bit older than he was. The rest were children."

He handed his phone over to Esther to let her scroll through his notes. "This is incredible," she said. "I can't believe you found this much information. But why would I need a passport?"

"Ah, yes, that." He leaned back and draped an arm over the back of the sofa. "Adam took me to this quirky little junk shop on Turnbull's Lane, which is just off Main Street, which your Vella may have called La Calle Real—that's the Spanish name for it."

"What's the Spanish name for Turnbull's Lane?" Lorena asked.

"Detrás de los Cuartos, which means 'behind the rooms.' Not sure which rooms, but there it is. Certainly sounds as though perhaps there was some business going on there that was not entirely aboveboard, doesn't it? And truly, after visiting this shop, that name seems to fit. The shopkeeper did not strike me as the most honest of chaps—there was a good deal of merchandise there that was priced as though authentic when it was clearly just a poor knockoff of a better brand. Anyway, as you know, Esther, I am always on the lookout for paintings, and there was one hanging behind the desk—which was why Adam brought me there, of course."

At any other time, Esther would have enjoyed Perez's meandering way of telling a story, but right at this moment she wanted to shake him into getting to the point. She took a sip of cappuccino and held it in her mouth to keep herself from interrupting,

"I asked about it as nonchalantly as possible," he continued, "so as not to seem too interested in it and thereby drive up the price. He said it was by a native artist, but it wasn't signed anywhere I could see, so I asked if I could see the back. 'Nothing but brown paper back there,' he said. 'All the same,' I said, 'I'd like to get a look at the back.' So he took it off the wall, but the only thing on the back was a tag with a number, which he explained was the way he identified the person who had consigned it."

Perez paused to take a sip of cappuccino.

"Long story short, he gave me the name of the person, which Adam and I agreed sounded familiar, so we went up to see her and recognized her as one of our old grade-school teachers. Which didn't surprise us at all. I've been gone for decades and I can't walk down a street on Gib without running into someone to whom I have some connection or other, however tenuous. We chatted a while and learned that the painting had been in her family for a few generations. Her great-grandmother"—he picked up his phone and began scrolling through his notes—"Josefina Santos had it, then her grandmother Luna, her mother Juana, and finally her. Her name is Gertrude, of all things."

"This is long story short?" Lorena said.

Thank you.

Perez laughed. "Yes, well, as short as a loquacious chap like me can make it, I guess. Anyway, here is the point. Gertrude—Ms. Hernandez, as I knew her—has fallen on hard times. It's become outrageously expensive to live in Gibraltar. I'd once planned on retiring there, but I'd never be able to afford it now. Ms. Hernandez consigned the painting, among a number of her other possessions, in an attempt to make a bit of money. I asked her what she knew of the artist. She told me that she couldn't remember exactly because it had been so long since she'd heard the story—and of course, she is rather old. She remembered her father reframing it at one point and thinks perhaps the painting was cut down to fit this particular frame—which would explain where the signature went. She also remembered seeing writing on the back of it when her father was reframing it. But that was covered up with the brown paper backing to finish it. So Adam and I go back to the shop, but of course the shopkeeper won't allow us to remove the backing without buying the painting. He quoted us a ridiculous price, not knowing who painted it or when, but we went ahead and bought it—though I am still worried that Ms. Hernandez is probably being cheated out of most of the profit."

Perez finally took a breath and swiped through his photos again.

"If it had been painted on a wrapped canvas, I could have simply removed it from the frame, rolled it up, and brought it to you. But as it's on an oak panel and rather cumbersome, I'm afraid this will have to do for now."

He handed the phone over to Esther, and there on the small screen was a man, suntanned and with dark hair, reclining against a large rock and writing in a leather-bound journal. It was a lovely scene, very much in keeping with the style of the paintings at the museum, and Esther zoomed in to examine the brushwork.

"So what was on the back?" she said. "Anything?"

"This is where it gets interesting. Go to the next photo."

She swiped to find a close-up of some writing on the back of the panel, and her breath caught in her throat. "Francisco Vella, 1881." Her heart started thumping. Was it possible that after all this time, the plain silhouette at the beginning of the Vella exhibit at the museum could be filled in with a picture of the artist himself? "But wait. Is this him? Is this identifying the subject or the artist?"

"That is indeed the question," Perez said. "And I believe perhaps it can be answered, should an expert on Francisco Vella be able to study it closely."

She looked up from the phone. "Where is the painting now?"

"It's at my cousin's house, hanging on the wall . . . waiting for you."

Chapter

TWENTY-FOUR

◆

GIBRALTAR, 1881

"There!" Cosmo pointed out across the strait toward the African continent. "That's where the monkeys came from. They're the only monkeys in all of Europe. And as long as there are monkeys on Gibraltar, the British will hold it."

"Is that so?" Viviana said, trying to catch her breath. She shaded her eyes and took in the rolling hills across the strait that receded into the far distance, getting fainter and cooler in tone as they went.

"Yes," the boy said solemnly.

"What do you think of them?" she asked.

"The monkeys? They're great. But you have to be careful. You can't corner them or they might attack you."

"No, the British."

Cosmo cast furtive glances at the other people taking in the view and came close to her. "You should be careful with them too. Some of them understand a little Spanish."

Viviana looked around, but it seemed to her that the pale ladies under their parasols and the sunburned men in their absurd wool coats were giving them a wide berth. She had hoped after the arduous hour-long walk that they'd have the place to themselves, but there really was no escaping the British.

"You know Emilia works in an officer's house," Cosmo said quietly.

"Does she like it?"

"Not at all. They're not very nice to her. But we need the money. She was rolling cigars before, like Tía Madalena, but this job pays a little better." Cosmo glanced around again, then leaned in close to whisper in Viviana's ear. "Emilia said they have a mean little dog that eats beef every day."

She pulled back and hoped she looked properly scandalized at the dog's beef intake. Though Emilia was still a bit standoff-ish, Cosmo had warmed to Viviana quickly. His curious dark eyes and easy smile reminded her of Ignasi, and his desire to roam fit perfectly with her desire to spend as much time out of the claustrophobic Vella house as possible. After a week spent mostly inside trying to be sociable and answer everyone's questions for her without getting herself or Vella in trouble, she was more than ready for an outing.

So, on this already-warm morning, Cosmo had taken her up winding roads past the Moorish Wall and Mt. Misery to the pin-nacle of the Rock, the only place in the world where one could see two seas and two continents at the same time—or so he had promised her before they left. Cosmo made big claims, so Viviana was getting used to taking what he said with a healthy measure of skepticism.

And yet, from up there on the top of the world, it did appear to be true. To the east she could see the Mediterranean Sea. To the west, her first glimpse of a sliver of the Atlantic Ocean. To the north lay the hills of Andalusia, Spain, a place that Cosmo said was full of robbers and assassins and bull fighters. To the south lay Morocco and the source of the Barbary apes that lived in caves on the eastern side of the Rock.

"How do you suppose they got here?" she asked Cosmo as he squatted down to examine something on the ground.

"The British?" he said.

"The monkeys."

"Oh, they have a tunnel. It starts in St. Michael's Cave and goes all the way to Africa."

"A tunnel?"

He said it so quickly and so matter-of-factly Viviana thought he must believe it.

"A tunnel?"

He stood and looked at her seriously. "Under the water. They can come and go as they please."

She tried to keep the turn of her mouth from revealing her skepticism. "And they are the only African creatures that use this tunnel? Why aren't there elephants or lions on Gibraltar if there's a tunnel between here and Africa?"

He screwed up his face. "They're too big. The cave is big but the tunnel is small. And only monkeys are clever enough to use it."

"Okay, who built the tunnel?"

He turned away and kicked at a stone. "Gee, I don't know."

Viviana felt a little petty for pressing him. There was no harm in believing something fantastic. It had been a very long time since she'd let herself just believe something delightful without some measure of suspicion. "So where are these famous monkeys, anyway?"

Cosmo looked around. "They're not always out. It's really hot today. Sometimes they like to stay in their caves where it's cool. They come out of the caves when the Levanter appears, but there isn't one today."

"Levanter? Is that a kind of beast? Like Job's Leviathan?"

He giggled. "No, silly. It's a cloud. They don't like it. No one likes it."

"A cloud with a name?"

"Sure. It's this cloud that settles just over the Rock and nowhere else." He waved his arms around. "Everywhere else you look it's blue skies, but overhead it's this hot, heavy cloud."

After the past week of living in the Vella house, with its crowded rooms and its whining dog and its mix of odors from cooking, refuse, and too many bodies, Viviana felt that she already lived under a hot, heavy cloud. Vella had been right about the sleeping arrangements. At night, Viviana and Consuela would ready themselves and then climb into their respective beds, which were encased in mosquito netting to keep out the bloodsucking insects that continually hummed around them, threatening them with yellow fever, a malady that visited the Rock almost as frequently as cholera. When the lamp was turned off, Vella would come in and join Viviana. She turned herself toward the wall, he to the room, and they lay still and separate until morning signaled another hot day had begun. Often Vella would already be gone when she woke and Consuela would be up preparing breakfast.

Her conversations with Consuela were inevitably awkward as she tried to tell the truth as much as possible while still maintaining the lie that she and the woman's son were happily married. She filled in her fake mother-in-law with true information from her past, including how her parents had died, how she and Ignasi had escaped the orphanage and joined the Carlist rebels. She told Consuela that her brother had been shot, though she left out the detail that she was the one who had shot him. She told her about her escape to France, the painted cave in the Pyrenees, her work in the Renaud household, and how she met the dashing and charming Francisco.

This was where the fabrication began. It was easy to do. She simply told the story of the next year or so as it might have happened had she gone with Vella when he'd asked her. It was a good and romantic tale, full of adventure. It might have been a good life.

"What are you thinking about?" Cosmo broke in.

Viviana blinked. "What?"

"You got all quiet and your eyes glazed over like my cousin's did when he died."

"What happened to your cousin?" Viviana deflected.

"He got sick."

"I'm sorry to hear that."

"Yeah. Lots of people get sick here. Abuela Consuela says it's because too many people are living in too small a space. That's why my grandfather died. That's why I'm going to move to Spain to be an outlaw someday. There's lots more room there. And lots of work for outlaws." He was quiet a moment. "I don't think we're going to see any monkeys today."

"Maybe not," she said. "But I do like this view. Do you think we could come up here again and I could bring my painting supplies? I think this would be a beautiful place to paint. And I wouldn't mind spending more time out of town, out where the air is a bit easier to breathe." Out where she could maintain a proper distance between herself and Vella.

"Sure," he said. "I'll bring you here again. And other places. Like the beach! We'll go to Catalan Bay. You should like that place because it's named for where you're from." He put his small hands on his narrow hips. "Maybe next time we're up here the monkeys will be out. But you've got to watch them if they are. They like to steal stuff."

Viviana laughed. "Do you think they'd steal my paintbrush?"

He nodded emphatically. "Oh, yes. They love taking people things."

"Perhaps we could teach them to paint?"

He seemed to consider this. "I don't know. They're not very patient." A pause. Then, "Could you teach me to paint?"

"Are you very patient?"

He screwed up his face. "I think I could try to be."

"Then yes, maybe I could teach you to paint."

He nodded once and with finality, like it was a formal agreement they had just struck, then took her hand in his. "Let's go home and get some lunch."

Viviana wanted to stay where they had labored so hard to reach and wait for the monkeys. She wanted to stay up where the air was fresh with the sea breeze and the horizon stretched out in every direction. Where everything felt a little more possible. Down below, in the winding and crowded streets, her horizons shrank to mere meters. She already knew, after less than a week, that she could not stay here. She could not allow her real self to be held captive by Vella's stories and lies. And she could not leave again on another trip with him.

She took another lingering look at the Atlantic. Then she let her young chaperone lead her back down the Rock.

TWENTY-FIVE

◆

MICHIGAN, PRESENT DAY

Esther could not go to Gibraltar. She didn't have a passport, she didn't have the first clue how to go through customs, and she certainly didn't have enough money to fly internationally, let alone buy what might be the only portrait ever painted of her ancestor and the center of her life's work. Who would run the museum while she was gone? Kylie? Who would look after Lorena?

Rhoda. Maybe Rhoda would come stay at the house for a while. That wasn't completely absurd. They were friends, of a sort. Rhoda was nice and accommodating and responsible.

But who was Esther kidding? There was no way she could make that ask. And there was no one to run the museum anyway, so getting someone to watch her mother was pointless.

Perez drained his cup and placed it back on the saucer. "Well, you have a lot to think about, and I have to get on the road soon." He looked at Esther expectantly.

It took her a minute to emerge from her internal calculations to figure out what he wanted. "Oh! The painting."

Perez smiled. "If that's all right."

"Of course." She rose and retrieved the small painting from the dining room table. She'd pulled it off the gallery wall, wrapped it in paper, and brought it home after receiving Perez's text. Now she handed it to its rightful owner.

"I know just where I'll hang it," he said. "I'll send you these photos and Adam's contact information. I've already told him all about you and your family connection to Vella, so he'll be expecting your call or text or carrier pigeon."

Perez shook Lorena's hand, then Esther's, holding on to Esther's just a little longer than felt normal. Or was she the one reluctant to break it off?

"I can't tell you how much I appreciate you taking the time—to say nothing of actually *buying* a painting to make sure I'd have a chance at it," Esther said. "It's really kind of you. Really kind."

"Of course," he said. "Happy to help out a friend. And frankly, it's added a bit of excitement to what has become a rather predictable life, wouldn't you say?"

Esther tried to say yes, but the word caught in her throat. It was unnerving how this person she hadn't interacted with in twenty years could penetrate so quickly and completely through her composed surface and see the chaos beneath. Like a good teacher, he had gone out of his way to open an avenue for her to expand her view, to experience a thicker slice of what life had to offer. To paint on a bigger canvas.

She closed the door behind him, took a breath, then turned to face her mother.

"Well?" Lorena said.

"Well, what?"

"Are you going to Gibraltar?"

Esther gave a despairing laugh. "In what world can I go to Gibraltar?"

Lorena looked around. "This one."

Esther started picking up the empty coffee cups. "It's ridiculous to even consider. I can't leave you here. I can't leave the museum. We can't afford it. And there's no guarantee it's really Vella's work anyway. And why couldn't this cousin of his just ship it here? Wouldn't that be cheaper than flying to Gibraltar? Ian didn't even suggest that."

"So now he's Ian?" Lorena teased.

Esther rolled her eyes.

"You should take a step out of your comfort zone," Lorena said. "Get out of this town for a while. Goodness knows you could use a break."

Esther bit her tongue to keep from pointing out again the reasons she would never be able to leave town. But then Lorena said something that opened the floodgates.

"And frankly, I could use a break from you."

Esther put down the cups—hard—on the kitchen counter and scuttled back out into the living room. "From me? You could use a break from me? I had no idea I was such a burden on you. How I make sure you eat and take your pills and take you to the hospital to save your life when you overdose. I had no idea how oppressive it is to have someone keeping an eye on you, keeping you levelheaded and safe and supplied with paint and canvases and your preferred snacks. So you can just make your own coffee with the machine you have no idea how to operate, is that it? You can go to the grocery store with all those conniving people who are out to get you and buy the food you need? You can go work your heart out at the family business and make barely enough money to keep the lights on and the trash picked up? You don't need me to do any of that anymore? Is that what I'm hearing?"

Esther stopped. She couldn't believe what had just come out of her mouth. Those were the things you didn't say. Those were the things you didn't think. Or admit to thinking.

Her mother was looking at her blankly, which was somehow worse than looking hurt. "I don't need a chaperone."

"I'm sorry," Esther said. "I'm sorry. I didn't mean all that. I'm just—I'm just tired." She plopped down on the couch and put her head in her hands.

Lorena sat down next to her. "I've never asked you to do any of that, you know."

"Yeah, and who was going to do it?" she said into her hands.

After a beat, Lorena said, "I thought when you came home from school to work at the museum, it was because you wanted to, because you were passionate about Vella's art and about the gallery and it was a way to use your art history degree—which, despite its outrageous price tag, is otherwise pretty useless, in my opinion. I never asked you to come home and babysit me."

Esther sat up. "You were alone when Gina left—sorry, when you drove her away."

Lorena scoffed. "I didn't drive her away. She moved to be closer to her new grandchild. She still calls me from time to time to update me on how things are going. You don't know because you're not here during the day. You have no idea what my life is actually like, you know that? You treat me like a patient, but I actually manage my condition pretty well most of the time."

"See, it's the 'most of the time' that worries me. What about the times you don't? What about not taking your meds? Or taking too many? What about being able to go outside on your own and come back safe? What if your mood shifts and the people around you don't understand why and something happens to you?"

She sighed. "Esther, I'm your mother. I'm not your responsibility. But the museum, you're right. That is your responsibility. And a good museum director would take this opportunity to add to the collection. She wouldn't be looking for excuses not to go examine and procure that painting. She'd be buying airline tickets and packing her bags right now."

"Mom, there's no extra money anyway."

"Says who?"

"Says the books. Which I have kept meticulously for the past twenty years. There's no arguing with them."

"Psh." Lorena stood and started toward the stairs. "You just aren't looking at the right books."

Esther flopped back on the couch, refusing for the moment to follow her mother into whatever scheme she was cooking up. Then she was on her feet and taking the stairs two at a time to catch up. She found Lorena in her studio, digging in the bottom drawer of the cabinet that held many of her supplies.

"I know it's here somewhere," she was muttering. "Aha!" Lorena pulled a yellowed envelope from the drawer and then pulled a little paper card from the envelope. "Here's the account number."

"What account?"

"Your grandfather was no fool when it came to the museum, you know. He made investments to ensure there would be money available in the future—for building maintenance, acquisitions, stuff like that. This is the account you can draw from for your trip."

Lorena waved the card at her and she took it.

"Why is this the first I'm hearing of this money?"

"Because it's the first we've heard of in decades."

"The museum's been struggling for a while, and you know this. Why didn't you tell me about there being money available when the pipes burst that one winter we had the ice storm and the polar vortex? Or when we had to get the asbestos removed? Or when the roof was leaking? I scrambled and begged and borrowed from anyone who might possibly still care about our family."

"And you got what you needed, right?"

Esther couldn't believe this. "That's not the point. There was money all along!"

"And now there's still money because we didn't use it on those things."

"But you said yourself that's what it's for!"

Lorena brushed past her and started down the hall. "I don't

ERIN BARTELS

know why you're complaining. You've been a good steward of what's been entrusted to you."

Esther followed her down the stairs.

"And now," Lorena continued, "you've been entrusted with the task of examining and hopefully buying that painting." She went into the kitchen and began rinsing out the cups. "So you need to get a passport—see if you can get them to expedite it—and then get yourself on a plane. I can manage on my own for a couple weeks. I can even keep the museum open if you tell me what you need me to do. Eddie can help me remember how it all works. And you have a student working there?"

"Kylie, yes. Though I wouldn't say she does much actual work. And when the new semester begins, she's probably going to quit, if my experiences with past student employees are any indication. I'll have to find another one."

"Fine. Students love me. I'll help you interview them. We'll get along just fine."

Esther stared at the piece of paper in her hands, at the numbers that marched across it in a precise line in her grandfather's handwriting. "You really feel confident that you could be on your own for a few days?"

"A few days, nothing. You'll need a week at least. The flights alone will probably take up two whole days."

Esther shook her head. "How would you feel if Rhoda came over every once in a while? Not to check up on you, but just in case you want some company."

Lorena's expression said she knew that of course it would be to check up on her, but still she said, "I'm sure that would be nice."

Esther bit her lip. "How long does it take to get a passport?"

223

TWENTY-SIX

GIBRALTAR, 1881

Six years ago, this place looked very different," Vella said, motioning to the small town perched precariously between the towering gray cliffs and the lapping blue waves of the Mediterranean. "Most of the village was wiped out in a flood, and the church was gutted. These boys were too young to remember."

"I remember," Emilia said.

Viviana and Vella, along with several of Vella's nephews and his niece, had spent the morning making their way to Catalan Bay on the eastern side of the Rock so the children could bathe and Viviana could paint. It had been a lengthy walk, much of it along a narrow dirt path strewn with rocks that had fallen from the cliffs above.

Viviana was glad to see that the little village seemed to have recovered. A new chapel and school had been erected. There was a small barracks to house the thirty soldiers who were stationed there, as well as a number of modest homes for the Genoese fisherman who had settled there with their families. Compared to the crush of souls on the other side of the Rock, Catalan Bay felt positively expansive despite the fact that it was actually quite small.

"Where did the name come from?" Viviana asked.

"Some say it is named for the Catalan detachment that fought with Hesse and defeated Susarte in 1704," Vella said. "Others think it is probably just a corruption of the Spanish word *caleta* for 'cove.' Who knows? But whatever the reason it got its name in the first place, it is clear to me that it was fated to be immortalized by a beautiful Catalan painter such as yourself. Now, where do you want to set up?"

"I like this view," she said. "So perhaps I'll start here."

"The view from the southern end of the cove is better," Vella said. "You can see the coast of Spain from there."

"I'll start here," she repeated.

Vella set down the easel he had strapped to his back and the bag he'd carried for her. "Suit yourself."

He removed his hat and placed it upside down on the sand, putting a stone in it so it wouldn't blow away should the wind pick up. Then he took off his shirt, tossed it at Emilia, and headed for the water, where the rest of the boys were already thrashing about.

Viviana longed to wade into the crystal-blue water, longed to dip beneath it and feel it close over her hot, sweaty scalp. But she couldn't do so with men and boys around. Besides, the sea frightened her a little. The story of the washed-out town—to say nothing of Vella's story about the shark bite—hadn't helped. It was one thing to bathe in a quiet mountain stream. Quite another to surrender to the capricious waves of the sea. Vella had spoken of teaching her how to swim, but she didn't actually believe that would happen. Vella said a lot of things that never came to pass.

Instead, she and Emilia spread a blanket and set up the easel and the paints and brushes. Then Emilia took out a charcoal pencil and a drawing pad her Tío Francisco had given her and settled down on the sand a few feet away, leaving Viviana to consider the scene before her. There were men in skiffs, men pulling in nets, men repairing the hulls of boats, men patrolling the shore. Where were the women of the town? In cellars and kitchens? Stuck inside with babies on their hips and spoons in their hands? All the while a fine and beautiful day was progressing right outside. Without them.

"Emilia," Viviana said, "why didn't you go into work today?"

The girl did not look up from her sketching. "I've been dismissed."

"What happened?"

Emilia looked out at the sea and back to the pad in her hands.

"The lady of the house does not like me there."

"Why? I've seen how hard you work at home. I can't imagine you conduct yourself any differently in their household."

"It wasn't my work she was dissatisfied with."

"I guess that shouldn't surprise me," Viviana said. "I once served in a household where there were women who didn't want me there, even though I worked hard."

Emilia scooted a little closer to Viviana. "Why didn't they like you?"

"I don't know exactly," she said. "They looked down on me because I wasn't French."

"The English look down on us."

"Yes, I see that."

Viviana pondered again the question that had vexed her for so many months of travel across Europe and Africa with Vella. Why had Madame Dorset and Lisette despised her so? Why did people have such strong feelings against those they didn't even take the time to get to know?

"I suppose sometimes people like life just as it is, and they resent someone coming in from the outside who changes it," she finally said. "I think when I came into the household where I worked in Toulouse, I upset the balance. Perhaps that's what happened in your situation."

Emilia looked thoughtful. "No. Not exactly. I think in my case it was because my mistress didn't care for the way her husband looked at me. I didn't care for it either. But my mother says it goes with the territory."

Viviana frowned. "Well then, perhaps you are better off in a different profession."

Emilia nodded but seemed unconvinced. "I wish I could do what Tío Francisco does. I am good with numbers and money, and I can get a good deal at the market. But girls can't be merchants. He'll probably take Cosmo as his apprentice when he turns thirteen. He's already showing him how to handle the less dangerous pigments."

Viviana wondered if Vella knew of Cosmo's plans to become an outlaw. It was such a shame that a girl who wanted to learn his trade from him would not be given the opportunity while a boy who showed no interest in it would be compelled to take it on.

Emilia rose and pulled something out of her apron pocket. "I nearly forgot. I snagged this for you from Tío's inventory."

There, cradled in her palm, was a full tube of paint marked *Bleu outremer/Azul ultramarino. Ultramarine blue.*

"You'll need it for the sea and the sky," Emilia said.

Viviana took the tube from her hand. "How incredibly devious of you. And thoughtful."

Emilia smiled. "I don't dare use it myself. I'm not good enough at drawing yet to be allowed to paint, though Tío said he would teach me. I saw the painting you did of him. It looks exactly like him. You're very good. And you need a good blue to paint the Mediterranean."

"Ultramarine is the best blue. So now I have all I need, thanks to you. Time to get started."

The women settled into their individual attempts to capture the spirit of the scene in front of them. Viviana sketched the big shapes upon the burnt sienna–toned board with diluted raw umber, then blocked in the darkest darks. She worked her way around the painting, adding more colors, more shades, more details, until her experience of this sunny, breezy summer day on Catalan Bay was indeed immortalized.

When she had first attempted plein air painting—on a fresh

spring day somewhere in Bavaria—it had felt like pure chaos. The clouds kept moving, the shadows kept shifting, the light kept dimming and brightening, changing the greens from warm to cool and back again. Leaves shivered, grasses waved, and sheep and cows walked about wherever they pleased. How could she pin any of it down to one moment when it kept changing? Painting in a studio, where objects on a table or a model in a chair did not move and light could be controlled, was almost easy compared to this wild and capricious world of plein air. Viviana had wondered if Mary Cassatt and her Impressionist friends were silly for attempting it.

Yet now, after months and months of practice, it was becoming second nature. Viviana did not worry about the changing shapes of the clouds or the inevitable movement of shadows. She painted faster, looser, and with more joy than she ever had in the studio. She strove not to copy what she saw—which was difficult in the most controlled of environments—but to represent it in all its moods.

At first, she hadn't thought the same methods could be applied to portraiture, despite what she had seen in the homes of Mary Cassatt and Berthe Morisot. But Emilia was right. Her painting of Vella did look like him. Irritatingly so. Why could she represent him so truly and yet still not be able to paint herself to her liking?

"Nice picture," came a voice in English. "Do you have a permit to do this?"

Emilia stood and came close to Viviana. She translated the soldier's question and then answered him. "No."

"You must have a permit to draw or paint here," he said.

"A permit?" Viviana said. "That's ridiculous. Who are we hurting by doing this?"

"It doesn't matter," Emilia said without relaying the question in English to the soldier. "They require permits for everything here. It's a way for them to make money off of us, another way for them to show they are in charge."

"You will have to pack all of this up," the man continued. "And the next time you want to paint, you will have to secure the required permit first and be prepared to show it when asked."

Viviana searched the beach and the water. Where was Vella? He could sweet-talk his way into or out of almost anything. Surely he could get this man to allow them to continue what was a completely harmless activity. But Vella was nowhere to be found, and Emilia was already packing the paints into the bag.

The soldier reached for the wet painting.

"No!" Viviana said. "This is mine."

The man drew back slightly, startled at her response, then chuckled. "Calm down, señorita." He looked her up and down, then subjected Emilia to the same assessment. "Maybe we can work something out."

Emilia did not need to translate for Viviana to understand the spirit of what he'd said. Emilia spoke to him submissively in English, handing over her drawing pad. He ripped out the pages she had finished, folded them, and stuck them in the inside pocket of his jacket. Then he handed the pad back to Emilia and looked expectantly at Viviana.

She could not give up this painting. All of that expensive ultramarine blue paint. And yet, what choice did she have? She removed it carefully from the easel, holding it gingerly at the edges, and held it out to the soldier. He looked momentarily disappointed that they had both complied. Then he took the painting, clasping it clumsily, his thumb smearing the decorative V that served as Viviana's all-purpose signature. It had worked for her whether she was Vivienne, Veronica, or Viviana. Now it seemed to signify other things. Vulgar. Violence. Victim. Ugly words for an ugly situation.

The man stalked off, painting in hand. They watched him until he disappeared into a building with their work of the last two hours. Then they packed away the easel and waited for the boys to finish playing and come in from the sea.

Chapter

TWENTY-SEVEN

❖

GIBRALTAR, PRESENT DAY

Esther dragged her oversized suitcase across the gray expanse of the Gibraltar International Airport's tarmac. Though other people were casually walking or driving alongside her as if it was all very normal to build a road across a runway, she couldn't stop checking the skies. Was that a plane coming in from across the sea, moments away from pancaking them all? No. It was a bird. Just an ordinary bird going about his bird business.

The moment her feet hit the sidewalk on the peninsula side, she breathed a sigh of relief and texted her mother that she'd arrived safely. She hadn't enjoyed the long flights, the hectic connections at O'Hare and Heathrow, the anxious waiting at customs. She had almost no experience traveling and absolutely no confidence in herself that she could get from point A to point B—something that any other adult would know how to do but of which she was ignorant—without making a catastrophic (or at least embarrassing) error. More than once she had found herself wishing, inexplicably, that her mother had come with her.

Yet here she was, exhausted but in one piece, luggage in hand, in a foreign land. It was a sunny October day in the low seventies, and what awaited her promised a level of excitement and freedom she hadn't felt since leaving for college at age eighteen.

She passed a skate park and a petrol station, then crossed the street when she spotted the small enclosed park with the war memorial where she was to meet up with Ian Perez's cousin Adam. She rolled her suitcase through the open gate, then picked it up when she realized that the ground surrounding the memorial was crushed limestone. It was tamped down and smooth, and she would not be the one to introduce a flaw in the form of a roller bag trail.

There were pines and palms and other spiky plants all around, hemmed in by the pointed iron pickets of the fence. She put her suitcase down by the monument, a stark stone cross inlaid with metal in the shape of a sword. On the octagonal base was the inscription "In Glorious Memory of Those Who Died for the Empire," and on either side of that were the years 1914–1918 and 1939–1945.

Esther wondered how many of the young men this cross memorialized had truly died *for* the British Empire. How many were considering their place in world history as they marched and fought and slogged through the mud? How many were thinking of their government or their principles or even their way of life as they went down in planes and ships? How many of them, in their last moments, had had glory on their minds rather than hunger, pain, loneliness, or regret?

Then she reminded herself that she was entering a place that had been fought over, fought upon, and fought from for more than a millennium. Whatever the reasons, countless souls had met the end of their earthly existence on this rock or in the waters around it. One at least had to admire the passion that had brought them here.

"Excuse me, miss, are you Esther?" came a male voice.

Esther turned to see a strikingly fit man who looked to be in his forties, with dark hair that was slightly silvered at the temples, hazel eyes, and a complexion that was a couple shades darker than Dr. Perez's.

"I'm Adam de la Paz. Ian's cousin." He held out his hand and closed the distance between them.

"Pleased to meet you." She shook his hand then realized she was staring. "Sorry. For some reason I thought you and Dr.—Ian—would be the same age. I guess because you had the same teacher."

He laughed lightly. "Ah, yes, Ms. Hernandez. She was brand-new when Ian had her in school. She seemed old by the time I had her. And yet it turns out she is still around. You see, my mother and Ian's are half sisters. Mine was actually born not long before Ian was. So she was technically his aunt, but like a cousin or a sister to him. I'm more like a nephew." He indicated a parking ramp just down the road. "I'm parked over there. Can I get your suitcase?"

"Thank you."

He picked up her bag. "I thought this would be heavier."

"It's big but not full. I wanted to leave lots of room."

"For the painting?"

"That and anything else I might happen to pick up."

He seemed to be repressing a smile, and Esther felt color start to rise in her cheeks. Honestly, she had to get better at talking to men without accidentally coming on to them. They stood there for an awkward moment until she said briskly, "Well, I certainly appreciate you being willing to meet me and let me look at the painting."

"Of course." They started walking to the parking ramp. "It's your painting."

She stopped. "My painting?"

"Yes. Didn't Ian tell you that?"

Esther hurried to match Adam's stride. "He said the two of you bought it. I assumed I would make you an offer if I thought it was authentic."

"Ah," Adam said, smiling fully. "Perhaps you should clarify things with him. But as far as I can see, it's yours. So where are you staying?"

"The Holiday Inn Express."

He looked at her. "What? No."

"Is that bad? It was one of the cheapest places I could find where I thought I wouldn't regret it."

"No, you don't want to stay there. You'll have a view of either a cliff or a cemetery. And it's too close to the airport."

"That's one of the reasons I chose it. So I'd be close to the airport."

"No," he repeated. "You can't stay there."

"Okay," she said slowly. "Do you have a better suggestion?"

"I have many better suggestions. I'll show you some of them. I'll show you all around and you'll see why you wouldn't want to spend your time in Gibraltar at the Holiday Inn Express." They reached the car, an older-model Mercedes, and Adam popped the trunk. "I'd offer for you to stay at my place, but I only have one bedroom and the sofa doesn't pull out." He set the suitcase inside, shut the trunk, and smiled. "And it also overlooks a cemetery."

Esther opened the passenger door. "Isn't Gibraltar only like three square miles? How do you have more than one cemetery?"

"Two point six. The cemetery by the Holiday Inn is the modern one. Stark but orderly. The one by my apartment is older." They got in the car. "Some of the graves date from the eighteenth century, mostly British soldiers and their families, and some yellow fever victims from the 1814 epidemic. I go for a walk there some evenings. It's quite charming. If you like, I'll show you around there tomorrow when you're over to look at the painting."

"Tomorrow? We aren't going there today?"

He pulled out of the parking space and headed for the exit. "No. No business today. This evening we are finding you a better sleeping arrangement and going to dinner. Then sometime tomorrow you can see the painting. But I'm also going to be showing you the wonders of the Rock. Ian told me you needed a vacation, and I promised him I'd show you a good time. We'll eat some good food, you can visit some shops, and Ian said I should take you to the beach. I told him maybe he's been gone too long and he doesn't remember temperatures in October, but he insisted that people from Michigan go to the beach even when it's cold out."

"Yes, I guess we do. The last time I was at the beach, there was ice on the lake and it was well below freezing." At his incredulous look she added, "I didn't go swimming. And anyway, I didn't bring a swimsuit on this trip."

"What? You came to the Mediterranean without a bangyadó?"

"If that's what you call a swimsuit here," she said, "then yes."

He leaned out the window to pay the parking fee. "In English we call it a bathing costume."

She laughed. "Really? That sounds so Victorian."

"It may be."

"Anyway," Esther said, "despite what Ian told you, I wasn't looking at this as a vacation."

The mechanical arm raised in front of the car, releasing them from the confines of the ramp. "Hmm. Then it's clear you need one."

Adam first drove them through the newer developments on the waterfront, built on land reclaimed from the bay since the 1970s. High-rise apartment buildings and hotels in white, yellow, and turquoise competed for space overlooking the harbor, where cargo ships and pleasure craft waited for goods and people to load or unload. The water beyond the pier was peppered with boats of various sizes, and beyond them was Spain. Esther admired all the bright and shiny things, but quick searches on her phone told her that this area was too expensive by half.

They wound their way toward the older parts of the city through narrow one-way streets, passing various hotels and hostels that had potential to be a more suitable place to sleep than the Holiday Inn Express. Adam had a strong opinion on each of them. This one had a beautiful lobby but spartan guest rooms. That one was overpriced. This one was run by a man who was not to be trusted. That one was on a street that was very loud at night.

"I really just need somewhere somewhat cheap and clean to sleep," Esther said, struggling both to keep her eyes open and to care all that much at this point. As long as there weren't rats, she was getting less picky by the moment.

They finally settled on the Eliott Hotel, which was clean and modern-looking and not too far from a coffee shop. When Esther was checked in and in her room, all she wanted to do was fall into bed and sleep away the busy day of travel. But it was nearly seven o'clock and time for dinner. She looked for a text from her mother—none—then texted Rhoda, who quickly put her mind at ease with a reply that they were just finishing lunch at YumYum Bento and were off to Studio C in a few minutes to catch a movie. Esther couldn't picture how either one of these activities would look with Lorena involved, but it wasn't her problem. She changed out of her travel clothes and felt a little more alert, though she wished she had time for a shower.

Adam drove them a few blocks south, weaving through one-ways to do so. Along the way he pointed out his apartment building and the charming old cemetery. Then they parked and walked to Casa Pepe, where they were greeted enthusiastically—Adam was clearly well-known and well-liked here—and seated immediately on the patio overlooking the Queensway Quay Marina. Sailboats lined up along the docks, and beyond them the sun was sinking lower in the sky.

Without looking at a menu, Adam ordered wine and tapas in

rapid-fire Spanish, peppered here and there with an English word or phrase. As plate upon plate arrived at the table, he explained each one to her in English. Paella negra—rice with seafood, blackened with squid ink. Corazón de alcachofas con jamón—hearts of artichokes with ham. Langostinos con crema y espinacas—king prawns with spinach in a creamy wine sauce. Boquerones—deepfried anchovies. None of it was food she would have ordered for herself, but everything looked and smelled incredible.

"Why is it that you have a Spanish accent while Ian sounds so British?" Esther finally asked.

"Oh, do you mean like this?" he said in an affected posh British accent.

"Yes!"

"You have to understand, when Ian grew up here, the border with Spain was closed—from 1969 to 1982—nearly his entire childhood. Naturally he spoke Llanito then, as I do. That's our local dialect, mixing Spanish and English, with a heavier emphasis on the Spanish sounds. But growing up so restricted in your movement makes you want to get out, you know?"

Oh yes. Esther knew all about that.

"Many people of his generation left for university in London as soon as possible. He left in the Eighties and never returned, except for visits. And in the UK, especially at that time, anyone with darker skin and the wrong accent was looked down on. To the people in Great Britain, Gibraltarians are colonials, conquered people who have to be managed, you see? Which isn't exactly true, but then why let a little thing like truth get in the way of narrative, eh? The faster Ian could speak 'proper' English, the better it would go for him. Then he moved to the United States, where a British accent made people think you were intelligent and a Spanish accent made people think you were a migrant worker or an illegal immigrant. Naturally, he kept the accent that served him best. But when he is back here visiting, he speaks as I do."

All the time Adam had been talking, Esther had been sampling the tapas, pleasantly surprised to find that everything was exquisite.

"You never left Gibraltar?" she asked.

"No, I did. For university. Then I came back to work."

"What do you do?"

"I'm a professor of marine science at the University of Gibraltar."

"So teaching runs in your family."

"I suppose it does. I have a sister who teaches Spanish in secondary school. Kids today don't grow up speaking Spanish—they all sound like Ian, posh British accents, speak only English."

"I've always wished I could speak Spanish. I took it for a couple years, but I was never very good at it, and now it's been so long I've lost most of the little I knew. I always thought if I could speak Spanish I'd feel more connected to Vella. I mean, Markstrom? You couldn't sound less Spanish than that, and my mom and I don't even tan all that well—though that may be because we don't spend much time outside."

Adam took a sip of wine. "I have to say, I was as surprised at your appearance when we met up as you were at mine."

"Oh?"

"I hadn't expected someone with such fair skin and light eyes. When Ian said you were Vella's descendant, I pictured something altogether different."

"I don't blame you. Nevertheless, there his name is in our family tree. Of course, he was married to a French woman, and I guess I always assumed we took after that side. Plus Markstrom is Swedish. And there's a lot of German in our family as well. Once the family was in America, they might have easily mixed with any number of different ethnicities."

"True." He leaned forward. "Have you ever thought of doing one of those DNA tests?"

Truthfully, she had. But something had stopped her anytime

it crossed her mind. What if it told her something she didn't want to know? Her father had left the family so long ago, she might have any number of half-siblings out there. She didn't know where he was or even if he was still alive. And she didn't think she'd like to know. Life was complicated enough. She didn't have the energy for long-lost relatives or absent fathers.

"Sure. I've been meaning to get around to doing that," she said.

"Could be enlightening."

The conversation drifted on at a leisurely pace as the sun set over the bay, silhouetting the tall masts of the sailboats against a pink and purple sky. Esther took a mental picture she could access later when she was back in her little studio at home. When she didn't think she could keep her eyes open for one moment longer, Adam insisted on paying the bill and drove her back to the hotel.

"I'll stop by tomorrow around lunchtime," he said. "I have to teach a class in the morning, but my afternoon and evening are free. Go around the corner there to Marks & Spencer to buy a bangyadó in the morning. I'm taking you to the beach tomorrow afternoon."

Esther thanked him for dinner and for carting her around and helping her find a better hotel. Then she went up to her room, sent her mother a short update on the day, and succumbed to sleep without even looking for a reply.

Chapter

TWENTY-EIGHT

GIBRALTAR, 1881

The Levanter arrived suddenly one day in early September. It didn't roll in from the sea as clouds are wont to do in other areas of the world. It gathered on the east side of the Rock, then spilled up over the summit like a waterfall turned upside down. To those in the Spanish quarter, it simply appeared overhead, heavy and hot and wet, a shroud of damp darkness made all the more difficult to bear for how the horizons on all sides of the peninsula still shimmered in exuberant white light. Everyone was in a foul mood. Strangers on the street, Vella's many relatives in the house, even the goats and the chickens and the mournful dog that haunted the small courtyard seemed irritable. Everyone, that is, except Viviana. Because the same day the Levanter appeared, Viviana received her permit.

After complaining to Vella about the soldier and the stolen art at Catalan Bay, Viviana prevailed upon him to get her whatever papers she needed in order to continue to paint. If Rosa Bonheur needed a permit to wear trousers, Viviana could accept that she needed a permit to paint in a public space. And now that she had it, she was getting out of the stuffy, smelly apartment to exercise her right to create.

Because he was too busy to accompany her to Europa Point at the far southern end of the peninsula as she desired, Vella directed Viviana to the much closer—and more lovely, he insisted—Alameda Gardens. Though painting in gardens was something she was not interested in doing, she went anyway rather than stay home and wait for someone to be available to take her farther afield. She asked Madalena and Emilia to come along, thinking it would be safer traveling in a group with someone who could speak English, but Madalena was elbows deep in laundry and Emilia was off looking for a new job.

So, early in the morning, Viviana walked alone down the busy street, repeating in her head the directions to the gardens so she would not forget. Take Buena Vista to Calle Comedias to Cuesta de Sandunga, then cut through to Calle Real. Comedias, Sandunga, Real. Comedias, Sandunga, Real. She knew she would pass Sacred Heart Church, a soaring new cathedral that had been under construction since Cosmo was a baby, and the old cemeteries, where victims of war and pestilence lay cold and quiet underground. Then she would come upon Kingsway, the wide promenade where finely dressed folk would spend Sunday afternoons, and next to that, the botanic gardens themselves. "There will be so many lovely things to see there, you won't know what to paint first," Vella had insisted.

Viviana was doing fine initially, treading ground she had already grown familiar with during the days she had been on the Rock. She passed the cathedral, but where she was expecting more busy streets, she instead came upon a set of stairs leading to a footpath behind the eastern edge of the city. She followed it a ways before hesitating and turning around. Surely this could not be correct. Viviana got back to the stairs, walked a little farther, and found herself at the intersection of several streets. She recognized the place, but then she didn't, because she'd never approached it from this direction. She was turning slowly in a circle, wishing she could read the street signs, when she heard a familiar voice.

"Señorita Torrens?"

Viviana recognized Dario from the crossing from Morocco.

"What are you doing wandering around in the street alone?" he said, approaching her.

"Dario, I am so glad to see you. I'm afraid I am a bit lost."

He smiled at her and held out his hand in greeting. "Where are you trying to go? And with all those things on your back—here, let me carry something."

"That's not necessary. You already have your own bag, and I have everything in hand. I am trying to find the Alameda Gardens. I'm going there to paint today."

"I see. Well, you won't find them in the direction you're heading."

"Yes, I think I missed a turn somewhere."

He put his hand on her elbow and rotated her slowly. "You'll want this road. Prince Edward. We call it Cuesta de Sandunga."

"Oh, yes! That's the one. And then Calle Real?"

"Correct. That's Main Street. You'll find the gardens if you go that way." He gave her an appraising look. "But why are you all alone today?"

Viviana sighed. "No one could come with me, and I didn't want to wait. I don't actually even want to paint at the gardens. I wanted to go to Europa Point. But Francisco said it is too far."

"He is right, especially if you are going alone and carrying all these things." He paused and stroked his chin in thought. "You know what is more interesting than the gardens and not as far as Europa Point?"

"What?"

"St. Michael's Cave."

Viviana thought a moment. "Isn't that how the monkeys got here?"

Dario laughed. "Who told you that?"

Viviana stiffened. "Francisco's nephew Cosmo. I didn't believe him. That's just what stuck in my mind. I know there is no tunnel to Africa. I'm not a simpleton."

Dario smiled. "I know you're not. I could tell that the moment I first saw you." He considered her. "Come. Give me that pack on your back at least, and I will take you to St. Michael's Cave."

"That does sound more interesting than a garden."

"And along the way, I want to hear more about you and your painting."

They adjusted the bags, and Dario led the way back to where she had gotten off track in the first place. They climbed the steps and headed up the path.

"I guess you were going the right way after all," Dario said when she told him her error.

After a couple switchbacks, they ended up on a narrow road. To their right, the city spilled out into the bay. To their left, the green western slope of the Rock stretched up to the cloud that covered it. The walk was steadily uphill, and Viviana was glad that Dario was carrying the pack with the easel and all the paints while she carried only the wet canvas case. With the climb and the steady conversation, they had to stop a few times for Viviana to catch her breath.

"I never used to have this problem with hills," she said, hand at her chest. "I lived in a mountainous region for so long. But I suppose for much of the past few years I have been sitting. Sitting in rooms, on trains, on ships, in carriages. I've traveled further than I ever imagined I would, but I was sitting still nearly the entire time."

"You'll get used to it again."

"I guess so. How much further?"

"Not too far ahead we'll get to Charles V's wall. That's about halfway."

They traveled on in silence for a while before Viviana resumed her life story. She held nothing back, painted nothing with a kinder brush than she deserved. She was utterly and completely honest about all of it, including her part in Ignasi's death, Vella's forwardness and her increasing discomfort with it, and her true desire to live and travel and paint freely. To be her own person, make her own decisions, and make a name for herself as an artist. Her name.

By the time they reached the wall, an imposing relic of a bygone era in a land full of such things, Viviana had run out of things to say and breath to say it with. She leaned against the stone and breathed deeply, in and out, feeling her lungs.

"We're only halfway?" she asked.

"I'm afraid so. If it's too much, we can go back."

She waved his words away. "I haven't come this far to turn back." She looked out across the city below to the bay and thought of where all those ships had come from and where they might be going next. "How far have you sailed?"

Dario took off the pack and leaned on the wall next to her. "Only between Spain and Morocco. Back and forth. Again and again. Taking things from one place to another and back again." "Did you ever want to work on a big ship? Sail out across the ocean?"

"Sure."

"Where would you go if you could go anywhere?"

"I don't know. America, I guess. Whenever I encounter Americans in Gibraltar, they're always happy. They buy a lot of things here, so they must have a lot of money. They just seem to love life."

"Of course they do. They're on a holiday."

He tipped his head to acknowledge her point. "It's more than that, though. They're . . . optimistic. They think good things will happen to them. And they must think that because good things do happen to them." He shrugged. "It just seems like there's more room for good things over there."

"There's certainly more room there than in Gibraltar," she said. "For everything. I've seen maps. It is a wide-open country."

243

He nodded. "More space for people."

"More space for dreams."

Their eyes met for a moment, and Viviana felt a connection with Dario she had never felt with Vella. When Vella looked at her, he seemed always to be assessing her in some way. There had been something a little thrilling in that at first, but it had quickly grown old. Dario seemed to actually *see* her.

"Whoops," he said, pointing up the slope. "We'd better be careful."

Viviana looked up. There, farther along the wall, was a small group of monkeys approaching them. They took a few steps away and watched as the monkey family scrambled down the wall to where they had been leaning a moment ago.

"They're so adorable," Viviana said. "I've never seen monkeys before."

They watched for a few minutes as the older monkeys settled down to groom each other while the younger ones frolicked about. Then one of them noticed the pack and began probing its skinny fingers under a flap.

"No!" Viviana said, waving her arms. "Shoo! Get out of there!"

Dario grabbed her hand out of the air. "Don't antagonize them. They have extremely sharp teeth and short fuses."

"But they'll steal my things. Cosmo said they would."

Dario laughed. "There's a better way to get monkeys to do what you want." From his pocket he produced a pouch of nuts and dried fruit. The monkeys immediately abandoned the bag and crowded around him. "Take the bag," he said to Viviana, who leaped into action as Dario passed out the rations to the greedy monkeys. "Okay, now let's get moving," he said.

They continued along the road, Viviana looking behind often to see if the monkeys were following them.

"What keeps you from going to America?" she said when she was confident they had given the monkeys the slip.

"You mean what keeps me on Gibraltar?"

"Isn't that the same thing?"

"No."

"Okay, what keeps you here then?"

"What do you think? My family is here. My culture. My language. My life. I don't think I could leave that all behind. Could you?"

Viviana let out a humorless laugh. "I've just spent the last half hour telling you I have none of those."

"Yes, I suppose you did."

They were quiet for some time until they came, finally, to St. Michael's Cave. Instead of leading her inside, Dario invited Viviana to sit. They put down the things they were carrying, and he took a clay bottle with a wooden stopper out of the bag he'd had over his shoulder when she'd first met up with him. He pulled out the stopper and handed it to her.

"Drink slowly and save some for the way down."

Viviana hadn't realized until that moment just how parched she was. The Levanter had given them shade and a bit of moisture in the air, but it had still been an arduous walk. She took a few modest sips, though she wanted to guzzle it all down, and handed the bottle back to Dario.

"Do you mind if I say something to you, Viviana?" he said. "I haven't known you long, so it may be presumptuous."

Viviana laughed. "Presume away. I enjoy talking to you."

He smiled. "I enjoy talking to you as well." He took a drink from the bottle and put it away. "Though it is the biggest and most impressive, this is not the only cave on Gibraltar. And while Cosmo was wrong about a tunnel to Africa, there are tunnels through the Rock. Some were made naturally, by wind and water and time. Some were made by the military, using picks and drills and explosions. On the outside, the Rock looks solid. And it is, to some degree. But inside it is honeycombed with empty spaces."

He paused, then said, "I think you are much the same way."

For a moment, Viviana could not breathe. She felt something

flutter behind her rib cage. Something like fear. Like a small black bat flying around in a dark cave. She sucked in a breath and let it out but said nothing.

"On the outside you appear to me to be solid and determined," Dario said. "But I hear the echo of emptiness inside you. All those things that make up a person's being—our family, our home-town, our language, our traditions, our songs, our history—are things you have either never experienced or experienced in such a broken way that they don't fill the spaces in you that they should."

Viviana squinted as if into the sun, but there was no sun there. She bit her bottom lip to keep it from shaking. "And what am I to do about that?" she said, bitterness and sorrow fighting for dominance in her voice.

"I don't know," Dario said. "Perhaps put down roots and build a life and a family here?"

"With whom? Francisco?"

He winced slightly, then said, "Sure. Why not?"

She let out a mirthless laugh. "He's married, for starters."

The look on Dario's face clearly showed that he had not known this.

"Secondly, I don't love him. I like him. He is a good friend. Most of the time. But I don't have any romantic affection for him."

She paused, weighing her words, trying to decide if she could admit out loud what she really, truly thought, no matter how selfish it might sound, no matter how much judgment it might bring down upon her. Then she said it anyway.

"And thirdly, if I have a husband and children and a home to keep, when do I paint? Never. Until I am an old woman and I finally have nothing to do and can barely hold on to a brush for my weary bones. But then what if I do not grow old? My father, my mother, my brother, my aunt, Monique Renaud—none of them were allowed to grow old. What if I am not allowed? What if I am fated to die young? Then shouldn't I use every moment I have to do what I'm passionate about? The only thing I'm good at? Any woman can raise a family. Not every woman can paint. And not one of them sees through my eyes. They are not looking as I am. They are not noticing the things I notice. Or if they are, they are quickly distracted by a crying baby or something burning in the kitchen, and it's lost. That moment is lost forever. And no one will be able to share in it. No one will see its worth. It will just be gone."

She stopped talking abruptly, wiped her eyes, and looked away from Dario, away across the bay below. Was there nowhere on this rock where one couldn't see the horizon beckoning?

"Maybe painting won't fill the empty places inside me," she continued. "Probably it won't. But surely it can make them more beautiful."

Dario came up beside her. "Of course it can," he all but whispered. "Of course it can."

She looked at him then and knew without a doubt that she would soon leave this place. So she had better use her time well.

"Come," she said. "Show me this cave."

Chapter

TWENTY-NINE

◆

GIBRALTAR, PRESENT DAY

Esther woke from a dreamless sleep at seven o'clock the
next morning, grateful Adam had insisted she recon-
sider her accommodations. The bed at the Eliott Hotel
was heavenly, and the view of the city and the bay beyond was
far more stunning than the view she would have had of the
cemetery and the airport. She opened the double doors to the
little balcony and listened as the city came alive and began going
about its business—voices and footsteps, the sounds of cars and
scooters, and beyond those the calls of seabirds and the occasional rumbling horn of a ship announcing its presence.

She showered and dressed and headed out to get some coffee,
her attention divided between the directions her phone offered
and everything around her, trying to take it all in and tuck it
away for later recall. The narrow streets, the strange plants, the
varied people. It was all so delightful. She walked down Library
Street past government buildings and a Tommy Hilfiger to an
alley that led her to Costa Coffee, where she ordered a chocolate

muffin and a café bombón without knowing anything about it except that she liked the name. When it came out it was in a glass cup in three layers: heavy sweetened condensed milk on the bottom, rich brown espresso in the middle, and a thin layer of foam on the top.

After her dessert-for-breakfast, she walked back down the alley to Marks & Spencer to try on bathing costumes. She was pleasantly surprised to see a lot of one-piece options that a woman in her forties could wear without feeling she'd tipped over into old age. Modest-yet-not-frumpy was a dwindling category when it came to clothing, and the few times a year she went shopping in East Lansing, she was always reminded that she did indeed live in a college town and that was the demographic that was catered to. For a reasonable price, she found a navy one-piece swimsuit with removable shoulder straps that she would never remove, as well as a long white textured cover-up that kind of reminded her of pajamas. Then she went back to a pharmacy she had passed earlier to get sunscreen. It being the off-season, she had to dig a bit but finally found some SPF 70 in a sale bin.

With a couple hours to kill and no agenda, Esther dropped her purchases off at the hotel, tucked her phone firmly in her purse, and began to wander. She had little inkling of which way was which, and she was fine with that. She was surrounded by water on three sides and an airstrip on the fourth, and the city was significantly smaller than the already smallish one she lived in. There was simply no way to get too lost.

In her wanderings she passed restaurants, bars, and bakeries. Museums, monuments, and memorials. Apartments, shops, and parks. A church, a synagogue, and a Hindu temple. The narrow one-way streets were choked with cars and bikes and foot traffic alike, and Esther was so grateful she did not have to drive here. The people she passed displayed nearly every shade of skin there was, their ancestors hailing anywhere from Scotland to Spain to the Sahara. Which got her thinking about Adam's surprise at her pale skin and eyes. And the darker tones of his skin and Ian's and of many other people she saw walking out of shops or heading off to work.

It did seem like if she had ancestry in this part of the world, she might expect to look a little more like the people who lived here. She had always taken her family story for granted. But then, not everything her mother had told her over the years turned out to be true. Was it possible that her family tree—and its connection to Francisco Vella—might be a fiction? Could her mother be deluded, lying to herself and others for decades? What evidence did Esther actually have that she was Vella's descendant?

She was just doing a search on DNA tests when Adam messaged her. He was leaving the university to get her, and she should be ready for the beach. She shut the search window and opened her GPS app to figure out where she was, then she turned herself in the direction of the hotel and walked with purpose until she arrived, just as Adam was pulling into a parking spot.

"Perfecting timing," he said, getting out of the car. He was in slacks and sandals and a loose-fitting sky-blue button-down shirt.

"Not quite. I'm not ready. I just have to run inside and change."

"You have sunscreen?"

"Absolutely. Oh, but I don't have a towel."

"I have towels."

"I'll just be a minute."

Up in her room, Esther ran a brush through her wind-tangled hair, changed into her new suit, and put the cover-up on. But weren't they eating lunch? She couldn't go into a restaurant like this, right? She took off the cover-up and pulled on a yellow sundress she had bought on clearance from an online store as she was planning her trip. When she'd seen it on her phone screen, the color reminded her of lemonade, but in person it was more like lemons. She almost sent it back, but when her mother saw it she said it was a great color for her. Lorena's compliments being so rare, Esther figured it must be true.

She slipped on a pair of sandals and stuffed the sunscreen and the cover-up into the bag she'd used as a carry-on. She caught a glimpse of herself in the mirror and wished her hair looked as nice as the woman's who'd wanted to buy that footstool back in May. But she didn't know how to make those perfect waves. All she knew how to do was a French twist, which she quickly did. She put her sunglasses back on and decided she almost looked good enough to belong at the same table as Adam de la Paz.

THE DRIVE TO THE BEACH took them down some of the streets Esther had walked that morning, then back up to the monument where they had met the day before. They followed Devil's Tower Road around the north end of the Rock to the Mediterranean side where the limestone cliffs shot nearly straight up out of the ground. Within just a few minutes, Adam was parking his Mercedes near the beach.

"Welcome to Catalan Bay," he said.

The sky was achingly blue, the water turquoise and sparkling. When Esther had flown out of Detroit two nights before, the skies were gray and the trees were a tapestry of reds, browns, oranges, and yellows. This blue, blue, blue place was surely another planet.

"It's lovely," she said. "I thought it would be busier."

"Once school is in session, the beaches empty out. You should have been here in July."

They got out and walked along a boardwalk past a staggered line of condos and hotels painted in petal pink, soft peach, pale blue, and buttery yellow. A few umbrellas and towels, as well as a handful of people, were scattered across the sand like confetti that hadn't been swept up after a party. A couple walked hand in hand along the beach. A woman with two small children sat in the sand. There were a few younger men in American-style swim trunks and one older man in a tiny Speedo, his hairy belly bulging over the top. Everyone was still sporting their summer tans.

"Lunch first?" Adam said.

"Yes, please. I'm starving."

They passed a plaza anchored by a small cream and white chapel. When he noticed her looking at it, Adam provided the name. "Our Lady of Sorrows."

"This seems like an odd place to feel sorrowful," Esther said.

"It should be Our Lady of Sunshine or Our Lady of Vacation."

"Mm," Adam said. "The town here has actually been washed away more than once, with much loss of life."

"Oh," she said. "Never mind." Then, "Recently?"

"Not recently, no. This particular church building has been there since the late nineteenth century. It had to be almost completely rebuilt after a flood and rockslides."

Lest she stick her foot in her mouth again, Esther said nothing more until they were seated on the patio of the Seawave Bar. They ordered olives, cheese salad, and the mixed fish platter. Esther wanted to try the paella, but that was only served after seven o'clock.

For a moment they were silent, staring out at the sea. Then Esther felt Adam looking at her.

"Did you already put sunscreen on?" he asked.

"No."

"You may want to now. Even though it's not hot, you could get burned even under an umbrella because of the glare off the water and the sand. And you don't have much of a base tan."

She dug in her bag for the sunscreen. "Well, where I'm from, we're wearing coats and scarves and drinking apple cider and picking out pumpkins for Halloween right now. Before I got here I hadn't seen the sun in a week. Sometimes it snows in October." She squeezed a blob of white cream onto her hand and began smearing it on her arms and shoulders, then carefully rubbed some on her forehead, nose, and cheeks under her sunglasses.

"Don't miss your neck."

Esther rubbed the sunscreen on her neck, straining to reach as far down her back as possible.

"Need help?" Adam said.

"Um, yeah. Sure."

Adam stood and motioned for her to lean forward. He slathered the cream across his palms and laid his hands flat on her bare upper back. He was quick and efficient, and a moment later he was sitting down in his chair again.

Esther sat back. Other than a handshake—there had been lots of those—it was the first time a guy had touched her bare skin since . . . college? Had it really been that long? And while there was nothing sensual in the way Adam had helped her with the sunscreen, there was something about warm skin against warm skin that felt so . . . essential.

Suddenly and with ruthless clarity, what Esther had given up for her mother's sake came crashing down on her like a landslide into a seaside town.

"Excuse me a moment," she said and headed into the restaurant to find the bathroom.

She locked herself into a stall, leaned on the door, and bent over, hands on her knees. She breathed deeply, in and out, three times, then stood up and covered her face with her hands, her fingers probing beneath her sunglasses. She moved the sunglasses out of the way on top of her head and rubbed hard at her eyes. A few more breaths and she pulled herself together.

She left the stall and rinsed her hands with cold water, staring at the sink rather than in the mirror above it. If she looked at that, looked herself in the eyes, she knew she would start to cry. She tapped cold damp hands on her face and neck, then walked back out to the patio where their waiter was just placing the lemonade she'd ordered.

Esther stopped him in the doorway on his way back in. "I think I'd like a vodka tonic."

"Right away, miss."

Esther sat back down at the table and took a sip of lemonade. Adam placed a hand on the table between them. "Is everything okay?"

"Of course." She smiled to prove it and slipped her sunglasses back over her eyes.

"I'm sorry," he said.

"For what?"

He lifted his hand and placed it in his lap. "I don't know. You just left so abruptly, I thought maybe I—"

"I just had to use the restroom."

"As long as everything's okay."

She nodded. "Yep."

He held her gaze a little longer, as though offering her a chance to say more. To explain.

"So when will I see the painting?" she said.

Adam accepted the subject change gracefully. "I thought we'd go for a swim after lunch, then I can take you to my place to see it."

At this point, Esther didn't care how much she needed a vacation. She just wanted to pack up the painting and walk back across the tarmac to the airport. "I really can just take it if I think it's real?"

"Certainly. And if you like, I can take you to meet Gertrude Hernandez as well. Maybe you can learn more from her than Ian and I were able to. We spent a lot of our time there talking about our school days. And anyway, it might be nice to meet a long-lost relative."

Esther had not considered this. Gertrude Hernandez was family. Distant family, but family nonetheless. "Yes, I'd like that very much."

"Wonderful."

Their food began to arrive, and Esther remembered her hunger. She focused on eating and again kept her lunch companion doing most of the talking with a barrage of questions about his work at the university. It was so much easier to get through being sociable if she didn't have to talk about herself. She had always chalked this up to having a boring life and therefore not having much to say, but after her near breakdown in the bathroom she began to wonder if it was not something more, something deeper.

Perhaps she couldn't talk about herself because she didn't actually know herself very well. She had not known that she could feel so sharply the absence of something she'd never experienced. She had not realized just how much she resented her mother until Lorena had said she needed a break from her. She had never allowed herself to think too long about what could have been had Lorena been a normal mom.

Who was Esther Markstrom, really? What did she want out of life? Was there any hope of getting it?

"What would you do if you could do anything?" she said as she and Adam walked back out into the sun after lunch.

"You mean what career?"

"I mean anything. What haven't you done that you wish you could do? Maybe travel somewhere or learn something or make some sort of mark on the world—beyond teaching, I mean."

"Hmm . . . does it have to be in this day and age? Or could it be any time in history?"

"Okay, sure. Any time in history."

"I think I would have liked to live in an earlier time and been a part of discovering something significant—the New World or a new species or a lost city or something."

Esther considered this. "I think they're still discovering stuff. In space, at the bottom of the ocean, in the human body, places like that."

He laughed. "I suppose so. What about you?"

Esther had heard the question, but she couldn't quite think to answer. They had come once more to the little plaza and the white chapel. Our Lady of Sorrows.

Adam retraced his steps. "Do you want to go in?"

"Can we?"

"Sure."

They approached an iron gate, which swung open at Adam's touch. Above the heavy wooden church door, the Virgin stood in an alcove. Adam tried the door.

"Locked," he said apologetically.

"Oh," Esther said. "That's okay." But she was disappointed. There was something about the little chapel and its sorrowful guardian that spoke to her now after lunch in a way they hadn't before. She had sorrows of her own she thought perhaps the lady above the door might understand.

They were walking back down to the boardwalk when a slight old man came around the corner and said, "Can I help you?"

"No," she said, "thank you."

"Can we see inside the church?" Adam said.

The man came near. "Thinking about having your wedding here?"

Esther was about to correct him when Adam spoke up, "Considering it." He gave her a wink. "But we can't be sure until we see the sanctuary."

The man pulled a set of keys from his pocket and opened the door. "Of course. Let me show you around and you'll see what we have to offer."

After the brightness of the Mediterranean sun, the darkness just inside the door was palpable, even after Esther removed her sunglasses. They entered the small chapel with its dark wood pews and colorful stained-glass windows set deep in the white walls. The man was telling Adam about how many people the room could hold and how many months out they were booked. At the front of the sanctuary was the altar, and behind it on the

256

wall was the crucifix—a wooden cross with a painted corpus hanging on it. Below the cross were angels, and on either side were two figures looking up at Jesus. Mary and someone else.

Esther tried to pull the story from her mind. Didn't one of the disciples stay when all the others had abandoned Jesus to his death? One of the Jones. John? Was it John? And didn't Jesus ask him to take care of his mother for him? She wondered if John liked taking care of Mary, if he ever resented the job. Probably not. He was a good person. A saint.

The men kept talking, and Esther drifted away to explore on her own. Down a short hallway, a door had been left partially open—an invitation if she'd ever seen one. She peeked inside what turned out to be a small office. A desk, a couple chairs, some bookshelves. And on the wall behind the desk, a small painting of sand and sky and sea. Esther opened the door the rest of the way and took a step into the room.

Two-thirds of the painting was sky, starting bright and strong at the top and slowly lightening until it reached the horizon. Out there the sea was at its darkest, getting lighter and greener—she guessed by adding a bit of viridian to what was almost certainly ultramarine blue—as it approached the shore. In the middle distance, several figures populated the land and the water. Fishermen and their boats. A passel of rambunctious boys splashing at the shoreline. In the foreground was a three-quarter view of a girl drawing the scene before her on a pad. Overall, the effect was what she had been trying to convey in her own painting of a summer day that Dr. Perez had bought—heat and breeze and expanse. But this painting had something hers did not. A sense of possibility. A feeling that somewhere beyond that horizon, something else waited. Something grand and fun and free.

"There you are," the old man said from behind her. "This is just the office."

"Yes, sorry," Esther said. "I was just admiring this painting. Is this the beach just out here?"

"Yes, but I'm afraid I can't tell you much more about it than that. It's from before my time."

"It's beautiful." She got closer, examining the brushwork, looking for a signature. But there was none. Just a smudge of a thumbprint in the corner where one might expect to find a name. A glaring flaw. How could a painter of this sensitivity make the mistake of grabbing it by the corner before it was dry? And why didn't he fix it when he realized his mistake?

"Well, what do you think of the space?" the man said.

"It's quite lovely," Adam said, "but I'm afraid it might be a bit too small, wouldn't you say, darling?"

"What? Uh, yes. It's a bit too small."

The men kept talking, but Esther was now fixated on the figure of the girl with her drawing pad. There was something about her that reminded Esther of the picture Dr. Perez had showed her of the painting that even now hung in Adam's apartment. She pulled out her phone and snapped a few photos of the seascape. As she was closing the camera app, she saw she had left the website open from her earlier search for DNA tests.

"Ready to take your first dip in the Mediterranean, Esther?" Adam said.

"One second," she said. With a few swipes and taps, the DNA test was on its way. She only hoped it would not arrive at the house before she did. She could imagine the kind of scenarios Lorena's mind might concoct around her daughter ordering a DNA test.

Back outside, Esther put her sunglasses on again and they made their way to the car.

"So," Adam said, "what about you? What would you do if you could do anything?" He was standing on the driver's side of the Mercedes, pulling off his slacks to reveal a pair of red, yellow, and white swim trunks.

Esther stood on the other side of the car, turned away, and pulled her dress off over her head. "I don't know."

"What do you mean? You asked the question."

She pulled on her cover-up. "That doesn't mean I have the answer."

He took a cooler from the back seat and shut the door. "You must have had some idea. Otherwise you wouldn't have brought it up."

They started toward the beach.

"It's hard to answer that question. Because there's not really any hope that I'll be able to do anything I'd think of. Your answer was about wanting to discover something. You could do that. You're a professor. I'm sure you do research, and being between an ocean and a sea, I would imagine you can do a lot of hands-on stuff. There is the possibility that you could discover something. A new species, a shipwreck, the lost city of Atlantis. That urge is not unrealistic."

"Traveling through time was, though. Here okay?"

She nodded, and they laid out the towels and set the cooler down between them.

"I don't accept your non-answer," Adam said. "'What would you do if you could do anything?' is a question anyone can answer, because it's *if* you could do anything. Obviously people's lives are such that they can't do just anything they want. But this is a hypothetical. So if you could start over and your circumstances were different or your family was different or your place of birth was different or even the century in which you were born was different, what would you do? If absolutely anything and everything were an option, what would you do?"

Esther put her hands on her hips and looked out at the glittering blue sea. "First, I'd go swimming."

259

Chapter

THIRTY

✦

GIBRALTAR, 1881

Viviana tapped the tacks into place, stretching the canvas around the wooden frame Vella had made for her in the small room behind the house that served as his shop. Just a few more and she would be ready to start. Nearby, Vella stood at the table grinding pigments from the raw materials he had gathered over their months of travel or ordered from even farther afield. Some of the pigments he would sell in their raw form in jars or tins. Others he would mix with oil and package as ready-to-use paint.

They had been working side by side for the past several days, after Viviana indicated her desire to learn how to make her own paint. She thought perhaps he might be hesitant to reveal trade secrets, but of course no man had to worry about a woman usurping his business or horning in on his market. Vella was generous, showing her step-by-step how to work with the safe pigments first before moving on to the special handling required by the more hazardous materials. Viviana wondered why he couldn't teach Emilia these things.

Now it was time to try out some of the paints she had made. The best place to do so was over top of her many-layered self-portrait, which was ever her testing ground. It had been painted over so many times she didn't worry about ruining it. After all, despite her many attempts at rendering herself accurately, she was still dissatisfied.

"What do you think?" she asked Vella. "Should I just paint over the whole thing again and start from scratch?"

Vella put down his pestle, wiped his hands, and came over to the area by the small window where Viviana had set up her easel. "Why on earth would you do that?"

"Because there is so much that is wrong. The nose is too long, the mouth is too small, the eyes don't line up correctly. The shapes are close but the positions aren't quite right, are they?"

Vella looked from the painting to Viviana and back again. "I don't think you want to start over completely. What I would do if I were you is use the right eye as the fixed point—it's perfect, absolutely perfect—and then just make small adjustments to fix the positions and sizes of the features around it."

"Oh, it needs more than that," Viviana said.

"No, I don't think it does. The hair is beautiful and lustrous, the dress is the perfect texture, the hand—"

"I do like the hand."

"And the background is fine. I wouldn't change that."

"The background is nothing."

"I like it that way. A background shouldn't draw the eye away from the subject in a portrait."

Viviana conceded the point with a nod. "Fine then. I'll start with the eye and stick to the face for now."

For the next hour, Viviana mixed and thinned the paint and applied it to the canvas, using her own eye as a fixed point. She glanced back and forth between a mirror and the canvas, measuring distances with her thumb against the end of the brush, trying to get everything in the right place. Every so often, Vella would drift over to see her progress, but he didn't comment on it. Soon enough, the light had moved and Viviana was forced to pause her labors and go help Consuela and her daughters with the evening meal.

While she got along well with Vella's sisters, Viviana had yet to figure out what his mother thought of her. Consuela was cordial, but she did not seem to like her as much as Vella had insisted she would. Viviana did her best to make herself useful when she was in the house and spent as much time out of it as possible. She did not want to be in the way. In fact, she didn't want to be in the house at all if she could be almost anywhere else.

The following day, when Vella was back at his worktable and she was back at her easel, Viviana asked him outright whether or not his mother approved of her.

"Certainly," he said. "Why wouldn't she?"

Rather than press the matter, Viviana let it go, concentrating instead on putting the finishing touches on her lips. "What do you think of this now?"

Vella examined the painting. "Very good. Closer than ever, in fact. It captures your spirit. Only you've forgotten your scar."

"Why would I want to include that? It's ugly. That is the beauty of painting: I can remove it."

"I thought this was a self-portrait."

"Obviously."

He pointed at the painting. "But this isn't you. This is an idealized you."

"So?"

"So that scar is part of who you are, isn't it? Part of what makes you *you*. All that we've been through in the past is what makes us who we are now."

"It's easy for you to say that. Your scar is always hidden beneath your clothes. A portrait of you would just be a charming man who knows he is handsome."

Vella smiled. "While I am deeply flattered that you would call me handsome—"

"No, what I said was that *you* think you're handsome."

"That's not what you said."

Viviana started to object, but he continued talking.

"While I am deeply flattered, I think you're wrong. If my portrait had been painted a year ago, yes, perhaps there would be a sparkle to my eyes and a twist to my mouth that would indicate that I and others thought highly of me. But that would not be the expression you did of me when the expression now. Look at the painting you did of me when we were in Tunisia. Is that the expression you painted?"

Vella riffled through a number of painted panels lined up against the wall and pulled out the one Viviana had painted of him on the Mediterranean's southern shore. He handed it to her and stood back.

Viviana was surprised to see that he was right. The face she had painted did not quite have the level of swagger of the man she had met in Renaud's studio two years prior. The man she had painted was slightly less sure of himself than the man who had whispered with her on the settee. He was chastised, perhaps strained . . . but not defeated. There was still a fire there. She could still feel the heat of it.

"You see," Vella said, "you captured not what I want people to see when they look at me, but what they actually see. This painting has been hard for me to look at, because it shows me as I am, which is less than I wish I was. Your self-portrait should show you how you are. I think you've done a marvelous job with the expression, but you could not have had that strong yet vulnerable expression on your face without the scar on your neck—and a hundred other scars on your soul that none of us can see."

Viviana looked at herself in her painting. Then she looked away. Because if she stared too long into her own eyes, she might cry.

"I truly hate it that you're right," she said. "I wish you were as bad a person as you have the potential to be."

He smiled. "Why is that?"

*Because it would be so much easier to leave you behind. "Because then I would finally be done with this painting. As it stands, there is more work to do. And not just the scar. Now leave me alone before I lose the light."

THIRTY-ONE

✦

GIBRALTAR, PRESENT DAY

Esther did not want to admit it, but Dr. Perez had been right. She did need a vacation. She needed to buy new clothes and eat delicious foods that someone else prepared and float in the ocean and get a bit of a tan. She needed time with people other than her mother. She needed time for herself where she was not watching the clock, wondering if she'd been gone too long or if she was neglecting her responsibilities.

She and Adam spent two hours at the beach, alternating between the sand and the surf, talking about everything under the sun, from Gibraltarian history to Michigan winters to the proper way to cook a steak. They cracked open a couple bottles from the cooler, beer for him, Coke for her. For a while, Esther even forgot about the painting she had been so eager to see when she landed the day before. The painting that might be the only representation of a man whose work and legacy filled nearly every space in her life that Lorena left open.

A mentally ill woman and a dead man. That's who controlled her days. Had it not been for the two of them, where would she be? Who would she be? What would she do if she could do anything?

When they packed up the car, it was already nearly four o'clock. Now as they rounded a bend and plunged into a tunnel, Esther felt a deep darkness despite the artificial light that illuminated the way ahead. If nothing about her situation changed, the days laid out before her looked exactly like the days she had already traveled. An endless routine of keeping the gears moving simply for the sake of keeping them moving. She was building nothing, striving toward nothing.

She twisted around in the passenger seat to see the light at the beginning of the tunnel, but they were already around another bend. The light at the end of the tunnel was not yet in view. They were just there, under hundreds of thousands of tons of rock, and Esther could feel the weight of it.

"You know there are more than thirty miles of tunnels under here?" Adam said. "Used to be that the military could sustain sixteen thousand men under the Rock. There was a hospital, a telephone exchange, a power station, a water distillation plant, ammunition holds—even a bakery. They could wait out almost any enemy."

Indeed, one could live under a great weight for a long time. But not forever. And if the enemy was monotony, there was certainly no escaping that as long as you remained bivouacked in the dark.

They turned another bend, and the light at the end of the tunnel came into view. And then they were out in the blinding sunlight once again, the sea on their left, the Rock on their right. Straight ahead was the end of the peninsula, then the beginning of Africa, a continent Esther had never laid eyes on until that moment.

"Can we stop out here somewhere?" she said.

"Of course. We'll take a short detour to Europa Point."

Adam veered left at a roundabout. They passed a gleaming white mosque and an enormous soccer stadium and parked in a lot by a playground. Esther quickly took off her beach cover-up and slipped her yellow sundress back over her head. Her hair, which had started the afternoon tucked neatly into the French twist, had come loose in the Mediterranean Sea, so she had pulled out the remaining pins and let it fall, wet and wavy, to her shoulders. The wind whipped through it, but her sunglasses at least kept it from getting in her eyes.

They walked down perfectly kept paths and gentle steps that led them to a white railing. Though the true southernmost point of continental Europe lay nearby in Spain, for Esther this was close enough. Beyond a small white and red lighthouse, Esther bellied up to the railing. Europe was at her back, Africa was laid out dimly before her, only eight or nine miles of seawater dividing them. It was like looking back at Michigan's Lower Peninsula from the Upper Peninsula. And it was as close to Africa as she was ever likely to get.

With the light tipping toward evening, Adam and Esther got back into the car. In the ten minutes it took to finish the drive to his apartment, Esther refocused her mind on the task at hand. Examine the painting and determine if either the subject or the artist or both was Francisco Vella.

When she entered Adam's apartment, she understood immediately why he could not accommodate houseguests. It was breathtakingly small. The living/dining area was little bigger than the foyer at her big old house in East Lansing. The kitchen—complete with sink, stove, washer-dryer combo, and fridge—was like someone had repurposed a narrow pantry.

"Allow me to give you the tour," Adam said grandly. "Sofá, mesa, cocina." He pointed at them in turn, then to two doors. "Cama, baño."

Esther turned slowly. It was like looking at an IKEA showroom. "How many square feet is this place?"

"Fifty square meters, a little over five hundred square feet."

She wanted so badly to ask how much he paid for it. "It's . . . Sorry, but everything that's coming to mind sounds like an insult, when it really isn't."

He laughed. "It's cute, it's adorable, it's efficient, it's perfect for a bachelor, it must be easy to keep clean. I've heard it all, and all of it is true."

"Yes, all of that." She peeked into the bathroom. "I don't mean to be rude, but my living room is nearly as large as this entire apartment."

"Well, I think that's pretty good for me then," Adam said, still smiling. "Considering your country is probably a few million times larger than mine."

"Touché."

He clapped his hands together. "Okay then. Let's get a look at this painting." He led the way into the bedroom. The painting hung above the bed, the only available wall space as the other walls were lined with custom closets and drawers or were home to windows that looked out over the cemetery, just as Adam had described.

Esther stood at the foot of the bed and took in the work as a whole. A rather simple, masculine frame bordered a simple, masculine scene. A man reclining in the shadow of a rock, one leg bent, propped on one elbow, leather-bound book in hand. Behind the rock, a strip of bright shoreline and a ribbon of pale-blue water faded seamlessly into a pale-blue sky—cerulean and lead white, if Esther was not mistaken. Though one might expect the figure to be head down, concentrating on the pages of his book, the man's head was raised, his features finely rendered in bold brushstrokes, his eyes looking directly at the viewer. Which meant he had been looking directly at the painter.

This one detail suggested that it *could* be a self-portrait. Most self-portraits Esther had seen had the artist looking directly out at the viewer because the artist would have been looking at himself in a mirror. Anyone could have modeled the posture—or if the artist was particularly adept at drawing, he could have done the figure with no model at all—and the artist could have done the face in the studio at another time.

"Could you take it down so I can get a closer look?" she said.

"Of course." Adam stepped up onto the bed and carefully lifted the painting from the nail. He handed it to Esther, who looked around for a good place to lean it. "Over here," Adam said as he stepped back onto the floor. He slid open one of the closet doors to reveal a set of drawers and pulled one out a few inches, then he took the painting from her, set it on the open drawer, and leaned the top against the rest of them.

"Perfect."

Esther looked into what might be the face of her ancestor, the man whose work had occupied so much of her life. He was undeniably handsome and unnervingly modern. With his unkempt hair, piercing eyes, stubbled face, and that wry turn to his lips, he looked like someone she might pass on the street back home. For all she knew, he had been sitting at the bar at the Graduate the night she'd stayed out too late with Dr. Perez.

Whoever had painted this man, his personality came through. If it was a self-portrait, she would have to revise the picture she had in her head of Francisco Vella. To her, his paintings had suggested a sensitive, sympathetic soul, someone who could look at prince and peasant alike and find the humanity in them. Someone who opened himself up and drank in everything around him. Someone who gathered and sorted and made beautiful all the broken and disparate parts of his world, like a child who collected birds' nests that had fallen out of trees. But this man—these eyes—didn't seem open and curious. They were laser focused. This was a man who knew what he wanted—and what he wanted was just out of his grasp. If he just stretched a little farther, schemed a little more, tried a little harder, it might come within reach.

Were these intense eyes the ones that had witnessed the scenes that hung in the Vella-Markstrom museum? Were they the ones that had seen the caverns within the woman who sat for *La Dama del Cabello Oscuro*?

Suddenly it occurred to Esther that *La Dama* may not just be la dama at all. What if that painting was not merely a portrait but a conceptual representation of the very land upon which she now stood? Adam had said that the Rock was riddled with tunnels. And using women to personify myths and concepts and disciplines and yes, places, was a common motif in past centuries. What if the lady with the dark hair wasn't a person who existed at some point in the past but instead was an anthropomorphism of Gibraltar itself? What if she showed up in multiple paintings because the itinerant man who painted them in every important city in Europe was longing for home? Would that explain the difference in style that had bothered Dr. Perez? If so, was it a hearkening back to an earlier style—an homage? Or was it a critical commentary on that style? And what of the woman in Mary Cassatt's watercolor? Who was Veronica Vella?

The possibilities were thrilling, and Esther wished she was already back home so she could look at the painting she had examined more than any other with new eyes. Could she look at it with the shrewd eyes depicted in the painting before her now?

She leaned in, studied the brushwork, searched for a signature that might have gone unnoticed in the tiny cell phone pictures she'd been shown. But there was none that she could see.

"Can we turn it around?" she said.

Adam turned the painting and set it back down on the open drawer. There were tiny holes in the frame where the paper had been tacked on. The wood panel was held in place with small nails.

"Do you have any pliers?" Esther asked.

Adam left the room and returned with a pair of pliers, which Esther used to carefully remove the nails on three sides, dropping them one by one into Adam's open palm. Then she slid the board from the frame.

"Hmm. This wasn't cut down like Ian thought it might have been. All four sides show the same age, all are smooth, and all have paint on them. So it's not that there was a signature that was cut off. There just wasn't a signature from the beginning."

She saw the handwritten name, Francisco Vella, and the year, 1881. She looked for any other marks. A place name, a shop name—anything. But there was nothing.

"I suppose it's possible that if some chemical testing was done on the writing, there's a small chance of figuring out about when this label was actually written—maybe. If it was written at the time it was painted, it might be more reliable than if it was written a hundred years later by someone who just *thought* it was Vella or had heard family stories passed down about it. But even if we could determine that, it wouldn't really answer the question of whether the name is of the painter or the subject. Or both."

She turned the panel over, careful to touch only the edges so that no oils from her fingers would rub off on the surface.

"The brushwork is promising." She sighed. "I just wish it was more cut-and-dried. I don't know what to do with this at this point except include an explanation of all the possibilities. Which I suppose would make for an interesting and instructive part of the exhibit—to explain the common problem in the art world of identifying without a doubt the correct person as the artist."

Adam helped her return the painting to its frame.

"You mentioned it might be possible to talk to Ms. Hernandez about it?" Esther said.

"Yes, I think she'd be happy for the visitors. Let me give her a ring."

He dialed his phone and stepped out to the living room. Esther continued to stare at the painting as Adam spoke in Spanish to the person on the other end of the call.

Who was this self-assured person looking back at her? And if he was her ancestor, why couldn't she have inherited whatever gene it was that made him so driven?

Adam popped his head into the room. "We've been invited to dinner."

Chapter

THIRTY-TWO

◆

GIBRALTAR, 1881

W e're heading out in two days, Mama," Vella said around a mouthful of rice. "We'll bypass Spain and land at Marseilles. We'll also miss Toulouse, but that can't be helped. I'll look for new markets in Lyon and perhaps a side trip to Geneva, then on to Paris and all the rest. I'll have some of the boys help me take the supplies down to the port tomorrow. The boat will leave the following morning."

Consuela nodded at her son but said nothing. She had been silent and brooding of late. Though Viviana had not told Vella that she was not going to accompany him on his next trip, she worried that his mother somehow suspected. How the woman could have found out was a mystery. Viviana had been careful to keep her intentions secret, telling only Emilia and Dario, and only out of necessity as they were key to her plan. She had sworn each of them to secrecy and she trusted both of them. Perhaps it was only a mother's intuition that Consuela had. Just a feeling that things were askew.

Vella certainly showed no signs of suspicion. With Dario's help, Viviana had timed her departure to coincide with Vella's. So as he was packing up paints and pigments and other goods, she was packing up her clothes and her painting supplies as though she would be going with him. Emilia had amassed a respectable stash of food, pilfered little by little from the family stores, as an emergency supply for the woman she believed to be her aunt, just in case the crossing was delayed by weather and the ship's hold ran low. The girl had even saved back some of the wages of her new position to add to Dario's donation and Viviana's own earnings from selling a couple recent paintings to pay for her passage.

The last piece of the puzzle would be secured tonight.

"I can pack up your clothes for you, Francisco," Viviana said.

"I'm sure I can make more efficient use of the space in your trunk than you could."

"You're probably right, my dear," he said. "What a thoughtful gesture."

"Of course," she said, avoiding eye contact with her pretend mother-in-law. "I know you still have much to do to prepare."

The conversation for the rest of the meal centered on the trip, with Vella's nephews peppering him with questions about the places he would be going. The women occasionally talked quietly among themselves in the intervals between serving and cleaning up after the men. Paulina, Teresa, and Madalena all made it a point to wish Viviana well and tell her that they would miss having her around. Consuela said nothing.

After dinner was over and the dishes were all clean and put away, Viviana found herself alone with Consuela. She folded and refolded Vella's clothes and tucked them neatly in his trunk while the older woman watched from the chair in the corner.

"You are not any better at that than my son is," she said.

Viviana chuckled. "No, I probably am not. But I wanted to help him."

Consuela was silent a moment. Then, "You wanted to steal from him."

Viviana's insides turned cold, but she continued folding as though she had not just been accused of breaking the eighth commandment. "I don't know why you would say such a thing."

"I know what is going on here," Consuela persisted.

Viviana turned to face her. "What? What is going on here?"

The older woman raised her finger toward the ceiling. "God is watching you more closely than I am, and I am watching you very closely."

Viviana put her hands on her hips and sighed. "I am sorry, Mama Vella, but I don't know what you're talking about and I do not appreciate being accused of stealing from my husband."

Viviana's heart beat against the wall of her chest. "How do you know that?"

"She wrote to me." Consuela produced from her apron pocket a folded-up letter and handed it to Viviana.

"I cannot read," she said.

"It is written in French on the one side and Spanish on the other. She must have gotten someone to translate it for her to make sure I would be able to read it. This letter warns me about a young woman with dark hair who is traveling with my son, pretending to be his sister. A woman named Veronica."

Viviana sat down on the bed, toppling a stack of hosiery.

"I assume that is you."

Viviana nodded. "It is."

Consuela pressed her lips together and looked like she was trying not to cry.

Viviana hung her head. "Oh, Señora Vella. I did not want to

lie to you. I didn't want to lie to anyone anymore. I just wanted to be myself."

"Why would you pretend to be his sister? And then his wife? Why did he lie to me?"

Viviana crossed the small distance between them and knelt at Consuela's feet, bowing her head in shame. "It is such a long story."

Consuela tipped Viviana's head up with her fingers under her chin. "I deserve to hear the truth."

"Yes. Yes you do." Viviana glanced toward the doorway, then shuffled closer on her knees. "And I will tell you everything."

THE NEXT MORNING, Vella and his nephews brought everything down to the docks and loaded the boxes, crates, and trunks on the schooner that would take them to Marseilles. Viviana did not go with them. Instead, she went with Emilia and Consuela to Sacred Heart Church, a Gothic-style structure that was still mid-construction. Though the church building had not yet been formally consecrated, Viviana thought it would do in a pinch. And it was closest to the house, which would leave them time for the day's other tasks.

Together, they prayed about all that was to come, both for Vella and Viviana. They prayed for safety despite treacherous waters. They prayed for guidance and protection once the destination was reached. They prayed for understanding and forgiveness in the face of the deception they were now all undertaking.

Before Vella and the boys returned, Consuela and Emilia bound Viviana's chest with strips of cloth, then Viviana put on the shirt and trousers and boots she had taken from among Vella's things. Over top of them she layered Monique Renaud's old whalebone corset and a new bustle to restore her feminine shape. And on top of those, Monique's blue dress, which she had worn to tea with Mary Cassatt, Berthe Morisot, and Marie

Bracquemond. Though it was far too fancy for the activities of a normal evening at home, it was the only one big enough to fit over all the extra layers.

Though she caught Vella looking at her rather curiously at the evening meal that night, he did not ask why she was so dressed up. After dinner, Consuela requested his help to repair two chairs for her before he left town again for many months. He did not need to know that his mother, his niece, and his friend-sister-wife had broken them on purpose while he was at the dock.

While Vella was thus occupied, Emilia and Viviana hurried to the waterfront, where Dario was waiting for them. Just as he promised, he had removed Viviana's trunk from the schooner after Vella left that day. With Dario standing guard, Viviana and Emilia ducked into an alley and removed the dress, the bustle, and the corset and packed them into the trunk. Then Emilia took a pair of shears from her apron pocket.

"Are you sure?" she said, her voice catching.

"It must be done," Viviana said, trying to push all her courage into her own voice. "It is only hair. It will grow back."

Emilia tied a ribbon around Viviana's beautiful dark hair at the nape of her neck, quickly braided the length of it, and tied another ribbon at the end. Then Viviana closed her eyes as Emilia cut through the rope of hair right at the base of Viviana's skull. Emilia handed Viviana the braid and trimmed what was left on her head until it resembled Vella's hair.

Viviana gave the braid back to her young friend. "Sell it and buy yourself something nice to remember me by."

Emilia was crying, but she nodded and tucked the shears and the hair back into her apron. Viviana gathered up the loose hair from the ground and hid it beneath an empty crate.

"Hurry," came Dario's voice. "The ship is leaving soon."

The women emerged from the alley, and Viviana stood for his inspection.

ERIN BARTELS

"Not bad." Dario removed the hat from his head and placed it over Viviana's shorn head. "Better. Now come. We must go."

With the help of a porter, Dario got Viviana's trunk aboard the ship. Viviana hugged Emilia tightly and whispered, "I shall never forget you. And I will pray for you daily." She turned away from the girl lest she begin to cry. Men did not cry. Then she shook Dario's hand. "Don't forget."

He pulled an envelope partway out of his vest pocket. "I have it here. Do you think I would forget a letter I transcribed myself?"

"I know you will do just as you said. I trust you."

Viviana knew she should board the ship, but she could not get her feet to move. She understood clearly at that moment the impulse that had led Vella to ask her to come with him on his travels after only knowing her for two days. She felt it now. A powerful urge not to be alone. A yearning for someone to share this journey into the unknown. A friend for the long, lonely days ahead.

"Are you sure you can't leave this place?" she finally said.

Dario smiled sadly. "I am sure. As sure as I am that you can. There are great things in store for you beyond the sea. You will find plenty of room for happiness."

She bit back her emotions and gave a little nod.

Dario put his hands on Emilia's shaking shoulders and gently turned her away from the ship. He would see her home and leave with her the letter to give to Vella. The letter Viviana had dictated three days ago. The letter that would explain her deception, ask for his forgiveness, and thank him for getting her this far. The letter that would ask him to take her finished self-portrait with him to give to Monsieur Renaud in Toulouse—whom he could now visit since she would not be along. The letter that encouraged him to forget her if that should prove less painful than remembering.

When her coconspirators were lost in the crowd, Viviana Torrens turned around and boarded the *Prometheus* under yet another borrowed name—Francisco Vella.

277

Chapter
THIRTY-THREE

◆

GIBRALTAR, PRESENT DAY

Gertrude Hernandez was a small, bent woman with a beatific smile and a strong handshake that belied her age and stature. Her gray hair was pulled into a smart bun and her dress was a riot of colorful flowers. Esther adored her immediately. She radiated warmth and welcome as she physically pulled Esther into her tiny apartment toward a small table pushed up against a wall and overflowing with food. There was barely room for two people to sit at the table, but a third chair had been added as well.

"Sit, sit!" the old woman kept repeating, until her guests obeyed. "I am so happy to have you in my home again, Adam. And what a beautiful young lady you've brought with you this time."

It had been some time since anyone had referred to Esther as beautiful or young, but compared to this ancient woman she supposed she might be a bit of both.

Once the three of them were seated, Gertrude reached out

278

for their hands to say grace, which she did in Llanito and then in English. "God speaks Llanito," she said with a wink, "but I thought that you might like to know what I was telling him."

For the next twenty minutes or so, the talk was all about the food that God, via Gertrude, had set before them. The fish soup, the flatbread, the yellow rice, the white beans, the rainbow of vegetables, the olives, the meatballs. As she delighted in the smells, tastes, and textures of everything she ate, Esther kept thinking of the poverty that had led this old woman to sell her personal belongings, at least according to Ian Perez. They should have offered to take her to a restaurant rather than invading her home and emptying her cupboards.

On Esther's plate, all the different delicacies tumbled over into the next, mixing with and enhancing one another. Beneath the tiny table, Esther was finding it tricky to keep her personal space from tumbling into someone else's. If she wasn't careful, her knees drifted and touched Adam's or Gertrude's. Holding them in just the right position so as to avoid any contact felt rather like holding a pose for her mother.

Her mother. Esther hadn't texted Lorena all day. She should check on her. Soon. As soon as they left this tiny apartment, hopefully with some useful information to go along with their full bellies.

It struck her how her interactions with Ian, Adam, and now Gertrude were saturated with food and drink and a generous spirit. It seemed a given to them that they would treat both friends and strangers with gracious hospitality, even if the table was too small and the cost would be felt. By contrast, the enormous table in her dining room in East Lansing was always empty—she and Lorena ate in the kitchen on stools on the same side of the counter, not even looking at each other.

"Adam said you are a descendant of Francisco Vella?" Gertrude said.

"Yes," Esther said, "and I understand you are as well?"

"He was my great-great-great-uncle."

"And he was my great-great-great-great—I think that's enough greats—grandfather."

Gertrude laughed. "It sounds like he was pretty great!" Esther and Adam joined her laughter for a moment. Then Esther felt her own laughter turn in tone from genuine to uncomfortable. Was he indeed her fourth great-grandfather as she had always believed?

"Ian told me about your museum when he was here this summer. It sounds marvelous. And I am delighted you have a new addition to bring home to it."

Esther smiled. "It makes me so happy to hear that, Ms. Hernandez. I was worried that you'd be sad about the painting leaving the country in which it was painted."

"Oh no, dear. It wasn't painted here."

Esther's pulse picked up. "You know where it was painted?"

"It was painted in Africa."

"How do you know?"

"I was always told it was."

"And do you know who painted it? There's no signature. Ian said you thought maybe it was cut down to fit the frame it's in now, but I removed it from the frame and there is no sign that it was cut down at any time. So the signature was not cut off. There never was a signature, as far as I can see."

Gertrude looked apologetic. "I'm afraid we never talked about who painted it. To us the important thing was the inside of the frame, not the outside." Esther's disappointment must have shown on her face because Gertrude rose from the table and said, "Now, now. Just give me a moment." Then she disappeared into the bedroom.

Adam caught Esther's eye and offered a sympathetic smile. Gertrude returned, holding something behind her back.

"Come over here and sit on the sofa."

Adam and Esther obeyed—Adam with perhaps a bit more

dignity than Esther, who nearly tripped as she rushed over to the couch.

"After I spoke with Ian and Adam about the painting this summer," Gertrude continued, "I called a few cousins to ask them if they had ever heard anything about it. One of them said he didn't know about the painting, but he did have something of Francisco's he could share with me. It had been handed down in his line like the painting had been handed down in mine." She produced a leather-bound book that looked strikingly similar to the one the subject in the painting was holding. "My cousin David said that this came originally from his great-great-grandmother, Emilia."

Gertrude held the book out to Esther, who wiped her hands on her lap before taking it. She gingerly released the deteriorating leather strap that held it closed, thinking that she should really be wearing gloves, then carefully opened the front cover and turned the first few pages. Spanish words in a slanted script filled each page top to bottom, side to side, not a margin in sight. She turned a few more pages to find that there were also sketches—many sketches.

"My eyes are very bad now and the writing is very small, so I haven't been able to read it," Gertrude said. "But perhaps with Adam's help you can find your answers in there."

Esther pulled out her phone. "It shouldn't take too long to photograph each page."

Gertrude laughed. "Oh, my dear, there's no need for that. It's yours. David was happy to pass it on to someone who would appreciate it."

"I can keep it?"

"Absolutely. You are family, after all."

281

Chapter

THIRTY-FOUR

◆

As the *Prometheus* sailed from Gibraltar southwest along the coast of Morocco toward the Canary Islands, Viviana kept to her own berth as much as possible, leaving only for meals with the other third-class passengers and for an occasional glimpse over the starboard rail. There, somewhere beyond the western horizon, her future awaited her, and she wished they were sailing straight for it. When she arrived in America, she would find some sympathetic and trustworthy person who could write a letter for her to Mary Cassatt. She would reveal her true identity, not as Francisco's sister Veronica but as his friend Viviana, and ask for introductions to people Cassatt still knew in America. Until those introductions came, she would have to find a place to stay and a way to survive. But she was not afraid. She had done it before and she could do it again.

She was fearful, however, of her true identity being discovered on the crossing. It took a couple days to remember how to move as a man, how to eat as a man, how to meet the eyes of

282

the men she encountered on the ship rather than glancing demurely away. When she had lived as a man with men in the past, it had been as a fellow soldier in a time of war, not as a civilized member of society. She was grateful none of the Englishmen on the ship expected anything but poor manners from a rock scorpion, which was all Francisco Vella was to them.

During the month Viviana had spent on that rock, Vella had been occupied with much work and she had busied herself with observing and painting her world. Though she did not learn the skill of swimming as he had promised, she had learned a few English phrases from her observations, which she hoped would prove useful when she reached her destination.

Good day. Goodbye. Good morning. Good evening.

So much "good" that it was hard to believe the English behaved so badly. She knew basic colors and how to count to ten, how to ask someone's name and how to ask for help. If she continued to listen carefully at meals on the ship, she might pick up a few more phrases before she disembarked at Norfolk. There were many days to pass between now and then—at least a month. After the Canary Islands, they would ride the trade winds west to the Bahamas before sailing along the North American coast to Virginia.

All that time, Viviana could not socialize for fear of suspicion and could not paint for lack of materials, for though she had packed her brushes and as much paint as she dared, she had nothing to paint on. Yet she did have a drawing pad—a gift from Emilia—along with a few charcoals and pencils. Sketching the other passengers and then giving them the drawings would be a way for Francisco to endear himself to them without having to say much. It would also be a way to pass the otherwise monotonous hours.

And so, one fine morning three days after leaving the Canaries, Viviana found herself sitting on a wooden cask above deck, sketching the sailors at their work. Dario's hat was pulled down around her head, shading her eyes from the sun and obscuring most of her face from any curious onlookers. At first, no one noticed her, quiet as she was. But in a place filled with hard physical labor and starved of art, a person sitting still and sketching will be noticed eventually.

Word spread around the ship, and soon she had people calling at her quarters belowdecks, wanting her to draw their portrait. Some were content to sit quite patiently as she strove to capture their features as precisely as possible. Others were squirmier and more loquacious. Sometimes Viviana got the feeling that they only asked to be drawn because they were bored and wanted someone to talk to. They must have been rather disappointed when the man with the sketch pad proved a foreigner—and a practically mute one at that.

Most of the time, Viviana wasn't really pretending confusion at their words as she had in Paris. It was, after all, an English ship, and she couldn't speak much English. But there were a few other people on board who spoke Spanish, including a thickset man with a mustache who always seemed to be looking at her when she raised the brim of her hat.

On day sixteen of their journey, when all were tiring of the same scenery and the same food and the same routine, this man sat on the chair in front of Viviana to have his portrait drawn. Then she began to draw.

"Hello," she said in a low voice in English. "Would you like me to draw your picture?"

"Yes," he replied in Spanish. "I hear that Francisco Vella is a very good artist."

Viviana kept her head tipped toward her pad. "My reputation precedes me," she said in Spanish. "Keep as still as possible."

After a moment the man said, "That will look more like me if you actually look at me."

Viviana forced a low chuckle and glanced up briefly.

Another minute or so went by, and the man said, "You must have a very nice razor. I've never seen such smooth skin on a man's face after weeks at sea."

Viviana said nothing, but drew faster.

"And I know for a fact," the man continued, "that Francisco Vella lets his beard grow out when he's traveling."

At that, Viviana stood and turned to leave, but the man caught her by the arm and forced her to face him. He removed Darío's hat from her head and gripped her chin, forcing her to look up at him.

A nearby British sailor spoke sharply to the man, who answered in English in soft tones. Apparently placated, the sailor moved on and returned to his tasks.

The man put the hat back on her head. "Now then, why don't we sit back down and you can continue?"

Viviana lowered herself slowly to the barrel. "So you know that I am not Francisco Vella." She still spoke in her artificially low voice. "This man may know she was not who she said she was, but that didn't mean he knew she was not a man.

"I knew it the minute I heard his name spoken aboard the ship. I have known Francisco long enough to know he has no business in the Americas. But it took me a few days to discover that you were the one using his name. Who are you really, and why are you pretending to be someone else?"

Viviana cleared her throat and spit on the deck. She had never understood why men had to spit so much more than women, but apparently they did.

"Francisco prepared me to take this journey," she said, "and it is his name we used to make it possible. Beyond that, it is none of your business. Francisco knows who I am. You do not need to."

She stood again, and this time the man did not stop her as she returned belowdecks and shut herself into her tiny sleeping quarters. If she had to, she would stay locked in the berth for as long as it took to get to Virginia. She did have some food hidden away, after all. If she ran low, she'd sneak out at night to get more, or she'd feign sickness and food might be brought to her. But she did not intend to meet up with that inquisitive man again.

Chapter
THIRTY-FIVE

❖

GIBRALTAR, PRESENT DAY

As Esther and Adam prepared to leave Gertrude's apartment, the old woman pulled Esther into a tight embrace. "I am so glad that Francisco's legacy lives on with you. I am sure he never dreamed that his work would ever be in a museum way over across the ocean. Looking through that book, I got the idea that drawing was just a hobby, a way to remember his many travels. But maybe I was wrong. It must have been much more than that."

Esther pulled away. "I am so grateful to you—and to Adam and Ian—for making it possible to get a couple more pieces to the puzzle. I promise I will take great care of both the painting and the journal."

"Of course you will," Gertrude said. "And I want you to visit me again if you are ever back to Gib."

Esther promised she would, knowing full well how unlikely it was that she would ever return and feeling rather sad at the thought of not seeing more of this place and these people.

ERIN BARTELS

Especially Adam. He had been such a lovely host, giving up his time and schlepping her all around town to help solve a mystery that was not even his. Esther felt she had barely scratched the surface of who this man was. They might have been great friends in other circumstances.

In the car, Adam motioned to the journal in her hand. "I suppose you'll put me to work now?"

She laughed. "I know I can't ask you to translate this entire journal. Maybe when Ian is done with classes for winter break he would have some time to help me. Or maybe someone at Michigan State can help. It could be a graduate student's special project or something."

"Or you could learn Spanish. Really learn it. And then when you come back to visit, I can teach you some Llanito and we'll make a real Gibraltarian out of you."

"Maybe," she said, wondering if Ian had told his cousin anything about her mother.

"So," he said, "what are your plans now?" He still had not started the car.

"I guess now we pack up the painting and I go home."

Esther was glad that Adam looked as disappointed by this as she felt.

"When is your flight?"

"My flight leaves Sunday, but I'm going to see if they have room on an earlier one. I may be able to leave as early as tomorrow."

He pursed his lips. "Or you could stay the weekend. I don't teach again until Monday, so I'm free to entertain you."

She tried to hide her pleasure at the thought that she was not the only one who wanted to spend more time together. "I suppose so," she said slowly. "I do have enough money to stay longer. Especially since I don't owe you anything for the painting—though I should save enough to pay Ian for it. But what would we do? I feel like I've already seen most of the peninsula."

287

"You most certainly have not! You went to Marks & Spencer and the beach. You can go to a department store almost anywhere, and as I understand it, you have plenty of beaches in Michigan."

"Not that I get to them much."

"Regardless, you haven't even begun to see what Gib has to offer." He finally started the car. "We'll start tonight."

"Tonight?" She checked the dashboard. "It's nearly nine o'clock."

"Which is only three in the afternoon for you."

Esther did the calculations. Was it really earlier at home? It felt like it must be later. "I'm all turned around."

"I mean, if you're tired, you're welcome to hit the sack at the hotel, but what I'd really like to do is take you out tonight."

He wanted to take her out. Not "my cousin told me to show you a good time." What he'd *really like to do* was take her out.

"We've already eaten dinner," she said.

"Who said anything about dinner?"

THE CLUB WAS CALLED THE VICEROY, and it was packed and loud and somehow both dimly lit and blindingly bright at the same time. Adam led her through the crowd, his fingers just barely touching hers so they would not be separated. He found an empty U-shaped booth curving around a small round table and motioned for her to sit. Then he scooted in beside her.

"So, I guess this is not a place people come to talk," she all but shouted.

"Of course not," he said. "People come here to dance."

"You come here a lot?"

He shook his head. "This place didn't even exist until last year. There used to be a nightclub here called Dusk, but it closed right before the pandemic. Then for more than three years, nothing. Nothing to do after hours."

A waitress came around and took their drink order.

"I don't think I've ever done anything after hours," Esther said.

He laughed. "Not even in college?"

"Nope. Holland, Michigan, in the late 1990s was not a nightlife hotspot. And truthfully, I've never been a nightlife person."

Adam glanced down at her dress. "Well, you look like you belong here."

Esther did not own even one garment suitable to wear to a nightclub, but when she was packing her suitcase for this trip, her mother had come into her room bearing a dress in a zipped-up nylon garment bag that looked like it hadn't been out of the closet since the Sixties.

"Look," Lorena said, "I know you think you're just going there to see a painting, but no one should travel to Europe without something nice to wear. You never know if you're going to get invited to a fancy dinner or a museum opening or something."

Esther pooh-poohed this, but when she saw how annoyed Lorena was at her refusal and how little space the dress would take up once it was out of that awful garment bag, she consented and tucked it in among her other clothes.

"Don't forget shoes," Lorena said, tossing a pair of open-toed leopard-print kitten heels on the bed.

"What are these?" Esther had asked.

"Those are the shoes I bought to wear with that dress."

An hour ago, Esther had pulled the dress out of the suitcase and onto her body, sure that it would look terrible or be too small or smell weird from having been in a bag for so long. Instead, she was amazed at how perfectly it fit and wondered what her mother might look like today if she had not spent the last several decades on antipsychotics. The dress was black and fitted, ruched on one side at the waist, with a boat neck and no sleeves, and reached just to her knees. The tag indicated it had been purchased from Hudson's, the Marks & Spencer of Old Detroit. The tag also indicated that Lorena had never actually worn it, her invitations to fancy dinners and museum openings having dried up in the wake of her illness.

The dress did smell a little stale, but with the amount of cologne and perfume wafting around them right now, Esther didn't think it would be noticeable.

"I doubt you'll think I look like I belong here if you can get me out on that dance floor," she said to Adam.

"Is that a challenge?" he said.

She laughed. "It will be, yes!"

Their drinks arrived, and rather than try to talk over the music and the other people, Esther contented herself with watching the crowd. She couldn't imagine a world in which she'd ever paint a club scene, but she still enjoyed the act of noticing all the little details. The group of heavily made-up girls in the corner, cupping their manicured hands to one another's ears to comment on the guys they were tracking at the bar. Said guys revving each other up and egging each other on until they got the nerve to break off from the pack in pursuit. The waitress whose smile didn't reach her eyes. The bartender who never stopped moving.

For the first time in memory, Esther did not look for a flaw, something that would allow her to separate herself and stand in detached judgment. She simply admired—without envy, without coveting a quality or an ability or a life she did not have, open instead to the wondrous variety of people and experiences around her. She could appreciate that their various paths had led them to this place, at this moment, and this moment would never come again. Other people who were not there right then were having their own moments elsewhere. They might be missing this one, but they were not missing out. They were busy with other things. And all those things she had missed over the years as she stayed close to home—travel and romance and adventures—were not things she could never have. They were just things she hadn't had yet.

She turned to let Adam know she was having a good time and

found that he was already looking at her, a small smile on his face. He sipped his negroni. She sipped her French 75. Then they both turned their attention back to the crowd.

The moment Esther finished her cocktail, Adam stood and held out his hand to her. "At least one dance," he said. "Then, if you want, we can leave."

"There's no 'one dance' in a place like this," she said, rising. "The music never stops."

As Adam led her out to the dance floor, Esther wished she'd spent more time observing the dancers than the drinkers and dalliers. The last time she'd danced in public was at her high school prom, which she'd attended with Justin Reynolds, a boy with pimples and braces who was at least four inches shorter than her if she was wearing flats, which she was not that night. They had sat on the sidelines most of the evening, getting up for two slow dances. During the second of those, he'd tried to kiss her but only succeeded in knocking his forehead into her nose.

Thankfully, the leopard-print shoes her mother had thrust upon her were only kitten heels, and Adam had enough northern European genes in his own DNA to match her height.

When they'd claimed a spot on the floor, Adam took her right hand in his left and placed his right hand just below her shoulder on her upper back. "I'll make it easy on you," he said. "I'll teach you to salsa."

"Okay," she said, deeply relieved that she would not have to make up dance moves on her own.

"This is very easy, very basic. I step forward with my left foot, you step back on your right, then back to neutral and switch weight. Then I step back and you step forward."

Esther immediately did something wrong.

"No, no, it's not a waltz. Don't count in threes, count in eights. The four and the eight are pauses."

They tried again, with Adam counting out loud, but Esther still messed it up.

"So, the main thing to remember here is that with every step, you switch your weight from one foot to the other." Adam demonstrated. "No just tapping your foot when it moves. You want to put your whole weight on it and then switch your weight to your other foot. Like this."

They started again, about half speed. After a few repetitions, Esther could feel the movement becoming more natural, more intuitive, in much the same way that a new drawing or painting technique started out uncomfortable and unnatural but eventually, when practiced enough, felt right. There was a fluidity to the dance, and as the minutes ticked by, Esther felt like her body was a thick, stiff paint that just needed a bit of medium added in order to make it flow.

"Very good," Adam said, stopping her. "Now, shall we try it in time with the music?"

Esther nodded.

Adam counted out eight quick beats, then they started to move. Esther immediately lost all rhythm and ran smack up against her partner, stepping on his toe and narrowly avoiding kneeing him in a sensitive area. They doubled over laughing.

"I'm sorry," she said. "I'm no good at dancing."

"It's okay. It takes a little practice." He took her hand. "How are you at walking?"

"One of the best."

"Okay, then let's get out of here."

Hand in hand, they made their way to the door and out into the night.

THE KITTEN HEELS were not the best shoes for walking, but they weren't the worst either. Still, by the time she and Adam had made their way out to the North Mole, she was ready to give her feet a break. She slipped the shoes off and carried them as they strolled along the east side of the cruise liner terminal and looked back across the water at the glittering city lights and the dark monolith rising up behind it. This was a view worth painting.

"It really is a beautiful place," she said. "I wonder why Vella would leave it behind. I mean, I understand traveling around Europe and Africa and coming back to Gibraltar as a home base. So many exciting and beautiful places, and he had a good business going. But why do you suppose he left for America? Why would he leave his wife and child behind in France? And why is there no trace of him in the US if the ship landed safely?"

"I suppose the journal might shed some light on that," Adam said.

They came to a stop and leaned over the rail.

"I can't believe I let you convince me to go out dancing rather than stay in and start poring over that journal," she said. "I don't even know myself anymore."

"I guess the vacation is doing the trick. It's not healthy to work all the time."

"I don't work all the time. The museum's not even open all that much compared to most businesses."

"But don't you take care of your mother as well?"

Ah. So Ian *had* told Adam about Lorena.

"I do, I mean, I keep an eye on her. She seems to think she can take care of herself."

"But you don't think so?"

"No. I mean, she never really has."

"Hmm. Has she ever been given the chance?"

Esther examined the shoes in her hands. "No, I guess she hasn't. First it was her parents, then just her father and a nurse, then—briefly—my father. Then me."

"So she's been constantly chaperoned her entire life?"

Esther had never really thought of it that way, but yes, she supposed that was true. Lorena Markstrom had had a babysitter for sixty-six years. No one trusted her. No one believed in her. She was always being watched . . . but never being seen.

Esther stood straight and turned toward Adam. "You know what I would do if I could do anything?"

"What would you do?"

"I would find some way to set my mother and me free from each other. Some way where we could both live on our own terms."

Adam smiled. "Well, that seems solidly within the realm of possibility."

Chapter

THIRTY-SIX

Atlantic Ocean, 1881

Viviana had spent three days in the belly of the ship when they ran into rough waters. She lay in her narrow bunk, gripping the sides and swallowing back vomit, for as long as she could manage, but finally decided that she must get up above deck where the air might be a little fresher.

With some difficulty, she scrambled up the steps, down a narrow passage, and past the mess hall where a small group of terrified Englishwomen clung to one another, looking as green as Monique Renaud's poisonous bedchamber. Up on the main deck, a cold rain pummeled the ship and everyone on it. The crew were hard at work, hoisting and lowering various sails, tightening and loosening ropes. Several male passengers were on deck as well, heaving up the contents of their stomachs. Viviana pitched against a rail and threw up what little food she had consumed that day.

A sailor placed a rope in her hand and shouted what must have been instructions, but she could not understand what the

man was saying. Then another man was right behind her, grabbing the rope, his meaty hands just inches from her slight ones.

"We need to hold this line," he said in Spanish close to her
ear. It was the man who had accused her of not being Francisco
Vella. "I bet you wish you were down with the ladies right now,"
he continued. "But you made your bed, so I guess you'll have
to sleep in it."

Viviana made no answer, merely held on to the rope as the
rain pelted her face and chest. A bolt of lightning split the sky,
followed immediately by a crack of thunder louder than all the
gunfire at Alpens, and she felt at that moment how the Liberal
army must have felt when she and her fellow Carlist soldiers
had cut off all escape routes and fired at them from walls and
bell towers and steeples. There was no way off the *Prometheus*
either, no way to quiet this storm. They must sail through it or
perish in the attempt.

For the next several hours, she followed the man from Gibraltar as he followed the orders of the English sailors. What
he did, she did, and when she did it wrong, he corrected her,
until finally the clouds broke up and the waves settled and the
men on the deck sighed a collective prayer of thanksgiving to
God for sparing the ship and their lives.

After a short respite, during which a bottle of brandy was
passed from man to man, everyone was given a cleanup task.
Viviana and her Spanish-speaking companion mopped the deck,
and afterward he led her back down to the lowest level where
they both had rooms. They sloshed through an inch of water to
Viviana's berth, where he followed her inside and shut the door.
She was too exhausted to be afraid. And anyway, he looked too
exhausted to pose much of a threat.

Viviana sat on the bunk in her wet clothes, feeling like a
wrung-out rag. He sat across from her on the trunk.

"Nice work up there," he said once he'd caught his breath. He
held out his hand. "I'm Juan Caetano."

Viviana shook his hand and said, "Thank you for your help," but nothing more.

He regarded her. "Okay, you don't have to tell me who you really are. But you're not going to be able to fool the others from here on out unless you get yourself another set of clothes."

He pointed to Vella's shirt, which was torn in two places, revealing the loosened strips of cloth beneath. Viviana quickly crossed her arms over her chest.

Juan held up a hand. "I'm not here to expose you, señorita. I'm sure you have your reasons."

Viviana relaxed but did not uncross her arms. "This is the only shirt I have to wear," she said in her own voice.

Juan stood. "Stay here."

He left the room, and Viviana quickly assessed the damage to her disguise. A moment later, Juan was back with a short stack of dry clothes and a towel.

"These will be much too big, but you can cinch everything up with a belt or rope." He placed the stack on top of the trunk. "You'll have to dry those strips of cloth before fixing yourself up. Otherwise, your skin's liable to get red and itchy. You can hang it up on the beams for a day. That ought to do it. Better let your boots dry too. I can bring you your meals."

Viviana looked at him curiously. "Thank you."

Juan nodded and left, closing the door securely behind him.

Viviana took his advice, hanging everything up on the beams above. Then she put on the too-big shirt and pants he had brought her, rolling the pant legs up above her calves to keep them dry.

Later that night, Juan returned with a plate of food, as well as a mop and a bucket. While she ate, he mopped up the water on the floor. Then he left again.

True to his word, the next day he returned with breakfast, lunch, and supper. On the third day when he was delivering another breakfast of biscuits and dried fruit, Viviana invited him in. She had re-bound her chest, though perhaps not quite as well as Consuela and Emilia had done, and had tucked and cinched Juan's donated shirt into Vella's now-dry pants.

Viviana asked him to sit and handed him the pants he had lent her. "Thank you for your kindnesses. I can manage without these, though. And I imagine you'll be glad to have them back."

He accepted them and waited for her to continue.

"Can I assume that you still do not intend to expose me?" she said.

"I fail to see how turning you in would benefit either of us. And anyway, you have a cabin, so you paid for your passage. You're not a stowaway." He scratched at his beard. "You're a mystery, but not a criminal as far as I can see."

"No, I am not a criminal."

He nodded. "So where are you headed?"

"Virginia."

"You clearly don't speak English. How will you make your way in America?"

"I speak French."

"Good for you. They don't. Or at least the people who would associate with someone of your status don't."

Viviana frowned. Mary Cassatt had spoken three languages. She had just assumed that this was common for Americans.

"Can you teach me English?"

Juan laughed. "Not much in the time we have left on this voyage."

Viviana sighed. "Doesn't anyone there speak Spanish?"

"Some. In Texas and California and other places in the west."

"Are they far from Virginia?"

"Very far."

"Have you been there?"

"No."

"Well—" She hesitated. She did not want to be dependent on yet another man to lead her around and translate for her. "Where are you going?"

"I disembark when we stop at the Bahamas. From there I join a merchant vessel heading for Brazil."

"And what will you do in Brazil?"

"I am leaving behind trade in tobacco and cotton for coffee and rubber."

"I see." Viviana was quiet a moment. "Do they speak Spanish there?"

"Portuguese." He must have seen the disappointment in her face because he went on. "You know, I hear they speak French in New Orleans. That's in a state called Louisiana. It's closer than California or Texas. If you want to leave the ship with me in the Bahamas, I'll help you find a ship headed for New Orleans." Viviana brightened. "Really?"

"Sure, why not?" He assessed her. "Will you be continuing your little ruse once you reach your destination?"

"No," she said firmly. "I would like to finally be myself."

"Then we're going to have to find a way for you to get off this ship undetected."

Chapter

THIRTY-SEVEN

◆

Esther slept in the morning after her night at the Viceroy with Adam and their walk down to the pier. In order to save her from having to walk any farther in heels, Adam had called a taxi to take Esther back to the Eliott Hotel while he walked back to his car and drove home to his apartment. Upon returning to the hotel, Esther had planned on starting to pick through the journal with the dubious aid of Google Translate, only to realize she had left it in the Mercedes.

Instead, she lay in bed in the dark, thinking through possible scenarios where she and her mother could live independently. Each line of thought quickly ran into trouble. How could she trust Lorena to live alone? What would happen if she didn't take her medication—or if she took too much? How often would Esther feel the need to check in on her? And wouldn't that mean she was still tied to the place her mother lived? Who would stay in the house? Lorena owned it, so probably her. And then where would Esther live? And how could she afford it?

She fell asleep frustrated and woke up late and with a headache. She messaged Adam, but he did not respond right away, so she walked to Costa Coffee for another muffin and café bombón. When he still hadn't responded a half hour later, she walked to his apartment building following the directions in her GPS app and knocked on his door. There was no answer. She knocked harder and longer, and a moment later the door swung open.

Adam was bleary-eyed and shirtless, his hair disheveled, his legs and feet bare. And even though she'd already seen him thus disrobed when they were at the beach, Esther was profoundly embarrassed to see what he looked like when he'd just rolled out of bed.

"Sorry," she said, looking at nothing in the room beyond him. "I didn't think I'd be waking you up at this hour. It's nearly ten o'clock."

He rubbed a hand over his face. "Come on in."

Esther hurried past him into the small living/dining room. She sent a furtive glance his way. "Did you go back to the club or something?"

"No." He slapped both sides of his face lightly. "I stayed up to get a head start on the journal."

He seemed to realize how little clothing he had on and stepped into the bedroom, then reemerged a moment later with jeans and a T-shirt on. In one hand he held the leather journal. In the other was a spiral notebook.

Esther took an involuntary step toward him. "Did you get very far?"

He motioned for her to sit on the sofa and then set the two books next to each other on the coffee table. "About halfway."

"You're kidding." She snatched up the notebook and opened the cover.

Adam yawned. "I didn't intend to work on it that long, but once I got going I thought about how nice it would be if you had the whole thing to read on your way home rather than having to wait for Ian to have time to translate for you."

"Adam, that's amazing," she said, flipping through the notebook pages. "When did you finally go to sleep?"

"Probably about three hours ago."

"Oh my gosh, I am so sorry!" Esther stood. "I need to let you sleep."

He stopped her with a hand on her arm. "It's fine. All I need is some coffee. Would you like some coffee?"

"Are you sure? I can leave."

"Nonsense. Sit." He walked a few steps into the kitchen. "I don't want to miss spending the day with you. I was going to take you to see the Moorish castle and the monkeys and St. Michael's Cave today."

Esther sat. She was torn between starting to read the translation and watching him make coffee. She put down the notebook. Better to start reading it when she could give it her full attention. She turned in her seat to face the kitchen. "I'd like to see all those things, but don't you think you should get some more rest?"

"I can sleep when you leave. I don't want to waste the time you're here in bed."

Esther was happy that he wanted her to stay, that he didn't want to miss out on time they could spend together. Because she felt exactly the same way. Adam was charming and good-looking and thoughtful and fun.

And he lived four thousand miles away from her.

"Is the painting still in your bedroom?" she asked.

"Yes. I hung it back up so I wouldn't accidentally knock it down. You can go in there and get it if you like."

"I just want to look at it."

Esther went into Adam's bedroom to the sound of the coffee grinder. The painting was hanging above his unmade bed. She looked at it from that short distance first, then stepped out of her shoes and onto the bed to get a closer view. She walked up the length of the mattress and placed one hand against the wall to the right of the painting to keep her balance.

Where was the signature? There had to be one. There was always a signature.

Her eyes scanned the edges of the painting, starting at the bottom right corner and traveling counterclockwise around the perimeter, until she was back where she started. Then something caught her eye. Something she hadn't noticed the day before when the painting was propped on the drawers. Whether it was the position of the painting or the light at that time of the day or both, something looked odd in that bottom right-hand corner. The color seemed . . . off. And the craquelure was different. Which suggested that the paint content or technique was different.

Esther now methodically scanned the entire painting top to bottom to see if any other parts showed this secondary craquelure pattern or other discolorations. Perhaps the artist had simply made later corrections with inferior paint. But she could see no other obvious differences. Which seemed to suggest that perhaps someone had painted over just one corner of the painting. Why would someone do that—except to cover up a signature?

"Coffee's ready," came Adam's voice from behind her.

Esther turned to find him leaning in the doorway, hands in his pockets, as though he'd been hanging out there for a while.

"Oh, sorry," she said. "I'm stomping all over your sheets."

"It's no problem."

He came a few steps into the room and held out his hand to help her step off the bed. She took it and hopped down to the floor next to him. She loosened her grip to release his hand, but he maintained steady pressure as he led her out of the room, only letting go when they reached the couch. Two steaming, fragrant mugs sat on two coasters on the coffee table, as did a sugar bowl.

"I'm sorry I don't have cream or milk," he said. "I drink it black."

"Black is fine," she said. "I'm surprised you don't drink tea."

"I do drink tea. But three hours of sleep calls for coffee. And I know you Americans tend to like coffee more, so I picked some up before you came into town."

"You got coffee just for me?"

"Of course. I wanted you to feel at home."

Home. Bizarrely, Esther did feel at home here in this compact, colorful place. Which was unfortunate, since it most certainly was not her home.

"Now then," Adam said, "I know you want to dig into that notebook—I can see this sort of crazed quality behind your eyes that wasn't there yesterday. But I am curious to know what you were looking at so closely in that painting."

She blew across the surface of the coffee. "I am too. It looks to me like someone painted over the corner at a later time."

"To fix some sort of damage?"

The seascape with the thumbprint at Our Lady of Sorrows popped into Esther's mind. "Maybe. Or to cover something up." Adam leaned back. "Intriguing. Go on."

"Every painting we have of Vella's has his signature. It's always on the bottom right, always in what appears to be chrome yellow, which would have started out vibrant and bright but weathers over the years to a kind of dull yellowy brown." She motioned to the bedroom door. "This one doesn't. So my immediate suspicion was that maybe this was a portrait some other artist did of Vella. But then I noticed a different craquelure—"

"I'm sorry, what is that?"

"Craquelure is the pattern of cracks you see in old oil paintings. Usually there is more cracking if the artist used inferior paints or if he failed to paint fat over lean, using thinner glazes first before adding thicker paint. If you start thick—fat—and top it with thin—lean—it tends to crack more."

"I see."

"But this painting looks like it was done all in one short sitting, en plein air, right at the spot depicted."

"Which Ms. Hernanadez believes is Northern Africa."

"Right. So if it was all done at once in this sort of Impressionistic style, you'd expect all the craquelure to be the same. But in this one corner, it isn't. The color is a little different as well."

"So is there a way to determine what's beneath that spot?"

"There are methods to x-ray paintings to see what's beneath the topmost layer. But I'd have to get someone at a major institution to help me."

They both sipped their coffee in silence a moment.

"So someone painted over the signature," Adam said.

"It seems possible."

"But why would someone do that without adding their own signature if they were trying to take credit for it?"

"Exactly."

All at once and in nearly perfect synchronization, Esther and Adam put down their coffee cups and reached for the two books on the table.

"You start at the beginning," Adam said. "I'll grab another notebook and pick up where I left off."

Practically trembling, Esther opened to the first page of Adam's translation and began to read.

THIRTY-EIGHT

BAHAMAS, 1881

The rocking motion of the trunk was not unlike the rocking of the ship during the storm, and Viviana concentrated on breathing slowly and shallowly, as she would wearing a corset, as Juan and an unsuspecting dock worker transferred the trunk from the ship to a hired mule-drawn wagon. Then the slow, jostling ride away from the waterfront to a spot behind some buildings, where Juan finally released the clasps and oxygen came flooding into Viviana's hiding place.

She was already dressed in her own clothes, Juan having thrown Vella's ruined shirt and his pants overboard the previous night. Her short hair was covered with a cap that was filled out by the tangle of strips that had bound her chest on the ship, making her appear to have much more hair than she actually did.

Juan helped her out of the trunk and onto the ground. "Welcome to the Bahamas, Señorita Torrens."

She smoothed out the wrinkles in her skirts and held out her hand to him. "Señor Caetano, I cannot begin to thank you for your help."

"Don't thank me yet. We still have to get you to New Orleans." He handed the wagon driver some coins to cover the extra cost of keeping silent about what he had just witnessed. "The driver will stay here with the trunks while we secure rooms. We will get you on your way as soon as possible."

The arrangements were made quickly at a nearby inn. Viviana went to her room to clean up from spending more than three weeks at sea while Juan booked her passage on a schooner headed for Louisiana the next day. They met in the evening for dinner, where Viviana had her first taste of coconut milk, mango fruit, and stewed conch.

"How does it feel to be a woman again?" Juan asked. "An uncommon woman, perhaps. But a woman all the same."

Viviana took a deep breath. "Good in some ways."

"But not in others?"

She smiled. "Until you've lived as a woman, I'm not sure I could explain it to you."

Juan laughed. "Then I guess I will never know."

She joined in his laughter. "I guess not." Then she sighed and looked out the window toward the harbor.

Juan followed her gaze. "You're a long way from home."

"Yes." Her voice hitched. "A long way from home. But perhaps I am closer to home than ever. My new home. A place I can call my own. A place where I can be myself."

Juan lifted his glass of rum. "To your new home, Señorita Torrens. And to you. May you never feel the need to be somebody else ever again."

Viviana raised her glass to his. "Salud."

EARLY THE NEXT MORNING, Viviana stood at the rail of the *L'avenir* and raised a hand in farewell. Juan stood on the dock, gave a single wave, and then put his hands behind his back. She kept her eyes on him until his form melted into the crowd.

Then she walked to the front of the boat, fixed her eyes on the horizon, and took a deep draught of the salty air. Behind her lay all the grief and pain and confusion of her life up to this point—all the people she had lost, all the times she had felt abandoned or betrayed. Behind her lay the Old World with its old ways and old ideas. Ahead of her . . . only God knew.

Above her head, the main sail caught the wind, and Viviana Torrens skated across the beautiful blue waters of the Caribbean toward possibility.

Chapter

THIRTY-NINE

❖

GIBRALTAR, PRESENT DAY

The sun was going down on Esther's third day in Gibraltar. She was lying on her stomach on the couch in Adam's apartment, reading pages as fast as he could translate them from his position on the floor and hand them over. The dining table was strewn with the remains of Filipino food from Tina's Takeaway, which they'd eaten as quickly as possible before getting back to the task at hand—figuring out who had painted the portrait in Adam's bedroom and why the signature might have been covered up.

Yet, in the course of the day, that question had been overshadowed by so many other pieces of information that Esther was having trouble holding it all in her mind at once. Yes, Francisco Vella had been a Gibraltarian merchant who dealt in pigments and dyes. Yes, he had traveled throughout Europe and Northern Africa during his time on this earth. Yes, he had had dealings with Valentin Renaud, from whose estate *La Dama del Cabello Oscuro* had come. But who was this woman who suddenly showed up in his writings? This servant girl who so bewitched him? Who was Viviana Torrens?

"Oh my," came Adam's voice from the floor. "This just gets better and better."

Esther popped up and swung her legs to the ground. "What?"

"Just a minute. I'm not done with this page yet."

"I told you not to do that," she whined. "Don't make any comments or noises until you're ready to hand it over."

"Give me a moment," he said. "Take five. Use the bathroom or go look at that painting again. You're making me nervous, hovering over me like that."

Esther stood. She did have to pee.

She was washing her hands when she heard Adam say, "Um, you're going to want to see this."

Esther rushed back out to the living room, wiping her hands on her pants. Adam handed her the translation he had just finished. Esther sped through the words, then doubled back and read them again.

"She's Veronica? Viviana Torrens is Veronica? The woman in Mary Cassatt's painting?"

Adam turned the journal toward her. "And look here."

There, sketched in what could only be described as loving detail, was the woman who hung above the Markstrom mantel—scar and all. Viviana Torrens. The lady with the dark hair. The lady who had to hide her identity when her past came to light.

Esther plopped back down on the couch, translation in hand.

"This whole time he's been mooning over this girl, it's the one in my painting. The one I've been looking at my whole life." She looked at Adam, who was already reading the next page. "And she was a painter?"

"Oh—" He stopped himself. "Sorry."

"What? Just tell me. You can write it down later."

His brow furrowed, and he set his mouth in a hard line before looking at her apologetically. "I don't know how to tell you this."

"Just tell me."

"He married that French woman, Dolorés."

"Yes?"

"Because she was pregnant."

"Yes, with my great-great-grandfather, Didier."

Adam made a face like he'd bit into something sour and rubbed the back of his neck. "That wasn't his child."

Esther felt the floor drop out from beneath her. "What?"

"Didier. It wasn't his child. The father was a man named Émile." Adam grabbed up his pencil and shook the stiffness from his fingers. "Here, let me write it all out so you can read it yourself."

For the next few minutes, Adam translated while Esther sat stunned. Didier Vella was not Francisco Vella's son? But if that was true, it would mean that she was not related to Vella at all. That she and her mother were not the last living leaves on Francisco Vella's family tree. That they were on some other tree—some common, everyday, non-artistic, non-genius tree. That they had spent their lives in service to the memory of a relative who didn't belong to them. That all those works the family had amassed over the years, their heritage and legacy . . . belonged to someone else. Someone like Gertrude Hernandez. To whom she was also not related.

On the coffee table in front of her, the new pages piled up as fast as Adam could write. But she was no longer reading them. This trip, the painting in the other room that Ian had purchased for her, the rooms full of paintings in East Lansing, the painting above her mantel—none of it meant what she had thought they meant. She had thought her family was special. She had thought that, in some small way, that made her special. That in spite of how small and boring her life was, she had this thing that other people didn't have.

But she didn't. She was ordinary. Utterly ordinary in every way. Just a middle-aged woman taking care of her mentally ill mother. Alone.

Esther stood. "I have to go."

Adam got to his feet. "Why? Wait."

"No, I have to go. Now."

"Do you want me to drive you back to your hotel?"

Esther grabbed her phone and her purse and slipped on her shoes. "No, I just need to get out of here."

"But where are you going?"

Esther was already out the door, heading for the elevator. Then she changed her mind and entered the stairwell. She didn't want to wait for the elevator, didn't want to give Adam a chance to catch up with her. She just needed to be alone.

She rushed from the stairwell and out the front door of the Trafalgar House apartments. Traffic was thick, but an opening presented itself. Esther jogged across the street toward the old cemetery. She pulled at the iron gate, but it was locked. She yanked again, shaking the gate harder and harder until she felt a hand on her arm.

"Esther," Adam said. "Esther."

She turned to face him. "I'm not related to him," she blurted.

"So?"

"It's all just . . . wrong." Her voice broke on the last word. The one thing in her life that made her interesting—that made her life even somewhat interesting—was a sham. She knew this was nothing to cry about, that adults shouldn't need to find validation outside themselves, that her intrinsic worth hadn't actually changed. But all the same, her vision blurred as tears built up on the surface of her eyes.

He took her hand. "The fact that you're not related to him doesn't diminish his art."

She blinked hard and pulled her hand away. "It's not that. Well, it's not just that." She struggled to put words to what she was feeling—that a chasm was growing wider and wider within her stomach, and she was also on the edge of it, teetering. "Either we were just mistaken all these years . . . or someone lied about it."

312

She clamped down on her next thought—that this was something Lorena would lie about. Maybe not deliberately, but in the way she did about lots of things. Because she had convinced herself it was true.

Adam looked at her hard. "I think we should take a break. We've missed our window to see the Moorish castle and the monkeys today. But we can still see St. Michael's Cave. It's closed for tours at this time of night, but there is supposed to be a concert there this evening."

"A concert?" What was this man talking about?

"Yes, there's an auditorium in the largest chamber, the Cathedral Cave. They have events down there every so often. Symphonies and operas and comedians. The acoustics are phenomenal."

She nodded, numb. "I don't know if I'm dressed right."

"It's a cave."

Esther allowed herself to laugh at that.

Adam held out his hand to her. "Come along. Let's get you some tissues and I'll get my wallet. And my shoes."

Esther looked down at Adam's feet. He indeed was barefoot. He had chased after her into the city streets barefoot. "I hope you've had a recent tetanus shot."

He looked thoughtful. "So do I."

DURING THE DRIVE UP THE ROCK to St. Michael's Cave, Adam finally said, "So . . . what happened back there?"

Esther was glad it was nearly dark so he would not see the color in her cheeks. "I guess it just hit me all at once that my whole life has been a lie. Well, not a lie—that's a bit dramatic. But a mistake at least."

"How so?"

"I've been working for more than twenty years to preserve the memory of an ancestor that's not really my ancestor." She laughed bitterly. "I guess I don't need that DNA test after all."

Esther stared out the window at the glittering lights of the city below them. Earlier, she'd almost felt at home here. Now she felt utterly lost. Utterly pointless. She couldn't imagine staying any longer. Neither could she imagine going back to 1745 Chesterwood Parkway. How could she tell her mother what she'd learned? How could she return to the museum? How could she look *La Dama* in the face again?

Viviana. Viviana Torrens. Who was she? And why, if Francisco Vella was so smitten with her, had he wed a Frenchwoman who was having another man's baby?

"Do you like the paintings?" Adam said.

"What?"

"Do you like Vella's paintings?"

"Of course."

"Do you think they're worth educating others about?"

"Yes."

"Then why does it matter that you're not related to him?"

She was quiet a moment. "I guess it's just always been this enormous part of who I am, part of my identity. Part of my family's identity. It's . . . weird. To realize you've been so fundamentally wrong about something that is so fundamental to who you are. It's like someone coming up to you and telling you that you were switched at birth or you have a twin you never knew about or your father is a secret serial killer. It's like the opposite of those stories where the destitute orphan girl finds out she's actually a princess."

Adam chuckled. "I guess so. But it doesn't really matter who your ancestors were or where you came from or whether you had a perfect childhood or a crummy one. The beauty of the day and age we live in is that the question you asked yesterday is based on a false assumption."

"What question?"

"You asked me what I would do if I could do anything. Which assumes that I *can't* do just anything. That I am somehow restricted, that there are possibilities that are just off the table. But what, really, is closed to me? Or you? If you decide you want to do something, you find a way. You find the right school, you find the right teachers, you find the right friends to help you along. You decide what you want, and you pursue it. It doesn't mean you'll always be successful—I mean, sometimes life intervenes or health fails or accidents happen—but the *pursuit* is open to you."

He pulled into a parking spot and turned off the engine.

"Ian grew up restricted to less than three square miles of this earth. And it was too small for him. So he left and made a different life for himself. He left his mother and his father and his brothers and his sister. He left his culture and his first language. He left people who loved him and supported him to live among people who looked down on him in a climate that he loathed. But he did it because he wanted to teach. And at that time, there was no university in Gibraltar."

Adam put his hand on hers and squeezed.

"If you like what you're doing with your life, it doesn't matter if you're related to this man or not. And if you don't like what you're doing with your life, change it."

A few people walked by the car toward the entrance to the cave.

"Okay then," Adam said. "Let's go in. The show starts in fifteen minutes."

THE CONCERT WAS INCREDIBLE. A string quartet accompanied by a male and female vocalist performed selections from Verdi's *Simon Boccanegra*, Massenet's *Hérodiade*, and Offenbach's *Les contes d'Hoffmann*, three operas that had little in common beyond being written in 1881. Esther understood none of the words and didn't even bother reading the synopses in the program. She didn't have the energy to figure out someone else's story when she was busy trying to sort out her own.

The drive back down the Rock afterward was silent. It seemed vulgar to talk after experiencing music like that. And, Esther was sure, they both had a lot on their minds. Finally, as Adam approached the Eliott Hotel, he asked what time she might want to get back together the next day to finish up the journal translation.

"I don't know," Esther said. "I'm not sure I can stand any further revelations. Anyway, I was wondering if perhaps I ought to give it—and the painting—back to Ms. Hernandez. They shouldn't leave her family."

"But you are family, even if you're not a direct descendant. He is still your great-great-great-whatever grandfather by marriage."

Esther shook her head. "I just don't feel good about it."

He pulled up to the front of the hotel. "We don't even know the answer to the question of who painted that picture or why the signature might have been painted over. Aren't you curious?"

Yes, she was curious. How could she not be? But she was also exhausted and deflated and just wanted to go home.

When she didn't answer, he put the car in park. "I tell you what. I'll pick you up tomorrow morning at nine o'clock and we'll have breakfast."

Esther opened her car door. "Thank you for a wonderful time tonight. And last night. And the night before. You have truly been a gracious host. I really appreciate it."

He frowned. "You're welcome. It's been my great pleasure."

She stepped out of the car, but before she could shut the door, Adam got out as well.

"Nine o'clock," he said.

She smiled at him. "Good night, Adam." Then she walked through the hotel doors and headed straight for the elevators.

Once inside her hotel room, she leaned back on the closed door and found a seat on an earlier flight.

Chapter

FORTY

✦

F rancisco Vella stared at his own face across the room.
What had briefly been to him some small proof that
Viviana Torrens actually did care for him as deeply as
he cared for her was now little more than a torment. She was
gone. Spirited away by his own flesh and blood and a man he
had considered a friend.

That Dario and Emilia and even his own mother had played
a part in Viviana's departure so enraged him that upon reading
the letter that morning, he had lashed out at anyone who approached his workshop, assuming that they all must be in on it.
He nearly came to blows with his brother-in-law Gasparo, whom
he accused of raising a wicked and deceitful girl. Manual and
Teodoro had had to pull the two of them apart.

Now Francisco had isolated himself in his workshop, ignoring the food Madalena brought to the door. He swayed between
anger and despair, between plotting Dario's death and his own.
How could she leave him in this way? Why didn't she just tell
him what she wanted? Why didn't she trust him to help her?

317

Because he wouldn't have, he knew. He would have convinced her to stay. He would have reasoned and cajoled, even begged, until she acquiesced. The letter said as much. And he knew it was true. He needed her far more than she needed him, despite the way their lives had been thrown together—by fate, by God, by something, Francisco was sure. He had been so sure.

And now? Now life would carry on as it had before he'd met the beautiful Catalan girl with the short hair in Valentin Renaud's studio.

He tore his eyes from Viviana's portrait of him to look at the portrait she had made of herself. She had fixed every feature so that it was absolutely perfect, so that it was almost as if she was there before him in the flesh. And she had reclothed herself in lustrous, ethereal blue. The blue from beyond the sea.

From the neck up, the portrait was a picture of serene beauty. But below the scar on the side of her throat, it told another story. All those empty spaces, those yawning, horrible empty spaces. It hurt to know that this was the way she felt. But what pained him most, what cut him so sharply he thought he could feel it in his gut, was that he had perceived that emptiness was there all along, just below her surface—and he'd ignored it.

He'd seen the expression on Viviana's face when she thought he wasn't looking. The grief and loneliness that lay beneath the mask she put on to get by. He had assumed, foolishly, that his charming company was all she was missing. That if he could make her smile or laugh, if he could show her the world she so wanted to see, she'd be whole. That if he had him to watch over her, she would find happiness.

But she hadn't. Her happiness had not been in his hands. Had never been in his hands. It was not something he could bestow upon her, no matter how good his intentions. Her happiness, the letter said, lay within her own mind, her own will. She desired to make her own way in the world. To live on her own terms. To see the world through her own eyes and to show others what she saw through her paintings. And to do it all under her own name.

Francisco crossed the room to Viviana's self-portrait and lightly touched his fingers to hers along the bottom edge. Then he tested a few other spots, relieved that everything seemed dry to the touch. He was leaving soon for Toulouse, to carry out Viviana's request that this painting be given to her teacher, Monsieur Renaud. Once he delivered it, he did not intend to pass through that city again. He just could not fathom having to look into those eyes—those beautiful, perceptive, sorrowful eyes—ever again.

Using a pocketknife, Francisco carefully pried up the tacks that held the canvas to the frame, then rolled up the painting and secured it lightly with a piece of twine. He placed it on his worktable and looked again at the portrait she had painted of him. In the corner, where it always appeared, was her signature, a graceful *V* done in chrome yellow. And though he could not bring himself to destroy or give away the painting Viviana had made of him, he also could not look at the mark Viviana had made on it, claiming it as her work. If she could not be his, neither would he be hers.

Francisco pulled out a brush and his last tube of mummy brown paint. He mixed a bit of the paint with thinners, trying to get as much out of it as possible since he was unlikely to ever make more. Careful to mimic her brushwork, he covered Viviana's signature and washed out the brush. Then he picked up the rolled canvas and left without a backward glance.

FORTY-ONE

✦

EAST LANSING, PRESENT DAY

Esther wheeled her mostly empty suitcase into the foyer at 1745 Chesterwood Parkway at nearly 1:00 a.m. on Sunday morning. She had left the Eliott Hotel at 3:00 a.m. Saturday to catch her flight and had slept little before that, tied up inside as she was. She felt bad about leaving early, about not saying goodbye, about leaving behind what she had gone to procure. She felt bad about what she would have to explain to her mother. And she felt especially bad that being home did not feel as good as she had hoped it would.

She walked into the living room, turned on the light, and screamed. There, on the couch, Lorena was locked in struggle with a man—or was it an embrace? Both figures shot upright and wheeled to see the intruder.

"Esther!" Lorena said. "You're home early."

The man put on his glasses and smoothed back his thinning hair.

"Eddie?" Esther said.

The maintenance man from the museum? Eddie the maintenance man was making out with her mother?

"What is going on here?" Esther demanded.

Lorena straightened her shirt. "What does it look like?"

"Why is Eddie here?"

"I invited him over."

Esther was about to ask her mother who told her she could have people over to the house when she was gone—then realized how ridiculous that was. She was not her mother's mother. Her mother was an adult. And this was her house.

"As you well know, Eddie and I go way back," Lorena said, looking to Eddie for confirmation.

Eddie nodded.

"He's the one who paid for our dinner at the State Room," she continued.

An older man with thinning hair and glasses and no accent.

Esther took a deep breath. "Well, I'm sorry to have barged in on you two. I'll just go upstairs."

"Wait," Lorena said. "Where is it?"

"Where is what?"

"The painting."

Esther sighed. "We can talk about it in the morning."

"I want to talk about it now."

"Mom, I have been up for nearly twenty-four hours and I am exhausted and I need to go to bed."

"You can't just go to bed. At least tell me something about your trip."

Esther drew a hand over her face. "Fine." She pointed to *La Dama del Cabello Oscuro*. "Her name is Viviana Torrens." Then she dragged her suitcase, thump-thump-thump, up the stairs and into her bedroom.

THE NEXT MORNING, Lorena was waiting for Esther in the kitchen. "Why haven't you called that Adam fellow back?"

Esther rubbed the sleep out of her eyes. "I beg your pardon?"

"Adam has been trying to get ahold of you and you're ghosting him—is that what they call it? Ghosting?"

"Yes, it's called ghosting."

"Well, why are you doing that? Ian says he's frantic to get ahold of you."

Esther shuffled her way over to the espresso machine, wishing she had some sweetened condensed milk so she could make a café bombón. "I sent him a text from the airport right before my plane left and one when I touched down in Michigan so he'd know I made it okay."

"I can't believe you just left him. That is so profoundly rude and unfeeling. What is the matter with you?"

Rude and unfeeling? Who did her mother think she was talking to here?

"Look, if you'll stop freaking out and let me make some coffee, I'll tell you everything."

"I already know everything. Adam told Ian and Ian told me."

"When did you talk to Ian?"

"I called him this morning. I told him you were back and you'd left the painting there and he needed to get ahold of his cousin to figure out what was going on."

"Why didn't you just wake me up?"

"Well, you were so touchy last night about how little sleep you'd gotten, I wanted to let you catch up."

Esther sat down at the counter without making any coffee.

"What did Ian tell you?"

"That you left the painting and that there was a journal—which you also left—and that you found out we're not actually related to Vella and that you flipped out—"

"I did not flip out. Who said I flipped out? Did Adam say that?"

"No one said that. I read between the lines. You flipped out and got all sad, and instead of digging deeper and finding out more, you just gave up and came home! Without even saying goodbye!"

"Yes, I think we've established that part. Look, Mom, I just need some time to think about everything I learned. It's hard to find out that everything you ever thought about your life is a lie."

Lorena rolled her eyes. "Oh, please. It's not a lie. It was a mistake, a small mistake. One little flaw in an otherwise beautiful thing."

"One little flaw? One little flaw is how forgeries are discovered. One little flaw is never one little flaw. It's just the red flag that turns you on to all the other problems that were staring you right in the face the whole time, only you couldn't see them."

Esther stood and walked into the living room. There, on the wall above the fireplace, hung *La Dama del Cabello Oscuro*. Viviana Torrens. A servant in the household of Valentin Renaud. Painted in an older, less Impressionistic style than the rest of Vella's paintings.

Are you sure it's his? Dr. Perez had asked.

Truthfully, Esther wasn't sure of anything anymore.

Lorena came in from the kitchen holding out her phone. "Someone is on the phone for you."

Esther eyed her. "Who?"

Lorena crossed the room. "I called him and I've already told him you're here."

Esther swallowed down the guilty feeling in her throat, took the phone from Lorena's hand, and sat down on the couch before remembering that she'd caught her mother making out on it the night before. She relocated to a chair.

"Hello?"

"Esther, I am so glad to hear your voice."

"Adam, I'm sorry. I—"

"Never mind that. Time for that later. I need you to listen to me closely."

"Okay . . ."

"I finished the translation. I worked on it all Friday night so I'd be able to give it to you Saturday when we met for breakfast."

As if she needed to feel worse for blowing him off.

"There's something important you need to know and I wanted to tell you in person, but I couldn't get a flight out until next weekend because of my class schedule."

Esther's heartbeat ticked up. "What could possibly be so important that you would actually fly to the US to tell me?"

"There's no way to prepare you to hear this, so I'll just come right out and say it. Francisco Vella didn't paint that portrait that Gertrude Hernandez had. He didn't paint any of the paintings in your museum, and he didn't paint the one in your house."

Esther felt like she was going to throw up. She could not take having one more rug pulled out from under her. "What are you talking about?"

"Viviana Torrens did. She's the one who painted all of them. The V isn't for Vella. It's for Viviana. And Vivienne. And Veronica. All the names she used to try to hide her identity. There is so much more to her story and it's all in the journal. Including the fact that she left Vella behind in Gibraltar to travel to America. So that portrait in my bedroom is no more Gertrude's than it is yours. Neither of you are related to the person who painted it."

Esther could not speak. She could not process. She could not feel the phone in her hand. She felt like a tiny speck of pigment suspended in oil.

"But of course, it is yours," Adam went on to fill the silence. "All of them are yours. They're just not painted by the man you thought they were. They weren't painted by a man at all."

Finally, Esther laughed ruefully and sighed. "Why did I change that flight?"

Adam laughed. "I wish you hadn't. I wish you were still here. We could have made this discovery together."

"Yeah," she said. Then she noticed that her mother was staring at her and wringing her hands. "Listen, Adam. I'm so sorry, but I have to call you back. I have to tell my mom."

"Of course. Take your time."

"I'll keep an eye on the time difference."

"Don't. Call me anytime, day or night."

She smiled but tried mightily not to read too much into that. "I'll talk to you soon." Then she turned to Lorena. "You're going to want to sit down for this."

TWENTY-TWO

Chapter

FORTY-TWO

◆

Esther kicked her mother's leopard-print kitten heels off her feet and collapsed into the chair behind her pristine desk. It had never been this clean before and never would be again. But she'd wanted to make a good impression on the folks from the Detroit Institute of Arts, to say nothing of the photographers from the *Detroit Free Press* and the *Lansing State Journal* and even the *New York Times*. It wasn't every day that one got to be a media darling, and Esther felt a bit like the old footstool she'd seen at the flea market nearly a year ago. The value of an item—even a news item—was entirely dependent on interest, and she knew that the media's interest in her collection would fade quickly. But for now, the Torrens-Markstrom Museum and Gallery was hot.

It wasn't simply that a forgotten artist had been rediscovered. It wasn't simply that a body of work that had been misattributed to a man had finally been properly identified as the work of a woman. It wasn't even that the permanent exhibit space had been expanded to include the never-before-seen life's work of

326

an incredibly talented living female artist, whose piercing self-portraits told the story of living successfully with a mental illness that had killed so many others.

Any one of those things would make for an interesting story. But that all three had happened concurrently was uncommon indeed. This was what was capturing people's attention and imagination.

The possibility that there was some undiscovered thing out there, just waiting for the right person to start digging, was an intoxicating prospect indeed. Who else might we have been wrong about? What other unsung genius or sensitive soul might be awaiting discovery? Who might be right in front of our faces, right now, that we haven't taken the trouble to see?

"There you are," came Adam's voice. "Why are you in here with the lights off? There are still a lot of people out there who want to talk to you."

"You've answered your own question," Esther said. While the last several months had been exciting and the last week had been exhilarating, the last few hours of chatter and incessant smiling had been exhausting.

Adam closed the door behind him and leaned on her desk. "I think Ian's connected with people from three different university presses who've shown interest in his next book."

Esther shrugged. "When you hang out with a mover and a shaker like me, you have to expect those things."

Adam chuckled. "I suppose so. Seriously, though, you do need to get back out there. Your mother is insisting. She has some sort of unveiling to do."

Esther groaned. "Hasn't everything been unveiled already?"

Adam took her hand and gently pulled her to her feet. "Now, now. None of that. Your public awaits." He bent down. "Come, now, let's get these lovely shoes back on and we'll just go out there, do a turn about the room, and then we'll escape and go dancing."

"Ha," Esther said flatly, but she slipped on the shoes all the same.

Adam led her back out to the area in front of the information desk, where there was something hung on the wall and covered with a piece of black silk fabric. Lorena and Eddie stood on either side of it.

Oh, Eddie. Totally-out-of-left-field Eddie. Was he why women in the Victorian era weren't allowed out without a chaperone?

Lorena beckoned Esther over and positioned her for maximum exposure to the cameras and phones pointed their way, which also conveniently hid Lorena from the same. She cleared her throat and started talking. "As was said earlier, this museum has been my family's pride and joy since the 1940s."

Her voice was shaky, and Esther took her hand and squeezed it. *You can do this.*

"It was run by a capable man—my father—for years," Lorena said. "But it was not until a woman was at the helm that it became what it is today. That woman is my daughter, Esther Markstrom."

Applause came quickly and heartily, and Esther caught her mother looking at her the way she had always wanted. And in that spark of true love, true pride, true appreciation, true understanding, Esther felt her relationship with her mother brighten and sharpen, like varnish bringing dry, dull paint back to life.

"She is not only a superb museum director and curator," Lorena continued, stronger now, "but a fine artist in her own right. She is also a good detective. She was the one who noticed the inconsistencies in craquelure that led to the discovery—with the help of our friends at the DIA—that Viviana Torrens is the artist of the portrait of Francisco Vella that now hangs in the exhibit. She was the one who pushed for X-rays to be done on *La Dama del Cabello Oscuro*, which led to the discovery of earlier self-portraits that Viviana Torrens had completed, beneath the painting you now see at the beginning of the exhibit. And she, along with her colleagues Dr. Ian Perez and Dr. Adam de la Paz, was instrumental in the discovery that what had been wrongly attributed to Francisco Vella—a merchant who could draw well but who did not, in fact, paint any of the works within these walls—was actually painted by a young woman from Catalonia who studied under French painter Valentin Renaud."

Applause erupted again, and Esther wished the floor would swallow her whole.

"Now then," Lorena said when the crowd had quieted. "It did not seem right to me that the portraits of Francisco Vella and Viviana Torrens—to say nothing of the dozens of portraits of myself—should grace the walls of this old building and yet neglect to pay homage to the woman who has made this all possible. So, without further ado . . ." She nodded at Eddie, who gently pulled the black silk from the picture on the wall. "I give you Esther Markstrom, director and curator of the Torrens-Markstrom Museum and Gallery," Lorena had to shout her last sentence to be heard over the applause.

There, hanging so as to be the very first thing museumgoers would see, was Lorena's portrait of Esther. It was simple and elegant, and even Esther had to admit that it made her look like the person she always wished she was—strong, savvy, and yes, even striking. This was how her mother saw her, had seen her all along. And it expressed the essence of Esther herself.

The applause went on uncomfortably long. Esther's face burned, and she shuddered to think how bad she would look in all the pictures and videos people were taking. Finally, though, Lorena's waving free hand managed to quell the adoration.

Esther looked at her mother with tears in her eyes, squeezed her hand, and took a step forward. "Well then. This is all deeply embarrassing, as I'm sure all you Midwesterners can imagine."

Laughter.

"You New York folk will just have to take us at our word on that."

More laughter.

Esther cleared her throat. "While I appreciate all that my mother said just now, it would be disingenuous to take all the credit she is giving me. If it weren't for Dr. Perez and Dr. de la

Paz, none of these discoveries would have been made. In fact, if it weren't for a nice little old Gibraltarian woman, Gertrude Hernandez, and her cousin David, none of these discoveries would have been made." She pointed into the crowd. "The lesson here is, don't throw out all the old stuff your grandparents are keeping in shoeboxes!"

The crowd laughed again.

"Seriously, though," Esther said, "much more research must be done to learn about what happened to Viviana Torrens once she reached the United States. And as my former professor recently reminded me, my research is— What did you call it, Dr. Perez?"

"Sloppy."

More laughter.

"Yes, sloppy. Which is why Dr. Perez and I will be working together to learn more about Viviana Torrens's life both in Europe and in the United States. I am so pleased you've all come out tonight to celebrate with us, and I hope you'll continue to support our efforts as we move forward into what promises to be exciting times in the years ahead."

As the crowd voiced their approval and support once more, Esther turned to Lorena and mouthed the words *Thank you*. Lorena gave her a little nod, and Esther marveled at how competent and normal and *happy* her mother seemed, not only this evening but in the months leading up to it. The new medication must be working. Eddie must be good for her. Being involved at the museum must be good for her.

Not long after the unveiling of the portrait of Esther Markstrom, the crowd began to break up. The reporters and guests trickled out to their cars and their hotel rooms. Eddie took Lorena back to the house. Until finally it was just Esther and Ian and Adam.

"Well then," Ian said. "I am going to head back to the hotel if either of you would like to join me for a drink. My treat."

"You know that under other circumstances, there's nothing I'd like more," Esther said. "But I am completely worn out. I am going home and going to bed."

"Of course," Ian said. "Adam?"

Adam clapped his cousin on the back. "I'd love to. Tell you what—I'll meet you there soon?"

Ian looked like he was about to ask a question, but then he nodded. He held out his hand to Esther. "Good night, Ms. Markstrom."

Esther ignored the hand and gave him a hug. "Good night, Ian. We'll talk soon, I'm sure."

"Of course. Lots to talk about."

And with that, Ian Perez walked out the door and headed west.

"Can I take you home?" Adam said. "You look positively exhausted."

"I am. But I can drive. It's just a mile or so away."

Adam nodded. "Okay then. But text me when you get there. So I know you're safe at home."

"Sure," she said. "Let me get my coat, then you can walk me to my car."

"Splendid."

Esther went back into her office and slipped on her spring coat. Her desk looked so bare. So stark. So stylish.

She opened a drawer and pulled out a stack of unfiled papers and magazines she'd stuffed into it in preparation for the day's interviews. From another she pulled a few trinkets she'd squirreled away. From another the stained Hope College coffee mug she'd bought her freshman year and the fanny pack she always wore to flea markets. She spread it all out over the desk. Then she dumped the plant she'd bought for the sake of the photographs into the trash. She wasn't a plant person. And she wasn't organized. And that was okay.

Because she knew who she was. And when you know who you are, you don't feel the need to strive to be somebody else.

Author's Note

Long before I was a writer, I was an artist. Or, at least, I was *artistic*. In fact, the class of 1998 voted me as one the girl Most Likely to Become President, which seems less and less likely as the years go by.

As a child I drew countless unicorns, dogs, horses, and other animals. I sketched people I found in photos. I painted watercolor flowers and landscapes, made collages from pictures cut from magazines, sculpted clay pots and figures, wove baskets, and made hideous jewelry out of something called "friendly plastic." As a twenty-something, I added other artsy pursuits like photography and creative stamping, as well as making mosaics and non-hideous jewelry out of beads. When they finally put my old pal Bob Ross on Netflix, that's when I decided that no matter how "messy and expensive" oil painting was, as I had always been warned, I was going to try it. Spoiler alert: it's neither, really, and it has become my preferred medium.

One of the best things about writing novels is that I get to draw on and plunge myself further into my own interests as I develop characters, plots, settings, and themes. For *The Lady with the Dark Hair*, I immersed myself in all things painting. I attended special exhibits at museums, including the incomparable Detroit Institute of Arts and the Cleveland Museum of Art. I read books about artists, artistic movements, art history, and colors and pigments. (Find those, as well as many other resources, in the "Books for Further Reading" section.) I watched painting demos on YouTube, followed artists on Instagram, and took a Domestika course on portrait painting from one of my favorite Instagram artists. I participated in a life drawing class as both an artist and a model.

And I painted. *A lot*. During each month of 2022, I painted a self-portrait as I tried to improve my skill at painting people. It was sometimes frustrating, sometimes exhilarating, sometimes somewhere in between. Beyond those twelve self-portraits, I painted many other things as well—landscapes, still lifes, frogs. You know, the basics.

I am indebted to my art teachers, including Mrs. Visser, Ms. Engels, and Mrs. Dresser (and Bob Ross), for teaching me the fundamentals, allowing me to be creative, and offering praise and encouragement to a budding young artist. I am also indebted to my mother and father for supplying me with materials for many years and paying for extra classes outside of school, and to all my extended family members who bought me instructional books and supplies for birthdays and Christmases, or just gave me gift cards to Michael's and Hobby Lobby (all those glorious gift cards). Thanks especially to my husband, Zach, for multiple easels, constant encouragement, and bearing with me annexing various spaces in the house over the years when I didn't have a studio space.

I would be remiss if I did not mention my most cultured friend, Valerie Marvin, whose membership at various artsy institutions has meant free admission for me, her frequent "plus one," during our day trips to museums.

Beyond my personal experiences and reading a bunch of books about art and artists, which, frankly, I would have read for my own pleasure anyway, much research had to be done to develop the characters and settings in this book. For this reason, I am especially thankful to my friend and fellow author Susie Finkbeiner for her insights about living with someone suffering from schizophrenia.

My deepest gratitude goes out to my former professor and favorite Gibraltarian, Dr. David Alvarez, not only for the loan of too many books about his home Rock but for answering my countless questions. This book would not have been possible without his gracious assistance and willingness to let me pry into his personal history and library. He even sent several of my inquiries to his Gib WhatsApp group (which includes the attorney general of His Majesty's Government of Gibraltar himself!). These folks conferred among themselves about such things as what kind of car a guy like Adam might drive, whether Gibraltarian men in their forties wear jeans, and whether a certain monument was ever moved as articles online seemed to suggest (it was not—yet). The members of the Little Bay Rovers Chat Group, as they are called, also proved a rich resource when it came to naming characters according to what century or even decade they were born. Any accuracy I achieved in presenting the land, people, and culture of Gibraltar, both past and present, is due to Dr. Alvarez and his cronies. Any mistakes, I own completely.

Lastly, I'd like to thank the many female artists over the centuries who have striven to create despite tremendous restrictions, opposition, and condescension, to say nothing of the rampant misattribution and devaluing of their work. Your fiercely independent spirit and your tenacity in the face of so many obstacles inspire me.

You are my muses.

Books for Further Reading

Besides relying on personal interviews and personal experience to bring the world of *The Lady with the Dark Hair* to life, I did a *lot* of research into the lives of female artists, the Impressionist movement in art, the origin of the colors and pigments artists have used over the millennia, schizophrenia, and the histories of three political crossroads: Gibraltar, Catalonia, and Alsace-Lorraine. If you want to dig deeper into any of these subjects after reading this novel, here's a list of the books I consulted as part of my research.

On Female Artists

The Mirror and the Palette: Rebellion, Revolution, and Resilience: Five Hundred Years of Women's Self Portraits by Jennifer Higgie (Pegasus Books, 2021).

Women Artists in Paris: 1850–1900 by Laurence Madeline (Yale University Press, 2017).

Artemisia Gentileschi by Jonathan Jones (Laurence King Publishing, 2020).

Berthe Morisot by Anne Higonnet (Harper & Row, 1990).

On Impressionism

The New Painting: Impressionism 1874–1886 (Fine Arts Museums of San Francisco, 1986).

On Color and Pigment

The Secret Lives of Color by Kassia St. Clair (Penguin Books, 2016).

Color: A Natural History of the Palette by Victoria Finlay (Random House, 2002).

On Gibraltar

Gibraltar: The History of a Fortress by Ernle Bradford (Open Road Integrated Media, 1971).

Georgian and Victorian Gibraltar: Incredible Eyewitness Accounts by M. G. Sanchez, ed. (Rock Scorpion Books, 2012).

Community and Identity: The Making of Modern Gibraltar since 1704 by Stephen Constantine (Manchester University Press, 2009),

The Prostitutes of Serruya's Lane: And Other Hidden Gibraltarian Histories by M. G. Sanchez, ed. (Rock Scorpion Books, 2007).

Rock of Empire: Literary Visions of Gibraltar, 1700–1900 by M. G. Sanchez, ed. (Self-published, 2001).

Deadly Visitations in Dark Times: A Social History of Gibraltar by L. A. Sawchuk (Gibraltar Government Heritage Publications, 2001).

The Streets of Gibraltar: A Short History by Tito Benady (Gibraltar Books, 1996).

Civil Hospital and Epidemics in Gibraltar by Sam Benady (Gibraltar Books LTD, 1994).

The Rock of the Gibraltarians: A Short History of Gibraltar by Sir William G. F. Jackson (Ashford Press Publishing, 1990).

Innocents Abroad, vol. 1, by Mark Twain (Harper & Brothers Publishing, 1897).

On Spain and Catalonia

Catalonia: The History and Legacy of Spain's Most Famous Autonomous Community (Charles River Editors, 2021).

Spain: 1808–1939 by Raymond Carr (Clarendon Press, 1970).

The Spanish Labyrinth by Gerald Brenan (Cambridge University Press, 1943).

On Alsace-Lorraine

Alsace and Lorraine from Caesar to Kaiser, 58 BC–1871 AD by Ruth Putnam (Knickerbocker Press, 1915).

On Schizophrenia

The Complete Family Guide to Schizophrenia by Kim T. Mueser, PhD, and Susan Gingerich, MSW (Guilford Press, 2006).

Liner Notes

I never wanted to live at my Uncle Mike's. Partly because I swore I'd never have anything to do with my dad since he clearly wanted nothing to do with me. (Being my dad's twin brother, Uncle Mike is about as close to my actual dad as anyone could be). And partly because he's the type of guy whose entire life screams *failure*, and the more your path crosses with his, the more likely you are to become a failure yourself. Truthfully, I do a good enough job of that on my own.

But then, if Uncle Mike hadn't taken me in when Rodney and Slow kicked me out, I wouldn't be covered in mud and standing in this pit with Natalie Wheeler.

Yeah, that Natalie Wheeler. Daughter of reclusive guitarist-turned-producer Dusty Wheeler and onetime-flower-child-singer-songwriter Deb Wheeler, who also happened to be Mike's across-the-street neighbors and long-suffering landlords.

Mike's house was never meant to be a house. It was just the break trailer for the construction crew that built the Wheeler estate twenty years ago back in 1970. Mike was on the crew, and the Wheelers rented him the property cheap after their sprawling contemporary glass and stone house was finished. I guess because one of them liked him and one of them pitied him.

I'm not one hundred percent sure which impulse first inspired Natalie Wheeler to give me the time of day, but right at this moment, I don't really care. Right at this moment, I'm seeing more clearly than I ever have in my short and rather disappointing life that maybe I'm meant for something . . . better. It doesn't really matter to me how we got here.

That said, it probably matters to you—or if it doesn't yet, it will shortly—so maybe I should start earlier. Maybe the night I first made it through the door of the Wheeler house. The night I first saw Natalie. Even if she didn't see me.

Track One

I wasn't invited.

I should probably make that clear right off the bat. Because I don't want you to get the wrong idea about me. I'm nobody special. I don't know anybody important, and nobody important knows me. I just happened to know somebody who knew somebody. Or rather, I happened to have the same name as somebody who knew somebody.

The invitation I pulled out of the rusty mailbox did say Michael Sullivan, but it wasn't for me and I knew it. It was for my uncle, who I happen to be named after. Not because my dad wanted to honor his brother, but because my mom preferred his brother to him and wanted to get back at him for missing my birth twenty-two years ago. Only I go by Michael, not Mike. The invitation said Michael. Probably because Mrs. Wheeler has class.

It arrived on Wednesday, December 27, 1989. I knew Mike wasn't going to be around for New Year's. I hadn't been living with him long, but it was long enough to notice a few patterns.

One: he smoked a pack of Camels every day.

Two: he never slept at home on weekends.

Three: he was bad with money.

Four: he listened almost exclusively to Lynyrd Skynyrd.

Five: he was wildly superstitious.

When it came to ringing in the new year in style at the Wheeler house, four out of five of those facts worked in my favor.

As I came back inside with the mail and knocked the snow off my boots, I heard Mike on the phone talking to his friend Carl. I knew it was Carl because of the voice Mike was using. He used one voice for work, another voice for girls, another voice for friends, and another voice for Carl, who was a friend but also someone who routinely loaned Mike money and rarely got any of it back.

I slipped the thick envelope (which had been sent through the post office even though I could see the iron gate at the end of the long Wheeler drive from the kitchen window—like I said, classy) into my pocket and listened as Mike convinced Carl to pay for gas for a road trip out to California, where Lynyrd Skynyrd was playing the Cow Palace on Sunday the 31st. Then they'd swing by Vegas on the way back to Michigan, where Mike was certain he'd win enough money to cover what he owed Carl as long as Skynyrd opened with "You Got That Right" and closed with "Sweet Home Alabama" (see also: superstitious). When he hung up the phone and started throwing some underwear and jeans into a duffle bag, I knew what I was going to be doing on New Year's Eve.

Mike left the next morning without so much as a "Stay out of my room"—which the lock rendered unnecessary anyway. You might think he could have invited me to go along with him. I liked Lynyrd Skynyrd okay. The guys and I occasionally threw in a cover of "Simple Man" when we played gigs, which wasn't as often as Rodney had wanted but proved to be more often than I managed to show up (see also: being kicked out). A good uncle might have made an effort to bring his aspiring rock star nephew out to California to live it up a little at a big concert. And I was over twenty-one, so I wouldn't have been a drag on them in Vegas. But I knew he wouldn't ask me to come. I was bad luck.

The day I was born and my mom named me after him, Mike lost half of his squad in a firefight somewhere west of Quảng Ngãi. For the next couple decades, whenever something went wrong in Mike's life, which seemed like it was more often than in most other people's, there was some way in which I was to blame. He routinely cheated on his girlfriends, but they dumped him because it was my eighth birthday or I had talked to him earlier in the day or I was watching the same TV show at the same time. When he got injured on a construction job, it was because my baseball team got mercied, not because he had been up drinking the night before. The day I got my first guitar—a right-hander even though I'm left-handed—he was sentenced to one hundred hours of community service after his third drunk and disorderly offense. The night I first kissed a girl, he was stranded in Detroit with a dead car battery.

The only reason he let me come live at his place when I found myself homeless back in August was because I promised to pay him rent and he needed the money. He always needed money. Most of the time he tried to stay out of the house—which was just fine with me—and when we were there at the same time, he was always looking at me sidelong, like I was contagious or something.

So when he left without me on Thursday morning, I was nothing but relieved. I had three boring days of work at Rogers Hardware in downtown West Arbor Hills to get through, days when I'd be marking down Christmas lights and stocking gardening supplies that people would look at for the next three freezing, snowy, slushy months but no one would actually buy until after Easter. Then it would be New Year's Eve and I would finally see what was on the other side of that iron gate across the street.

WHEN SUNDAY ROLLED AROUND it was windy and warm, nearing forty degrees in the afternoon. I'd spent the morning sleeping late and eating three bowls of half-stale Cocoa Puffs because the milk was going to expire, then digging around in my drawers for something to wear to the party.

The invitation had been printed in gold on heavy paper, but it said "Come As You Are" at the bottom of it. "As I Was" usually meant ripped jeans, a concert T-shirt, and a denim jacket, though I'd been trying to save up for a leather one I'd seen at the mall. But that didn't seem right for a party announced in gold lettering. I had khaki slacks for work, but that wasn't really "As You Are" for me. That was just something I had to do to keep a roof over my head and gas up the car and pay for pedals and strings and maybepleaseGod a better amp someday.

However, Uncle Mike had a closet over on the other side of the thin wall, and for all his faults, he always looked cool. Actually, maybe that was the problem with him. What you saw was not exactly what you got. It fooled people into trusting him when he was only slightly more dependable than his brother—which was not at all.

He'd locked his bedroom door, as always, but it wasn't hard to pick the lock. I had plenty of experience doing just that to get into various houses or apartments when I either lost my keys or was accidentally-on-purpose locked out by the people I was crashing with.

Mike was a middle-aged contractor and I was a skinny wannabe rock star built more like Steven Tyler than Henry Rollins, so most of his clothes would be too big on me. Definitely I'd have to wear my own pants. But Mike was also secretly sentimental, so he never got rid of certain things, even if he couldn't stretch them over his growing gut. He had faded T-shirts from concerts I wish I'd been old enough to go to, a black motorcycle jacket I assume he must have worn during his glory days of roving across the country following bands and girls and pipe dreams, his old army junk from Vietnam.

I settled on a pair of my least ripped jeans, Mike's Goose Lake

Music Festival tee—nothing said I'm a legit Detroit musician like a nod to the legendary 1970 concert—and the black leather jacket, which I knew would land me in either the hospital or, more preferably, the morgue if he ever found out I'd touched it and gotten my bad luck all over it. I tied my finally-shoulder-length hair at the back of my neck and pulled out a few strands around my face so it didn't look too polished or purposeful—cool wasn't cool if it wasn't effortless—and laced up my black motor-cycle boots. No, I didn't own a motorcycle, though when I was little I apparently rode on the back of my dad's once. According to my mom, there's a picture of it somewhere.

I was ready to go. It was 4:59. The party didn't even start until 9:00.

I caught the tail end of a football game I didn't care about, half watched the news talking about Panama and Israel and some bomb threat on some airline, then turned up the volume when *Life Goes On* came on, but it was a rerun. I killed the TV and turned on the radio instead, but it was mostly year-end junk. Top songs of 1989, but not actually being played in full, and most of them were pop shlock—Paula Abdul and Debbie Gibson and Milli Vanilli.

I secretly did like some of that crap—it was just so catchy—but synthesizers and drum machines wouldn't get rid of the churn-ing I'd started to feel in my stomach when I thought of walking through the door at a party I wasn't really invited to and where I wouldn't know anyone.

I turned the radio off and popped *Slippery When Wet* into the tape deck, following it up with *Hysteria* and then *Appetite for De-struction*, which I turned off after "Sweet Child O' Mine." Axl's pinched, perfect whine still rang in my ears as I crossed the dark street and approached the open gate of the Wheeler house. I thought of how Axl would walk into a party, shoved my hands into my jeans pockets, and put a friendly sneer on my face, the kind of expression I used to get through gigs without a panic attack.

The winding driveway was already lined with cars at 9:15. Nice cars. Some new, some classic, all perfectly shiny except for the spatter of salt water just behind the tires. Who washed a car in the winter? Rich people. What did "Come As You Are" mean to rich people? Ties and sport jackets? I didn't own a tie, and I'm not sure Uncle Mike did either. Well, maybe. For court dates.

I could feel my heart rate tick up and sweat gathering on my scalp and my palms. I almost turned around and called this what it was—a bad idea. But then the last thing Rodney had said to me when he and Slow gave me the boot from our crappy apartment in Plymouth (which he always told people was in Detroit) replaced Axl's aching E-flat in my brain. *"The minute you're not a drain on this band, the minute you actually have something to offer, that's when you can come back. Not one second sooner."*

Knowing Dusty Wheeler . . . that would be something to offer. That might make up for me missing the odd gig or five. That might make up for the fact that my equipment kind of sucked. That might make up for Slow's girlfriend hitting on me right in front of him, which, hey, wasn't my fault to begin with but also didn't bother me all that much because she's pretty cute and is one of the few people who makes me feel kind of good about myself in kind of a bad way.

If I could get a demo to Dusty, I'd be worth something to those guys. Maybe they'd even give a few of the songs I wrote the time of day. Maybe I could actually sing lead once in a while instead of Rodney, who was always a little flat and on the unintelligible side.

I picked up my pace and pushed through the panic. I wasn't going back to that trailer right now. That trailer was the past, evidence of a forgettable life in a disappointing family. My future was waiting for me at the end of this driveway.

Erin Bartels writes character-driven fiction for curious people. Her readers know to expect that each of her novels will tell a unique story about fallible characters so tangible that it's hard to believe they are not real people. Whether urban, rural, or somewhere in between, her settings come alive with carefully crafted details that engage all the senses and transport the reader to a singular time and place. Her themes of reckoning with the past, improving the present, and looking with hope to the future leave her readers with a sense of peace and possibility.

Erin is the award-winning author of *We Hope for Better Things*, *The Words between Us*, *All That We Carried*, *The Girl Who Could Breathe Under Water*, and *Everything Is Just Beginning*. A two-time Christy finalist and winner of two 2020 WFWA Star Awards and the 2020 Michigan Notable Book Award, Erin has been a publishing professional for more than twenty years. After eighteen years in Michigan's capital city, she now lives with her family in a charming small town surrounded by farm fields and pasturelands.

Find her online at ErinBartels.com, on Facebook @ErinBartels Author, or on Instagram @ErinBartelsWrites.